Switching Gears

by

Rhavensfyre

Switching Gears (2nd edition)

Copyright © 2013 by Rhavensfyre

This is a work of fiction-names, characters, places and incidents are a product of the author's imagination or are used fictitiously. Any resemblance to actual persons, living or dead, business, events, or locales is entirely coincidental.

Acknowledgements

As always, a big shout-out to our beta readers, Tammy, Gail, Dava, and Marion.

A very special thank you to singer/songwriter Marion Dries for permission to use her song "I'm Confused".

Switching Gears was Rhavensfyre's first novel and it carries a special significance to both the author and the readers. In it's second incarnation we hope all of our readers, both new and old, take something fresh away with them with the retelling.

Micah and Olivia's story is one of passion, pain, and eventually, acceptance and love. It was not an easy book to write and for some, not an easy book to read, but it is an amazing journey.

Chapter One

What the hell am I doing here?

Micah Connolly strolled through the halls of Holden, Holden & Barr, Esq., repeating that question like a mantra. The seemingly nonchalant gait was a total farce and made her hips protest at being held back.

Back in a building she swore she would never enter again, she was too nervous to do anything else. The minute she walked through those doors, her legs decided to betray her by turning into barely controllable rubber bands held together by super glue. It was either put her normally purposeful stride in check or risk looking like an idiot by tripping over her own feet. She was expected to appear harried and in a rush, but she refused to make a spectacle of herself in the process. What she needed to do was calm down. Micah took in a deep, cleansing breath and held it for a second before blowing it out. It was best if she tried to keep her thoughts on the job at hand, she decided, and not dwell on the past.

The heady aroma of expensive colognes mingled with equally expensive and even more cloying perfumes until they hung heavy in the high rise's recycled air.

It assaulted her senses, offending her in a way the smell of exhaust and foul city odors never did, not even the ones that occasionally defied explanation.

Her comfortable Merrells scuffed silently across thick, royal burgundy carpet as she moved closer to the executive suites along the back wall. Micah smiled in childish satisfaction when a woman in ridiculously stylish high heels tottered over to the water fountain, almost tripping on the unrealistic flooring choice. She remembered how difficult it had been to walk in heels on that very same carpet almost a year ago, right before she left without notice and without explanation.

Despite her best attempt not to, she couldn't help but berate herself for failing to realize her new job might send her back here—the last place on earth she wanted to be. As a bike messenger, she delivered packages all over the city. Foolishly, she hadn't thought her new job would require her to step foot into this particular building again, an oversight she was paying for today.

A few questioning looks from the impeccably dressed corporate drones as they passed her by was starting to upset her. *Haven't they ever seen a bike messenger before?* Granted, baggy shorts and a t-shirt wasn't exactly corporate dress, but still, she wasn't used to downright rudeness. Then she realized that they could hear her displeased muttering under her breath, and she was probably scowling, to boot. She forced a pleasant, if neutral smile and bit her tongue to stop her grumbling, then caught a glimpse of her reflection as she walked past a large painting hanging on the wall.

Micah didn't care for the modern abstract style, but the glass protecting the almost sterile office piece was spotless and shiny enough to reflect back her image, revealing a tan face hidden behind mirrored wraparound sunglasses. Her hair, as black as a raven's wing, was cut short and tight across the back beneath her messenger service cap. The cap used to be just as black but was faded to a dull grey from sun exposure and marked with bright blue lettering proclaiming her status as a bike messenger. A stylized speeding bicycle logo sprinted across the brim as if trying to escape the worn fabric. She almost laughed aloud when she realized that she had dressed entirely in black today, a fitting color to her mood right now.

The farther in she went the fancier the cubicles got until she ended up in the back corner where all the primo offices sat. Spotting her old friend Amanda sitting at her desk, she smiled and quickened her steps. Amanda was a friendly face, and she just might be able to help make her delivery a little less painful.

"Hey, A."

Amanda looked up from her computer and gasped, no doubt startled to hear her voice let alone see her standing there. Micah didn't blame her. Ever since she left the law firm she had been consistently declining Amanda's offers to meet for lunch, so her reaction was understandable. They had struck up a casual if competitive friendship when Micah started working at the law firm. Over time, the two women found out that they truly liked each other and actually had a lot in common, an appreciation of women for one thing. If anyone had asked her, Micah would have listed Amanda as one of her closest friends—a good friend, but like a lot of things from her past she had been avoiding her. A quick memory check and some simple math told her it had been months since they last hooked up for a night out on the town, and that wasn't fair to Amanda.

"Whatever are you doing here?" Amanda flashed a nervous glance towards the office door before leaning over her desk to give Micah a brief hug.

"Hell if I know, A." Micah shrugged, pulling off her cap and tossing it on Amanda's desk before nervously raking her fingers through her hair. All it took for her already barely tame locks to turn into something completely unruly was a hot summer day and that damned hat. Micah pulled her sunglasses up onto the top of her head, effectively undoing her finger combing and not really caring to repeat the effort. She was too busy pulling out a large envelope from her messenger bag.

"Apparently I have a delivery for Olivia, so if you will just sign for it?" She tried to shove the large envelope toward Amanda while offering her the clipboard and pen. *Only a signature away from escaping*, she thought, feeling the itch of imaginary eyes watching her right between her shoulder blades. She rolled her shoulders and tried not to twitch. Standing this close to Olivia's office was threatening to overwhelm Micah's ability to remain calm and cool; she knew the door was open but resisted the urge to check over her shoulder. Hopefully the woman was busy at her desk and not standing in the doorway watching the show. If Olivia didn't see her, Micah wouldn't have to risk explaining her sudden disappearance.

The memory of the last time she was in Olivia's presence kept surfacing despite her best efforts to push it far, far down into her subconscious. Micah felt her face go red hot. The object of her soul's darkest fantasies and the source of her heart's deepest betrayal, Olivia still held some sort of power over her, tapping into every uncertainty she usually managed to keep at bay.

***

Micah had met Olivia Holden during her second interview for an intern position and was surprised that she had been accepted for the job after her embarrassing and tongue tied performance. She had walked into the office an assured and confident graduate student with a promising future in law and sat down in front of a woman so beautiful and elegant that the power to speak drained right out of her along with her ability to think straight.

Olivia Holden was known to be a formidable woman, and at thirty-eight was one of the youngest and most influential female attorneys in the New York area. She was also absolutely, and without any doubt in Micah's mind, one of the most stunning creatures she ever laid eyes on.

Olivia wasn't a large woman; in fact, she was a couple of inches shorter than Micah even in heels and ran closer to the willowy side of slim. She had pale blond hair and high cheekbones that framed her most striking feature, ice blue eyes that were as dangerous as a late winter storm. Depending on her mood, they could run as pale as cold frost or as deep as the darkening sky before twilight fell. When Olivia looked at you with those piercing eyes, it was as if she was stripping you down to your bare soul. During her interview, with those cool as ice eyes assessing her from across the desk, she was sure that Olivia could read her thoughts as clearly as the words on the legal brief laying in front of her. She had been so excited and honored to meet the infamous and oh-so-untouchable Olivia Holden, and then found herself overcome with the desire to do just that, touch. It was a cruel turn of fate that she found her desire fine-tuning itself towards the one woman she couldn't approach, let alone have.

***

Shifting nervously, Micah just wanted to give Amanda the envelope, get her signature so she could get paid, and get the hell out of there before Olivia saw her.

"Micah, bring me the packet," Olivia's imperious voice floated out of the office and crushed that brief hope. Cool like silk with a subtle Brandywine undertone, Olivia spoke with a quiet intensity that was easily heard, even across the distance between her office and Amanda's desk.

"Dammit," Micah cursed under her breath. Of course Olivia noticed her. Amanda tossed a sympathetic grin in her direction but sat back down and started typing. It was pretty obvious she wasn't going to get in the middle of it, friend or no. Micah grimaced and tapped her sunglasses down off her forehead to rest on the bridge of her nose. Armored with all the attitude she could muster and shielded behind tinted glass, she kept her expression hidden behind the mirrored lenses of her Ray-Bans. The midnight black tint would ensure that there was no way for Olivia to see the apprehension in her eyes. It would have to be sufficient. Amanda twisted her head enough to see her. She raised an eyebrow at the change and whispered good luck just before Micah turned and sauntered into Olivia's office as cockily as she would make her grand entrance at the club.

"Here ya go, Olivia." Micah again held out the offending envelope. She tried to project insolence and boredom, but a slight tremor in her hand threatened to

6

expose her nervousness. She almost dropped the envelope unceremoniously onto Olivia's desk when her fingers went numb and stopped working completely.

"Sit," Olivia commanded, not bothering to look up at Micah as she reached her hand out for the envelope. Olivia examined the envelope intently before ripping it open, pulling out a thick folder as she sat behind the polished teak wood desk that was the centerpiece of her expansive office. It was only after she leaned forward in her chair and started looking through the contents of the folder on her desk that she even bothered to look up at Micah.

"Is there something wrong with your hearing today?" Olivia asked in a voice that on a different woman could have sounded peevish, but on her, it held an air of command that made you ask yourself why you hadn't done as she asked in the first place. It was the air of a Queen sitting on her throne, and in this office, that was exactly who Olivia was.

***

Leaning back imperiously, Olivia placed a well-manicured finger along her bottom lip and contemplated the younger woman standing in front of her. Micah's thick black hair was short, much shorter than she remembered. The new hairstyle complemented her face well, bringing out her cheekbones and adding an androgynous look that she found intriguing. Micah was dressed in loose-fitting black cargo shorts and a very tight sleeveless shirt that left no doubt she was keeping very fit. Letting her eyes wander over the sleek muscles and shapely physique, Olivia wondered why Micah had hidden such a remarkable body under the drab loose clothes she seemed to favor when she worked for her. There was no way she could have developed that body since she left. Mirrored sunglasses finished the outfit, hiding expressive hazel eyes that Olivia knew could change in an instant, revealing every emotion and thought. That Micah kept her eyes hidden from her irritated Olivia instantly; she needed to know what the woman was thinking.

Taking in the complete picture, Olivia realized that this was a very different Micah than the one she remembered. That realization left her with more questions than answers. What would account for such an extreme change in appearance and attitude? She felt unsettled, more than she thought she would be at having Micah back in front of her.

"I said sit," Olivia's voice cracked whip like across the room, betraying her irritation at having to repeat herself.

Micah did not sit at Olivia's command. Instead, she simply refused to look at her, focusing just to the left of Olivia's shoulder and staring out the large panoramic window behind her.

"I don't want to ruin your chair, Olivia. It's ninety-five degrees outside and, um," she paused as she gestured at her dusty street clothes, "I'm very sweaty." Micah stopped speaking when she realized she was making excuses. She didn't owe Olivia either explanation or excuse, and found that she was getting annoyed with the direction their fledgling conversation was heading. Olivia was treating her as if she was still a new intern, and that was not who she was anymore.

"Besides that, you aren't my boss. So I don't really think you can tell me to do anything." Micah's words bit like sharp steel through the tension in the room. She clenched her teeth together until her jaw popped and she could feel her muscles jump in protest. What else could she do? Olivia seemed to be doing everything in her power to upset her or mentally throw her off, but all it was actually doing was pissing her off.

"No, I am not." Olivia's cool words might have agreed with Micah's, but the weighted look attached to them begged for an argument. Both women narrowed their eyes in challenge to the other, knowing where the argument would start and where it would lead.

Olivia felt at a disadvantage with Micah's eyes hidden behind those damnable sunglasses but she could tell by the set of her jaw, her normally full lips pale and thin against her tan skin, that Micah was primed for the pending argument.

Micah had been trying to hold her tongue this whole time, but Olivia was really getting under her skin...in more ways than one. She crossed her arms in front of her, the defensive posture broadcasting her desire to be done with the conversation.

Micah's gesture refocused Olivia's attention onto the skin-tight black shirt that she wore, the thin fabric accentuating her muscular physique while leaving no doubt that her female attributes remained very much intact. The fight drained out of her, only to be replaced by something more primitive and very physical.

A very subtle shift in the air caught Micah off guard, but not for long.

Holy shit! Micah couldn't believe it. Somewhere between Olivia trying to maintain her cool and somewhat prickly façade, and flashes of irritation with Micah's stubborn refusal to cooperate, Olivia failed to control her face for one revealing second. For one unguarded moment, she looked hungry, for lack of a better word.

And not just any hunger, either, but that insatiable hunger Micah was so familiar with that was born of secret desire and need. Olivia wanted her and no matter how fleeting it was or how quickly she managed to shut it down, Micah hadn't imagined that look. Trying to take that look back was like slamming the lid back down on Pandora's Box—it was too late to stop what had been released.

Her heart raced in response to the familiar rush of adrenaline she lived and breathed for. After all this time, she still wanted Olivia; her absence hadn't changed a thing. If anything, she wanted her more, and now that she knew Olivia desired her as well, that was a potential game changer.

Olivia closed her eyes, took a deep breath and then tried to start over. She was being a royal bitch, and that was not how she wanted Micah to see her. Gesturing at the chair nearest to Micah, Olivia softened her tone. "Please, sit down?"

Micah's eyebrows climbed above the edge of her sunglasses at the unexpected mild tone. *Olivia asking and not telling? Now that was a change.*

"Amanda, a bottle of water for Micah." Olivia's voice turned cold and impersonal again.

Poor Amanda. Evidently polite and mild was something Olivia was trying on Micah alone. She nodded to Amanda, thanking her for the chilled bottle, but forgoing the offered glass. She twisted the cap off the bottle and drank almost half of it in one go. Cycling was thirsty work.

Olivia looked up from the paperwork in front of her to study the younger woman. The rhythmic movement along Micah's long neck as she drank deeply fascinated her. When she tipped her head back to finish up the last

10

few ounces at the bottom of the bottle, a single drop of water slid down and along her throat before disappearing between the deep vee of her neckline. Olivia blinked rapidly, trying to convince herself that she was not thirsty as she ached to follow that single drop of water.

Embarrassed at her obvious ogling, she managed to tear her eyes away just as Micah finished drinking. Clearing her throat, Olivia tried to retake control of her rebellious thoughts and the situation.

"Do you have any more deliveries today?" she asked casually, subtly pressing her palms against the cool, hard surface of her mahogany desk. The desk was a tangible presence between her and Micah, one she seemed to need right now. Sitting behind her desk always allowed her a certain modicum of power. The one behind the desk was always the one in charge. That Micah's presence made her feel like she was hiding behind its broad surface made her feel uncharacteristically off balanced. It was an unfamiliar sensation she wasn't especially comfortable with, and it made her want to fall back into the professional persona she used to keep her distance from others.

At the negative shake of Micah's head, Olivia responded in her best business-as-usual voice.

"Good, then you can take this paperwork back to the office you got it from. Just give me an hour or so to go through it first. I will, of course, cover the cost of your waiting," she said, holding up the bundle of legal papers Micah had just delivered.

Confused at the sudden shift in behavior, but glad to get the hell out of Olivia's office, Micah stood up to leave.

"Sure thing, I'll just hang out with Amanda until you're done," she said, but before she could escape,

Olivia caught her with a warning look that didn't need any explanation. Evidently, Olivia expected her to just sit there and stay for the hour she needed to review the paperwork.

Micah considered leaving anyways. Then she thought of a better idea. She slid back down in the chair, not even trying to hide the wide grin spreading across her face.

Okay, Olivia, two can play this game. Micah figured she could ignore Olivia for an hour, but not without something to focus on. It was time to pull out her MP3 player. Earbuds in and she quickly lost herself in the music of one of her favorite artists, Lily Allen. The songs were lighthearted and made her smile, a sure way to irritate Olivia even more. *It's only fair,* she thought, since she was being forced to do something she hated. Sitting and doing nothing.

A quick glance up verified her assessment. Olivia was expending more energy than was needed on the simple draft in front her. Micah was willing to bet that the deep frown leaving a thin furrow across Olivia's forehead was more frustration than concentration, since she just spent ten minutes going through a document that she hadn't managed to make a single mark or correction on. Evidently, Olivia did not like being ignored.

Micah was only partially correct. As Olivia shuffled through the draft in front of her, she spent more energy focusing on how to get Micah back than on the work at hand. Just being in the same room together made her realize just how much she missed Micah since she had left. What she needed was a plan.

Her resolve solidified to the sound of her pen tapping out a slow rhythm on her desk. She would get Micah back in her life. Not as an employee or intern.

That wasn't how she wanted her and something told her a resounding no would be the only thing Micah would say to that offer. Thinking about how she did want her made Olivia lose her place again, and she was forced to re-read the last paragraph. She found an error she should have noticed the first time and took her pen to it a little too energetically, crossing out the offending language hard enough to leave a dent in the paper. That simply wouldn't do. She had an audience that knew her well enough to realize she was either stalling or having trouble concentrating, and she really did need this document sent off immediately. So, while she couldn't completely ignore how she was feeling, she could keep her eyes where they belonged—firmly on the draft laying in front of her.

When she finally did look up she found Jonathan Barr, her junior partner, standing in her office poised to tap Micah on the shoulder. It was a good example of just how badly Micah distracted her. She hadn't even noticed him coming in and for all she knew, he could have knocked and said hello.

Micah was into her music and ignoring everything around her until she felt a tap on her shoulder. She twisted to see who it was and found Jonathan looking down at her with a bemused expression.

Micah smiled and took out her earbuds. You could hear the music blaring from them for just an instant before she dialed the volume down. She glanced down at her wristwatch and was surprised to find that an hour and a half had actually passed.

"Really Micah, they let you up here dressed like that?" Jonathan drawled, affecting a horrified tone.

"Yeah, go figure. I was sure they would turn me away at the door."

13

"Well, at least they are designer," Jonathan sniffed before flicking dismissive fingers towards her shorts.

"You are such a snob, and they should be designer since I snagged them from your closet this morning," she said, laughing at Jonathan's attempt at humor.

Olivia's gasp interrupted the friendly banter. They both turned to find her staring at the two of them. A face caught between shock and disbelief with a tinge of confusion tossed in turned speculative when Olivia's steady gaze focused on Jonathan. Their less than careful words had sparked Olivia's curiosity and Micah had no choice but to let her in on their well-kept secret. If she didn't do it now, she knew Olivia would just grill Jonathan once she left. She couldn't do that to the poor man, not after all he had done for her.

"I live with Jon now. He gave me his spare room a few months ago and in return I introduced him to Adam." A quick understanding glance passed unnoticed between the two friends. Jonathan's relief at being saved from that conversation was plainly written on his face.

"I see. Thank you for the explanation." Olivia's terse response left no opening for further conversation. Micah stood there, feeling awkward as hell while Olivia returned her attention to her paperwork, effectively ignoring the two of them. The awkward moment drew out long enough for Jon to glance over at her, as if looking to her for guidance. She just shrugged. It was just Olivia being Olivia, they both knew that.

Olivia had no idea that Micah and Jonathan were so close or that he even had a new boyfriend. Jonathan was someone she actually considered a friend, and she had no idea what was going on in his life. Making a show of flipping through the paperwork once more, Olivia scribbled a couple of quick notes on a piece of paper, put it and the documents back into the folder with more energy than required and handed the folder back to Micah.

"I'm finished with this. You know where to take it." She dismissed the two of them with a glance and a wave of her hand before turning to the next task on her desk. She needed time to digest this unexpected revelation.

She waited until Jonathan and Micah walked out of her office before throwing down her pen and swiveling her chair around to stare out at the City skyline. If she turned her head just a tiny bit she could hear them chatting out in the hall, then argued with herself about the nuances of the definition of eavesdropping before siding with the argument that supported her actions. It wasn't really eavesdropping if they chose to talk right outside of her office, right? Olivia smiled triumphantly. Especially if they didn't bother closing the door behind them.

"Are you coming for drinks with us tonight?" Jonathan asked Micah.

"Sure, I don't see any reason why not."

"Perfect, but Micah, can you please try to dress up a little?" Jonathan clapped his hands together in delight before giving Micah his best lost puppy dog expression.

"Oh, don't worry, I will dress Dyke chic. Who knows, maybe I'll get lucky." Lighthearted laughter followed the slightly off color remark. Olivia's head spun around so quickly she felt her neck pop.

"Hey, A! See you tonight," Micah called out. And then she was gone, disappearing down the hall as she headed for the elevators. Jonathan, however, wasn't so lucky. Before he could make it past Amanda's desk, Olivia called him back into her office.

"Jonathan, a moment?"

"Yes, Olivia. Of course." Jonathan followed Olivia back into her office.

"Is there something you need?" he asked meekly, knowing that this had everything to do with his young friend and nothing to do with work, other than how the next few minutes were going to affect the rest of his day. His heart didn't race, but it certainly stuttered a bit as he walked back into the office.

"Come in and close the door. Have a seat and make yourself comfortable."

***

That was easier said than done. Sitting in the chair Micah had just vacated, he couldn't help but worry. After this morning, he would forever think of it as the "chair perilous" in honor of this day. He never expected to see Micah here let alone in the same room with Olivia, and up until ten minutes ago, he would have placed a hefty bet against those odds without a minute's hesitation.

Olivia was obviously trying to gather her thoughts, ignoring his presence while she tapped a nervous drumroll out on her desk with her manicured nails. He was genuinely surprised at what Olivia said to him next but it was the pain and fear reflected in her eyes that was the most disconcerting. He couldn't remember Olivia Holden ever revealing a moment of weakness in front of anyone, not even himself.

"Please, don't let her go home with anyone tonight?" Olivia didn't care that she sounded like she was begging, or that Jonathan might realize just how much she cared for the other woman, she just didn't want Micah to find someone else before she had her chance.

Jonathan stared at her blankly. He couldn't decide whether to look concerned, surprised, or just plain shocked at the blatant request. He opted for squeezing the bridge of his nose between two fingers to ward off the coming headache and sighing. *I so do not want to be in the middle of this.*

"She never does, Olivia. She was just joking around." He didn't lie to her, not exactly. Then, because she still looked upset about the pending night out, he added more gently, "Probably because she knew you could hear what we were saying."

A long look passed between them, a moment of understanding that Jonathan knew he could never talk about, not to Adam, not to anyone. He was sure that if he tried to bring it up to Olivia again, she would deny everything, especially her motives.

Olivia took in a deep, shuddering breath then exhaled fully. Her eyes cleared and paled until they held the familiar ice blue shade that typically sent people running for cover. This was the Olivia he knew, all business and iron will, showing no weakness to the outside world and giving no quarter to her opponents.

"You can leave now," Olivia spoke gruffly, but he forgave her for it instantly. Her voice betrayed her, and he found that he enjoyed his knew found knowledge. There was a vulnerable side to the great Olivia Holden. She had kept it well hidden behind the steely gaze and stiff back she had inherited from her father, but he was relieved to find there was a softer core beneath that hard exterior.

Olivia waved her hand towards the door, dismissing him from her office without speaking again. Perhaps she was afraid her voice would crack. All he knew was that tonight was going to be quite interesting, if he had a chance to corner Micah and she was in a mood to talk to him.

Chapter Two

Monday arrived to a world as gray and dull as concrete. Raining off and on all weekend and muggy in between, the dreary weather matched Olivia's mood to a tee. She rarely worried about bad weather, but knowing that Micah would be out in it on her bicycle made her imagination run wild. She knew how many crazy drivers there were out there, and how dangerous it could be for pedestrians and cyclists alike. Unable to stop worrying, Olivia had made a few calls from her house on Saturday.

Her plan of action would keep Micah safe and out of the weather for the most part, *and near me,* she added. However, she wasn't looking forward to how Micah was going to feel about her "new" assignment. For the first time in a long while, Olivia felt nervous walking into her office. Her heart pounded beneath her calm demeanor and she could feel a slight tremor in the pit of her belly that made her hands tremble much like they had the first time her father had given her the lead in a major negotiation.

Not too long after she settled behind her desk Olivia looked up to find Micah approaching her office with sure strides. Olivia quickly dropped her gaze back where it belonged and forced herself to concentrate on the paperwork sitting on her desk.

Micah strode into Olivia's office and plopped down into the guest seat then crossed her long legs in front of her before leaning back and linking her fingers behind her head. She hadn't bothered knocking, and she hadn't given poor Amanda enough time to let Olivia know she was there before wandering, uninvited, into the private office. It was difficult, appearing outwardly relaxed and at home in Olivia's office when she was anything but calm, but she didn't want to give Olivia the satisfaction of knowing how pissed she was. After the phone call she got this morning from Street Slicks, the Bike messenger company she worked for, she felt manipulated by the other woman. Worse yet, she didn't have a clue what Olivia's agenda was, and she wasn't sure she wanted to. *Yet, here I am to find out.*

Without waiting for Olivia to acknowledge her, Micah spoke first, knowing her attitude and lack of manners would irritate Olivia to no end. Maybe she could get out of this gig if Olivia would fire her from it. She had already given the manager an earful over cheerfully assigning her to such a choice gig. He thought she would appreciate the offered bonus, which was twice her normal daily pay. The thing was, she really didn't need the money as bad as he thought she did. Micah had enough saved up to get by for quite a while. Working as a bike messenger satisfied two other needs: it was a very physical job so it helped keep her in shape while doing something she loved, and more importantly, the constant activity served to keep her too busy to start rummaging around in her own head.

"Good morning, Micah." Olivia put down her pen and gazed over that huge desk towards her. Every movement she made was precise, down to the exact right angle of the pen in relationship to the sheaf of papers beneath her left hand.

Micah felt the shock of that simple, cool greeting all the way down to her toes. Her fingers flexed, wanting to form into tight balls of anger. *Good morning?* She managed to grumble something close to a greeting before getting to the heart of the matter.

"So, I get a call from my work today only to be told I am being loaned to you, and to report here every morning." Micah paused and leaned forward, aggressively sweeping her arms out in a grand gesture that took in not only Olivia's office but the entire building. "Well, here I am, and I am curious as to why."

Micah's voice held a cadenced, almost lyrical quality that reminded Olivia of windblown cliffs and sun dappled Irish glens that sheltered shadows of darkest greens within them. She remembered Micah telling her once that her grandparents had come over from Ireland years ago, and her voice still held a tinge of that lilting accent. When she was angry, it had a habit of taking over, the lilt evolving into something harsher.

When Micah directed that harsh, almost insolent tone towards her, Olivia felt herself recoil internally. She began to wonder if she had made a terrible mistake. Uncharacteristically flustered, Olivia's gaze wandered where it shouldn't until it landed directly on an unfamiliar dark pattern on the underside of Micah's upper arm.

"What. Is. That?" She spoke each word distinctly, her extensive vocabulary reduced to single syllable sentences and stabbing her finger in the air towards Micah's upraised arm.

Micah twisted her neck to follow Olivia's finger and found the source of her wide eyed stare and incredulous expression. Her shirtsleeve had ridden high up along her bicep. Sliding back into a catlike slouch, she dropped her arms, effectively hiding the intricate loops and lines of black calligraphy marking her skin.

"It's a tattoo," Micah stated flatly.

"I didn't know you had a tattoo."

"There's a lot you don't know about me, and I actually have two tattoos." Micah volunteered the information as if issuing a challenge, fully expecting Olivia to express disapproval at something as vulgar as a tattoo.

"Where is the other one?" Olivia asked, sounding more curious than anything else.

That response threw Micah thoroughly off balance. That was so not the response she had expected. Momentarily speechless, she vaguely gestured towards her side. More ink lay hidden there, just beneath her shirt, a lot more ink than the tiny one Olivia could see.

"What does it say?" Olivia asked, focusing on the safer location, the visible one on Micah's arm.

"Fiontar Agus Duais." Micah's mild Irish brogue became more pronounced as she spoke the tattooed words.

"What does that translate to?" More curiosity.

"Basically?" Micah asked, shrugging off Olivia's obvious impatience. "Risks and Rewards."

"And what about the other one?" Olivia asked, her eyes travelling along the lines of the other woman's body, finding no evidence of the second tattoo anywhere she could see.

"It doesn't say anything," Micah said, drawing her eyebrows together in confusion. "It's a design."

Why would Olivia care about her tattoos?

"Show me." Olivia's voice rang out between them. She stood up so suddenly her chair rolled away from her, the padded leather thumping against the wall behind her.

"Um." Micah looked back at the open door, nervously considering the best avenue of retreat.

22

"Close the door, and then show me." Olivia amended her initial demand, noting the other woman's nervous glance back at the door, the faint flush of color creeping along her neck.

Automatically responding to the commanding tone, Micah closed the door and then turned towards her former boss. Olivia captured Micah's attention with one impatiently raised eyebrow hovering above piercing blue eyes, demanding control of the situation.

Micah felt caught in a strange spell she couldn't break out of. She turned away from Olivia, breaking their eye contact before pulling her T-shirt up to reveal the intricate design snaking along her back and ribcage. She clutched at the thin fabric along her waist with her other hand so it wouldn't ride up above her beltline and stood there, awkwardly waiting for Olivia to say something while she struggled with the how's and why's running through her head like a herd of frightened cattle. Micah was exposing more skin than she ought to, and, she was doing it in her former boss's office, in front of Olivia of all people.

Seriously, what the fuck am I doing?

Caught up in the chaos of her own fractured thoughts, Micah was startled to find that Olivia had left the safety of her desk. She was now standing so close to her the perfume she was wearing wove itself through and around the air about her. It made her dizzy, but that didn't stop her from filling her lungs with the intoxicating scent. Micah practically jumped out of her skin when unexpected warm fingers started travelling over the sensitive flesh along her back and ribs, following the lines of the large tattoo that started along her right shoulder and dipped along her flank, following the line of her slim waist, and disappearing into her waistline at her right hip. Serpentine and delicate, the large tattoo slithered across her skin, organically following the curves of her body so that the tattoo seemed to shift and move when she moved.

"How far does it go?" Olivia questioned breathlessly. Micah twitched, jumping nervously beneath her questing fingertips and awakening the scaled form obviously designed to flex and twist with the slightest movement. The black ink was so realistic, so finely wrought, she expected to feel rough edges sharp enough to cut her, but she found only smooth skin that warmed beneath her touch.

"Far enough," Micah said, using Olivia's question to her advantage by moving away and giving her some much-needed space. The tormenting exploration made her feel raw and exposed, as if Olivia was stroking the lines of her soul, rather than lines of ink pushed into her body by unforgiving needles. She pulled her shirt down before twisting around to face Olivia, then lifted the bottom of her cargo shorts to reveal the design trailing down her thigh to end just above the knee. She couldn't trust her voice; showing Olivia was much easier than speaking. She wouldn't have been able to form words right then anyway. Her mouth had become a desert, refusing to add moisture to her tongue at the first touch of those tentative fingers. She could still feel the lingering echo tingling along the path of Olivia's fingers as she traced the lines of her tattoo. She was sure if she checked every hard line on her back was raised, welt like, in response to the unexpected caress.

Olivia's gaze flickered down to what was literally the tail end of Micah's tattoo, then travelled up. She was an intelligent woman and quick. It wouldn't take much for her to consider what she was missing, nor to fill in those missing pieces of data. Calculating eyes narrowed as they journeyed along the hidden paths Micah had desperately kept from her sight. When she gasped and clutched at the necklace dangling between her breasts, those pale blue eyes locking onto hers with all the force of laser beams, she knew Olivia had connected the dots...so to speak. Micah glared at her, defiantly refusing to address the unspoken question behind Olivia's gaze. They stood there for a moment, neither willing to give way until Olivia nodded, not quite acceding defeat but showing a willingness to let it go for now, then turned and walked away. Micah found that the air in the room had miraculously returned. She inhaled deeply, filling her deprived lungs with much needed oxygen after holding her breath for way too long.

Olivia picked up her pen and sat down before addressing Micah again. "We're considering using bike messengers from now on rather than keeping deliveries an internal function. I expect it will be more cost effective, but I wanted someone that knows how we operate and is trustworthy. I thought you would be perfect, so I talked to your boss and he agreed for you to be loaned out here."

Micah found the explanation odd. Her ex-boss very rarely explained her actions to anyone, and only when it was necessary to make sure everything was done exactly as she wanted. *Except that didn't always apply to me, did it?* Micah asked herself. With Micah, Olivia had always been friendlier—and more forgiving, even to the point of asking her to babysit her daughter. It was this blurring of the lines between them, of strict rules broken by the very woman that lived by them that had made things difficult between them, and was a big part of the reason she had to leave.

25

"And what am I supposed to do while I wait to be, ah..." Micah searched around for a moment to find the exact word to describe what Olivia was suggesting without it sounding sarcastic. She didn't quite fail, but she didn't succeed, either. "Utilized?"

"You get to sit over there on the couch and wait."

"What? And how will you explain that, or me, to your father?" Micah half expected to find the unforgiving and overly strict senior Holden lurking just around the corner. His persistent disapproval at his daughter's inappropriate friendship with one of their interns had left Micah at the receiving end of his icy blue eyes glaring at her with what she could only call disdain. It didn't help one bit that his daughter had inherited those cold eyes, the color of an arctic storm and just as capable of freezing a room or cutting into an adversary when needed. And that was the thing, too...Olivia didn't need to get angry to win an argument. She did what was needed, without passion or heat, and she had become very good at it. After all, she had learned from the best.

Until that last night.

Micah shied away from where that thought would lead her, mentally shaking those painful moments out of her head and concentrating on what was happening now. What she had let happen now.

"Micah!" Olivia exclaimed, her initial shock at Micah's insolent tone subsiding into a resigned sigh. Of course Micah hadn't liked her father; not very many people did. He had very specific ideas about what he considered proper behavior, and he made sure that Olivia understood her position as his daughter.

"My father is no longer actively involved in the firm. He retired six months ago and I am running it now. Which means the firm operates under my rules, not my father's." No longer constrained by her father's presence, Olivia was free to bend or break any rules she wanted, or make new ones.

"Okay." Micah rubbed the back of her neck, trying to release the tension there. Sitting still was not her strong suit. "Well, do you have anything for me to do right now?"

Olivia shook her head. "No, I'm afraid not. Not for a while."

Frustrated, Micah sat up straight and tried a different tactic. "So, can I at least run and get a coffee while I wait? I haven't had my morning fix yet."

Olivia nodded in agreement and Micah bolted from the office. She grinned at Amanda on the way out and got a sympathetic wave in return.

God, she needed that coffee—not that she needed the caffeine at this particular moment; she was still buzzing from the adrenaline rush generated by the last fifteen minutes in Olivia's office. But, she did need an excuse to extricate herself from the very confusing and overwhelming scene she had just left. She was breathing too fast, as if she had just run a mile at a fast pace, and her heart continued to thud loudly in her chest in response to Olivia's gentle touch. Her skin felt electric, the lines of the tattoo tingling wherever those soft fingers had wandered. She felt dizzy and lightheaded and turned on all at once and she needed to regain control of herself before she could even think of drinking coffee. She managed to keep her cool until she made it into the bathroom. It was empty, which was a good thing because she needed a moment of privacy. The wraparound mirrored sunglasses came off, and she had to squint against the harsh fluorescent lighting until her eyes adjusted.

Micah splashed cold water on her face then leaned on the sink and stared at her reflection. It was frightening how normal she looked, especially when there was so much turmoil chewing her up on the inside. *What the hell am I doing?* She couldn't believe what she had just let Olivia do. Her brain had just turned off, and she had gone on autopilot, letting Olivia do whatever she wanted to her.

Normally she was the one in control, the one giving the commands and it scared the crap out of her that this woman could strip her of that control with just one sentence. Micah took a deep breath and searched the mirror for some kind of answer. Troubled hazel-green eyes stared back at her, mocking her attempt to see past all the padlocks she herself, had placed there. She growled in frustration. Her reflection didn't have an answer for her, either. Lacing her hands behind her neck, she tilted her head back until the fluorescent lights on the ceiling flashed bright in her eyes. Groaning at the unfairness of it all, she gave up fighting herself. She just had to admit it, she wanted it to happen. If she hadn't, she sure wouldn't have let Olivia touch her like that. She had wanted to feel something for so long, and now she knew what that something was.

***

Olivia sat for a few minutes, ignoring her work while she reviewed what had just taken place in her office. She had no idea what had come over her, acting so unprofessional in the office by having Micah show her the tattoo. She wasn't normally a visual person, but when she saw that wonderful piece of art she just had to touch it. Shaking her head, she laughed at her own delusion, then snapped her mouth shut before her secretary heard her chuckling to herself in an empty office.

Her fingertips still tingled with delicious memory. She wanted to touch Micah, had wanted to touch her for so long that the tattoo was just an excuse to do exactly that. To be perfectly honest, she had been making excuses for herself all week, ever since she had arranged for Micah to come to her office.

Olivia had missed her chance with Micah last year, before the young woman had dropped off the face of the earth without a single word or explanation. "My fault," Olivia whispered, lightly touching lucky fingertips to newly jealous lips. How do you explain to someone who thinks you are straight that you aren't? Especially if that someone knows you were once married and have a child as well?

Olivia groaned and rubbed her temples against the maddening questions that had plagued her for the last year, and for which she still didn't have an answer. How do you tell someone like Micah that you are attracted to them? That bit didn't even have anything to do with her being a woman. She wasn't good at being single, period. The subtleties of dating and all that it entailed eluded her. It simply wasn't a part of her extensive skill set, not now and certainly not back then and there was nothing she could do about that.

Then there had been that little issue of Micah being an intern. It wouldn't have been ethical, that was what she kept telling herself, despite knowing it was a lie. She had wanted Micah and made every excuse in the book not to act on her feelings, but it was because she was a coward. She had been uncomfortable with acting on her attraction. A big part of her identity, of who she was, would change forever the minute she accepted that part of herself and she had been absolutely terrified of taking that life-changing leap. It was only after the other woman was gone that she came to regret her decisions. Micah's presence had made her realize that she wanted to be with a woman, and not just with any woman; she wanted Micah.

The dark-haired woman who walked into her office today was everything she had committed to memory and yet, was so much more. She had changed her haircut, her style, even her attitude, and Olivia found every bit of it intriguing. Not to mention that tattoo! Taking in the whole package, she had to admit that the new and improved Micah was beyond alluring. Sexy in a half-tamed way that didn't diminish her interest, but rather reminded her of how addictive the thrill was when there was a bit of danger in the game.

Despite trying to keep her attention on her work, she remained distracted. Olivia was still having trouble NOT thinking about the parts of the tattoo she couldn't see. Her imagination ran wild, allowing her to draw her own conclusions as to where those lines ran and how far. She was startled out of her daydreams of soft skin and sculpted muscles when a steaming hot cup of coffee was set in front of her. She didn't take her eyes away from her paperwork, just picked up the cup and sipped carefully, expecting something mediocre and getting something else, altogether. It was good, better than her normal fare, and she doubted Amanda had suddenly developed barista quality skills. She looked up to find Micah settling in on the couch with her own steaming cup in hand and that made her unaccountably pleased.

"That is still how you take your coffee, isn't it?"

"Yes, thank you." Olivia smiled softly, touched that Micah would still remember something so inconsequential as how she liked her coffee. Micah returned the smile with one of her own before putting in her earbuds and pulling out a notebook and pencil.

After an hour or so of productive work, Olivia put down her pen with a satisfied snap and subtly stretched her shoulders before tucking the sheaf of papers into a legal envelope. Micah had shed the cap and sunglasses and was intently scribbling in her notebook. She had also made herself at home, stretching out on the small couch sitting below the requisite wall of fame every good attorney's office held. Photos with local bigwigs, award ceremonies replete with plastic smiles were interspersed with oversized diploma's written out in rolling script, all announcing her travels through the academic world and ending with the right to add more letters behind her name.

Twirling her gold Mont Blanc between manicured fingers, she took advantage of Micah's concentration to watch her work. She really did like the new haircut on her. Longer in the front but very short in the back and tousled where she periodically ran her fingers through it, the new cut gave her a rakish, almost androgynous look that suited her well. Curiosity got the better of her. She wanted to know what was keeping Micah so studiously occupied and decided it was time to find out.

"What are you doing?"

The question startled Micah.

"Um, drawing," she said, pulling out her earbuds first so she wouldn't yell over the music. She tapped her sketchbook with the flat end of her pencil, just in case it wasn't obvious enough.

31

"I realize that," Olivia drawled. Now that Micah had shed those damnable sunglasses, there was no hiding the obvious humor dancing in those eyes. Micah was being purposefully obtuse for the sheer pleasure of it, knowing how much that bothered her. "Let me rephrase that. What are you drawing?"

"A picture." Micah responded with a laugh, "Do you need me to deliver or pick anything up yet?"

Olivia handed over the envelope with an address attached. "Have Amanda copy this first, then off you go."

"Thank God, I'm not used to being this inactive," Micah exclaimed, throwing her messenger bag over her head and settling it on her shoulder before dashing out of the office.

"Don't forget, Amanda first!" Olivia called out just as Micah cleared her door. She shook her head at the other woman's exuberance. *So much energy,* she thought, turning her chair to face the wide expanse of glass behind her to gaze out at the city. With Micah gone, her office felt strangely empty and dull, more like an old library or even a tomb, rather than a place of business. Micah's presence created a sense of vibrancy that electrified the room and made her feel more alive. A pleased smile spread across her face. She had made the right decision bringing Micah back.

She stood up and stared down at the panorama laid out before her. The rain had left wet runnels streaming down the glass that distorted her view and made the various city lights appear melted mockeries of their normal iridescence, but she still strained to see a lone biker whipping between yellow cabs and darker sedans overpopulating the street below her. She frowned, her brow furrowing against the concern for Micah's safety that she couldn't easily dismiss. *It's her job, she knows what she's doing out there,* she thought, but that didn't ease her worry.

She stared down until her eyes ached from the strain and she had to give up. She had tried to wait until the rain had passed before sending Micah out. While the sun had yet to make an appearance, the rain that had steadily pelted the window all morning had finally given up, leaving the city cast in a depressing shade of dull, wet grey. *Would Micah realize what I had done, or would she think this was all some sort of power game, me holding her in check until I chose the time to let her go?* It was a troubling thought, but there was nothing she could do about it. All she could do is wait and see if she would come back.

***

Micah looked down at the address Olivia had given her and sighed in disappointment. *Only a mile away.* At least it would give her some time to clear her head, just not as much as she had hoped for. It would be back to the drawing board, literally, as soon as she returned. That wasn't exactly a horrible thing to contemplate. It had surprised her, how much sketching she had done while sitting in Olivia's office. Maybe this sitting and waiting on Olivia's couch would be good for her, her muse certainly seemed to think so. But then again, maybe not. Being in love with someone who doesn't love you back is hard enough; sitting in the same room with that person all damn day can be torture. *This job is going to give me enough angst and emotional torment to fuel every creative fire within me.*

Trying to figure out what Olivia's motive was in keeping her around consumed the rest of Micah's thoughts as she walked out the door and onto the rain-dampened streets. Unlocking her bike, she tried to erase the vision of sapphire blue eyes and travelling fingertips from her mind—she had to stay focused on the busy city streets.

On autopilot, she flew through intersections on her way to her delivery, zipping between honking cab drivers and oblivious pedestrians who maintained a studious lack of awareness of the traffic around them as they scanned their iPods or talked on their cell phones. She slid to a stop in front of the drop off location and whipped her lock out, securing her bike with the same swift, practiced movements of a champion calf roper.

On the way back to the office, Micah took a different route that extended her ride. She wanted to enjoy the feel of the speed-induced breeze on her face for a few more minutes before heading back to the couch. Her muscles were stiff from sitting all morning and she wasn't ready to go back indoors. Enjoying the burn in her calf and thigh muscles, Micah pedaled as fast as she could go until an idiot driver unexpectedly made an illegal turn right in front of her, leaving her nowhere else to go except the sidewalk.

Jumping the curb wasn't an issue, she had done it a million times before, but the garishly dressed tourists planted solidly in front of her definitely were. Their faces frozen into cartoon like "O's", they didn't have a clue that moving out of the way might be a good idea or that she was yelling for a damned good reason. Forcing the bike to make a hard right turn, she felt the single speed wobble and she went down hard. Sharp pain shot along the right side of her body as she felt bits of New York pavement scraping through the fabric of her shirt and into the flesh of her right shoulder and hip. Ignoring the burning pain, Micah cursed loudly.

GODDAMMIT! If my tattoo is fucked up, I swear to God!

Chapter Three

Now that the initial adrenaline rush had worn off, a persistent throbbing was making itself known with every step Micah took. The pain in her hip and shoulder competed with the exquisitely unique burning sting of scraped skin and exposed nerves that only road rash could offer.

Micah made a beeline for Jonathan's office and tried not to bleed onto the expensive carpet. His door was wide open, and she unceremoniously strode in, not bothering to look first.

"Hey Jon, can you help me...?" The rest of her sentence trailed off into the air along with her idiotic assumption that Jon would be available to help her. There was someone else in his office. *Of course,* Micah muttered, cursing her bad luck.

Jonathan launched from his chair the second he realized it was Micah standing in the middle of his office, disheveled and bloodied and a bit unsteady on her feet, with a look on her face that told him she wasn't thrilled to find Olivia in his office. "Jesus, Micah, are you okay?"

"Fucking dandy, Jon." Micah tried to make light of the fact that she was bleeding all over the place, but sarcasm got in the way. She just wanted to get patched up and get out of there, originally with the hopes of avoiding Olivia in the process. She would deal with the pain in her hip and knee when she got home, but the road rash was another thing. She knew she couldn't

reach the worst of it, which is why she headed straight for Jon. She could
trust him to tell her how bad it was without worrying about what he saw. She could also bully him into informing Olivia that she wasn't coming back today, preferably waiting until she was long gone. A sharp pain made her grimace, but she managed to pull a wry grin out of it.

Her plan to avoid Olivia had failed miserably. The woman was staring at her, normally ice blue eyes containing something dark and storm-ridden as she stared at Micah's tattered shirt and exposed skin. Micah couldn't get a good read on her expression, but it didn't look good for her. She hunched her shoulders, physically protecting herself from the imminent explosion. Olivia couldn't be happy about her getting hurt on the job.

"What happened?" Jon asked, carefully exploring the worst of the shredded fabric along her shoulder.

"Some jerk didn't know he was supposed to get out of my way. It was either eat pavement or run him over," she said, leaving out the part where the 3,000 pound cab tried to occupy the same space she'd been rolling through.

"Uh, huh," Jonathan murmured, then positioned himself between Olivia and Micah before pulling the dirt and blood encrusted fabric away from her skin. "It could be worse, but this shirt is definitely done for."

"It is?" Micah twisted to see for herself, then winced and gave up before Olivia saw her. She was trying like hell not to let on how uncomfortable she was, and Olivia's eyes hadn't left her since she walked in.

"I thought you might have a first aid kit?" she asked, trying to ignore the constant sting of torn fabric rubbing painfully against already raw skin. *Jesus, it's starting to feel like someone was taking a potato grater to my back.* That thought generated a genuinely toe curling visual image inside her head. A residual thread of nausea returned to coil around her gut. Sometimes being an artist wasn't a good thing, not when your imagination could turn any random thought into an image you didn't want to see. Contrary to popular belief, you can't just take an imaginary eraser through there and wipe it clean like chalk on a blackboard.

Micah gave Jonathan an expectant look. He turned to find Olivia ignoring everything but Micah. He sighed and rubbed his eyes hard enough to feel the back of his eye sockets.

"Fine, I'll find it," Jonathan muttered. He wasn't keen on leaving those two particular woman alone while he searched the break room for the small first aid box they were required to keep, but it was either do it himself or stand and watch them glare at each other. All they needed was some bad dialogue and some cheesy spaghetti-western music playing in the background to make their little Mexican standoff complete. Troubled and more than a little worried about what he would find when he returned to his office, he hustled back as quickly as he could, his silk tie flapping over his shoulder and his Dulce & Gabbana patent leather dress shoes complaining to his feet over the pace.

Olivia intercepted him before he managed to gain a foothold in his own office.

"I'll take care of this, Jonathan, just keep working and make sure you get that contract to me by the end of the day." Olivia held out one perfectly manicured hand in his direction, palm up, and waited with barely concealed impatience.

Jonathan's eyebrows shot up to where his hairline used to be, but he gave up the small box without another word, then shot Micah an apologetic look that wasn't going to save him when he got home.

"Hey, don't I get a word in on this?" Micah protested.

"No, not when you've been injured on my time. I need to make sure you don't need more than a Band-Aid before I let you go home."

Faced with the realization that she could either make a scene right here in front of everyone, or go along with Olivia's overbearing motherliness, Micah chose to shut her mouth. She had already put Jon in a bad situation by coming to him first, she wasn't about to make him choose between them or end up playing referee between his boss and his best friend. Now, if he volunteered, that was a different matter altogether. Micah threw one last blatantly desperate look in his direction as she was unceremoniously escorted out of his office, but he just shook his head. *No help there.*

Despite her best intentions she balked at the door, but Olivia wasn't having any of it. She just took her by her uninjured arm and led Micah down the hall to her office.

"Ow, ow... Olivia, you need to slow down! I landed on my hip," Micah protested. Olivia on a mission was an unstoppable force, and Micah wasn't immune. She was being pulled along in the other woman's wake far faster than her abused muscles were willing to go.

Olivia did slow down, but she didn't stop until they were both in the luxurious private bathroom that she shared with no one. It was Olivia's one treat to herself. She insisted on it when she made full partner, among other demands, even going so far as having her father put it down in writing while she smiled, overly pleased at her creative negotiations. Her father had laughed, then told her how much like her mother she was. She had agreed with him then, but deep in her heart she knew he was the one she took after, had emulated for so many years that she had managed to overcome the one defect she couldn't overcome. He had wanted a son to follow behind him, but had only managed to produce a daughter. Since he still raised a topnotch attorney to follow in his footsteps, she felt he should have been happy about that. His refusal to retire until this year, years after he promised to, was a pretty clear indicator he wasn't. *Arghh...why am I thinking about this now?* Olivia berated herself. There were more important things going on now than rehashing the past, and right now that important thing was watching her warily, like a wild animal debating if the meal you just threw at them was some sort of trap.

Olivia started sorting through the first aid supplies, dumping items out onto the marble countertop. Focusing on the task gave her time to try and control her rampaging emotions. Seeing Micah injured bothered her more than she cared to admit, especially because she had been the one to send her out. She felt responsible. A sick feeling passed through her, realizing how much risk Micah took out there on her bike. She could have been injured, much worse than she had been. The thought of not ever seeing Micah again caused her to pause, frozen in place as she considered the possible outcomes before her hands reacted to the cold feeling. Her hands shook violently for a second before she was able to school them into performing for her, until only the slightest tremor remained that would give away how absolutely terrified she had felt when Micah walked in. *At least she had walked in on her own power*, she consoled herself.

"Olivia, are you mad at me for something?" Micah asked. She could feel the tension coming off the other woman's body in waves like heat on summer pavement, could see it in the jerky way she moved as she dug through the miscellaneous first aid supplies.

"No, Micah, I am not mad at you," Olivia gritted out between clenched teeth, then almost dropped her gauze before turning around and pointing at the toilet seat. "Sit."

Micah didn't really believe her, but she sat anyways, then looked around. Olivia had done some redecorating since she'd been gone. The room was extravagant, both in its décor and size. Too big to fit in a broom closet, she had speculated whether someone had lost a private office so Olivia could have her folly. Deep marble tiles accented the floor and set off the cloth wallpaper set in an elegant gold leaf pattern fit for a queen. The marble countertop Olivia was using as a first aid station doubled as a make-up station. Micah wondered why she was sitting on an uncomfortable toilet seat when there was a very comfortable looking chair available—then she saw her reflection and snorted in amusement.

I wouldn't have put me in that chair either.

The upholstery looked expensive and that meant it was; Olivia wouldn't suffer anything less than the best. It certainly wouldn't have survived the grimy and bleeding woman looking back at her in the mirror.

"This might hurt." Olivia hesitated before she began. That first glimmer of uncertainty in her eyes was somehow reassuring and Micah relaxed minutely.

"I know."

She had to give it to her. Olivia was being incredibly gentle as she bandaged her shoulder. There wasn't much left of her shirt where she had hit the cement; a simple tug had been all it took to widen the gap large enough to expose the scraped skin. The rest of her sleeve lay tattered and as ragged looking as her skin felt.

"Why do you do it?" Olivia asked. She was applying tape to a large white bandage.

"Do what?"

"Bike messenger, it's dangerous."

"It's all about risks and rewards, Olivia," she stated with conviction, her voice clear and purposeful.

"Is the risk worth it then?" Olivia's sharp blue eyes captured her in a hawk like gaze and refused to let her go.

"I'll let you know when I find out." Micah sighed, exhaustion settling in as the last remnants of the accident fueled adrenaline rush left her. Rising a little unsteadily from the toilet seat, she winced when her hip protested, stiff from sitting on the cold porcelain.

"Let me see your hip." Olivia immediately stepped closer, her gaze flickering down Micah's body, searching for more signs of injury.

"Um, no," Micah stated flatly, wishing Olivia hadn't moved so close to her.

After she had hit the pavement, the acrid scent of fear had invaded her sense of smell. That bitter smell of sulfur and ozone had burned into her nostrils so completely she hadn't been able to smell anything else— until the heady aroma of Olivia's favorite perfume chased it away. The close confines were concentrating the enticing scent, invading her thoughts and sending

Micah's hormones rampaging like an enraged bull to overrun her already overstimulated system.

The urge to take the woman before her into her arms and lay her down onto that oh, so cool marble floor was an almost palpable force. Her hands trembled with the overwhelming desire to act out the scenes playing out on the back of her eyelids. *Probably an after effect of the adrenaline rush,* she thought, trying to find a logical explanation for her sudden arousal.

"Micah?" Olivia's voice startled her out of her reverie. "Show me." Tinged with impatience, it was more of a demand than a request and it sent ice tumbling through Micah's veins.

"No," Micah repeated. She had other reasons than just her hormones for not wanting to disrobe in front of her ex-boss. This morning was a mistake she wasn't going to repeat.

"Are you prepared to be sent home for this?" Olivia sounded cross now. Knowing Micah, she would try to work injured and not take care of herself.

"Yes," Micah answered without hesitation, lifting her jaw stubbornly. There was no way she was giving in to her, not on this.

"Then just leave," Olivia sighed, gesturing towards the door gracefully. Turning her back to the door, she stared into the mirror at her reflection. Micah stood there for a moment, then raised her hand. She wasn't sure what she was planning to do. Turn her around? Apologize? Take her into her arms and do all the things she had fantasized about doing for the last year? She hesitated and Olivia spoke, sounding so resigned it made Micah flinch.

"Please, don't." Olivia turned her face away from Micah's gaze.

Micah closed her eyes against a different sort of pain that creeped into her heart, a razor sharp pain she hadn't felt in over a year, then left the bathroom and the office without a backward glance.

Chapter Four

Back at her apartment, Micah gently laid her damaged bike out on the covered balcony then crouched down in front of it with a sad sigh. The poor thing looked pitiful. Its front wheel was twisted and warped from the spill, a solid reminder of the dangers of riding in the city that she not only ignored, but relished in a way only another adrenaline junkie would understand.

A quick inspection showed the frame was still true, and luckily the Hurley fixed gear set and chain tensioner had escaped as well. The nondescript frame was covered in an explosive collage of paint, stickers, and scuffmarks that defied identification. The purposeful defacement was the ultimate urban camouflage, a disguise meant to hide what it really was—a high-end Cannondale racer, modified and purposefully made to look cheap if not totally worthless. You can't bring your bike into the buildings with you and you can't have a bike that looks like its anything worth stealing, either. That was a sure way to end up walking back from a delivery, not a good idea when you're a bike messenger. Satisfied that her bike was at least mostly sound, she made a quick mental note to pick up a new wheel later on. Right now, she was tired and sore and all she really wanted to accomplish was to get out of her dirty clothes and crash for a while.

Getting back up took more effort. Her back and hip twinged when she tried to stand up, but she managed to get off the balcony without hunching over like a frail ninety year old. It wasn't until she was back in her bedroom and away from the apartments overly immaculate shared spaces that Micah was able to take a deep breath and unwind. She could be herself in the comfort of her own personal haven.

Her room was at odds with the modern, art deco theme that Jon favored for the rest of the apartment. More than one piece of her furniture had earned a raised eyebrow when she had moved in, a couple of items had made Jon clutch his chest and run away from the sheer horror of her lack of style. She had simple needs and even simpler requirements in furnishings. Everything matched but only because nothing really did, making it a theme. It was all comfortable and none of it would suffer from the occasional spilled coke or grease stain. A tall metal bike stand stood against the height of the far wall, showcasing two very different bicycles from the one she had left on the balcony.

The first was a bright yellow custom job. Her pride and joy, it had started its life as a high-end street bike she had personally customized into a cross comp. She took this bike with her on the rare trip out to the mountains. The second bike was an old Japanese road bike. Half dismantled, its frame rested in the arms of its bike stand like a partially reconstructed dinosaur skeleton, which wasn't far from the truth in bike years. The beast was over twenty years old, making its steel frame a rare creature in a world full of titanium and carbon. Micah was retrofitting the steel frame with modern parts, a project she kept meaning to get back to. A quick click of her remote and loud music filled the space around her from the speakers she had laid out strategically around the room. Taking advantage of Jon's absence, Micah dialed the sound up as high as she wanted, enjoying the sensation of the bass as it thumped through the apartment like a physical presence.

Humming snippets of the song blasting through the apartment, she stripped off her shirt and headed for the bathroom. The shredded garment was crusted with pavement, dirt, and blood. Micah curled her lip in disgust.

No saving that, she thought, tossing the ruined shirt straight into the trashcan, *and it was one of my favorites, too.*

Micah had spent a lot of time in the gym over the last couple of years improving her physique, so the form fitting tops she favored led to a lot of appreciative looks at work and on the street. She wasn't above enjoying the attention, and now that the boys at work knew which way she swung, they had stopped hitting on her and treated her like one of the guys. The girls, on the other hand, were somewhat emboldened by the knowledge. They weren't above an occasional bicep squeeze or brush-up along the tight corridors of Street Slicks. Even some of the straight women flirted with her, which didn't hurt Micah's ego a single bit.

Shoes and shorts went next. Micah padded into the bathroom, leaving a trail of clothing behind her like modern breadcrumbs dropped in a carpeted forest. Twisting her back towards the mirror, she reached over her shoulder and peeled Olivia's neatly placed bandage away to inspect the damage. She hissed as the tape peeled off her abraded shoulder, revealing angry red road rash gleaming wetly against her intact skin. The lower corner of the abrasion overlapped the tattoo travelling along her upper back, the intricate black ink work lost beneath the scraped and torn skin.

*Dammit, dammit, dammit...*Micah cursed roughly, beyond angry that her artwork was damaged.

The otherwise sharp edges of the black design licked up against the red of the road rash, making the tattoo look as if it was breathing bloody fire. There was nothing to do but let it heal and see what kind of touch up she might have to get done. Her next visit to the tattoo shop was definitely going to have to be put on hold. The tattoo wasn't complete, and this was going to keep her from getting her "fix" for quite a while. Not to mention the damage was going to piss off her tattoo artist to no end. *Great, this just gets better and better.*

She switched her attention to her other injuries, focusing on where it hurt the most. Pressing lightly with her fingertips along the crest of her hip, she found a tender area right along her right flank. It felt swollen and bruised, but it was the discolored patch across her lower back that concerned her most. She remembered landing on something hard and unforgiving when her bike went down and thought she had bounced off her bike chain. Now she wasn't so sure. Further inspection revealed a deep, jagged scratch that lay across her lower back just above her underwear line, already scabbing over with dry blood. That one was going to hurt a lot more before it got better.

At least Olivia fired me since I couldn't go back to work today looking like this. How convenient. Other than being stuck at home for the rest of the day to recuperate, that thought should have made her happy.

So why does it hurt so much if that's what I really wanted?

Rubbing her chest against the deep ache growing beneath her breastbone, she tried to bypass that line of thought as she concentrated on injuries she could address.

Micah needed to get cleaned up, but the thought of water sluicing along her injured shoulder didn't sound particularly appealing or relaxing. A hot bath was more in order. Its calm waters seemed more welcoming to her sore muscles then a shower. She waited until the bath was almost full before adding her favorite oils, the smell of sandalwood and patchouli riding the heavy steam circling lazily over the hot water. Silently thanking Jon for his hedonistic ways, she greedily eyed the sinfully lavish oversized tub he had equipped her bathroom with. Micah slid her slim body along the pale cool porcelain of the edge of the tub, testing the steaming hot water with one foot before lowering herself the rest of the way in. She closed her eyes, blissfully losing herself to the music drifting in from her bedroom, intent on soaking the pain of the day away.

***

The following morning, Micah stood silently in front of a large drawing she had tacked against the bedroom wall. This morning ritual held specific importance to her, and it was something she did every morning since she came back from West Virginia. A stylized semi-realistic design with a hint of Celtic flair, the drawing was long and sinuous. The image of a dragon, unique in concept, lay hidden within an intricate pattern of sweeping black lines and interlacing negative spaces.

Micah followed the lines of her artwork, mentally noting how the design translated when tattooed along her body's planes. The path of an upraised claw, designed to appear to grasp her right shoulder, the mouth of the dragon biting along her neck line, were all designed to accentuate the shape and curve of her well-muscled body. Her hand travelling along her stomach, her fingers curling into a weak imitation of the strength drawn into the dragon's hindquarters. She could almost feel the deep pain of sharp claws digging into her lower abdomen while another leg sought purchase across her right hip. The long tail curved along her thigh, twisting to follow the muscles of her right quad until it curved and twisted into oblivion above her right knee.

The drawing was complete, but the tattoo was not.

The tattoo artist she had chosen was one of the best in New York. Cassandra Wolfe was highly sought after and very exclusive, but Micah's contacts had gotten her a choice meeting with the artist. She was sure that the well-known artist would jump on the chance once she saw her design. Instead, Cassandra had tried to talk Micah out of it. She was worried about working with a practically virgin canvas, but Micah was adamant in her desire. It was a challenge to convince her to change her mind, but once she was invested, Cassandra began to relish Micah's periodic visits to finish the large piece. Micah had laughed when Cassandra told her she was one of her best canvasses, impressed at her ability to endure the pain of tattooing along the most sensitive areas. Half-jokingly, she had grinned at the heavily tattooed artist, "Oh, but I like the pain."

Only a tattoo artist would accept a statement like that without wondering about your mental health, Cassandra didn't even blink an eye. More than likely, she was a kindred spirit who welcomed the challenge Micah presented. Now, her next appointment would have to be put on hold until her skin healed. For the first time since they had started, she was going to have to cancel on Cassandra. She wasn't going to be happy.

Turning away from the drawing, Micah glanced at her waiting computer. She really needed to get back to work on what she was writing. It was getting to a point where she was starting to feel guilty about it, but the prospect of sitting quietly at her desk was almost unbearable when she felt like this. She looked away from the black screen only to land on another source of frustration. A half-finished sketch sat on her easel, taunting her with its lack of completeness. She felt a little like that drawing today. Her tattoo unfinished and now damaged, she could feel where lines needed to be, and she felt their absence keenly. Her hand itched to pick up a pencil and start in on the drawing, but her mind felt too scattered. Her agitation a mental tremor she knew would frustrate her if she tried to do any work now.

Pacing like a caged tiger, Micah gave up and grabbed her bright yellow cross comp bike and headed out onto the streets. Her single speed needed a new tire, and she needed to RIDE! It didn't matter that every revolution made her hip scream, or that her shoulder hated every ounce of pressure she put on it. She could deal with the pain. What mattered was the crisp morning greeting her as she breezed out the front lobby and onto familiar streets that still made her heart race with anticipation. She headed for The Racked Bike, a basement bicycle shop she loved to frequent. Its current owners, Bethany and Sam, had left its dungeon theme intact from its prior life as an underground Goth club, but that wasn't what made the shop truly unique. The bicycle shop also doubled as an industrial art showroom. Bethany was an avid producer of metal art, her twisted but brilliant pieces giving new life to old bicycles and other bits of urban debris.

Micah grinned joyfully as she sped up, creating her own breeze as she whipped through the streets with wild abandon. Her path heralded by the honking horns and foul language of those less fortunate fools caught inside metal boxes with four wheels. Gridlock simply wasn't something that existed in her two-wheeled world. There was always a path around every obstacle. *Well, almost always*, she thought, the small twinges of pain in her hip and shoulder reminding her otherwise.

Chapter Five

Olivia woke up Wednesday morning eager to get back into the office and, although she would never admit it, her cheerful attitude had more to do with a certain woman than her vaunted work ethic. Micah hadn't come in to work yesterday after taking that terrible spill the day before, but when she called the manager at Street Slicks last night, he had assured her Micah was still slated to report to her office in the morning. She could tell that he was curious about the unusual arrangement, but her generous offer for Micah's "loan" was more than sufficient to keep those unspoken questions at bay.

Regina had been snooping around when she was talking on the phone and had overheard her mention Micah's name. Her daughter had been so excited to know that Micah was back in town that she had interrupted her phone call, first by squealing loud enough to make the neighbor's dog howl, then by following that horrendous noise up with a million questions—questions for which Olivia had no readily available answers.

That had only encouraged her enthusiastic offspring to push for more information, and she had to admit her juvenile attempts at cross examination were pretty impressive for one so young. Regina was smart and had learned a lot from listening to her mother, but she had been bound to lose that fight. Even so, she did manage to earn one concession before accepting defeat. Olivia had to agree to ask Micah over for dinner, in exchange, Regina had promised to go to bed on time and without complaining about it for an entire week. Their agreed upon compromise was a win-win in Olivia's book, but she still scowled and made a show of agreeing only after Regina had made her argument. Dinner was an excellent excuse to see Micah outside of the office and since it was Regina's request, she doubted that Micah would say no.

Regina hated the idea of being subjected to the occasional babysitter, but she adored Micah and had been brokenhearted when she left. Micah had been the one and only intern Olivia had ever asked to babysit for her. She wanted to say that she did it because she knew the younger woman needed the money for school, but she refused to believe her own lies any longer. She had invited Micah into her house because she wanted her there. Her father had been adamant about a lot of rules but he was absolutely tyrannical over one in particular— no fraternizing, especially with the interns. He wasn't thrilled about the babysitting, but he had relented when it coincided with his schedule. The senior Holden needed his heir apparent at a particularly important dinner affair, and she needed somebody on short notice. Micah had volunteered, and after that it was hard for her father to say no, not after allowing it once.

She smiled, but there was no humor in it. That was all she was allowed to get away with, and she had taken full advantage of it, even if all there was to it was a few quiet moments of conversation at the end of the night. She would come home after some tedious party or another and Micah would be there, studying or watching TV, and they would chat for a while before Micah had to leave. She would walk upstairs and kiss Regina goodnight, and the next day it was back to business as usual. It wasn't much, but it was something. *Something you royally screwed up in the end, didn't you?* She sighed at the heaviness of her thoughts, willing the self-accusations away as a useless exercise in regret. It was the past and there was no changing it.

Then Micah had left, disappearing before her internship was over and Olivia never had a chance to explain. But now she had Micah back and there was nothing keeping them apart. *Except for the past, isn't that ironic?* Her failure to be honest with the other woman about her feelings was coming back to bite her in the ass in a very big way.

On the ride in to work, Olivia had a lot of time to think about Micah. The woman who walked into her office the other day certainly wasn't the same woman that had walked away from her a year ago. Somewhere along the way she had lost a great deal of complacence and found her confidence, but not in the traditional sense she was used to. It confused the hell out of her. It was as if Micah had somehow remade herself, taking an over-polished gem and chipping rough edges in it, giving it sharp edges and difficult to navigate facets. In the process, she had become profoundly more interesting.

Olivia strode out of the elevator and nodded to the receptionist on the way to her office. Her eyes strayed to the elegant lettering proclaiming the firm's name above the receptionists' desk. That was one thing she could honestly say was a change for the better. The elder Holden had finally retired, removing the last external obstacle between her and Micah.

Her father's stern voice still echoed inside her head at times, reminding her of the need for decorum in her professional and private life. The private lectures about professionalism and proper behavior were so commonplace in her office, she swore the words were ingrained in the wood of her desk and along the book-clad walls. She could ignore that echo now that her father was retired and she wasn't subject to his disapproving glare, marking every unguarded glance and chance smile.

A mental snapshot of Micah slouching in her office popped into her head. Insolent, brooding yet arrogant...she oozed sexual tension with a touch of something almost dangerous. If he had an issue with Micah before, she was sure this butchier version would be met with abject disapproval. For some reason, that made her smile even more.

***

Olivia set her leather briefcase down on the only corner of her desk not filled with something. The pile of paperwork laying on her desk was ridiculous, and that wasn't even the half of it. She hadn't even turned on her computer to scroll through the dozens of emails she was sure were all marked urgent. It was amazing how much work mysteriously appeared on her desk after she left for the night but before she returned in the morning. Not that she was going to complain about the efficiency of her office. It was one of the things she could always count on. Efficiency and a level of detail orientation that would drive some people mad, but pleased her to no end, even if it meant walking into a stack of paperwork every morning. Diving into the pile, Olivia delegated a decent amount of work towards her intern, and then started in on what was important and couldn't be put off.

Two hours ticked by to the sound of papers rustling and her pen scratching out notes before Olivia finally looked up from her desk and realized that Micah still wasn't in. Getting some coffee and stretching her legs sounded like a good idea, so she took advantage and went in search of Jonathan.

"Jonathan? Is Micah okay? I figured she would be back in today." Jonathan looked up from his desk at the sound of Olivia's voice, his eyebrows knitting together in confusion.

"Yes, of course she is. She left the apartment and went to work like always," he said, peering past Olivia as if expecting Micah to magically appear behind her. "Why? Is she not here?"

"Would I ask if she was okay if she was here?" Trying desperately not to roll her eyes at her junior partner, Olivia couldn't keep the peevishness out of her voice. She wasn't sure if Jonathan was being purposefully dense or...? Or what? Olivia wasn't sure where that came from. Evidently, when it came to Micah she would have to watch her emotional responses. Somehow, everything was rawer, almost visceral. From the knowing look on Jonathan's face, she was also being incredibly obvious.

"Um, you have a point there, Olivia," Jonathan answered, a little worried himself now. He picked up his cell phone and speed dialed Micah.

"Hey, are you okay?" he asked as soon as Micah picked up the phone.

Olivia stood in front of him, arms crossed stiffly in front of her with barely concealed frustration.

That she was standing in the same power position she reserved for her opponents didn't help Jonathan's nerves one bit. He swiveled sideways in his chair so that the burning sensation from Olivia's laser like stare slid closer to his temple rather than right between his eyes.

"Where are you?" Jonathan inquired, then started laughing after hearing Micah's answer. "Okay, see you tonight."

"Well, what did she say?"

"She's at Street Slicks. Apparently, when you told her to leave on Monday she thought you were letting her go, permanently."

"Oh." Olivia made the word sound like she had been punched in the stomach.

"Olivia? This thing brewing between you and Micah, it puts me in a tight position."

"I know, Jonathan. I'm sorry." Olivia laughed, a sharp, humorless sound she immediately cut off. "I seem to be doing that a lot lately, apologizing."

"Does it feel as strange to you as it does to me?" he asked. Olivia wasn't known for backing down from anything, even when she was wrong. She was more likely to change the rules on you to prove a point.

Olivia shrugged, an elegant motion that relied more on a delicate flick of her wrist than her shoulders. "You could be right."

Jonathan rubbed his temple with his forefingers, silently contemplating what he should do next. He didn't want to see either woman hurt but he couldn't just stand by and not do what he could to help, either. *Meddling old fool, that's what you are.* Decision made, he stood up and walked around to where Olivia was standing woodenly, an odd, almost forlorn expression on her face.

"Olivia. Micah is different from the woman you knew a year ago. I know you have no idea but..." He stopped and laid a gentle hand on her shoulder before continuing. This was going to be hard. "That was stupid of me. How could you know?"

"I need to tell you about Micah's parents. To begin with, they aren't the nicest people in the world. Dogmatic, old-fashioned—call it what you will, but they chose their religion over their daughter. They turned on her after she came out to them. They used their beliefs to give them the excuse to betray her in the worst possible way and felt justified in doing it. They turned on her because she chose to be with a woman, and they couldn't handle the shame of her being that way."

His next words bore straight down into her soul, and she understood why he had looked so reticent about telling her about Micah.

"Because she chose you, Olivia. Even though she didn't think she could have you, she was true to herself, but not without consequence." Jonathan looked away then, unable to meet Olivia's eyes straight on. His throat worked several times before he was able to swallow properly, and when he continued, it was in a voice that held unspeakable sorrow. There was another story there, something he was holding back from her. He looked at her then with red-rimmed eyes with an unspoken plea to let it go. Olivia pushed down her normally bullish nature that made her want to demand to know everything. If Jonathan didn't want to tell her, it was for a reason. She didn't like it, but she had to accept it. She nodded at him, letting him know that she understood. A tentative smile ghosted past his lips before he continued.

"I can't tell you everything, I won't betray Micah like that. All I can say is they hurt her, badly, and it did something to her. It took her a long time, but she refused to let it destroy her. She became more independent. Hardening herself and yes, getting a little cocky in the process. She's angry and stubborn and unwilling to get hurt again, and she will run if she feels threatened or pushed into a corner."

Jonathan had one last thing to say before leaving Olivia to think about what he had told her. He spoke over his shoulder, unwilling to witness the headstrong and indomitable woman so overwrought. He had never seen Olivia as a frail woman, and he didn't want her to worry about having a moment of weakness in front of someone else. She needed to feel what he was about to say without walls around her, and she couldn't do that if he was there.

"I wouldn't even be telling you this, Olivia, if I didn't know how much she means to you. I care about both of you, and if there was anything I could do that would help you two find happiness, I would. Even if that means meddling just a bit." He laughed then, the sound harsh with irony. "If you truly want her, be prepared, you will have to fight her insecurities. But I can tell you, she is worth it."

And with that last bit, Jonathan walked out of his own office to give Olivia some privacy.

Olivia's mind and body felt raw, exposed—a glacier grinding against a barren landscape, impossibly hot and cold at the same time. Her throat felt as dry as the desert and she had to swallow hard several times before she could break her tongue free from the roof of her mouth. Unshed tears brimmed dangerously close to falling past eyes that burned with the effort to keep them at bay. Blindly finding the corner of Jon's desk, she allowed herself to lean heavily on the thick wood, bowing her head for a moment before gathering her tattered soul around her. Jonathan hadn't told her much, but the sadness in his voice had spoken volumes. There was so much more to Micah's story than he could tell, a story that included her and had changed Micah.

A couple of deep breaths later and Olivia was out the door, heading for her own office.

"Amanda! Cancel the rest of my appointments and have Robert come around with the car. Five minutes." Olivia whipped by Amanda, trusting her to get everything done, gathered up her things and left the office. A newfound sense of purpose fueled her. If she had to fight for Micah, she would; she refused to lose her over a simple misunderstanding.

Robert pulled up to Street Slicks, her sleek black town car looking very out of place outside of the run-down converted warehouse that housed the bike messenger service. The place was overrun with dozens of bikes and scruffy young men and women lounging outside an open roll-up door that served as the entrance. Large industrial windows lined the second floor above them. Too dusty to reflect the city skyline, they were dotted with broken panes that stood out like broken teeth, dark and jagged negatives against the dull grey glass and faded graffiti plastered across the walls.

Signaling Robert to join her, Olivia exited the interior of her car, her high heels and silk power suit out of place within a sea of cargo shorts, t-shirts, and sneakers. Approaching the group with Robert close at her back, she walked into a wall of loud music and infectious laughter. A group of people gathered around someone doing tricks on a bike on top of one of the tables placed along the sidewalk.

"Hey, Micah, you going to take a turn?" Olivia heard somebody yell over the raucous din. Loud voices competed with the rhythmic music blasting from the boom box that sat perched precariously along a shallow window ledge. The milling crowd did not prevent her from noticing the lithe figure peeling herself off the wall in response to the challenge from where she had been lounging. Micah moved easily, denying the fact that she had just eaten pavement a couple of days ago. Olivia noticed the cigarette held loosely in Micah's right hand, lazy smoke curling around long fingers that trailed off into nothingness. *How odd,* she thought, trying to remember if she had ever smelled cigarette smoke in their earlier interactions. She didn't know Micah smoked.

"Yeah, I'm up, but I want a different song." The sardonic smile and jaunty gait made Olivia hesitate.

Stepping forward into the crowd, Micah noticed Olivia standing across from her. Their eyes locked, hazel to blue. Micah's gait stuttered for a moment before resolutely changing direction. Stalking past the offered trick bike, she held Olivia's gaze firmly in her own, her expression intense.

"Which song do you want?" someone called out, oblivious to the tension crackling in the air between the two women.

Micah turned back to the disappointed crowd, walking backwards for a second.

"Sorry, guys, something else has come up." Tossing her cigarette to the ground, she put it out with a quick twist of her foot and strode past Olivia. She gave the haughty looking woman a barely perceptible nod, inviting the lawyer to join her in her own car.

"Robert, can you give us a few minutes, please?" Olivia asked.

"Yes ma'am." Robert opened the door and stepped back to let them in. "I'll be close by in case you need me."

The solid metal door closed silently, swallowing the noise from the outside. Micah heard a few disappointed boos and one or two catcalls rush in before the lush interior of the town car's back seat narrowed her world down to the smell of soft leather and Olivia.

Stretching her legs out before her, Micah slouched insolently against the soft black leather and waited for Olivia to explain herself. The tension between them thickened into something almost palpable, practically crackling like ball lightening within the shaded confines of the car.

"Where are your sunglasses?" Olivia asked, filling the silence with the first thing she could think of.

"They went missing when I hit the pavement the other day," Micah answered. "I didn't realize they were gone until I got home. They were probably scratched or broken, anyway," she added, shrugging her shoulders at the loss.

The conversation faltered then but the enclosed interior of the car left no room for uncomfortable silence.

"Look Olivia, is that what you came down here to ask me? If it is, I'm leaving, I have things to do." Shifting in her seat, Micah grabbed the door handle, making her intentions completely clear. If Olivia didn't have something important to say, she had no reason to stay.

"Micah, please, sit back down." Olivia patted the leather seat next to her.

It was the "please" that did it for Micah. Curiosity getting the best of her, she settled back down next to Olivia and waited for her to continue.

Olivia studied the woman sharing the back seat of her town-car, openly admiring the casual, almost catlike, slouch that managed to accentuate her sleek muscularity. Micah's baggy cargo shorts were a frustrating barrier to Olivia's desire. She wanted to see more than a perfectly formed set of calves emerging from the shadows of the heavy cotton cloth. Her t-shirt on the other hand, was form fitting. Snug against her biceps, the tight fabric left little to the imagination and made her want to reach out and touch the hard curves beneath it. A pair of trim leather bracers graced each sinewy wrist. The overall picture was very appealing, so much so that she was finding it hard to think clearly. This new Micah was breathtaking—androgynous, slightly dangerous looking, and so sure of herself. Olivia made the mistake of taking in a deep breath to calm herself. In the close confines of the car, Micah's scent, clean and earthy, practically overwhelmed Olivia and threatened her composure.

"I didn't mean for you not to come back, I just wanted you to take a day to rest," Olivia spoke quietly, her hands betraying her nervousness. She could barely look at the woman across from her, and that was so unlike her. She forced her fingers to relax as she willed herself to look up. Micah was watching her closely, patiently, as if assessing and weighing her every word. The weight of that gaze stripped her of any guile and left her with only one tool in her arsenal, raw honesty.

"You were supposed to rest and come back in today, or at least let me know if you couldn't."

"You told me to leave, I left. You never said to come back," Micah explained, a self-deprecating smile ghosting across her lips.

"Well then, come back," Olivia stated, as if it was as simple as that. Remembering what Jonathan had told her, she worked diligently to temper her normally impatient nature.

"Please come back?" Olivia found herself in an uncharacteristic position, one where she wasn't the power player. It was unfamiliar territory, and her request shocked her as much as it shocked Micah.

"I don't know what you want from me, Olivia," Micah growled and looked away.

It was Olivia's turn to be confused and angry.

"What do I want?" she asked incredulously, her voice raising several octaves in response to Micah's tone. She had been reduced to pleading, had opened her heart and let it rule her behavior. "What I want," she repeated, her voice firm now. She wasn't asking a question but making a statement. "What I want is..."

Trailing off, she let her actions speak for her.

Leaning forward, she wrapped her hands around Micah's neck and drew her in for a passionate kiss. It was a kiss born out of anger and desire, all wrapped up together into one confused mess that left her breathless.

Micah stiffened at the sudden onslaught of emotions, the unexpected physical contact, and the sheer intensity of Olivia's kiss. The sensation of those soft lips upon her own chased her anger away and left her wanting more. Leaning Olivia back into the soft leather, she removed the other woman's hands from her neck, holding them down for a moment before lacing her fingers through pale blonde hair so soft it could make silk weep. In control now, Micah deepened the kiss. She parted her lips, allowing her tongue to run along Olivia's bottom lip, coaxing her to let her in. Seeking entrance to the sweet interior of the other woman's mouth, she teased and enticed Olivia's tongue to dance alongside hers. A moan travelled up and through the two women. Unsure of who originated the sound of want and desire but caught up in its siren song, Micah felt the hot spark of arousal ignite deep inside her, threatening to burn through the thin thread of self-control she refused to relinquish.

Breathing heavily, she broke away from Olivia and retreated to the farthest corner of the back seat. It was almost humorous, the two of them making out in the back of a car like teenagers, but that didn't make it any easier. She pushed hard, fighting her body's demand to continue what they had started. Ignoring the sensation of an electrical storm rumbling deep in the pit of her stomach, she watched as Olivia worked just as hard to compose herself.

"What just happened?" Olivia's voice was a pale reflection of itself, breathless and full of wonder.

"You tell me, Olivia. You kissed me," Micah responded from the relative safety of her corner. Her heart was pounding almost painfully inside her chest. She had envisioned kissing Olivia many times in the past year, but not once had she expected Olivia to be the one to kiss her first.

"Does it matter? No, don't answer that."

"So, where do we go from here?" Micah asked.

"I still want you to come back, will you please come back?"

"I will, but if you tell me to leave again, it will be forever. I'm sorry if that sounds harsh, Olivia, but it's how it has to be." Micah relented. The "please" hadn't hurt, but the intensity of that kiss had sealed the deal. She would take the risk, but not without a safety net in place.

The air shifted in the cab, followed by a solid thunk, the sound of the front driver's door closing when Robert joined them. *Impeccable timing as always, Robert,* Olivia thought, shaking her head in amusement.

Micah bit her lip, but remained silent. Now that they had company, it was pretty obvious that particular part of their conversation was over.

Olivia coughed politely, then very calmly asked Micah a question she had meant to ask her before they got sidetracked. "I am curious. I called your boss yesterday and he reassured me then that you were still scheduled to come by the office this morning. How did you manage to come back here instead?"

"Ah, yeah." Micah's cheeks colored just the slightest bit. "I told him my bike was still in the shop. I wasn't working, I just came down to hang out with the guys.'

"So you don't have your bike with you?"

"No, I took a cab."

"Perfect. Then you can come have lunch with me," Olivia said, switching gears. She wasn't willing to give up her time with Micah just yet.

"I'm not really dressed to go anywhere," Micah said, gesturing at her clothes before taking out a cigarette and nervously fidgeting with it.

"Don't worry about what you're wearing."

"Olivia, I'll be shitty company." Micah desperately wanted to light up. She knew that wouldn't fly in Olivia's fancy car, though.

"I didn't know you smoked, I mean, I have never smelled it on you before." Olivia nodded towards the cigarette Micah was nervously tapped against her knee.

"I normally don't. It's just an occasional thing, although lately it's been a little more frequently," Micah admitted, ruefully glancing down at her unlit cigarette.

"I don't care what you're wearing, it won't matter." Olivia took the cigarette out of Micah's hand, then lightly ran her fingertips along Micah's jawline before kissing her so very gently. Olivia didn't try to deepen the kiss, now was not the time for that.

"Have lunch with me?" She breathed against Micah's lips.

"Are you going to kiss me again?" Micah could feel the distance between them, the merest fraction of a centimeter separating them. Each shallow breath danced across her skin, a heated promise of silken lips touching hers, yet she held back and refrained from tasting lips she already knew were as sweet as wine. Olivia closed her eyes and shivered against her. Micah wanted her to complete that distance, to be the one to give in and kiss her. For that reason alone, she waited to see what would happen next.

"Yes." Olivia sighed, disappointed that Micah had resisted her teasing. Somehow, Micah had turned the tables on her and Olivia found herself closing that fraction of an inch between them. This kiss, the third kiss of the morning, held an element of promise that left Olivia breathless and made her wonder about her next choice.

"Then let's go," Micah spoke playfully, her voice carrying none of her trademark sarcasm as she fell back into the soft leather behind her.

"Of course," she murmured, then hit the intercom button. "Robert, can you drive us home?"

Chapter Six

Micah cast a nervous glance out the tinted window. They had ridden in silence for that last ten minutes and now Robert was driving them past increasingly familiar neighborhoods. A few seconds later, Olivia's house came into view, and Micah's heart contracted into a tightly wound little ball.

The stone and brick home remained a painful reminder of the past. A year had gone by since she had last walked beneath the arched entranceway. A few hours later, furious and beyond upset she had run back out that same door, fully intending on going and never stopping. But, she did stop. She made it to the sidewalk and stumbled to a halt. *Surely Olivia wouldn't just let me leave like this?* She had asked, convincing herself that Olivia simply wouldn't do that to her. So she waited in the dark and shivered against the night chill and the longer she waited the colder she felt, until she felt frost gathering along the edges of an already brittle soul. She waited for as long as her pain and self-respect could stand, wanting more than anything for the front door to open and Olivia's silhouette to appear and chase away the shadows that surrounded her. She kept hoping that Olivia would follow her, to come after her before it was too late, but as the seconds ticked away she realized that wasn't going to happen. Any remnant of hope that she had harbored failed her in that moment, so she just ran and she continued running. And now, she had somehow come full circle, walking back into the same home that had played witness to such a heartbreaking tableau.

Micah made it as far as the foyer before her mind froze and her feet stopped moving. Then Olivia took her hand and led her farther into the house. To her surprise, Olivia headed straight towards the kitchen.

"Do you have any idea what you'd like for lunch?" Olivia asked.

Micah shook her head.

"Well, you'll just have to eat what I prepare, then."

"Olivia, you don't have to cook for me. A pizza or Chinese is fine," Micah said, realizing that Olivia had every intention of cooking for her. That was so unexpected, so unlike Olivia, that it made her more nervous than she already was. Olivia was more comfortable moving around the gourmet kitchen than Micah had anticipated, but it felt odd, watching the high-powered attorney acting so domestic.

"I insist," Olivia said.

She must have noticed Micah's discomfort because she stopped what she was doing and pulled out a cold bottle of water and handed it to her with a sympathetic smile. "Go sit down and relax. This is a treat for me, as well. I so rarely get the opportunity to show off my culinary skills."

"Are you sure?" Micah asked. She held her breath and stilled when it looked like Olivia was going to touch her again, then exhaled in disappointment when she didn't. Olivia just smiled and turned back to the task at hand and she was left standing in the middle of the kitchen with nothing to do and a lot to process.

She was having a hard time thinking about food. The passionate kisses they had shared in the back of Olivia's car were still fresh in her mind, awakening appetites that had nothing to do with the chicken and vegetables Olivia was preparing so neatly.

Micah allowed herself to taste the memory of that kiss and it made her heart race. Olivia wasn't like any other woman she had ever met. It had been a year since their last kiss and she still managed to pull passion from her without effort. A thrill ran down her spine. The woman was dangerous to her and she didn't even know it.

She let her eyes wander, following the subtle curve of her neck until it disappeared beneath her white silk blouse. It would be so easy to take a few steps forward and pull Olivia into her arms. The idea was so tempting. *This time it would be different,* she told herself. *And if it wasn't? What would you do if she turned you away, again?* Doubt managed to dampen her desire enough to warrant caution and Micah wisely decided to retreat. She wandered into the living room and stopped in front of a pair of French doors that looked out into the backyard.

A small deck marked the edges of the deliberately organized chaos of an English-style garden hidden within a line of privacy hedges. The greenery was a huge difference from the urban landscape that normally surrounded Micah. It made her think of her cabin in western Maryland. The small cabin, surrounded by deep woods, never failed to calm her. She took a deep breath, almost smelling the clean air that held the taste of soft pine and loamy earth. *It might be time for another visit soon. I feel the need to recharge, to get away from the concrete and noise for a while.* But as soon as she thought it, she reconsidered and discarded the idea. Olivia was acting so out of character. It gave her hope for the rest of the afternoon—and after this afternoon? She refused to move that far into the future yet. If only she could shake the cloying sense of déjà vu that clung to her like a spider's web.

Micah startled out of her reverie when Olivia called out from the other room. Her back and shoulders tensed, half expecting time to loop back on itself and replay her last visit. She turned, marking the place she had stood next to the couch, heard the echo of her voice raised in anger followed by the sound of her shoes hitting the foyer tiles—then she looked up at Olivia and couldn't help but smile.

***

"How are your injuries doing today?" Olivia asked, more relaxed now that she was within the familiar surroundings of her home. Since her work day was essentially over she had indulged a little and poured herself a glass of white wine. Chilled to perfection, small beads of condensation formed where the liquid warmed the crystal stemware and dampened her fingertips.

"They're fine."

Olivia frowned at the short answer. Laying one careful hand on Micah's uninjured arm, she motioned for them to sit down on the brown leather couch.

"The chicken needs to cook for a while. Do you mind if I look at your shoulder while we are waiting?"

Micah shrugged. She placed her water bottle down onto the coffee table next to Olivia's wine glass then carefully rolled back her shirtsleeve, revealing a tidy white bandage along her shoulder blade.

Olivia didn't wait for permission. She gently peeled back the edge of the bandage, then gasped when the wound revealed itself.

"Micah, this doesn't look good," she exclaimed. The wound was scabbing over but the edges looked angry. Swollen, red and raw, her skin felt hot to the touch, too hot for comfort. She took a closer look, peeling away more of the bandage to reveal yellow discharge and dried blood along some of the deeper gashes. It looked like someone had taken a cheese grater to the other woman's skin. Her stomach knotted into a small hard ball of queasiness.

"It's road rash, Olivia. It never looks pretty," Micah answered, dismissing her concerns with a shrug.

"No, it's not just that. This is starting to look infected. Micah, you really should have a doctor look at this, you might need antibiotics." Olivia probably spoke more forcefully than she meant to but she was concerned and Micah's blasé attitude had rubbed her the wrong way.

"No...I don't," Micah stated forcefully, pulling away from Olivia's prying fingers. "Olivia, I know how to take care of a little road rash, it's not like I haven't dealt with it before."

It was a simple fact: if you rode a bicycle, you were going to fall once in a while. It was usually someone else's fault unless you were doing something stupid, and you rarely managed to escape some kind of injury. That's just the way it was.

Olivia just looked at her.

"I've been soaking it in the tub at night, and I did put ointment on it before I bandaged it up. The only thing I'm worried about is if my tattoo is screwed up," Micah continued. She was starting to regret agreeing to this. "Don't worry about it."

"Someone needs to," Olivia grumbled, unwilling to give up on what was fast becoming a test of wills. She was starting to get angry. *What is wrong with this woman? She's acting like she doesn't care what happens to her!*

The spark of passion the two women had shared less than an hour ago was fast turning into something else. An argument just as passionate and as hotly contested was starting to brew in its place.

"Excuse me for a moment," Olivia murmured, then stood up and left the room, leaving Micah behind to stare at her retreating form.

What the hell are you up to now?

She stood up, becoming more and more agitated as minutes passed by, but still no Olivia. The woman was known to be brusque, a shrewd negotiator and a stickler for the rules, but never rude—not purposefully.

Micah started to walk in the direction that Olivia had disappeared, then changed her mind. She eyed the couch again, but couldn't imagine sitting in one place and waiting patiently. *I could just leave.* The thought had crossed her mind once or twice already, but it was too close to fulfilling that strange sense of déjà vu, and she wasn't willing to do that.

"I need a smoke." Micah unlocked the French doors leading to the back deck and let herself out. She needed to think and she couldn't do it inside Olivia's house. She lit up her cigarette, then leaned against the wooden railing and promptly forgot about it. She was too busy contemplating the mess her life had become. She was in love with Olivia and had been for a long time, but she was scared to death of letting the other woman in. It would destroy her if Olivia cast her aside after everything that had already happened. She had changed so much, what if Olivia couldn't handle who she had become?

Chapter Seven

"There you are," Olivia announced. "Sorry I had to leave. There was something I needed to attend to."

When Olivia had walked back into the living room and found it empty, she thought Micah had left without telling her. Then she caught a glimpse of movement out of the corner of her eye and breathed a sigh of relief. Micah hadn't left, she had just wandered out onto the deck. Her first impulse was to go to her, but what she saw made her pause. Her hand stilled, resting on the brass handle but not turning it. Unable to help herself, Olivia silently observed for a moment.

Micah's face was visible in profile as she leaned against the wood railing, the slight breeze blowing the raven-black hair away from her face. For a young woman, the weight of the world seemed to sit heavily on her shoulders. Her expression was wistful, bordering on melancholy, and she felt herself being drawn closer to Micah for having seen her in this unguarded moment. Gone was the cocky, devil-may-care persona she carefully cultivated. That was not to say that wasn't a part of who she was, but obviously there was much more to her than Olivia had even considered.

Micah turned at the sound of Olivia's voice.

"Yes. Here I am. Where else would I be?"

"Why are you smoking again?" Olivia answered Micah's question with one of her own.

"Sometimes I smoke when I get nervous or stressed out," Micah answered without thinking.

The candid answer surprised both of them.

"Which is it now?" Olivia asked softly.

"A little of both. It doesn't matter." Micah pushed away from the railing. Olivia could almost hear the hollow clink of steel and chain locking into place as Micah mentally armored herself with attitude and self-assurance.

"Did you get your problem taken care of?"

"Problem?" Olivia asked, pursing her lips in consternation before she realized what Micah was talking about. "Oh, that? Yes. I just needed to make a quick phone call. Did you think I left you to work from home?"

"Well, the thought had crossed my mind."

"Micah!" Olivia exclaimed.

"I know, I know. You invited me over for lunch. No mixing business with pleasure, right?" Micah's eyes flashed with a dry humor that was lacking a moment ago. "Is lunch ready? I'm starving and something smells really good."

Olivia's garden was too beautiful to litter in. Micah pinched her cigarette out and tucked the butt back into the pack rather than leaving it behind. She didn't see Olivia wince at the offhand comment and by the time she tucked the cigarette pack away in her pocket Olivia had already recovered.

"Yes, it is, actually. Come inside and eat while it's hot." Olivia took Micah's arm and led her back into the house, glad for the distraction the meal would provide.

***

Lunch was filled with talk about Olivia's ten-year-old daughter, Regina. The light and humorous conversation had both women laughing, although Regina might not have appreciated her mother revealing some of her more interesting antics. Micah, in continuing her theme of candidness for the day, revealed that she was helping a friend illustrate a graphic novel.

"That's one reason I'm working as a bike messenger. My evenings are free to write and draw, and I can stop anytime during the day to jot down ideas or do a quick sketch. I always bring my sketch pad with me."

"Jot down ideas for what?"

"Well, the work on the graphic novel has been going so well, I decided to try my hand at writing my own story. It seemed to make sense. My illustrations always have a story to tell, so why not try to put my art into my own words?"

"I didn't know you write as well," Olivia admitted. Hell, she hadn't even known Micah was an artist until the other day. Every time she peeled back a layer, Micah had more to reveal. Olivia was starting to realize just how little she knew about the woman she had been fascinated with for so very long. Obviously, the one-sided view she had of Micah as a studious law student and intern was woefully lacking in substance.

"It's always been something I enjoyed doing, but I really didn't get a chance to start again until I came to New York. My father always thought the creative arts were a waste of valuable time." Micah's grim smile barely touched her lips when she mentioned her father, a parody of happiness that never reached her eyes. "I guess it was a good thing I came here, otherwise I would have never found my muse." This time Micah's smile was genuine, flashing straight white teeth before tucking her head down in an oddly shy gesture.

Olivia got the strangest impression that Micah was somehow referring to her and filed that vague statement away for future analysis.

"Do you have anything finished yet?" Olivia asked, thrilled to see the spark that ignited in Micah's eyes when she talked about her art. That enthusiasm and glow was something she had never seen when Micah was working as an intern. It made her wonder why she had wanted to become a lawyer in the first place. It was obvious Micah enjoyed what she was doing now, even though it wasn't necessarily conventional.

"No, it's pretty much just an experiment right now. I'm not even sure who my audience would be."

"So, you are an artist and a writer? I would love to see your work some time."

"Um, sure." Micah sounded less than enthusiastic about that idea. "By the way, this is excellent, I had no idea you were such an accomplished cook."

Olivia blushed and took a sip of her wine. The not so subtle attempt at changing the subject didn't fool her in the least. Peering over the rim of her glass, she could tell from the slight tightening around Micah's eyes and mouth that she had somehow stumbled on another touchy subject. With Jonathan's warning still fresh in her mind, she let it go for now, even though her curiosity was piqued. She had to remind herself that Micah was slowly opening up to her, and no matter how hard it was for her, she couldn't rummage around in Micah's brain like a bull in a china shop. Patience was not one of her better virtues.

Just as Olivia was about to ask another question, the front doorbell chimed. She excused herself and went to answer it, coming back a few moments later with a well-dressed woman in tow.

***

Micah looked up, passing a steady gaze from Olivia to the visitor then settling back again on Olivia. Micah stood up slowly, pushing her chair away from the table.

"Hmm, what's this all about, Olivia?" Micah inquired, knowing the answer but wanting to hear it from her. A slow, creeping anger was seeping into her bones, chilling her spine and turning her voice to ice. The other woman's professional clothing and calm demeanor gave her calling away, even in the absence of a stethoscope draped around her neck. Micah had seen enough doctors to peg one, even in the unlikely location of Olivia's dining room.

"Micah, this is my friend, Dr. Claire Woods. I would like for her to take a look at your shoulder and hip." Olivia's pleased smile faltered after a moment when she realized Micah wasn't happy with the good Doctor's presence. She really had thought Micah was just being stubborn earlier. *Sure you did. This is why you didn't tell her who you had called earlier.* Olivia ignored the small voice inside her head calling her out for being a liar and squared off with Micah.

"Was I mistaken? I didn't think you would mind me calling in a favor, just to make sure you're okay."

"I do mind, Olivia." Micah threw her napkin down on the table, her appetite ruined.

Olivia stepped closer and lowered her voice. "She's already here, Micah, and I know you're worried about your tattoo."

The room was silent for a full minute while the two women appraised each other's determination, the tension in the room rising with each passing second. A cool voice interrupted their silent argument, forestalling an explosion of epic proportion.

"If this is a bad time, I can leave." Micah's heated glare turned on the innocent physician who just gazed back at her mildly, adopting that professional demeanor all physicians seemed to cloak themselves in. "But, as Olivia pointed out, since I am already here..."

Micah nodded tightly, acquiescing to the need to have her shoulder looked at without actually giving in to Olivia. The battle of wills wasn't so much won as put aside for the time being. *You couldn't change a leopard's spots any more than you could change Olivia's mind once it settled on a course of action.* Micah reminded herself, *besides, she's right. I am worried about the tattoo.* Resigning herself to the inevitable, Micah allowed the doctor to approach her.

Micah managed to roll her sleeve up without taking her eyes off Olivia. The caring and concern in those bright blue eyes cooled her anger but didn't take away the irritation she felt. Olivia had gone behind her back, forcing something that should never have been an issue.

The doctor stepped forward and pulled up the bunched fabric, pulling up the bandage much like Olivia had done earlier, shaking her head at what she could see.

"I can't look at this properly; you need to take your shirt off."

"NO."

Two sets of eyebrows rose simultaneously at the absoluteness of the refusal. The doctor stood fast under the full brunt of her patient's angry glare, hazel eyes that flashed closer to emerald-green bearing down on her before flicking past her towards where Olivia stood.

"No," Micah repeated, her tone flat and non-negotiable.

It was the doctor's turn to look at Olivia.

80

"Olivia, we need a little privacy." While stated mildly, the request still held all the authority of any doctor ensuring the privacy of their patient.

The shock on Olivia's face was priceless. Without a word, she turned and left the room, her friend following closely on her heels. To Micah's surprise, Dr. Woods closed the door behind Olivia and turned around.

"Now, as you've heard, I'm Dr. Woods, but please call me Claire. You must be Micah. It's nice to meet you," the doctor stated briskly, taking Micah's hand in hers for a brief handshake. "Shall we have a look at that shoulder?" Dr. Woods half asked, half-suggested in that odd manner that doctors had when they wanted you to do something but made it sound like you had a choice. Micah turned and pulled off her t-shirt, tucking the fabric in front of her so the doctor could examine her shoulder

"Wow, that's an impressive tattoo, how long did it take?

"So far, three sittings and it's not done yet."

"Well, the shoulder doesn't look as bad as Olivia made it out to be, but I'm glad you let me look at it. Just let me get it cleaned up and bandaged properly. Tattoos aren't my thing, but right here," Dr. Woods lightly touched Micah's shoulder blade, "right here you have some pretty deep road rash. You'll have to wait until it heals to see how badly it damaged your work."

Micah cursed lightly, earning an apologetic grin from the doctor. She already knew the area was going to need re-work, but hearing if from Dr. Woods made it official. That did not make her happy.

While Dr. Woods cleaned her shoulder wound, Micah kept a sharp eye out for Olivia. She was so caught up in making sure that Olivia stayed on her side of the door, she almost missed the doctor's question.

"I want to give you something for this infection, are you allergic to anything?"

"Just codeine," Micah answered absently.

"Thank you. Now, I would like to see that hip. I believe Olivia mentioned you hit something when you fell off your bike?" Finishing up with the shoulder, Dr. Woods placed a firm but gentle hand on Micah's arm. The light touch was meant to encourage Micah to turn towards her, but her patient wasn't cooperating very well. "Micah, I need you to turn around."

"Micah? Ms. Connolly? If you want me to help, I need you to cooperate a little."

"Fine." Micah huffed.

Lacking an examination stool, Dr. Woods sat down on one of the dining room chairs so she could get a better view. Micah slid the top of her cargo shorts down off her hip to reveal a long gash just below her belt line, allowing the doctor to examine the wound more closely.

"Unfortunately, I can't really see the extent of the bruising because of your tattoo, but your hip definitely looks swollen. Does this hurt?" she asked, exploring gently with her fingers.

"Ow. Ow. Yes, it hurts, stop poking." Micah jumped away from the doctor's probing fingers.

The action of turning and pulling away at the same time made her lose the grip on the shirt she had been clutching against her stomach. Dr. Woods gasped at the sight of Micah's exposed abdomen.

"Ah, yes. This looked bad at first, Micah, but it isn't as deep as I thought. No sutures needed and no signs of infection." Dr. Woods stumbled over her words. She bent down; picked up the fallen t-shirt and offered it back to Micah. She pulled her shirt back on, then tapped Dr. Woods on the shoulder. She had stopped talking and that wouldn't do.

"No, not deep at all," Micah said. She made sure she had the Doctor's full attention, then purposefully flicked her gaze towards the door where Olivia's shadow hovered. "Really nothing to worry about at all."

Quickly recovering from her initial shock, the doctor gave Micah a quick nod in understanding. There were things Olivia didn't need to see. Things Olivia didn't need to know about.

"You know, if you don't let her in soon, she may just blow up out there," Dr. Woods stated.

Micah grinned. "I do believe you're right about that, Dr. Woods, ah, Claire. If we're done here?"

"Okay, Olivia, I'm decent again."

Olivia practically bounded into the room. She felt like she had been sent off to the corner to sit things out while Claire examined Micah. With only a snippet here and there making it through the door, she had plenty of questions for the doctor and one for Micah. *Why was the woman acting so shy around her?*

Olivia barely opened her mouth to speak before the doctor held up one authoritative finger. Evidently, she was being allowed to listen in but not to interject.

"Your shoulder has a mild infection, so I am going to give you some antibiotics and something for the inflammation and pain in your hip. You really need to rest it for a few days until the pain starts to go away. If it keeps bothering you, you should follow up with your personal physician."

"Um, define rest...I make my living riding my bike," Micah said, studiously avoiding looking at Olivia.

"Well, not riding your bike would be recommended. Preferably for at least a week."

"A week? That's not possible."

"It's okay, I'll see what we can do," Olivia interjected. Micah looked like she was about to burst. If she clenched her jaw any harder, Olivia was sure she was going to crack some teeth. It was time to separate the two of them. "Claire, why don't I walk you out to your car?"

Olivia left a very unhappy woman standing in her dining room. She could see the logic behind Dr. Wood's orders and she was sure that Micah did, too. She just needed some time to digest the doctor's advice.

"I want to thank you again for coming out on such short notice." Olivia stood at the curb and waited while Claire put her bag away.

"Of course. You can call me anytime, you know that. Tell Regina I said hello, okay?" Claire turned and gave Olivia a quick hug. "Olivia, I don't know what you have gotten yourself into, but if you need to talk to anybody, just give me a call. Keep an eye on her; that one seems as stubborn as you."

***

Micah was not handling the news well and was seriously trying not to freak out.

I need to ride, it's how I cope. What the hell am I going to do for a week with no outlet?

Micah felt her stress levels rising to dangerous levels, making her skin crawl with the need to do something, anything to dispel the nervous energy that was feeding off her mood. Pacing only served to reinforce the feeling of being trapped in a very small space with nowhere to go. She didn't even notice Olivia until she stepped right in front of her and blocked her way.

From the expression on her face, she was expecting their argument to continue where it had left off now that the doctor was gone. Whatever residual anger Micah had left inside her fled when Olivia placed a tentative palm on her chest. Her heartbeat surged, pounding against Olivia's palm as if the woman held it cupped inside her very hand. Micah tore Olivia's hand away from her, pulling her into a rough embrace.

The kiss was chaotic. A feverish attempt to purge every ounce of the emotional overflow out of her system before it overwhelmed her. Micah realized what she was doing and pushed Olivia away with a tortured sob.

"Sorry, sorry, sorry." Micah collapsed onto the couch and pressed her hands over her face. Embarrassed at her loss of control, and appalled at the almost violent nature of the kiss, she couldn't even look at Olivia.

"What's there to be sorry about?" Olivia asked gently, sitting down next to Micah on the couch. Stroking her hair, Olivia reveled in the mink-like sensation of the short hair along the nape of Micah's neck. "For kissing me?"

Shuddering at the intimate touch, Micah glanced skittishly at the other woman. Wild with fear, she was afraid she had ruined everything. Not trusting her voice, she nodded.

"I enjoyed it, if you couldn't tell. If anybody needs to give an apology, it's me. I shouldn't have sprung Claire on you like that." Olivia slowly leaned forward and lovingly kissed her, displaying a level of tenderness that Micah could never have imagined.

"Thank you for trying to take care of me, Olivia," Micah whispered against her lips.

Using just her fingertips, Olivia traced Micah's face. "Sweetie, for you, anything."

Micah wasn't sure she believed her, but she smiled anyway. She appreciated the sentiment, but she just couldn't trust the words.

Micah kissed her one last time. Scrubbing her fingers through her hair, she threw her body back into the deep cushions of the couch and stared up at the ceiling. Every line of her body exuded frustration. "I don't know what I am going to do with that much down time," she confessed.

"Come into the office then. You can bring your laptop or sketchpad, whatever you need, and work there," Olivia suggested.

"Seriously?" Micah asked, considering the offer. *At least I won't be in the apartment by myself.*

"Yes, that way I can make sure you are actually taking it easy," Olivia said, borrowing one of Micah's smirks.

"That might work," Micah said, willing to give the idea a chance. Coping with the forced inactivity was going to be hard enough, trying to do it all alone for hours at a time was a sure recipe for disaster.

"All we can do is try. I tell you what. Why don't you stick around today and see how we do. Regina will be home from school in another couple of hours. She really wants to see you again and we can all have dinner together." Olivia shamelessly played her trump card, knowing Micah couldn't resist. "Please?"

Micah sighed. "I would love to see Reggie again, but I am feeling really wiped out after today. Plus, I really didn't sleep well last night."

"So? You can take a nap here. Regina really would love to see you again." She tried to make the suggestion sound as reasonable as possible. The simple truth was that she wasn't ready for Micah to leave yet. A small, frightened part of her held an illogical fear that if Micah left, she wouldn't come back. After all, it had happened once before, hadn't it? She felt driven to prevent that from happening again.

"Is that the only reason you want me to stay? For Reggie?" Micah leaned forward, waiting for an answer to her all too shrewd question.

Olivia swallowed nervously. Using her daughter as an excuse was a cowardly thing to do, and she felt her face grow hot in embarrassment. How she felt about Micah had been her own deepest and darkest secret for so long. Now that she didn't have to hide her feelings anymore she should be able to jump in with both feet, so why was she having such a hard time just telling Micah how she felt?

"No," Olivia admitted. "No, not just for Regina. I–I want you to stay."

Micah leaned back, more pleased by the admission than she expected. She grinned, refusing to let the moment be more serious than she was comfortable with.

"Okay, if you insist, but only on one condition," she said.

"Yes?"

"You have to join me."

"Done," Olivia quickly agreed.

Like it was really a choice, Olivia thought, *Let Micah walk out the door or have her in my bed. It's what I've wanted for so long.*

Taking Micah by the hand, Olivia led her straight to the master bedroom where an elegant four-poster bed stood as the centerpiece of the room.

"Um–I don't have anything to sleep in," Micah stuttered.

"What do you normally sleep in?"

"Nothing." She smirked, wondering what Olivia's reaction would be. It wasn't true of course. Even in the privacy of her own room, she normally slept in a t-shirt and shorts. It was just fun to mess with Olivia. From the look on her face, she had been immensely successful in her attempt at teasing her. Unfortunately, Olivia's temporary state of speechlessness was short-lived.

"Do you actually sleep in the nude, Micah?" Olivia drawled her name out slowly, teasing her with a lazy smile that bordered on seductive.

"Do you?" Micah shot back. Amused at Olivia's attempt at calling her bluff, she was more than willing to continue their little game, especially if Olivia kept smiling at her like that.

"No."

"That's a shame." Micah shrugged, affecting a nonchalance she wasn't feeling. Her eyes kept drifting back to Olivia's lips. After tasting them today it was going to be damn hard keeping herself from wanting more, but considering other things she didn't have much choice.

"A shame, really?" Olivia asked, boldly wrapping her arms around Micah's neck.

Olivia trembled, but her eyes smoldered with fresh desire. This was no longer a game, and Micah couldn't afford to pretend it was any longer. Realizing that she might have exceeded herself with her cocky attitude, Micah stopped Olivia before they started something she wasn't sure she could stop. "Olivia. Don't."

She reached up and captured Olivia's wrists, then pulled out of her embrace. "I can't. I wasn't lying about wanting to sleep with you, but I really meant sleep. I'm wiped out."

Olivia searched her face, and for a moment Micah thought she had ruined everything. She was about to offer to leave when Olivia's expression changed. She had expected resentment or embarrassment at being denied, but what she saw was relief.

"God, Micah. I'm sorry. I don't know what came over me." Olivia strode over to her dresser and pulled out a pair of silk boxers. "Will these work?"

"Yep. This way to the bathroom?" she asked, tossing her head towards a second doorway.

"Yes, help yourself to whatever you need."

The innocent offer slid across Micah's skin and sent a shiver down her back. She was already rethinking the intelligence behind her earlier banter. Letting her cockiness overrule her common sense had led her back into Olivia's life, her house, and now her bedroom. Her step faltered and she almost tripped over her own feet when another thought intruded on her and sent her heart racing. *Oh, my God! Olivia is waiting in bed for me. I have had so many fantasies that start that way.* Not for the first time that week, Micah had to ask herself what she was doing. She turned on the faucet and splashed cold water on her face, not to wake herself up but to cool down the barely restrained ardor threatening to make a liar out of her. She needed sleep and wanted something more, but the look in Olivia's eyes had told her what she needed to know. Olivia wasn't ready for what Micah had to offer.

***

Olivia was waiting for her to come to bed.

Micah sat down on the edge of the bed, then hesitated. The bedding looked so expensive, and she was a road-rash covered mess. "The bandages..."

"Are fine. Don't worry about the sheets," Olivia finished Micah's question for her. Pulling back the sheets, she waited for Micah to crawl in next to her, then scooted over until she could lay her head on her shoulder. "Is this okay?" she asked quietly.

"It's perfect," Micah stated, pulling Olivia into a tight embrace.

Olivia was surprised when she felt Micah relax beneath her, her breathing evening out and slowing almost instantly. She fell asleep within minutes, the stress of the last few days finally taking its toll. Olivia wrapped her arms around the solid form beside her, then quickly followed the exhausted woman into the land of dreams.

Chapter Eight

The sensation of someone watching her made its way into Micah's awareness. She pulled herself out of the cozy, velvet lined darkness that occupied the space between dreams and reality and opened her eyes. She looked down her nose. It wasn't Olivia, she was still curled up against her, fast asleep. A muffled giggle to her right gave her observer away. She turned her head and found Olivia's daughter, Regina, leaning on her elbows at the edge of the bed, her chin tucked in the palm of one small hand. She was desperately trying not to giggle again.

Micah waggled her eyebrows at her and smiled. Regina's eyes widened and she clamped her hand over her mouth. Taking the smile as an invitation, Regina climbed up onto the bed. Still giggling, she enthusiastically wrapped Micah up in a big hug.

"Hi, Reggie," Micah whispered, her heart warming at the sight of the little girl. She missed Regina; she was a good kid and Micah thought of her more like a favorite niece than someone she babysat on occasion.

"Hi, Micah. I missed you!" Regina whispered joyfully. You could tell she was trying to keep her voice down but she couldn't quite make it work. "Are you and Mom sick?"

"No. Why?"

"Because you're sleeping and it's still daytime. I only take naps if I'm sick," Reggie announced, puffing her chest out proudly before squinting at Micah thoughtfully. "I didn't know grownups took naps."

"Sometimes we do." Micah winked.

Olivia stirred next to her.

"Darling, you need to let Micah breath," Olivia yawned. Untangling herself from Micah's arms, Olivia slid off the bed with a bemused grin on her face. Micah noticed that Olivia's comfortable looking soft cotton yoga style pants and wide neck t-shirt were a lot less revealing than the short boxers she had found for her. She suddenly felt severely underdressed in comparison and made sure the covers were tucked tightly around her.

Regina bounced onto the bed as soon as her mother left and started asking question after question without taking a single breath in between.

"Where have you been? Are you and Mom dating? Are you staying for dinner? You know she missed you."

Good God! Micah had forgotten how quick Regina was. She truly was Olivia's daughter, capable of firing off questions as fast as any prosecutor.

Micah looked up to find Olivia leaning in the bathroom doorway, watching them. A gentle smile graced her face, her expression wistful. Regina kept rambling on, oblivious to her mother's presence.

Micah mouthed "What?"

Olivia just shook her head. How could she explain that she was just enjoying watching the two of them interacting together? Micah was different around Regina. She seemed happier, her soul a little bit lighter and her laughter a little easier. Regina was in rare form today, regaling Micah with stories from school that were downright hilarious. She was sure if she let her get away with it, her daughter would spend the entire afternoon catching Micah up on every interesting thing that happened over the last year, all done in one continuous breathless succession. Poor Micah.

Just then, Micah laughed heartily, her whole face lighting up with childlike abandon. Olivia peeled herself away from her vantage point, it was time to steal Micah back from her child.

"Regina, why don't you go downstairs and get a snack. We'll be down in a minute." Regina groaned, making a show of disappointment that earned her a stern glance from her mother.

"Are you going to be staying for dinner, Micah?"

"Yeah, Sweetie, I am. Make sure you get something healthy to snack on and not those cookies you prefer," Micah told her, ruffling the sandy blonde hair that was so like her mother's. She grinned at the child's enthusiasm as she bounced off the bed and out the room in a heartbeat.

Olivia closed the bedroom door behind her daughter, then locked it to ensure their privacy. She returned to the bed, crawling across the bed until she straddled Micah's hips.

"You are amazing, do you know that?" Olivia asked, then proceeded to kiss Micah soundly. Olivia moaned when she felt hot hands slide along her ribs, settling on her waist before pulling her down.

Without warning, Micah hissed in pain, causing Olivia to rear up.

"Oh, your hip, I am so sorry, did I hurt you?" Olivia attempted to untangle herself from the woman beneath her, being careful not to bump her hip again. Without warning, she suddenly found herself on her back with Micah hovering over her.

"Not enough to matter," Micah reassured her. She gazed down at the woman trapped beneath her, watched her lips part of their own volition. The longer she waited the faster Olivia's breath came and those pale blue eyes, usually so cold and reserved, now burned with the fierce blue flame of a gas jet that had the power to devour everything around it.

"When did you become so bold?" Micah asked.

"About the same time you asked to sleep in my bed," Olivia reminded her.

"Oh, yeah. I did do that." Micah grinned. "It's my turn now."

That was the only warning she was going to give. Micah resumed the kiss on her own terms, slipping her tongue along silken lips until Olivia opened herself to her, their tongues tasting and testing each other with equal abandon. Micah pulled back from the kiss after a very long moment, breathing heavily.

"Now that's how you properly wake up from a grown-up nap," she said, then crawled out of the bed and went in search of her shorts, the baggy ones she came with and were more suited for company. When she returned from the bathroom, her hands still busy tightening her belt, she was stopped dead in her tracks by the scene in front of her. Olivia was still lying in bed, flushed, tousled, and so obviously and thoroughly kissed—she was the very picture of temptation. Micah spoke without thinking. "Gods woman, you are too gorgeous."

She took a step forward, then backed all the way up to the door.

"I'm going downstairs. If I don't..." Micah stopped there, leaving the rest of her sentence unspoken. Two more steps and she was beyond the threshold. She closed the door behind her and took in several deep, ragged breaths. *This is not good, so not good,* she thought, then bounded down the stairs in search of a cold drink. Something cold with lots and lots of ice.

"I know," Olivia spoke to an empty room, too quietly for Micah to hear even if she had her ear pressed to the other side of the bedroom door.

She rolled over onto her back and stared at the ceiling. *What just happened?*

Micah had asked her when she had become so bold, and in that moment she had to ask herself that very same question. Olivia ran her fingertips across lips that felt swollen and bruised, delightfully so. How many times had she imagined what that would feel like, Micah's lips on hers like that? How many times had she asked herself what she would do if the opportunity ever presented itself again? That was the real answer, not the quick lie she had managed to come up with. Her body still thrummed with all the possibilities those kisses promised her.

"Mooooom," Regina yelled loud enough to pierce her sanctuary, the sound managing to travel right through the floor boards beneath her. Olivia sighed, then dragged herself out of bed. It was time to be the mom again and she needed to make herself presentable for what promised to be a G-rated night.

"Homework first, Regina."

Regina was not happy. She wanted to spend time with Micah, not do boring homework. Olivia completely understood where her daughter was coming from but she had to put her foot down. It was only after Micah volunteered to help Regina with her math that peace finally descended on the house. After that little hiccup, the rest of the night was filled with pizza and laughter.

After dinner Regina begged Micah to stay and watch a movie. She couldn't say no.

Olivia wouldn't let her help with the cleanup, and insisted she stay in the living room with Regina. "Don't let her pick something gory. She'll be up all night with bad dreams."

Olivia's admonishment was met with a dramatic show worthy of an Oscar. Regina threw herself back into the deep cushions and crossed her arms stubbornly, all the while denying that she still made sure she kept her closet door closed while she slept—just in case there were monsters hiding there.

Olivia rejoined them on the couch a few minutes later. Micah scooted to the corner of the couch and patted the cushion next to her. Olivia sat down, then slowly let herself relax. The close confines of the crowded couch made for a great excuse to lean against Micah's shoulder. Strong fingers surreptitiously found her hand. She hummed in pleasure when those fingers started to gently massage along her palm and thumb, easing the workday stress out of the surprisingly tense muscles.

The movie was funny, engaging, and didn't require a lot of thought to enjoy. Olivia settled in on the couch, enjoying the illusion of domestic tranquility as she split her attention between the movie, Micah, and her daughter.

The time passed too quickly for Olivia's taste. Before she knew it the movie was over and she had to resume her role as a parent.

"It's time for bed, Regina," Olivia announced the minute the credits started to roll. It was a school night, and Olivia had already let her get away with staying up later than usual.

"Awwww, mom!" Regina started to whine. She didn't want to go to bed, not with Micah there. A firm look sent her reluctantly scurrying for the stairs. Before she climbed the stairs, she turned around to say goodnight.

"Micah? Are you staying over tonight?"

The unexpected question caught both women off guard. Olivia looked at Micah with an odd combination of horror and anticipation. Micah twisted to look behind her. Reggie was poised on the first stair, waiting for an answer.

"You mean like a sleepover, Reggie?" Micah asked as casually as possible.

"Yeah..."

"No, I'm not going to sleepover tonight, kiddo."

"Okay, then bye!" Regina called out, then added hopefully, "But you are coming back again?"

"Yes, Reggie. I'll be back to visit again."

Reggie managed to sound like a tiny elephant running up the stairs, which made both women chuckle. Micah turned back around to find herself face to face with Olivia. Their position on the couch seemed suddenly a bit more intimate than a moment ago.

"I have to apologize for Regina. She has been a handful all night."

"Nah. She's just excited. She's a good kid, Olivia. You're doing a great job with her."

"But precocious."

"That she is," Micah teased. "A sleepover? And where did Reggie get that idea, huh?"

"I haven't a clue what you are talking about, Micah," Olivia exclaimed in mock offense. Her breath hitched when Micah leaned closer, her eyes glowing mischievously. It was damned hard to think when she looked at her like that.

"So, no um...sleepovers have been happening then?" Micah teased, grazing her lips along a delightfully pouting lower lip before nipping gently. That got Olivia's full attention.

"No, Micah...I haven't had anyone over like this, well not quite like this, since the last time you were here," Olivia spoke without thinking. The elephant that had just ran up the stairs reappeared, landing firmly in the middle of their conversation and squashing the intimate connection between them. *Stupid, stupid,* she berated herself. She felt Micah withdraw from her, both physically and mentally, and she desperately wished she could take back those careless words.

Olivia wasn't the only one suffering from regret. Micah was mentally kicking herself over asking such a thoughtless question. For starters, she had no right to ask such a thing. For another, it had sent their conversation into a direction she was not prepared or ready to go yet.

"Micah, I know we haven't talked about this, but..." Olivia started, only to have Micah interrupt her.

"No, it's in the past; I really don't want to talk about it." Micah retreated to the other side of the couch, running her fingers through her hair vigorously before adding, "Look, can we just forget about it for tonight?"

"For now." Olivia reluctantly agreed.

By carefully avoiding the one conversation that Olivia desperately wanted to have, but Micah was adamant about not starting, they were able to enjoy the rest of their evening together. Eventually, she couldn't contain her yawns any longer.

"I've really got to go, Olivia, or this really will become a sleepover," Micah joked, then she caught Olivia's speculative gaze. "Don't even think about it."

"Fine, fine," Olivia said. "But, at least let me call you a cab. I'd have Robert take you, but he's been off duty for hours."

Micah left soon afterwards with a firm promise to be at the office the next morning.

Chapter Nine

Micah walked into Olivia's office the next morning promptly at 8am with a searing hot Venti coffee from her favorite gourmet coffee shop in hand. Surprisingly, she offered the coffee to Olivia.

"Oh, thank you." Olivia leaned back and inhaled the aromatic steam, then took advantage of the break to take in Micah's appearance this morning. She couldn't help looking the other woman up and down, taking in the black jeans and purple silk t-shirt that transformed Micah from bike messenger to, well, casually elegant. She smiled at Micah over her cup. Taking a quick sip of her coffee, she hummed in approval and contentment. All seemed well with the world today.

Micah didn't seem to mind coming in this morning, even though she couldn't act as a messenger. They both knew it was just a pretense to have her spend more time with Olivia, although neither would ever admit it. Secretly, Olivia had another motive. She knew how stubborn Micah was and she wasn't about to let her stay at home alone and stew until she convinced herself it was okay to go back out on the streets.

She might get hurt again, Olivia thought, horrified at the prospect, then chided herself for being so overprotective. *So invested already? It's what she's been doing every day for months before you found her again.*

"Yes, I am," she murmured.

"What was that?" Micah glanced her way.

"Oh, nothing." Olivia sat up straight, her tone brisk and business-like to hide the fact that she had let her thoughts wander so freely in front of Micah.

It didn't take long for Olivia to find herself incredibly busy, but the occasional stolen glances out her office door kept her in a good mood all morning. Micah had camped out at an unoccupied desk so she could chat with Amanda while they both worked on their separate projects. Micah had her sketchpad but eventually abandoned it for her computer after drawing furiously for an hour or so.

The morning passed quickly, so quickly that Olivia didn't realize it was time for lunch until her stomach let her know it was empty. She looked up to find that Amanda had already left her desk to find her own lunch. She got up and stretched, her muscles were stiff from sitting in one position for so long, and went out to find Micah.

"What are you doing for lunch?" Olivia idly inquired. Micah had been typing away feverishly, her face intently glued to her computer screen. It took a moment for Micah to come back to her, her eyes shifting from an inward focus that wasn't really seeing the outside world. Micah's eyes were more green than hazel today, glowing brightly in contrast to the deep purple shirt. The mercurial nature of Micah's eyes always fascinated Olivia. They seemed to change color at will, or in response to what she was wearing or thinking.

"I was waiting for you to finish up."

"Well then, should we order something?"

"I already did, it should be here in a while." Micah smirked, closing her laptop and getting up to walk around her desk. Olivia held her breath; the desire to step into Micah's path and hold her in her arms was almost overwhelming.

"Come with me," she said, pulling Micah into her office.

Once inside, Olivia lost her momentum. She became uncharacteristically flustered, caught between wanting to speak, and seemingly unable to. A dark flush travelled up her chest to light her cheeks on fire, echoing the heated look in her eyes.

She wants to kiss me, but she can't do it, not here. Micah watched Olivia's silent struggle, intrigued at the woman's efforts to push down her personal desire, then found that that she cared a bit less about appropriate behavior and professional decorum than her old boss did.

She pulled Olivia into a close embrace and kissed her, soundly and without reservation. She did what Olivia wanted—what she couldn't bring herself to do in the office where her father once sat.

It was more of a thrill than Micah had expected, having daydreamed about doing that so many times before when she sat at that desk as an intern. Unfortunately, the sound of the elevator pinging its arrival to their floor marked their time.

Olivia untangled herself from Micah's arms and stepped away just as the delivery guy rounded the corner with a large paper bag in his hand.

"We should eat." Olivia stumbled over her words. Hair a mess, lips swollen with desire and gazing up at Micah with those ice-fire blue eyes, she looked more ready for the bedroom than the boardroom.

"I'll go get it. You wait here," Micah said, trying not to feel too disappointed. The elevator ping had sent

Olivia's pulse skyrocketing, panic driven at the possibility of being caught making out in the office like a teenager.

***

After finishing their meal together, Micah sat down in the chair in front of Olivia's desk. She hesitated, and then cleared her throat.

"Olivia, I won't be in tomorrow."

"What...why?"

"Um, I needed to make a doctor's appointment, and they called me right before lunch to let me know that they can fit me in tomorrow morning. I just didn't want you to worry when I didn't show up." From Olivia's reaction, Micah realized she wouldn't accept a general excuse. Rather than be grilled for information, she just came out with the real reason for not being there. She just hoped that Olivia would leave it at that and not want more details.

"A doctor's appointment! For what, Micah?" Olivia exclaimed. If anything, she looked more alarmed now.

Nope, no luck. The lawyer in Olivia wasn't going to let it go without details. Exasperated, Micah blew out her breath and briefly debated not answering. Then she relented. Olivia wasn't just being nosy, she was actually concerned.

"I need to go see my orthopedist for an old knee injury. It's been bothering me a lot since the fall and I just need to make sure that I didn't screw it up again."

"What time is your appointment?" Olivia asked. She pulled out her personal appointment book, already making plans in her head.

"Eleven in the morning. I am just going to head home today and get some work done there."

"Why can't you continue to work from here?" Olivia asked.

"I just need some time to myself, Olivia. I have a lot of thinking to do and I can't do that here. Honestly, it is just too distracting with everything going on between us for me to just sit here with nothing to do," Micah explained.

Olivia pushed down her own concern and concentrated on what Micah was saying. She seemed wound up, nervous, not at all like the woman that had shared her bed the afternoon before.

"You don't really need me here, so I will talk to you in a couple of days, okay?" Jumping up, Micah grabbed her laptop and bag and strode out. Olivia was left sitting in her office with the rapidly cooling remains of their lunch sitting on her desk.

***

It hurt Micah deeply to run away from Olivia. It hurt even more to admit to herself that running was exactly what she was doing. But, she didn't have a choice.

It was all getting to her. It had been a couple of days since she had been able to ride her beloved bike. She had also spent more time inside a building in the last two days than she had in the last three months. Thanks to the badly placed road rash, she wasn't even sure when she could get back into the tattoo parlor. Most of all, there was this intense and sudden intimacy between them. It was too much, too soon, but she couldn't have stopped that kiss if she had wanted to.

All the emotional upheaval, combined with everything else, was threatening to send her over the edge, threatening her need to feel in complete control of her life.

"I'm trying," she whispered, wondering who she was trying to convince. The distorted image reflected inside the polished metal elevator doors stared back at her. *I know, I know. I kissed her, not the other way around.*

***

Bright and early the following morning, an exceedingly groggy Jonathan answered the front door to find his boss standing there.

"Uh, hello, Olivia," Jonathan managed to mumble as gracefully as he could that early in the morning. Olivia ignored Jonathan's obvious confusion at her presence and promptly made herself at home.

"Good morning, Jonathan." Olivia nodded graciously and took a seat on the couch.

"I was making coffee, would you like some?"

"Yes, please."

Coffee made and not quite sure what was going on, Jonathan joined Olivia on the couch for the most unusual morning chat he'd ever had with his boss, one that included lounging around and sipping java on his own couch. The usual morning urge to rush to the office was absent, conveniently so, since his boss was sitting in his living room engaging in small talk.

Olivia didn't wait long before asking the question she really wanted to ask.

"When is Micah getting up?"

Jonathan shrugged. "I don't know. She was up most of the night. Apparently she's worried that they'll want to do surgery again."

Jonathan nervously ran his palm over his head at the look on Olivia's face. He suddenly felt very uncomfortable in his usually very comfortable abode. It was weird enough having your boss sitting in your living room at eight o'clock in the morning, it was worse having your boss asking questions you weren't sure you should answer.

"You did know that she had knee surgery almost a year ago, right?"

"No, I didn't."

Jon paused. He knew that Micah would be pissed as hell if he talked too much. Weighing the consequences, he settled on protecting his friend's privacy over the potential wrath of Olivia.

"Well, that's her story to tell, especially since I don't even know the details." It was a cop-out on his part, but Olivia seemed satisfied with the answer.

Just then, loud music erupted from behind Micah's closed door.

"She's up," Jonathan announced, shaking his head ruefully even as he offered a fond smile towards the practically vibrating walls.

"What in the world is she listening too?"

"I think it's Joan Jett," he replied after listening for a second. "Usually she starts up with something a little less, ah, aggressive. She likes Lily Allen. She's obsessed with English singers, but Joan Jett is definitely her favorite. I'm just glad the exterior walls in her room are soundproofed or I would never hear the end of it from the management."

Just then, the door opened, letting the music crash into the living room violently. A disheveled and half-asleep Micah closely followed the cacophonous noise. She emerged from the doorway in a pair of black boxers and a tank top, a dark green silk robe tied carelessly at the waist.

Micah didn't notice her audience as she limped her way straight to the kitchen, she reached blindly into the refrigerator and grabbed a can of Coke. Olivia's eyebrows rose perceptibly when her brain registered the lyrics that seemed to growl through the song. The music was raw, and the song was heavily laced with suggestive language.

Olivia followed Micah's progression with her eyes. She thought the younger woman was gorgeous first thing in the morning. Her hair was wild, untamed, partially due to her running long fingers through the dark locks. She took a long drink from her Coke before stretching. The motion was smooth, practiced, and utterly sexy as she rolled her head absently, exposing the smooth line of her neck to Olivia's delighted and unobserved view.

The dark green silk robe didn't hurt at all. Its color set off Micah's tan quite nicely. Olivia felt like a voyeur. Her thoughts ran to the physical. She wanted to run her own fingers along the smooth skin, imagine Micah's pulse quickening with her touch. She wondered what Micah's chameleon eyes looked like against the forest green of her robe. She imagined gold flecks dominating the hazel-green, much like Micah dominated her thoughts. *Damn, I have it bad*, she thought, feeling heat color her face at the appraising look Jonathan was leveling at her.

Micah returned to her room by simply turning around and retracing her halting steps. She seemed utterly unaware of her audience sitting on the couch.

"In case you couldn't tell, our Micah isn't really a morning person." Jonathan laughed. "Give her another five or ten minutes and she may actually acknowledge you."

"I thought I had seen a slight limp before, but never that pronounced," Olivia spoke absently. She was preoccupied with more troubling thoughts.

What happened to her? Seeing Micah in pain and limping so badly disturbed her greatly. No wonder she had been so insistent on leaving work yesterday. Micah cultivated such a devil-may-care attitude, it would be hard for her to admit pain or weakness. *Especially to me,* Olivia thought guiltily, knowing that she had a reputation for not tolerating weakness. That didn't apply to the people she cared about, but how would Micah know that?

"Is she having a lot of pain?" That question earned her a trapped look from her junior partner.

"You will have to ask her, I don't really know."

"Jonathan, how did she hurt her knee? She hasn't told me, and I have a feeling she won't if I ask her myself," Olivia asked Jonathan directly, letting her frustration show. She could tell he was reticent about giving away information about his friend, but at this point she really didn't care.

"Okay. All I know is that after she disappeared, two whole weeks passed without her contacting me, which was weird. I tried calling her but she never answered or called me back. She didn't respond to my text messages. So, I went to Amanda. I asked her to pull up her emergency information. She gave me the number listed as an emergency contact."

Olivia frowned when she heard that. She frowned because it wasn't exactly ethical to do what he did, even though he acted as a concerned friend. But mostly, she frowned because she hadn't thought of it herself. After trying to text and call for several days with no contact, she just gave up. She had assumed that Micah didn't want to talk to her; she never imagined that something might have happened to her.

"Please, go on," Olivia urged, her voice thick with guilt.

"Her friend Adam told me where I might find her. He wanted to go himself, but he didn't have a car and couldn't get time off from work right away. He asked me to go to the one place he hadn't checked yet. That was the personal week I asked off for. I went looking for her."

Pausing for a moment, Jonathan sipped at his morning coffee, his gaze wandering nervously towards Micah's closed door before continuing. He sighed heavily, as if already feeling the burden of Micah's anger.

"She was in a bad way, Olivia. She was bloody, and her knee had been injured. But, like I said...that's her story to tell." Jonathan stood up. His cup was empty and it was time to get to work, but he had one more thing to say before he left.

"The only reason I shared this much is that I know you really care about her, and she needs that."

"Love." Olivia corrected him, her voice so soft it barely made it to Jonathan's ears.

"Hmm, what was that?" he asked, turning back towards Olivia.

"Love, Jonathan. I love her, I have for a while," Olivia confessed, looking up at the man with fear and hope battling for dominion behind overly bright blue eyes.

"Well, that's even better," he said, a broad smile spreading past his lips and lighting up his face, "but Micah's the one that needs to hear that, not me."

Before the conversation could continue, the music stopped, the bedroom door swung open, and a dark head popped out.

"Hey, Jon! Do you know where my shorts are?" Micah called out blindly.

"You mean your cargos?" he inquired, drawing his words out too elegantly to be accused of deliberate sarcasm. She was always leaving her clothes about, usually forgetting them in the dryer.

"Naw, my other ones." Micah chuckled at the long running joke. "The black ones. I only wear the cargos for work..." her words trailed away when she finally noticed her unexpected visitor.

"Um, hello Olivia?" Micah stared at the woman perched on the edge of Jon's couch, then leaned against the doorframe and waited for an explanation.

Realizing that he was the third party in the middle of a tense stare down, Jon thought it might be a good time to head out.

"Well, I think that's my cue." Jonathan rinsed his cup out in the kitchen sink, then spun past Micah to give her a quick peck on the cheek. "Your shorts are in the dryer. Be good today."

"Good is subjective," Micah shot back, accepting his lighthearted scolding with a nod and a wink. She waited until he let himself out of the apartment before pushing away from the doorway.

"What are you doing here?" Micah called out to her unexpected guest as she went to retrieve her shorts from the dryer.

"I came to accompany you to your doctor's appointment," Olivia stated matter-of-factly, as if it was the most reasonable thing in the world to do.

"Why would you do that? You have a full schedule today," Micah asked as she limped back to her room. Olivia took the open door as an invitation to join her and followed Micah into the bedroom.

"I had Amanda reschedule everything. I wanted to be here for you," she admitted.

"Why now?" Micah sat down on the wooden stool in front of her dressing table.

Olivia bowed her head against Micah's challenging glare. Micah had every right to question her; she had always put her work before anything else. To do any less was unthinkable.

Olivia's heart pounded in her chest. Wrapping her arms around Micah from behind, she dipped her head down to brush her lips against Micah's skin where her shoulder met the curve of her neck. Her hair fell forward, slipping across Micah's collarbone and hiding her face from the mirror. Nibbling gently against the smooth skin, she was delighted when Micah tilted her head to give her more access. The fine hairs at the nape of her neck tickled Olivia's cheek, making her skin tingle.

"Gods, what are you doing to me?" Micah whispered. She wanted to close her eyes and drown in the physical sensation of their contact, but couldn't abandon the visual effect the mirror afforded.

Olivia looked up then, locking her eyes with Micah's through the mirror's image. She felt drunk on Micah's scent. The taste of her skin lingered on Olivia's lips, her tongue darted out to lick the traces from her upper lip. She felt Micah shudder, practically shivering in her embrace. Micah's lips parted, a sound part moan, part sigh, slipped out as almost an afterthought. It practically robbed Olivia of her ability to speak again. She licked her lips, suddenly dry from the thrill of the words sitting on the edge of her tongue.

"What I have wanted to do since you left yesterday. What I have thought about doing all night long," Olivia said. The bald honesty in her statement was a pale shadow of the emotions running wild inside her.

"Because I finally got you back, and I don't ever want to let you go again," Olivia answered Micah's first question, the one she had thrown at her like a challenge before continuing in a voice that was both intense and quietly demanding. "If you need someone to hold your hand, or to listen to your hopes, your fears, your random thoughts, I will be here."

She broke eye contact again to tease Micah with soft kisses, an occasional playful nip rewarded with a sudden gasp. She could feel Micah's pulse pounding along her neckline, her earlier fantasy made real. She placed her lips firmly along that line, feeling the effects of her lips on Micah's body.

Her hands moved of their own volition, seeking the soft hot skin she knew lay hidden beneath the cool silk. Hard muscles jumped along Micah's flat stomach when she ran her fingertips across the rougher tank top fabric that kept her from her goal. Micah's pulse quickened perceptibly, then seemed to falter. Firm hands grasped her own, interrupting her bold exploration. She felt Micah's body stiffen, becoming hard and cold in the instant it took her to stand and move away, breaking contact with her.

"Micah?" Olivia felt Micah's withdrawal like a cold wind blowing through her.

Micah leaned heavily against the dresser in front of her, bowing her head for a moment before looking up. Her haunted expression was so raw, so intense; it made Olivia step back involuntarily. Micah's eyes were dark and troubled, making her look younger and more vulnerable.

"Micah, what...?"

A quick shake of the dark head stopped Olivia's question. Bridging the distance between them, Micah caressed Olivia's cheek gently before brushing a light kiss against Olivia's full lips. "Thank you," she whispered, her warm breath tickling along Olivia's jaw.

Olivia was too confused to ask for what before Micah retreated again.

"Just let me get dressed," Micah called over her shoulder. Grabbing her clothes, Micah practically flew into the adjoined bathroom.

"If you must." The words, heavy with loss and regret, were lost in the sound of the door closing and the lock sliding into place with a loud snick.

***

Micah strode over to the bathroom mirror, staring at herself in the judging glass. Anger rose up from deep inside, painful, raw, and real enough to make her bleed inside. She sought purchase on the sink edge as a following wave of nausea washed over her. Gripping the cold marble until her knuckles turned white, she threw back her head. Wanting to howl in frustration, she breathed deeply, seeking calm in a storm of conflicting emotions. Unpeeling her fingers from their death grip, she untied her robe with angry, quick movements, then pulled her tank top up past her ribs.

Only a very few people had seen the full extent of the scars that covered her midsection. Even when she had showed Olivia her tattoo the other day, she had made sure to keep her shirt pulled down in the front. If she continued down this path, acting on this impossible attraction between them, Olivia would find out eventually. But was she ready to show and tell?

113

With a sigh and one last look at herself in the mirror, she proceeded to get dressed in comfortable but nice clothes. Exiting her bathroom, Micah found Olivia sitting at her desk browsing through her extensive CD collection.

Olivia looked up when she heard Micah return to the room. When Micah had walked away so suddenly, Olivia felt like all the oxygen in the room left with her, making it difficult to breathe. Her chest constricted painfully at the sense of loss she felt—it was too close to how she felt the last time.

One day Micah was there, and then she was gone. It was incredibly silly, since Micah had only gone into the bathroom, but it was more than that. It wasn't just physical. Micah had emotionally shut down and shut her out before she walked away.

Cocky Micah was back. The signature jaunty gait and lazy grin greeted Olivia as she walked out of the bathroom, although for her, it was apparent Micah had to work to minimize her limp. The black shorts Micah was so intent on finding earlier were shorter than what Olivia was used to seeing her in. Unfortunately for Olivia's current state of mind, they showed off a good portion of well-muscled, tan, and shapely leg. The stylized tattoo that curled around the lower part of her quad just above the knee was the same tattoo that graced Micah's flank and back. Her mind's eye followed those flowing lines up, her odd fascination with Micah's tattoo turning mildly sexual as she realized just where those lines travelled under her clothing.

Olivia coughed lightly, intent on not following that line of thought and failing miserably.

"Why have I not seen these shorts before?" Olivia asked, looking Micah up and down. The black polo shirt was plain, but it was well cut and didn't detract from the natural beauty that stood in front of her.

"Um, they aren't really appropriate for riding the bike."

"I'll have to take your word on that," Olivia said, trying to fill what felt like an awkward silence between them.

"I'm not going to be able to convince you not to go, am I?" Micah asked with a guarded glance in her direction.

"No." Olivia sucked in her breath, waiting to see what would happen next. She couldn't help but focus on her wording. *It wasn't what she said, it was how she said it. She didn't ask me if I would leave. She didn't ask me to leave...she asked me if I could be convinced to change my mind. That's important.*

Micah sighed and shook her head.

"We have plenty of time before we have to leave, could I interest you in some more coffee?" Micah asked as she walked past Olivia and out into the living room, leaving the more intimate confines of her bedroom.

"That would be lovely."

***

Despite it being her third cup of the morning, Olivia was content to sit at the kitchen table and watch Micah make coffee. She was delighted to find out that Jonathan had outfitted his kitchen with a professional looking barista setup. The smell of freshly brewed coffee travelled along the steam escaping from the polished copper. As Micah moved about the large kitchen, Olivia observed her carefully. Micah was still trying to hide her limp, and was doing so quite successfully. If Olivia hadn't seen how bad she was earlier, even she might have missed it. *So that's why I haven't seen it before, she is very good at hiding her pain.*

"Micah, you don't have to hide from me."

Micah turned so fast she almost dropped the mug in her hand. Eyes flashing, Olivia watched several emotions travel across Micah's face before she shuttered them behind a flat and emotionless gaze.

"I don't know what you're talking about." Micah set the mug down in front of Olivia and turned back to the machine. She dumped out the grounds forcefully, her movements jerky and quick.

The effect her words had on the other woman took Olivia aback.

"Your knee, the fact that you're in pain—you don't have to hide it from me," she explained quickly, thoroughly confused by Micah's extreme reaction.

"Oh." Relief washed across Micah's face, chasing away the shadows around her eyes.

Olivia frowned. *What else was Micah hiding? More importantly, what did she think I meant?*

Olivia took a sip of coffee and contemplated. There had to be a way to find out what Micah was being so secretive about without alienating the woman. Olivia knew that she didn't have the best history when it came to communicating. She didn't want to make that mistake again. She wanted a real relationship with Micah, and secrets weren't conducive to a good relationship.

"Would you care to explain your reaction just now?" Olivia asked, choosing the straightforward approach.

Micah remained silent. Her back to Olivia, she kept wiping down a countertop that was already overly clean.

Olivia abandoned her coffee to join Micah at the counter, then took her hand to stop the circular motions before she managed to rub an indentation in the marble surface.

"When I said you didn't have to hide from me, you looked...scared?" she asked. A subtle eye flutter gave Micah's inner thoughts away, confirming Olivia's guess.

Micah pulled her hand away and tossed the towel on the countertop.

"Micah, what are you scared of?" Olivia spoke as gently as she could, trying to get Micah to look at her.

"Can we just talk about this later, please? Just let me get through today then we'll talk."

"Fine, but we will have that talk later. We can't move forward," Olivia added, gesturing between them, "if we can't talk, and make no mistake I want to move forward."

She waited until Micah nodded, then dropped the subject. She gave Micah's hand another quick squeeze, wanting to reassure her before letting go.

***

A few hours later, Olivia was back on the same couch. Micah disappeared into her bedroom to change into more "comfortable clothes." This time, however, her retreat was followed by the soft snick of the door locking behind her. Micah was seriously unhappy. The doctor had told her to take at least another week off, if not more.

Olivia found herself mulling over what she had learned, which she had to admit wasn't very much. From what she had gleaned from Jon and Micah, she had sustained some injury about a year ago that had resulted in knee surgery. She must have had a good doctor because Olivia hadn't noticed the barely visible scars until today.

Micah had been worried that she had reinjured her knee and would have to go through surgery and physical therapy again. Luckily, it looked like she wouldn't. According to the Orthopedist, Micah's knee was hurting more because her hip injury was throwing off her gait. She had apparently bruised her hip pretty badly.

Micah emerged from her bedroom and joined her, sinking into the couch's soft leather with a relieved sigh.

Olivia had to smile; Micah did look more comfortable in her pair of faded jeans and tank top. The road rash on her shoulder was visible along the edge of the tank top. It looked better already, less angry and red. The abrasion looked like it was healing well, even to her unpracticed eyes.

She decided to see if she could get some answers now that Micah had gotten past the stress of seeing her doctor. Turning on the couch cushion, she rested her elbow on the back of the couch, her head resting in her hand. She brought her knee up onto the couch, tucking her foot under her leg, then studied Micah's profile for a long moment before the other woman noticed.

"What?" she asked, sounding a bit defensive.

"How did you injure your knee?"

"I fell. What can I say? I can be clumsy at times," Micah responded, ending the vague explanation with a self-depreciating chuckle.

Olivia didn't buy that answer for a second. Yes, Micah could occasionally be clumsy, although she hadn't seen that since the last time she had been in heels, but she had never caused herself bodily harm.

"Don't lie to me, I cannot tolerate lying." A concerned hand placed on Micah's knee softened the sharp words. Olivia felt like a huge hypocrite, internally wincing at her harsh words. Who was she to preach about lying?

"Trust me, I am not lying. I really did fall."

"But not because you're clumsy," Olivia stated her assumption as fact, her voice soft.

After taking a deep breath, Micah shook her head. "No."

Micah took a deep drink from her Coke can, then sat staring at it, refusing to make eye contact with Olivia. She didn't want to lie, but she also wasn't in the right frame of mind to explain either. Because if she did, she would have to explain everything and she hadn't figured out how to do that yet.

Olivia stood and started collecting her purse. It was pretty clear she wasn't going to get any answers today. "Well, I need to get back to the office for a few hours. I will call you later, maybe then you will feel like talking to me."

She made it to the front door. She twisted the knob and pulled back, then a strong hand appeared above hers, stopping the door from opening all the way. Intent on leaving, Olivia hadn't noticed Micah following her. Her anger and the thick carpeting had masked the sound. Now she was caught between the door and Micah's body.

Micah leaned forward and placed a light kiss on the Olivia's cheek. "Thank you for coming with me today, Olivia. It really meant a lot to me." She stepped back to let Olivia pass by her and out into the hall, then closed the door behind her.

Chapter Ten

"Goodbye, Olivia," Micah whispered, ignoring the pain in her heart.

Micah stood, blindly staring at the front door, her fingers splayed wide against the pristine white surface. Her body began to tremble, defying her control. Shaking her head back and forth violently, she launched herself away from the door to pace the confines of the apartment like a caged tiger. Her long strides quickly brought her into the living room.

It felt like the walls were closing in on her, she felt panic rise up into her throat, sour and burning all the way down to her stomach. The space seemed too small. She couldn't breathe here, she couldn't think. Everywhere she went, Olivia was there. Even now, her scent lingered in the air around her. It was too much. The intensity of it all threatened to overwhelm her. Digging her nails into the palms of her hands, she used the sharp pain as a focus to clear her thoughts.

"I can't do it." Every time Micah played the inevitable conversation in her head, she could feel the panic building up inside. This pain in her heart wasn't a pain she understood or could control. It was too intense; it beat like a wild drum inside of her, threatening to unravel months of carefully orchestrated change— change she had endured in order to find some small amount of solace.

She wasn't ready to explain her knee injury or her scars, and that meant she only had one option, one choice left. It didn't matter if it was right or wrong, good or bad. She had to move, had to act, she had to get away and regroup.

Grabbing her duffle bag, she stuffed some random clothes in it from her dresser. She needed a pen—so of course she couldn't find one. She tossed through her desk drawers until she found one hidden under a pile of old medical bills. Grabbing a sheet of paper, she wrote a quick note to Jon explaining that she needed some time away. He would be worried if he came home and she had just vanished again.

The last thing to go was her laptop and sketchpad, making sure she included a few fresh pencils in her favorite messenger bag.

"Sorry, Doc. I've gotta ride." Micah reverently removed her yellow bike from its rack, grabbed her cell phone and keys, and left the apartment. Making her way down to the parking garage, she tried to convince herself that she was doing the right thing. Even if it didn't feel like it.

***

It was a chore to squeeze the bike out of the tiny elevator, but a little three point turn action did it. It wasn't hard to find her truck, a shiny late-model Toyota Tacoma that gleamed under the sharp fluorescent lights. Bright cerulean blue, it stood out in sharp contrast to the boring gray compact cars and black town cars. Only Jon and Adam even knew she had a vehicle. Unfortunately, the truck was rarely taken out of its parking spot. She hated driving in the city, preferring her bike or her feet to get around.

She felt her feet get lighter with each step towards her truck. Micah had spent a bit of time customizing the small 4x4 and it showed. Oversized wheels gave the lifted vehicle an aggressive stance that was entirely out of place in urban New York, but ate up the dirt roads in the countryside. She carefully locked her bike into the bed mount before tossing her duffle bag and front tire in the back seat. Her laptop got shotgun in the front passenger seat, sufficiently camouflaged from inquisitive eyes tucked inside of her ratty looking and tattered messenger bag.

Micah headed straight out of the city. Heading south and west, she pointed her truck towards the setting sun. She didn't need a map or GPS; she knew exactly where she was going.

Around six that evening, her cell phone started to ring. Olivia's name flashed on the screen so she sent the call straight to voicemail then turned her phone off. Only a couple of hours left and she would be at her cabin. Thinking about the isolated rustic log cabin in the middle of its wooded acreage made her smile for the first time since this morning. She hadn't been there in quite a few months, and she craved its quiet solitude.

A little mom-and-pop store sat at the bottom of the mountain and she stopped there before continuing, it was one of those places left over from another time where you could buy anything from fresh local produce to farm boots and nails. It was the last place to buy supplies before the roads became hit and miss for pavement.

Climbing back into the truck, she flipped the Toyota into four-wheel drive, looking forward to the final leg of her journey. She wasn't really hungry, but still bought a few staples, just in case. The weather could change easily in the mountains, going from sunny and calm to stormy and wet in an instant. It wouldn't do to get trapped there with nothing to eat if the roads washed out or flooded.

Micah's smile widened the minute she made the final turn leading to the log and tin cabin. Coming here was just what she needed. Its quiet solace would help her get her life back on track...again.

Micah walked inside the cabin just before dark. She checked her cell phone and saw that Olivia had already called five times and had sent two texts. She ignored all of them.

Micah was so tired, mentally and physically, that she didn't even bother to change into her bed clothes. It was enough to just toss her boots off and flop into bed. The night was cool enough to be comfortable, but not so cold she would need a fire, for which she was eternally grateful. Tomorrow she would worry about getting the cabin back to fully functional, but for tonight it was enough to just sleep. Fully clothed, she tossed and turned, churning the bed covers beneath her into a tangled mess. Vivid blue eyes and soft pink lips haunted her dreams that night.

***

The next morning dawned calm and clear, unless you were anywhere near Olivia Holden. After a sleepless night and countless unanswered phone calls and messages, Olivia was livid. Walking into her office in full "boss from hell" mode, her staff moved out of her way, parting before her like the Red Sea.

She had held out hope until now. Her heart sank into that deep, dark part of her soul where loneliness and fear reigned, knowing without a doubt that Micah was not there. Intellectually, she knew she wouldn't be there, but her heart refused to believe it until she walked into an empty office.

Tossing her purse down on her desk, she had Amanda call Jonathan and tell him to get to her office, now. Unable to sit still, Olivia paced behind her desk as she tried to contain her nervous energy. At each turn, she would stop and look out her window, unconsciously running her fingers along her lower lip as she waited for Jonathan, then begin again when he didn't show up in a couple of seconds. With each revolution, Olivia's frustration and fear wound tighter.

What the hell happened?

Micah had ignored all her calls and texts last night. It was her own fault really, letting her stubborn need to know everything send her storming off yesterday. Unfortunately, by the time she had swallowed her pride long enough to call and apologize, something had come up at work that she couldn't ignore. She called as soon as she could, only to be greeted by the same recorded message over and over again.

Olivia was thrown back into her own dismal past, reliving the first time Micah had disappeared. Olivia had tried calling her then, too. She had come in to work much like today, expecting to see Micah at her desk, but she wasn't there. Then Micah didn't show up to work the next day, or the one after that, and she had just given up. Not this time.

Barely containing herself while she was forced to wait, Olivia felt like pulling her hair out in frustration. The whole situation was just unacceptable.

***

"Where is she?" Olivia turned on Jonathan the minute he hurried into her office.

"I don't know, Olivia. She was gone when I got home last night. All she left was a note telling me not to worry," he said, unsure what he could say to make Olivia feel any better. He doubted anything would.

"At least she left you a note," Olivia grumbled. It was a hard pill to swallow, knowing that Micah chose to leave a note with Jonathan rather than talk to her.

Rubbing her temples against an impending headache, Olivia sat down tiredly. "If you hear from her again, please let me know. I need to know that she's okay...at least...I guess that's all for now, Jonathan," she said, dismissing him from her office before leaning back pensively.

Her thoughts turned inward; mimicking the churning motion of her gold pen as she idly spun it between her fingers. A slideshow of conversations and interactions from the past week flickered through her mind, to be shuffled and catalogued while she searched for clues. Something had gone terribly wrong, something that had made Micah run from her.

I won't let this happen again.

A newfound sense of determination settled solidly on her shoulders. Yes, Micah had run from her before, but she had also let her go. Olivia had two choices now: let the past repeat itself, or change her actions. Now she just needed to find her and hopefully, find the right words to fix all of this.

During a mid-morning meeting with Jonathan, his phone finally rang. Micah's name flashed on the screen. Olivia raised one delicate eyebrow at him. He nodded and silently mouthed the words she most wanted to hear. "Yes, it's Micah."

Olivia remained silent and motioned for him to put the call on speaker.

"Sweetie, are you okay?" he asked, holding the phone out so that Olivia could hear.

The phone crackled with a bad connection. "Jon, take me off speaker or I swear I will hang up." Micah sounded tired, but firm. He looked over at Olivia and shrugged. What else could he do? A quick nod of acquiescence and he hit the speaker button then brought the phone back to his ear.

"Okay, you're off speaker. Now, are you okay?" he asked, watching Olivia carefully as he listened to Micah's response. "That's good, where are you? You know you have some people really worried here."

It was driving Olivia crazy only hearing half of the conversation.

"When are you coming back?" he asked, hoping to have good news for Olivia. "What? What does that mean, you don't know?"

Jonathan was becoming more upset by the minute. Olivia snatched the phone out of his hands, unable to stand by and just listen anymore.

"Micah, where are you? This is completely unacceptable!" she fired off rapidly. Olivia didn't hear a reply; the phone was disturbingly quiet and after watching the phone flip back to the screen saver, she realized that Micah had hung up on her.

"Tell me where she is," she commanded, handing Jonathan his phone back.

"She's okay. She is at her cabin in Maryland and apparently doesn't know when she is going to come back." He sounded angry, which surprised Olivia.

126

"I didn't expect you to just give in that quickly," she admitted. She had gotten the impression that Jonathan was more loyal to Micah than to her.

"When it comes to Micah, I do tend to be overly protective. But this whole situation changes things." Jonathan grimaced. "What are you going to do about it?"

Olivia looked up at the ceiling and weighed her options. She was a busy woman with a full day's work scheduled and locked in for at least three months. "Maryland?"

"Yes, and as about as far into the state as you can go before you hit West Virginia."

"In other words, far away from here."

"Pretty much." Jonathan grinned at her wryly, waiting to see what she would decide.

"This is ridiculous," she finally growled. She was the boss. Amanda could reschedule her appointments and whatever couldn't be moved around Jonathan could handle for her. He was more than qualified. "Give me the address."

"Thank God!" Jonathan felt like throwing his arms up in the air and yelling Halleluiah. He wrote down Micah's address and handed the slip of paper to Olivia. "Bring her home where she belongs, preferably in one piece."

Silently apologizing to Micah for revealing her secret hideaway, he left Olivia to figure out what to do next. *God, the drama*, he thought idly as he walked out of her office, *and people think I'm a drama queen!*

***

"Be ready in five." Olivia texted her driver Robert, then used the brief time she had to formulate her game plan. Regina was going to her father's house this weekend, so she didn't have to worry about her daughter. He was scheduled to pick her up after school today, but just in case, she gave him a quick call to make sure nothing unforeseen had happened. Then she made a call to her housekeeper, asking her to pack a few items for her so she could leave right away.

Punctual as always, Robert pulled up just as Olivia was hurtling out the front door. Surprisingly fast for a man his size, he bounced out and opened the door for Olivia, waiting for her to settle in before closing the door.

"Where to, Olivia?" he inquired.

"We need to stop at the house for a few minutes, but then I need a favor. Are you up to a road trip?" Olivia inquired. "I need to take an overnight trip, all the way to Maryland. I know it is a lot to ask, but I am unsure about finding this place by myself." If he wasn't available, Plan B included finding a rental car, gallivanting around the countryside and hopefully, not getting lost forever in the backwoods.

"Are we going after Micah?" Robert asked. His reflection in the rear view mirror was hopeful, almost excited as if he was thrilled to be involved in her little adventure. Maybe he thought it was romantic—her chasing after the girl of her dreams.

"Yes, we are," she admitted, returning Robert's steady gaze.

"Well then, just point me in the right direction and I'll get you there." Robert flashed a mouthful of straight white teeth, his grin sincere and infectious.

"Thank you, Robert. I need you to take me here," she said, passing him the address Jon had scribbled down.

"Yes, Ma'am," he said, tapping his black cap in a loose salute before pulling out into the heavy traffic.

Maria, her housekeeper, had outdone herself. By the time they arrived at the house, there were several full bags sitting in the foyer waiting for them. Robert made quick work of them, and they were off.

Rush hour kept them trapped in the city for longer than she liked, but happily the roads cleared up after they hit the main interstate. Several hours passed with nothing to do but watch the scenery roll by. Darkness gathered, sneaking up on her before she realized that it was pitch black outside. The Town Car's headlamps cut a short swath of visibility in front of them, light that the moonless night quickly swallowed up.

"How much farther, Robert?"

"Ma'am? We have at least another hour to go." Roberts face was nothing but a series of shadows partially illuminated by the dashboard.

She hadn't planned as well as she had thought. She couldn't just show up on Micah's doorstep in the middle of the night. "Damn. Find us a hotel, Robert. I'm sure we can find a couple of rooms."

"Yes, ma'am."

Within a few miles a series of roadside signs popped up, advertising hotels up ahead. Robert took the next exit so they could stop for the night. *This was a good decision*, she thought. It would be better to talk to Micah with a fresh mind and sunlight to back her up.

Chapter Eleven

Inhaling deeply, Micah took in the familiar woodsy smell of the countryside around her. The morning air was crisp and clean. It was so different from the constant assault of the city on your senses. For one thing, there wasn't another soul in sight, which suited her mood just fine.

Each breath seemed to cleanse and invigorate her soul. Leaning against the wood railing, she drank in the sunrise with every pore in her body, silently watching the deep purples fade into a glorious rain of red and gold as the round eye of the sun peeled away the night. The moon fought furiously to remain seen, but it inevitably faded with the arrival of the rising sun.

Micah didn't advertise it, but she owned the entire mountain. She knew every tree and hollow the property kept hidden within its valleys and hills. The view from the back porch, with the forest stretching out before her and a small stream bubbling briskly down the hillside, was worthy of a photographer's study. Even as a child the land had spoken to her. It was here that her artistic heart had been allowed to grow and flourish, even if it was only seasonal.

This was one reason she had kept her grandmother's cabin; the location was as close to paradise as you could get. No matter how tainted her childhood was or how broken and bruised she found herself, she would always have this place to come back to, to renew and reflect on her life.

When she was younger, her grandmother would bring her up to the cabin for the summer and during school breaks. She loved the quaint little cabin and the time spent there included most, if not all of her most cherished childhood memories.

The cabin always offered her peace. A temporary respite from a world she found harsh and cold. She wept when she learned that the gentle woman she loved so much had left the world. When they read the will, she had gladly accepted her grandmother's inheritance. Sometimes, she could still feel her grandmother's spirit, and she wished with all her heart that she was still here to talk to. It had only been a little over a year since she had died, and she could desperately use her sage advice.

Micah's jaw creaked as she fought another yawn; she hadn't slept very well last night. Actually, she had barely slept at all. Stretching as far as she could reach, she felt her back creak and snap. Her sore muscles and bones were the victim of curling up on a bed, fully clothed, after driving for hours without a break.

Thoughts of Olivia consumed her. Micah knew she wasn't being fair to her. Olivia had been nothing but caring and accommodating, even if she was a little pushy at times. *What do I do in return? I leave. Olivia didn't deserve that.* To make matters worse, she had ignored Olivia's phone calls and text's. Not one of her better moves.

She ran her hand across her stomach, absently tracing the slight ridges beneath the thin fabric of her tank top with her fingertips. She realized what she was doing and stopped herself. Clenching her fist in sudden anger, Micah fought the urge to take the poisonous emotion out on the wood railing. Every scar was burned in her memory, each one bearing its own special flavor of pain and release. She felt ugly in both body and soul, constantly haunted by the ghosts of her past, each berating her for succumbing to such weakness. Each mark was a testimony of every time she fell from personal grace, spiraling into a devastating loss of control on sun-singed wings. It made complete sense to her, but that didn't make an iota of difference; it was how Olivia would see her that mattered.

Micah knew Olivia thought she was beautiful, she could see it in her eyes, in the way she looked at her when she thought Micah wasn't watching her. Having Olivia see her as anything else would kill her. If Olivia saw the marks on her stomach, Micah was sure they would disgust her. When she found out how Micah had gotten them, her disgust would turn to disappointment and pity. She could not bear having Olivia look at her like that.

She didn't know what to do, and the hopelessness of the situation made her despair almost unbearable.

It seemed to be a theme of hers, to return to this cabin when her life was at its lowest, when her despair was most threatening to her psyche.

"You're quite the prize, aren't you?" Micah muttered. A bird chattered at her from a nearby tree, perhaps it was offering her some sage advice she couldn't understand. All she knew was that she felt cold inside, and no amount of summer sunlight seemed sufficient to warm her.

***

Olivia congratulated herself on last night's decision. The tiny road winding its way up the mountain towards Micah's cabin was too small for the county to even bother painting lanes on it. The drive would have been nerve wracking late at night. The driveway was even worse. Crushed stone, despite being tightly packed, crunched beneath the Town Car's tires like some prehistoric bird chewing rock. It crackled loudly inside the car's interior, and she was sure the noise would announce their presence long before they reached their destination. It didn't.

Robert parked the car and she stared out the window at the tiny cabin perched among tall pines. It sat silent, and for all appearances, empty.

"Should I go up and knock?" Robert offered.

"No. I'll go," Olivia said, leaving him with the car. Rather than head straight for the front door, Olivia followed her instincts and headed down a wide pea gravel path that ran alongside the quaint cabin.

She found Micah standing on a covered balcony overlooking the distant mountains. It was an impressive view, but that wasn't what held her interest. Olivia stopped, content to stand silent and unnoticed.

Micah was leaning on the railing, her steady gaze riveted on the sunrise. The contrast of deep shadows beneath the porch competed with the cold light of the early morning, accentuating the sharp angles of her cheekbones and jawline. Her black hair shone darkly, except where thin tendrils of sunlight highlighted the tousled locks along her brow with a bluish hue.

She appeared lost in her own thoughts. Micah's face was pensive as if she sought some shining answer to all her questions in the sun's glory. Barefoot and dressed only in faded old jeans and a blue tank top, the casual outfit showcased her long legs and powerful shoulders. As the rising sun gained access to the shadows beneath the porch's tin roof, more details emerged. The deep golden light brought Micah's still form out of the shadows. Olivia noticed how fine wisps of dark hair curled lightly against the tan skin at the nape of her neck. Bright motes of dust danced around her, transforming Micah into some ethereal creature of light and dark.

Micah shifted her grip on the wooden hand railing. A bright flash caught Olivia's eye, distracting her attention away from Micah's face. The sun had caught the edge of a heavy silver ring Micah was wearing. Olivia had never seen it before, but the bold design fit the image before her well. Despite herself, she had to smile in appreciation of the stark beauty in front of her. The woman was just too gorgeous for her own good.

"Micah?" Olivia called out softly.

Micah practically jumped out of her skin. She turned awkwardly towards the unexpected noise, then had to grab the railing to keep herself from falling. Here she was daydreaming about Olivia and suddenly, there she was. *Think of the devil...* an old saying her grandmother had been fond of bubbled out of her memories.

"Holy shit, Olivia, what the hell are you doing here?" Micah demanded, her right knee starting to throb. She refused to bend down and rub it, she didn't want Olivia to see any weakness.

"It should be obvious, Micah." The crunch of pea gravel beneath Olivia's feet was loud in the crisp morning air.

Damn. How could I have missed that? Micah asked herself. The answer was obvious and didn't make her very happy. *I was so caught up in my own misery I didn't even hear someone sneaking up on me.*

Olivia's gaze slid down her jean-clad body and rested on Micah's rebellious knee.

"You really should get off that knee," she said, after watching Micah carefully shifting to take the weight off her right leg. She was obviously in pain but was unwilling to admit it.

"How did you even get here?" Micah asked, then swiveled her head towards the sound of heavy footsteps crunching along the path from the front of the cabin. A second later, Olivia's chauffeur, Robert, emerged around the corner with her bags in tow. They looked heavy and there were way too many of them.

"Hey, Rob," Micah called out, her voice friendly and warm towards the overloaded chauffeur.

"Hey, yourself, kid." Robert smiled up at her then placed the luggage at Olivia's feet before retreating back a few feet.

"Were you planning on staying, Olivia?" Micah asked, her voice tinged with acid. Leaning casually against the railing she glared down at the woman from the elevated decking, her expression decidedly unfriendly.

"Micah, please sit down, I can tell you are in pain." Olivia started to climb the short stairway, one hand resting lightly on the wood railing.

"I don't need to sit down, Olivia. What I need to know is why you seem to think that you have been invited here." Micah crossed her arms, shielding herself from the stubborn woman who had the temerity to invade her personal haven. This was her place, her refuge, and the one person she had run away from was now here. Micah was pissed. If she ever returned to New York, she would have a thing or two to say to Jonathan.

"Answer me, Olivia. What are you doing here with your bags?"

Micah's voice rose with every syllable, until she practically shouted the last two words. The sound of Robert huffing around the corner, loaded down with another bag, interrupted Micah's rant. He stopped at the pile of bags but didn't attempt to mount the stairs after looking at Micah's face.

"Olivia?"

"I'm fine, Robert, you can head back now. Oh, and Robert? Thank you." Olivia dismissed her driver, daring Micah to say something. Rob tipped his hat to both women and left... quickly. He was a smart man.

"Well, I guess that answers that question," Micah grumbled, shaking her head. *Why had she let Rob leave? A better question would be why had she let Olivia stay behind?*

"I am not here to answer questions. I'm here to get answers!" Olivia exclaimed, letting her fury reign unrestricted now that they were audience-free. She boldly strode up the final stair to join Micah on the wooden porch. Micah was still taller, but she no longer had the advantage of standing above her.

"Damn it, Micah! You just left me in New York. You refuse to answer my calls. You stand there and ask me why I think I feel privileged to come here uninvited? YOU made me come looking for you. Then I find you here, hiding away from the world! What the hell is going on?" All of the stress and strain of the last day was let loose in a string of accusations.

Each sentence struck Micah in the heart like a physical blow. She bowed her head against the verbal onslaught, feeling the truth behind each and every one of Olivia's accusations.

"All right, you do deserve an explanation." Micah looked up at her, tears of anguish shining brightly in eyes that carried too much pain for someone that young.

The sorrow in Micah's voice made Olivia's heart contract painfully. She started towards the suffering woman, then held out one ineffectual hand, afraid to touch her. "Micah, I'm..." *What? Sorry?*

The moment passed where she might have found the right words to make things better. Micah gave her a sad look, then shrugged and shook her head as if to say it wouldn't matter anyway.

"I'll make us some coffee." Micah turned away from the warming light of the early morning sun and headed for the open door of the cabin. It was too beautiful outside for her story. That she was turning away from the light in order to go over all the sordid details of her past in the dark was appropriately ironic.

Chapter Twelve

Once in the kitchen, Micah pulled out the coffee and coffee maker, using the familiar motions to gather her thoughts about her. She turned off the small stereo sitting on the counter, throwing the cabin into absolute silence. The absence of her ever-present music rattled her, but it was necessary. Grabbing a can of soda out of the fridge and popping the top, Micah took a long drink to ease her dry throat. Having done everything she could think of to delay, she finally resigned herself to the inevitable. She gestured at Olivia, inviting her to sit at the small rustic table she used for the occasional meal.

"This is not a pretty story, are you sure you want to hear it?" Micah's face was grim but hopeful. "It's not too late to change your mind and leave, you know, you can still call Robert to come back for you."

She tried to give them both one last out but Olivia just waved her hand for Micah to begin.

"Alright. You might as well take a seat and get comfortable." Micah lit up a cigarette then boosted herself up to sit on the edge of the kitchen counter. Reaching over, she slid open the window that sat above the sink. Taking a long drag, she blew the smoke out slowly, her hazel eyes distant and unfocused.

Light grey curls of cigarette smoke drifted their way from Micah's lit cigarette towards the open window, joining the motes of dust dancing in the sunlight that pushed its way in against the gloom.

The kitchen table lay in the path of the sunbeams. When Olivia stepped forward to take the offered chair, she walked into the light, much like an actress stepping into the spotlight. Micah sucked in her breath, struck by the ethereal quality of Olivia's pale blonde hair.

Shit, I have got to get it together, Micah thought, taking another shaky drag on her cigarette.

It was a dual-edged blade, her feelings for Olivia. They cut both ways. A small part of her threatened to laugh uncontrollably at the irony. IF she didn't care, IF Olivia didn't affect her so totally and completely down to the very heart of her, she wouldn't have to go through this. Blaming Olivia was the easy way out. She knew that now, but it wasn't going to make the next few hours any easier.

Feeling heat against her fingers, she looked down at her forgotten cigarette and found it had burned down to the filter. Crushing it out in the sink, Micah lit up another smoke, still avoiding looking at Olivia directly. She took another deep drag and exhaled slowly, blowing the smoke towards the window so as not to offend Olivia. It was the best she could do. Olivia hated cigarettes, but there was no way Micah was going to make it through the telling if she didn't smoke.

"A lot happened all at once, just let me start with that," Micah said, taking a drag on her second cigarette. Her voice, thick with emotion, held the soft undertones of her Irish heritage, giving her words a slight lilt. She risked a quick glance at Olivia before looking away again.

"So anyway, about two months before I left New York, a lawyer called me out of the blue to tell me that my grandmother had died. She had been sick for a while and no one had told me. I guess she didn't want to worry me, she never let on that she was sick." Tears gathered at the painful memory, blurring her vision. Rubbing her eyes roughly, she pressed her fingers against her eyelids, wiping the moisture away. "I didn't even get a chance to see her one last time before she passed."

"My parents and I hadn't spoken much over the last few years; we didn't get along at all. My grandmother was more of a parent to me than they ever were. At least she offered her love without conditions." Her throat constricted from forcibly holding in her tears.

"You know, my parents have done a lot of shitty things to me, but waiting until my grandmother was gone and buried...they didn't even bother to call me themselves. They left it up to the law firm handling my grandmother's will to inform me." She stopped, unable to continue.

"That's horrible, Micah." Olivia's voice was husky with emotion. "I can't even imagine how awful that must have been."

Micah nodded and started in on the hardest part. If she verbally acknowledged Olivia's sympathy, it would be her undoing. She had too much left to say.

"I threw myself into school and work. I needed something solid, something firm in my life that I could rely on. Earning the intern position at your firm earlier that year had been a major break for me, but it meant a lot more to me after getting that news. The constant work allowed me to function, it kept me busy and let me forget all the crap going on in my personal life. And then, even that was gone."

Micah took a deep breath and held it until her lungs burned with the need to exhale. She still wasn't prepared to talk about the real reason she had disappeared the first time but there didn't seem to be any way to avoid it. Olivia seemed intent on following her wherever she went and obviously was willing to do whatever it took to find her. That sort of tenacity was uniquely Olivia, and Micah didn't seem to be able to say no to her.

"Do you remember that last day?" Micah asked, then shook her head at uttering such a stupid question. "Never mind. Of course you do. You asked me to watch Reggie so you could go out, just like you had a dozen other times. After you left, I received an unexpected phone call. I won't go into all the details right now, but needless to say, my father hadn't been making anything easy for me. I had to meet with the lawyers back home, something I had been stupidly putting off doing. I needed to talk to you, desperately. I waited until you got home, not really knowing what to expect, only that I had a few things I needed to say before I left. Then you came home, and it all fell apart."

She paused again, and then shrugged before continuing. "I won't apologize for leaving. You were so caught up in your own news, so excited with the prospect of taking over the firm, and more than a little drunk from the evening's celebration. I don't even think you noticed how upset I was."

Another drag on the cigarette, another quick swallow from the now lukewarm soda, and Micah felt like she could go on.

The can clicked metallically when she set it down on the wood counter between her legs. She turned the can around and around, idly watching the watermark appear and disappear with the motion.

"You were in the mood for celebrating and I was caught up in my sorrow. It was a bad combination. Too many emotions running high, you know?" Micah blinked, trying to dispel the images of the past barraging her. "You know what happened next. I was mortified, thinking I had misread everything and had just made a huge mistake. The look on your face, the denial, I just couldn't handle it. So, I just left."

The words were quiet, laden with pain and heavy with sorrow.

"I had been such an idiot, I had thought that you had feelings for me, that somehow, you had wanted me as much as I wanted you." Micah practically spat the words out.

"I went out to a bar later that night to drown my sorrows. What a cliché!" Micah barked a short and joyless laugh. "I was out to prove something, I guess. I needed to know someone wanted me, since you obviously didn't. I ended up having a one night stand with some woman who came on to me."

Crossing her arms in front of her, Micah rubbed her bare shoulders as if her own words chilled her, and then twisted her neck until a sharp crack echoed in the small room. "I just wanted to feel something. I felt like an empty shell, numb inside and out. Wanting a relationship hadn't worked for me; random sex didn't do it either. It was quite the epiphany. I couldn't have who I wanted, but I could have what I didn't need." Another humorless smile followed Micah's admission.

"It wasn't going to work, staying in New York and trying to stay away from you. I left that night and went home to West Virginia." Rolling her eyes at her own blindness, she smiled bleakly. "Not one of my best decisions, but I felt like I had to make an attempt. I needed to see if I could repair things with my parents. I was in pain and just wanted to go home, to feel loved. I mean, isn't that what parents are for?"

The question was rhetorical; she didn't expect Olivia to answer.

"I'm being a terrible hostess, I forgot your coffee." Grateful for the temporary distraction, she jumped down from the counter and grabbed a plain mug, then pulled creamer from the small fridge and sugar from the upper cabinet.

"Dammit!" Micah's hands were shaking so badly she almost dropped the creamer.

Olivia appeared at her shoulder, taking the container from her.

"Let me do this," she offered, pouring her own cup of coffee and preparing it herself. Then she sat back down and took a sip. "It's good."

A ghost of a smile flickered across Micah's face, not much more than a subtle twist of her lips, then was lost in the shadows again.

Micah slouched against the tile counter, one ankle crossed over the other and her hands buried deep in her jeans pockets. Now that she had started, the story had taken on a life of its own. It was demanding to be told. Her nerves practically crackled from the adrenaline coursing through her veins and nothing physical happening to expend the excess energy. She cast a fond thought towards her cross comp bike, still sitting in the back of her Toyota. A ride would be nice, but it wouldn't help solve the situation. It would only postpone the inevitable. Olivia would still be waiting for her when she got back.

Micah ran her fingers through her hair, roughly massaging her scalp in an attempt to regain her focus.

"So, I go home," Micah reiterated, starting up again where she had left off. "I'm not even there for an hour before we start arguing. First, it was about grandmother, then it progressed to them attacking me. They wanted to know why I had left New York, why I had left law school for no good reason. They pushed and pushed until I gave in. I honestly believe they had mapped out my entire life for me. Evidently that didn't include me informing them that I was a lesbian." Micah grimaced, taking another drink before finding her next words.

"I had no idea they were so homophobic, I mean, why would I have known? The subject had never come up before," Micah asked, not really expecting an answer. "I should have known," she added, condemning herself for her blindness.

"They hated who I was, or as they put it...who I had chosen to become. They couldn't believe that their daughter was gay. They raged against me verbally, trying to convince me that I was wrong, that I could come back to the right path, throwing words like 'sin' and 'damnation' at me. When that didn't work, they resorted to name calling...abomination was the least offensive." Micah pushed off from the counter; she couldn't stand still any longer. She paced the length of the small kitchen before stopping in front of Olivia. Her hands clenched and unclenched several times as she relived the last few minutes in her parents' house.

"Who I was and how I loved, that was not a mistake and I couldn't stand being told so for another minute. I let them have it. I told them very bluntly that I had fallen in love with another woman. I told them that I was in love with you."

Olivia's eyes went wide, her hand flying to her throat in response to the change in Micah's expression. Micah's expression became absolutely feral, her wide smile exposing bare teeth but never touching her eyes.

"I have to admit...the looks on their faces were absolutely priceless. Unfortunately, their shock didn't last long. I'm surprised your ears weren't burning. You were my boss. You had obviously corrupted me and led me astray. It would have been amusing if it hadn't gotten so intense. This was not the homecoming I had hoped for."

***

Micah closed her eyes, the scene vividly playing out behind her eyelids as if it was yesterday. She was sitting in the living room, trying to explain herself to her parents. Her mother kept looking at her father for guidance while he paced back and forth across the living room carpet.

"I won't have it, Micah, no child of mine can..." he *stopped, clamping his lips together until they were thin and white, refusing to even utter the word.*

"Can be what? A lesbian?" She shouted, watching him wince and turn away. It didn't matter, she had said it and what was said, couldn't be unsaid...or unheard.

"You have always been the difficult one, running off to New York to go to school when you could have stayed here instead. You left your mother and me to take care of your grandmother. You turned your back on your family and now you come back, and what? Expect us to hear this and just accept it?"

Shocked at the verbal attack, Micah spoke without thinking, "You blame me? Is this why you didn't tell me about grandma dying? How absolutely petty! You sit here, lecturing me about sin, you hypocrite!"

"How dare you!" Her father spat out venomously.

Micah looked over at her mother, waiting to see if she would pipe up or just sit there. Just once, she wished she would speak up, but it was becoming obvious that her inner fire had burned out a long time ago. Her mother was a dying ember, snuffed out by her husband's verbal abuse. Despite her urgent prayer for her mother to find her spark again, she just sat quietly, intent on examining her hands as they lay limply in her lap.

"Just dandy, Mom, thanks for the support." Sarcasm emerged, a much more comfortable emotion. This wasn't working. It was too much like her childhood, her father lording over them, and her mother sitting there and taking it. She never once took up for Micah against her father. In fact, her mother always seemed relieved when his temper landed on someone else other than her.

Her father's face turned beet red, anger contorting his face and making him a stranger, ugly.

"You-will-leave-now." Each word was spit out individually, the hatred in her father's voice chilling her to the bone. Clenched fists echoed the stiff posture and absolute stillness that should have set off alarm bells in her head.

Micah opened her eyes, blinking rapidly to wipe away the painful images.

"Before I could get up to leave of my own accord, my father took it upon himself to help me leave his house."

The unexpected act of violence still left her with feelings of disbelief. She could still feel his fingers digging into her skin like corded steel, the angry bruises that had taken weeks to fade.

"For the first time in a very long while, my father touched me in anger. You know, the whole county was aware of his penchant for violence. He was known for getting into fights at the bar or anywhere they made the mistake of serving him liquor. For a while he reserved his family, my mother and I, for a more insidious type of violence. He enjoyed the kind of pain you could cause with words. It's funny, you know. In a way, my interest in writing is because of him. His example showed me just how powerful words could be. They could hurt or heal, and they stay with you for a long time."

A faint smile ghosted across Micah's face. She truly did love writing, the ability to turn words into something that had the power to transform and illuminate. That was what had convinced her to go to law school. The law offered her the purity of words that protected and defined the world. Art had been her secret passion; something for her alone. It had taken more time to become comfortable sharing that part of her, but in the end, she was glad she did. Micah realized she had gone silent. "I'm sorry. I got lost in my thoughts."

Olivia stared up at her, her coffee forgotten as it cooled untouched after that first sip.

"Oh, Micah," Olivia whispered, overcome by the suffering Micah had endured. Micah's hazel eyes were rimmed in red, a testimony to her pain. It pained her heart to see her like this. She felt incredibly guilty that she had been so demanding, so harsh with this woman simply because she wanted answers.

"Micah, I didn't know. I can't bear this. You don't have to continue, not because of me." She had been cruel, perhaps unintentionally, but nonetheless cruel.

Micah almost laughed in her face. She couldn't take it? She couldn't bear to hear more? After pushing her to tell her everything, Olivia wanted her to stop. Well, she wasn't going to stop now, she couldn't. It was time for Olivia to know every sordid detail whether she wanted to hear it or not.

"No, Olivia. I need to finish this. You need to know what you are getting into. You need to know so you can decide if you truly want to be with me," she told her, finding the need to pace before beginning again.

"My father...he threw me out the front door so violently I fell backwards down the front stairs. He left me there, lying on the pavement. He turned his back to me and went inside. He didn't bother looking back, not once. He just locked the door behind him and turned off the porch light."

Her injured knee protested against the short laps across the hardwood floor, the pain another unwanted present from her father.

"That's how I hurt my knee. I wasn't lying to you, I did fall down. I just had help." Her laughter rang hollow in the small confines of the kitchen.

"I picked myself up and drove back into town to find a hotel room. I really didn't have the money, but what else could I do? I almost called you to ask for my internship back, I was that desperate. The reading of the will was scheduled for that Tuesday, so I held off until then. I spent two days hiding in my room, scared to death at the prospect of seeing my parents again. I couldn't leave without finding out what my grandmother had left me. I would have cherished any small token to remember her by and I couldn't bear the idea that it might go to my family by default."

"When I got there, you could have chipped ice from the corners of the room. My parents ignored me completely, trying to pretend I didn't exist. At least, they did until they read the will. My grandmother left me everything, this cabin, the land around it...whatever personal belongings she owned...all of it. My father was livid. He made a huge scene in the attorney's office, even going as far as threatening to sue me. He finally stalked out, slamming the door so hard it cracked when the attorney told him there was nothing he could do. The will was ironclad and had specific references that explained just why he was not to receive a dime from her. I thought it was over. I had to stay put for a few more days so the paperwork could be processed, then I was free to leave. At least one worry was taken care of; I had enough money to live on for a while and a place to stay."

"It wasn't over, though. My father made one last ditch attempt, and he used my mother to do it. She came to my hotel room, trying to convince me to sell the cabin. She tried to tell me that my father was sick, that they were strapped for cash from taking care of grandma, anything that would convince me to give in."

The entire conversation would have been ridiculous if it hadn't hurt so much. Her mother practically begged her to give up her inheritance, trying to make her feel sorry for them. It had been so obvious that her husband had put her up to it.

"I guess they felt like they were entitled to the money since they had taken care of her. It was like they expected to get paid for taking care of her." She muttered, resenting the emotional blackmail all over again. *I've avoided these memories for so long,* she thought, taking in a ragged breath, *and they still hold so much power over me.* Her throat burned from smoking so much, but it was nothing compared to the pain in her chest.

"I almost gave in, almost...letting my guilt over grandmother's death sway me. I almost gave in out of some bizarre idea that I owed my family for giving me life...for raising and feeding me and keeping me clothed. God knows my father reminded me about how much I owed them practically every day of my life. I told her I would sleep on it, mostly because I couldn't say no to her to her face. I mean, she was my mom, you know? Then I woke up the next morning. My knee was swollen to twice its size. The pain was excruciating and I could barely walk. I hobbled my way into the local acute care clinic, the closest thing to an ER we had. The Doc didn't have any good news for me. That little fall really screwed up my knee." Micah realized she was rubbing her bad knee, the remembered pain all too real at that moment.

"One of the worst and best things about living in a small town is that you know pretty much everyone. When the nurse walked in, she recognized me immediately. Sandy had been one of my closest friends in high school, and she treated me like the same friend I had left behind. It was as if those years since high school had never passed. She offered me a sympathetic ear and a place to stay until I could move to the cabin. Eventually she wheedled the truth out of me. How I got hurt, the will, my parents demands that I sell the cabin, their financial troubles. She was that kind of person that you could unload on and never worry that she would judge you. Seeing her again was the high point of my visit home, until she said she had something important to tell me."

Micah stopped pacing. She was breathing too fast. *Control.* She needed to calm down if she was going to get through this.

"What she told me. Gods, Olivia, what she told me sent me into such a fury." Micah's eyes flashed with something close to hatred. "My grandmother was only sixty-seven years old, Olivia...a spry and healthy sixty-seven-year old woman. She didn't die from old age, she died because she became sick and the people in charge of her well-being ignored her. They neglected her and let her get sicker and sicker until she died because she wasn't taken care of properly. My friend brought me the coroner's report; it was the most awful thing I had ever read."

"She died because my father didn't make sure she got the proper medical care when she needed it, and then he had the nerve to ask for her money after she died." Micah practically hissed that last bit, the tendons in her neck bulging as she grimaced against the pain of her grandmother's senseless death.

"I just completely lost it. It was either confront my father and risk getting hurt more, or run away. I ran. I don't even remember how I got here. I obviously drove; I just don't remember the trip. I remember grabbing my keys and the paper work from the lawyer, and that was it." Rubbing her forehead as if trying to bring those lost memories back to the surface, she sighed deeply. *Almost over.*

"I guess something broke inside."

Micah reached into the drawer behind her, pulling out a long, thin, leather clad item. Holding it between her fingertips, she held the long hunting knife out in front of her. Grasping the bone handle, she unsheathed it in one quick practiced motion, exposing a wicked looking blade about five inches long. The polished steel flashed dangerously in the sunlight.

Olivia paled. Her focus wasn't on the blade in Micah's hands, but on the strange expression on the younger woman's face. She had wanted this, pushed for Micah to be honest with her, to expose herself. Now, with her heart beating wildly against her breast like a frightened bird, she wasn't sure she wanted to hear anymore. Micah's expression shifted and changed in rapid succession. Fear, desire, anticipation, and guilt all fought for dominance, flickering in the shadows like an old black-and-white movie.

"This is what you wanted." Micah stepped forward, laying the knife carefully on the table between them. Micah captured Olivia's eyes with her own and held them by force of will alone. Stepping back away from the table, she pulled the bottom of her tank top out of her jeans, gathering the thin material in her hand. She slid the fabric up, exposing the flat planes of her stomach, pale against the dark tan of her arm.

Micah blinked, releasing her hold on Olivia. She shifted her eyes downward, inviting Olivia to follow her hand's movement.

"Oh, my God." Olivia's face held such horror.

If Micah hadn't been expecting it, it might have hurt more. As it was, the look on her face confirmed everything she had feared, everything she had been trying to avoid. The blade might as well have been a snake, the way Olivia stared at it.

"Now, do you see?" She smiled joylessly.

Micah's stomach was scattered with scars—some small, some not so small and one quite large. They were well-healed. Pale white lines crisscrossing the pale flesh, the larger ones ridged as if they had healed poorly at first. The outline of her tattoo lapped and curled around the edges of the scars, no doubt covering some of the lighter ones before dipping beneath the waistline of her jeans.

"I was never suicidal—let me make that perfectly clear. I just broke. It started small, just to feel something, something other than anger and overwhelming sadness. But then small wasn't enough. It becomes an addiction, you know, the endorphin rush that only comes with certain kinds of pain."

Micah pulled her tank top back down, but kept talking. Part of her needed to get the whole story out.

"Jon was the one who found me. I assume Adam told him since he was the only one who knew about this place. A couple of weeks had gone by since I had left. I had let my phone battery die. I didn't check my e-mails. I was here with my pain and sadness and nothing else mattered. One day I woke up and found my hair tangled too badly to brush it out, I can't even imagine how I must have looked. I found this knife and started hacking it off."

Micah ran her fingers through her short hair. "Evidently, I decided to keep the look."

Her wry comment was meant to defuse the intensity of the moment, but it didn't help.

"I can't..." Micah swallowed hard, then continued, "I'm not ready to tell you about what went on in my head after that. I can't promise you that I will ever be ready."

The admonishment was a warning. She hoped Olivia maybe, just maybe, would know not to push her on this subject.

"The day Jon showed up was a particularly bad one. He found me pretty bloody. I had gone a little too deep on this one earlier in the day." Micah ran her hand along the thin ridge hidden beneath her tank.

"He never said a word. He just cleaned me up, put me to bed, and tended to my wounds. He even risked the mountain drive several times to get food and medical supplies. I had no idea he even knew what a steri-strip was, but he patched me up pretty good. The knee was another issue. When he saw how swollen my knee still was, he told me he was taking me back home with him. I fought him tooth and nail about seeing a doctor."

She wasn't stupid. A doctor would have taken one look at her and sent her to a psych ward somewhere. It was only after he swore to keep her secret that she finally relented. She would see a doctor about her knee...and only her knee, period.

"Most of the rest of it you already know. I've been living with him ever since. I think he is still trying to protect me, be a mother hen." She smiled affectionately at the thought of the older man, stubborn to the end but fiercely protective of her.

"Some good came out of the whole thing, since that was how he and Adam met. I'm happy they got together; they should be rewarded for putting up with me. It turns out that it was a good thing that he had been so pushy about the doctor, too. I had to have surgery on my knee—twice. While I was in physical therapy I found that I really liked riding the bike, and three months ago I started working as a bike messenger."

Micah stopped. "That's my story. My life got out of control and I got it back the best I could. I started drawing and writing again to keep my brain occupied when I couldn't get outside as much. Now, the messenger job lets me be outside all day, keeping me fit and moving around. The people I'm with don't judge me, and as to the rest of society, I just blend into the background and that's fine with me."

Putting out her last cigarette, she realized that she had chain-smoked through the entire pack. Her voice was hoarse from smoking so much.

"I won't lie, Olivia, the need to do this again is still there. It will probably always be there. I try to control my urges by getting tattoos when the pressure gets to be too much. I can't promise you that it won't ever happen again, but I really do try."

It was enough. She was done explaining. She had survived the telling of the whole thing, but not without feeling raw and exposed at baring so much of her soul.

"So there you have it. Now you know."

With that final statement, Micah retreated back outside, leaving Olivia behind her. She honestly didn't know what to expect. She couldn't bear to see Olivia look at her with pity, she would rather just be left alone.

Chapter Thirteen

Olivia knew Micah was waiting for her to pass judgment on her. She sat at the table for a good five minutes, staring at the hunting knife and contemplating everything she had just been told.

Once, she had reached out to touch it, but pulled her hand back before her outreached fingers made it across the table.

To feel such pain, she thought...then rewound Micah's confession. *No,* she corrected herself, *to get to a point where you are so desperate to feel something that you would resort to hurting yourself. How horrible that must be.*

Olivia rested her elbows on the table and covered her eyes. She couldn't say she understood everything that Micah had gone through, was going through still, but she felt terrible that Micah thought she needed to go through all that by herself. None of what she had been told, or seen for that matter, changed the fact that she was in love with Micah.

It was a shock, seeing all those scars marring the perfection of Micah's body, but she found herself blinded to them. Yes, the scars were ugly, but they weren't Micah. They didn't define her. Micah was beautiful to her, not for her perfection but because of what she felt when they touched.

She did have a few questions of her own. Maybe not the ones Micah was expecting, but ones that she desperately needed answers to. Actually, there was just one question that really mattered. Micah had told her parents how she felt about her and she did this even when she thought there wasn't anything left to salvage between them. It had been an incredibly brave thing to do, and as Jonathan had alluded to earlier, that bravery had carried dire consequences. It was time for Olivia to honor that bravery by giving Micah back what she had demanded from her, honesty and openness.

She walked outside to find Micah standing on the porch, gazing out at the forest below her. She tensed up the minute Olivia stepped onto the wood planking, shoulder muscles twitching as if she was anticipating a physical blow.

"Micah?" Olivia joined her at the railing. When she didn't answer, she reached over and gently cupped Micah's hand in hers, half afraid she would pull away. "Micah, look at me please."

Again with the please. It made it hard for Micah to refuse. She turned and waited silently for Olivia's verdict.

"You said had, as in past tense?" Olivia fought the urge to hold her breath. So much of her future, their future, was tied up in the next few minutes.

"What?"

"You said, 'had fallen in love with.' Is that past tense?"

"No, Olivia, it's very much present, and future, too."

"Oh, Sweetie," Olivia said, gazing into Micah's eyes. "I love you, too. I have for a long time." Olivia placed a feather soft kiss on one palm before lifting it to her cheek. She captured Micah's other hand and she pressed it firmly against her heart. Head and heart. She had lost both of them a long time ago.

"I am so sorry that you went through all of that alone. I tried to call you the first time you disappeared from my life. I wanted to find you and bring you back but I stopped myself. I told myself that if you wanted to be with me you wouldn't have left. I intended to make my interest known as soon as your internship was up. If I had known why you left, I would have done anything to take back what had happened."

"Olivia." Micah's tone of voice carried a warning. Olivia would have to do better than rehash tired old excuses.

"I...I responded badly that night. I know that now, and it hurt you. I was so caught up in my own happiness that I didn't see your pain. When you kissed me, it was everything I had ever wanted, but you were still my intern. I just couldn't bring myself to break my father's rule; the behavior was too ingrained in me," Olivia's voice cracked. "Please believe me when I say that I never intended for you to think I didn't want you, or that you had made a mistake."

Olivia could see how her reaction might have been interpreted. Micah had needed her and she had turned her away. Worse, she had seen the horrified expression on Micah's face before she left, fleeing Olivia's house after they had kissed. No, she corrected herself, Micah had fled after the conversation that followed that kiss, a conversation that had left her feeling ashamed of both her words and actions.

"Just how far in the closet are you planning on living, Olivia? Are you willing to stay there for the rest of your life, just to please your father and some ideal of his?"

"Closet? Whatever are you talking about, Micah?"

"Oh, God...Olivia. Please tell me you aren't straight."

"I..."

"This can't be happening, I've seen you watching me. I know you want me, you wanted this as much as I did."

"Micah...I can't. Not with you," Olivia practically begged. She wished Micah would just try to understand where she was coming from. She had never done this before, never felt like this for another woman. Why couldn't she understand that she couldn't do this right now?

Olivia sighed deeply; wishing the past away was something she couldn't do.

"Not going after you was the biggest mistake I ever made. That's why I followed you this time. I couldn't let you go without telling you how I feel. I promise you, if you give me a chance I won't make the same mistakes. You will never have to feel alone again."

Too overwhelmed by Olivia's words to form a coherent response, Micah gently untangled herself from Olivia's hands. Gazing deeply into those brilliant blue eyes, she ran her fingers along the fine jawline, then gasped when Olivia tilted her head into the motion. Olivia appeared to genuinely crave her touch, something she could intimately understand. Her fingers followed the smooth skin of Olivia's neckline, and then gathered at her nape to draw her in for a kiss.

The kiss was sweet, questing, and tasted like the finest of wines.

Strong fingers slipped through her hair, gently massaging the base of her skull in slow, lazy circles. It nonetheless sent shivers down her spine, making her dizzy with anticipation.

Taking a jagged breath, Olivia whispered to her beloved. "Please, promise me that you will talk to me if you feel the urge to harm yourself again."

159

Micah pulled Olivia closer for a second taste of her lips. Olivia boldly ran her tongue along her bottom lip, seeking entry. Micah let her, then deepened the kiss, her insistent tongue demanding submission. A playful nip sent shivers of delight down Olivia's spine, breaking her concentration for a moment before she repaid Micah in kind, placing a trail of light kisses and nibbles along her neck.

Olivia wrapped her arms around Micah's waist, could feel the muscular back move beneath her fingers. Letting her fingers dance along Micah's lithe form, she slid her hands beneath the untucked tank top, seeking hot skin. Lightly caressing along Micah's flank, she continued her exploration, unable to stop herself.

***

Goddammit!

Micah broke away from the kiss when she felt Olivia's questing hands skim softly across her stomach.

"No, don't." She grabbed Olivia's hands and pulled them out from under her tank, then instantly felt guilty for manhandling her so roughly. She raised and then gently kissed each hand in turn, much like Olivia had just done a moment ago, apologizing for the faint fingerprints along her wrist.

Both women were still breathing hard. Olivia's chest heaved with every breath, her lips plump and full from being so thoroughly kissed. She was the very vision of sensuality. Every nerve fiber in Micah's body was tuned to the woman in front of her. Her brain, on the other hand, was screaming in her ears, playing to every fear she so carefully kept locked up. *Too much. Too much, too soon!*

Micah realized that it had taken well over an hour to tell her story. The sun was sitting higher in the sky now, the brilliant colors of sunrise had long abandoned the day. Now there was just a mutual intensity, a burning sensation that accompanied a cloudless sky that lacked any character.

Gods, it felt so much longer.

She was emotionally and physically exhausted, as washed out and pale as a faded old tee, she didn't have enough energy left to fight or explain any further.

Olivia looked thunderstruck, lost in the residual haze of her arousal and shocked by the sudden loss of contact. Micah felt slightly guilty for stopping so abruptly, but she couldn't help it. She couldn't shed her armor that fast. It had protected her for so long it had become a part of her. Trying to strip her of it now would be like trying to remove a second skin.

"What's, wrong?" Olivia asked.

"Nothing," Micah muttered. "I...I'm not..." she started, then gave up. Her brain refused to cooperate any longer. Rubbing her forehead tiredly, she backed up a couple of steps. That was better. At least she felt a little more in control. *What is it about Olivia? She's the only woman who can do this to me.*

"Look Olivia, I'm exhausted. I slept like shit the last couple nights and this morning has been a little...a lot emotional. Could I interest you in a short nap? Um. I mean, if you don't want one, that's fine, but I really need some sleep," she added, her cheeks warming when she realized what she had just asked.

Olivia pressed manicured fingertips to Micah's lips, hushing the awkward explanation.

"A nap sounds excellent. The motel had a horrible bed," Olivia said, emphasizing the word nap. She was rewarded by a rather confused looking woman screwing her eyebrows together at her.

"Huh, what motel?"

"I left yesterday, right after you called Jonathan, but by the time we got into the area it was getting late. I didn't think showing up uninvited in the middle of the night was a wise idea."

"Makes sense to me," Micah murmured, smiling gratefully at the consideration. She didn't think she would have been able to say what she had to say last night. It could have ended badly, even before it started.

Micah grabbed Olivia's luggage from where Robert had left them and carried them back into the cabin with her. Olivia followed closely behind, finally having the opportunity to see more of the cabin than just the kitchen. Micah pulled back a large Indian blanket hanging from one of the heavy log beams spanning the length of the cabin revealing a queen size bed tucked along the back wall.

Olivia stopped and stared at the unexpected luxury. Micah must have noticed, because she also stopped, then broke into a grin when she caught the look on Olivia's face.

"Did you expect bunk beds or something of the sort?" Micah smirked. "Maybe an air-mattress and a tattered old sleeping bag, hmm?"

"I, um..." Olivia stalled, choosing to ignore Micah's sarcasm. She pulled back the bedding, revealing smooth high-count cotton sheets and feather pillows. Her palm sunk into the thick pillow top mattress and she hummed in approval. "Definitely better than the motel."

Micah laughed.

"Surprised? Just because I choose to hide out in a cabin in the middle of nowhere, doesn't mean I don't enjoy my luxuries. Wait until you see the bathroom." Micah grabbed some cotton shorts and a t-shirt from a small wooden dresser and headed into what Olivia assumed was the bathroom to change.

"Are you always this modest?" Olivia asked the minute Micah returned.

"When I'm around someone as beautiful as you? Yeah, I am," Micah shot back, swiftly climbing into bed.

"I'm not sure how I'm supposed to respond to that," Olivia responded blandly. Since Micah had set the tone for the morning, Olivia decided to follow suit. She only had to search through two suitcases to find something appropriate to wear. "I assume that's the bathroom?"

"Yeah, help yourself."

Olivia changed into her silk pajamas and padded back into the other room. Micah lay there, already peacefully sleeping. Olivia climbed into the other side of the bed, then carefully scooted towards the center of the bed. Micah had one arm up above her head, tucked underneath her head. Scooting closer, she laid her head on Micah's shoulder. Micah moved fitfully and almost woke up, drawing Olivia into her embrace. A soft kiss brushed along her hairline. She sighed, content to remain curled up next to Micah while she slept.

Micah opened her eyes as soon as Olivia's breathing fell into the regular rhythm of sleep. She lay awake for quite a while afterwards, staring at the pine knots in the ceiling.

She felt wrung out emotionally. Lighter, but exhausted. She had shared something very personal with Olivia and instead of looking at her with disgust or pity, she had accepted her.

That didn't mean she was ready for Olivia to become intimately acquainted with her scars. To say that was problematic was an understatement. No matter how much she thought about it, she couldn't come up with an easy answer. There was nothing she could do to change things, and she couldn't bear to end what was between them. Micah's eyelids grew heavier by the minute until she finally gave into the fatigue that had been dogging her all morning. Pale blonde hair framed the last view of her cabin before entering the darkness of sleep. Only Olivia's weight wrapped around her kept her from moving restlessly, but it didn't stop her dreams.

Chapter Fourteen

Olivia woke up in a strange bed, her heart pounding until she woke up enough to realize where she was. At some point she must have turned over in her sleep. There was nothing but a blank wall in front of her, the regularly stacked shape of natural logs reminding her that she was sleeping in Micah's cabin. She rolled over, only to find she was alone in the bed. Propping herself up on one elbow, Olivia ran her hand over tousled sheets that still carried Micah's imprint. They were cold.

Micah had been up for a while.

Olivia sighed, finding she was starting to hate waking up alone, either that or she was learning to like going to sleep with someone else too quickly. Honestly, she was surprised that Micah was up before her, considering how exhausted she had sounded when she had asked Olivia to join her for a nap. Olivia smiled at the quaint term; it was endearing in a childlike way, but she had to admit it was very effective. Inviting someone to take a nap didn't carry the sexual overtones that asking someone to sleep with them did. Regardless, she had held a small hope that something might happen between them, a hope that unraveled the moment she returned to find Micah already sleeping. Asleep, Micah looked younger, more innocent. She could find nothing in that smooth brow and peaceful face that resembled the tortured young woman she had listened to at length this morning.

Olivia shrugged on her blue silk robe and followed the muffled sound of music past the thick wool wall hanging. Thick runners protected her bare feet from the cold wood floors and kept her footfalls completely silent. Micah sat on the couch, her feet propped on the coffee table and her laptop balanced on her thighs. She was typing at a rapid speed and didn't seem aware of Olivia's presence until she sat on the couch. Olivia folded herself onto the remaining cushion and turned sideways, stretching out on the couch with her feet just inches from Micah's thigh.

"Just give me a minute to finish this up," Micah said without looking up.

Micah was focused, her eyes plastered to the computer screen while she typed and then reviewed her work. She reached out absently, rubbing Olivia's calf as she hummed along with the music. Saving her document with a satisfying click of a button, she set her computer on the coffee table in front of them and fell back into the cushions.

"I didn't wake you with the music, did I?" she asked.

"No, Sweetheart, not at all. I do know how much you love to play your music loud. Does it prevent you from working, not playing it loud?"

"Honestly? Yeah, it does. A lot of time I need the distraction. The noise keeps the other half of my brain occupied."

"But not today?" Olivia asked as innocently as possible.

Echoing her thoughts, Micah quipped back, "No, not today. I am feeling quite inspired today."

Olivia felt inspired, too. She moved closer to Micah, then boldly slid one slim calf over Micah's thighs.

"Please, continue what you were doing," she suggested.

Micah stared down at the proffered calf, then cocked her head sideways at Olivia.

"You are absolutely gorgeous, you know that?" She didn't mean to ask that aloud but Olivia was watching her with those eyes, a soft smile on her lips and a dreamy, half-lidded expression on her face. It was hard not to notice how incredibly sexy she was. It also didn't help that Olivia was sitting close enough for Micah to feel her body heat, to smell her perfume scenting the air around them with every breath.

"Do I?" Olivia managed to agree while still leaving a twist of a question at the end. *Am I to you, enough to get past your stubborn resistance?* She reached out and took Micah's unresisting hand, bringing it back to her forgotten calf. "Rub," she commanded.

Olivia's breath caught in her throat at the hungry look in Micah's eyes. That look developed a life of its own, until Micah's eye's glowed darkly, any hint of green overshadowed by gleaming obsidian. Olivia's thighs trembled, but she managed to keep a firm hand on Micah's, guiding her towards the edge of her silk robe. *How far will she let me go?*

"Stop," Micah pulled her hand away from its inevitable path and stood so suddenly that Olivia fell backwards onto the couch. Micah stood perfectly still, looking down at her for the longest time. Frustration and arousal colored her high cheekbones. Before Olivia could move, before she could speak, Micah made a curt motion with her head, cautioning her not to do a thing.

"You've mistaken my intentions," Micah said finally, knowing she sounded cold.

Olivia could not be the one in charge, not if this was going to work. She returned to the couch, kneeling over the silk-clad woman before leaning down to kiss her. Her lips parted, bringing her tongue into play. Micah demanded and received the response she desired. Olivia arched up, her hands clasping at her as she tried to draw her down closer. The deep, low moan from the woman beneath her begged for more. She was happy to oblige.

Micah's hours on the bike and in the gym served her well. Powerful shoulders and biceps easily kept her propped up until she finally, blissfully, lowered the length of her body to meet Olivia's. She brought one knee up, her right thigh crumpling the thin silk of Olivia's gown between her thighs.

Micah lifted her head so she could watch Olivia's face, then rolled her hips just enough to make Olivia gasp again. "Is this what you wanted?"

"Ah, God, yes..." Olivia squirmed beneath Micah, something she immediately realized Micah found quite appealing.

Olivia ran her fingertips across Micah's upper back. Digging in without warning, she allowed her nails to rake across the broad shoulders. Micah's back arched into the pain. A deep growl, wild and untamed, escaped from her throat. Olivia watched, mesmerized, as Micah's passion flared with the addition of the sharp pain. Caught in the whirlwind, it took all of Olivia's power to speak one last time before the couch became their bed.

"Take me to bed, Micah," she whispered. "Please."

Micah held out her hand, and she took it eagerly. She was already willing to follow where Micah led her, and somewhere, deep down inside, she was beginning to understand this new Micah.

"Yes," Micah murmured, her vision bleeding into a red haze of arousal. *"Take me to bed,"* Olivia pleaded. *"Please?"* Olivia's voice continued to echo in her head, an oft repeated fantasy that had escaped paper and pen and long held secret desires.

Clothes, she thought...barely making coherent thoughts...*too many clothes.*

While utterly alluring in her silk robe, Micah wanted to touch bare skin, so much softer and hotter than silk. Olivia was right. They needed the bed, and now. If they didn't move now, Olivia would find herself naked and taken right there on the couch.

She pulled Olivia up and led her back to the bed they had shared not so long ago. Her steps were sure, requiring no thought to move through the familiar space.

The bed was still rumpled from their earlier nap; whatever happened now wouldn't change its appearance but it would change how she saw it from this day forward.

Such an innocent thing, sharing a bed to sleep, she thought. Micah doubted that Olivia would understand how that simple pleasure was far more intimate to her than sex. Sex was uncomplicated and easy. Or, it had been. Micah doubted that anything between them was going to ever be close to uncomplicated, nor was it going to be just sex.

She had lived so long in that guarded world she had created where she refused to be touched, either physically or emotionally. She didn't want that, not now, not with Olivia. Her heart lurched, fueled by a double dose of adrenaline and arousal. Fear, rage and passion were horrible bedfellows, one of them had to go. Micah hurriedly unclenched her fists before Olivia noticed, then closed her eyes and mentally chased away the demons she didn't want to deal with tonight. *I can enjoy this and still maintain control.*

Olivia faced Micah, taking in the flushed skin and hooded gaze. Noting only the slightest tremble in her hands, she was amazed at Micah's self-control. It was time to up the stakes. She slid her silk robe off her shoulders, exposing her flawless skin. Olivia gazed directly into Micah's eyes, all heat and hungry fire.

"Undress me." The command was tempered by need. "Please," she added, unable to help herself.

A long slow shudder passed through Micah, her posture changed perceptibly. Confident and sure, she ran her fingers along the smooth skin of her shoulder until meeting the offending silk. Olivia trembled beneath her touch, her lips parted as if to speak again.

Micah reached out and down with her other hand, grasping the thin flat belt tied loosely at Olivia's waist. One quick tug and the fabric fell open. The thunder in her ears picked up a notch, threatening to drown out all reason. At some point Olivia had shed the silk pajama bottoms and camisole she had slept in earlier.

"Naughty, naughty," Micah murmured, grinning at the view before her. Sliding one slim finger along the edge of the fabric, she ran the errant digit down from Olivia's collarbone, past the tempting rise of her breast and continued down, down, only stopping before she went anywhere...interesting.

Micah chuckled, the sound low and throaty. It was Olivia's turn to maintain self-control. She stood before Micah practically naked, albeit by her own design. Micah continued to weave a subtle pattern across her skin. When her wandering fingers changed directions suddenly, gliding blunt nails along Olivia's stomach, a soft moan escaped her.

Olivia's eyes snapped shut. She swayed, dangerously close to collapsing from the intense surge of arousal Micah's touch drew from her. Strong arms caught her and guided her onto the bed before she fell. Her silk robe remained tangled at her elbows, effectively limiting her movement. Before she could escape from the thin fabric, Micah captured her left breast with her lips while searching fingers found the right, rolling her nipple between unforgiving fingertips. Olivia arched her back into Micah's touch, begging for more contact. Micah obliged, lashing her tongue against the already sensitive flesh.

Micah enjoyed making Olivia's body writhe in pleasure. Captured beneath her, she had full view of Olivia's slim body, her skin smooth and pale in contrast to her own tanned skin. She could feel Olivia's hips moving beneath her, the sweet scent of her arousal filled Micah's nostrils and made her mouth water in anticipation. Reluctantly giving up her lavish attention to Olivia's nipples, she planted a line of teasing kisses down Olivia's abdomen towards her intended destination. Micah wrapped her arms around Olivia's hips, nibbling gently at the delicate flesh of her inner thighs to encourage her to make room as she slid down Olivia's body. Blowing softly, she couldn't help but tease Olivia for a moment longer before tasting her, slipping her tongue between soft folds that beckoned to her eager mouth. Dipping her head, she let her lips and tongue explore the sweet wetness, finally settling on the bundle of nerves that pulsed and hardened beneath her.

***

Olivia had a vague awareness of noises, and then realized she was the one making them. Passionate moans and gasps echoed the sensations Micah was drawing out of her. Her voice was no longer her own; it obeyed Micah's command of her body, responding to her tongue and hands as they explored her body. When Micah abandoned her breasts to leave a trail of hot, wet kisses down her abdomen, her breasts ached from the lost contact. Her nipples felt as hard and red as small berries, savored by Micah's talented tongue.

*Ah, God. I never...*her stray thought was interrupted, incomplete, lost to her forever, and in the best way possible when Micah's tongue slipped between her thighs for the first time.

"Unnggh," she moaned, her stomach muscles clenching as she brought her heels down forcefully. Bucking her hips off the bed, Olivia's hands sought the thick waves of Micah's short hair, trying to control the head that moved between her thighs. Strong hands grasped hers, carefully removing her threaded fingers and forcing her hands onto the bed by her sides.

Micah shifted her grip, grasping her firmly by the wrists then squeezing gently to reassure her. The teasing nature of Micah's slow tongue brought Olivia to a level of arousal that was so intense it was almost painful. She desperately needed release, but her orgasm remained elusive. Micah was being a horrible tease, her tongue bringing her to the edge then backing away just enough. Olivia's captured hands sought anything tangible to hold on to, her grasp on reality receding from being held at the edge of orgasm for too long. Her manicured nails dug into Micah's muscular forearms.

"Micah, oh, please..." The desperate plea was ripped from Olivia's throat. Micah moaned into her, bringing her lips and tongue back to bear on the tormented bundle of nerves, quickly bringing Olivia back to that deep precipice she had been balancing on for so long.

"Micah!" Olivia called out in a voice hoarse from screaming. "Ahh! Oh, my God, Micah!" she called out her lover's name once more, her voice rising in pace with the intense pleasure coursing through her body. Her entire body tensed, every muscle straining, begging for release. The thunder pounding in her head found its lightning as bright light broke across Olivia's vision, temporarily blinding her. Having been brought higher and farther than she had thought possible, she allowed herself to fall deep into that electric darkness.

"Move your leg, honey," Micah's voice, husky and breathless, whispered in her ear.

"Huh, what...?" Olivia tried to make sense of Micah's words; she was still caught in the afterglow of her orgasm. She felt electric, her body tingling with small aftershocks of pleasure.

Micah shifted position, capturing Olivia's leg between hers. Her lips found the pulse at Olivia's neck, sucking gently. Olivia felt an urgent hand run along her thigh, encouraging her to bend her knee. Micah moaned when Olivia's thigh rose up to meet her center, the feel of slick folds gliding along her thigh almost sending Olivia over the edge again.

"Ah, God...so hot."

Her arms free at last, Olivia took advantage by running her hands down Micah's back, reveling in the feel of lean muscles moving and rippling beneath her fingers. She slipped her other hand into the soft nest of hair at the nape of Micah's neck, massaging gently, encouraging her. Micah's movements became frantic, her hips thrusting rapidly against Olivia's thigh. A low moan, almost a growl, interrupted Micah's jagged breathing. Rising up on clenched fists, Micah pumped hard against Olivia's thigh, her movements losing their rhythm as she came undone. In that unguarded moment, her face reflected such fierce joy that Olivia lay stunned. She was so beautiful.

How had she earned the love of this incredible woman?

Chapter Fifteen

Micah stood in the shower, hot water beating down onto her neck and shoulders. She had left Olivia sleeping peacefully in her bed. The shower door opened unexpectedly, letting in cool tendrils of air that stole away the steam and made her shiver. A warm, very feminine body molded itself to her backside, instantly replacing some of that lost warmth with an entirely different sort of heat.

"You should have woken me, Sweetheart," Olivia purred, raising herself up on her toes to press hot lips to the back of Micah's neck.

"Hmmm...that feels good," Micah murmured, reaching back to stroke Olivia's hip. "I didn't want to wake you. You looked so relaxed."

Her explanation ended in a moan as slippery hands found her breasts. She allowed her head to fall back, resting on Olivia's shoulder. *How the hell did she find the soap so quickly?* Micah asked herself and then laughed. *Such an odd thought to pop up, considering the circumstances.*

"I was very relaxed, thanks to you," Olivia murmured huskily in Micah's ear. She shivered again. Olivia's voice, while always alluring, was downright sultry after making love. *Not to mention, damn sexy during*, she thought.

"But you could have woke me up for this," Olivia added. Micah's nipples hardened into small pebbles beneath Olivia's palms, begging for her attention. She brought her fingertips into play, teasing Micah's nipples mercilessly. A low moan escaped from the woman in her arms, reverberating against her exploring lips. Emboldened by the sensation of soap-slippery skin, she slid her hand down the taut stomach, intent on exploring further. Caught up in the scorching haze of renewed passion, Olivia didn't immediately register the feel of scarred flesh beneath her fingertips. She did feel Micah flinch, her body turning to cold stone a second before she pulled away.

"You know, I'll just let you finish up," Micah said, awkwardly snatching the towel from its hook as she practically jetted out of the shower stall. Holding the towel in front of her, she beat a hasty retreat out of the bathroom.

What the hell? Olivia laid her forehead against the cool marble shower wall, its smooth surface resistant to the hot water streaming from the bronze showerhead. It had felt so damn good, touching Micah. Olivia knew she had felt Micah respond, she wasn't mistaken, but then something changed and Micah was just gone. It was hard not to feel abandoned, and even harder not to leave the shower and demand to know what the hell was going on. Her emotions were running too high to do either, her body still too primed for sex to think logically. The washcloth felt too abrasive running across skin that felt too sensitive for anything as ordinary as cotton. She tried to avoid the most sensitive areas, but her attention was divided. The last few hours definitely took up most of her thoughts, all the way up to the point where Micah chose to leave rather than enjoy Olivia's loving attention.

Two things surfaced in her mind, tainting her memories and making her heart race in fear. *Micah did not let me touch her.* Their lovemaking had been decidedly one-sided, with Micah always the one in control.

That revelation led to another.

She didn't let me see her naked, not completely. That damnable tank top had remained a barrier between them. It was no wonder she had awoken to a vague, unsettling sensation that she had fallen asleep before filling an unspoken need. She had wanted so badly to touch Micah, and when she saw her, wet and naked in the shower, she couldn't resist joining her. Olivia bowed her head and let the water sluice over her aching head. *How did that become a mistake?*

***

Micah quickly dried off in the bedroom, roughly scrubbing her skin with the thick towel. She was furious with herself for how she kept flinching away from Olivia's touch. She had convinced herself that it would be different with Olivia.

After their talk, after showing her the scars, she had hoped it would be different. Hell, it had been until Olivia started touching her stomach. Her scars had cut deeper than just flesh; they had marked her spirit, her soul.

It was painfully obvious how much Olivia wanted to touch her. Micah had denied her that; she wasn't ready to give up her need for control. She wasn't sure if she ever could; would Olivia be able to accept that?

Uncomfortable with that particular line of thought, she started grabbing clothes from the bedside dresser. Catching her reflection in the mirror, Micah stopped dead in her tracks, not wanting to acknowledge the person gazing back at her. The person in the mirror looked drawn, haunted, and slightly guilty.

Geez...I am such a broken toy.

The shower turned off in the other room and Micah hurried to finish dressing. Sliding into her comfortable old faded jeans, she threw on a button up sleeveless denim shirt instead of her usual tank top, feeling the need to be covered a little more. She headed into the kitchen before Olivia could join her. The bedroom smelled like sex, heavy and intoxicating, and altogether too tempting.

***

Olivia emerged from the bathroom wrapped in her blue silk robe. Micah wasn't visible, but she could hear her moving around in the kitchen so she headed in that direction.

The minute she walked into the kitchen she felt the need to tighten her belt and pull her collar closer. She didn't expect to find Micah fully dressed and somehow that made her feel uncomfortably naked in her robe. Micah was also doing her best to avoid eye contact as she prepared a simple bowl of cereal for her dinner. Olivia shook her head at the sudden change in Micah's demeanor and found a seat at the kitchen table, then waited for her to settle down. That plan lasted less than a minute, mostly because she couldn't stand watching Micah trying to figure out what to do next to avoid sitting down.

"Micah, will you come sit so we can talk?"

Micah turned to study Olivia, her eyes dark and broody beneath the shadows of her still damp hair. She fortified her coffee with one last spoonful of sugar and spun her spoon through it before finally taking it and her bowl over to the table. Folding her long legs under her,

Micah sat down, holding her bowl in front of her like a shield.

"So, I guess you need to go back tomorrow?" Micah asked nonchalantly, trying to make the inevitable conclusion to their conversation as quick and painless as possible. Of course Olivia would leave. *Why would Olivia want to stay with a woman who had put up so many walls she couldn't even let her lover make love to her?*

"We, Sweetheart, we need to go back tomorrow," Olivia stated firmly. They were going back together in the morning and that was that.

Micah recognized the familiar iron in that tone of voice. Reminding herself that not everything had to be a disagreement between them, she conceded this one time.

"That's fine," she muttered. She couldn't expect Olivia to find her way back alone. That would be incredibly shitty to do to her, not when she had the truck sitting right there. Sure, there was a chance Rob was hanging out somewhere nearby on Olivia's orders, but she had a feeling the woman had gone all in on this one and sent him home. She was that assured of herself.

If only she had all of the data before making that decision, huh? She might not have signed up for a one way trip here.

Micah's mood became more morose and guilt-laden the longer she sat, silently staring at her bowl of cereal as if it would magically give her the answers she so desperately needed.

"Are you going to tell me what happened in the shower just now?"

Micah groaned. Leave it to Olivia not to let something go. The woman could worry something to death, like a dog with a bone. Well, she could be just as stubborn, if not more so. She just needed some time to work things out in her head. Things between them had moved so fast. If someone had said she would be spending her time this weekend in her cabin making love to Olivia, she would have told them they were insane.

The silence between them was deafening, broken only by the sound of a lone owl hooting softly as the sunlight outside faded into dusk. The forest surrounding the small cabin threw shadows across the windows, the gathering darkness reflecting the mood of the two women.

"You're not going to talk to me about this right now, are you?" Olivia tried again.

"No, not if I can help it."

Olivia sighed in frustration. The feeling of being underdressed intensified; it was silly lounging about practically naked when Micah wasn't. Olivia shivered, the evening chill reaching through the thin silk.

"It's getting chilly in here. I'm going to change into something warmer." She stood and tightened her robe around her, then fixed a keen scowl towards Micah's sullen exterior. "We will talk about this later."

"I look forward to it," Micah shot back sarcastically, watching Olivia retreat back to the warmth of the main cabin.

Micah shook her head as she took her uneaten bowl of cereal to the sink. It had become an unrecognizable mess. *Kind of like me*, she thought, rinsing the inedible goo down the sink.

How was she supposed to explain to Olivia that she couldn't just treat her like some anonymous fuck? Identifying the source of her guilt didn't make the sour taste in her throat go away. How do you explain to someone like Olivia that you haven't got a clue how to make something work that had been broken for so long, that before tonight it had been easy. She could give a woman what they wanted and not even have to worry about undressing. Olivia wasn't a stranger at a bar that she could screw in the back room and then go home, never to see again.

Olivia mattered. She mattered and she would expect Micah to let her reciprocate when they were making love, that little display in the shower was proof of that. As much as she wanted her, the thought of letting go like that scared the shit out of her. You can't hide then; walls get ripped down in that moment when another person touches you that intimately.

The simple fact was, that to her, Olivia was flawless and deserved someone who was the same. Nevertheless, she also knew that Olivia wanted her. She wanted her enough to find her, to come all the way out to her cabin, and then listen to her while she revealed a very painful time in her life. Olivia had opened herself up to Micah, offering both her body and her heart, a gift Micah had never expected. Love had its risks; was she ready or even worthy to accept this prize?

Micah realized she had been washing that one bowl for several minutes. Peeved with herself, she ran a quick towel over the overly clean pottery and put it away, then leaned against the sink and stared out the window. It was too early to see any stars, but she watched for them anyway, her mind working furiously. If she didn't want what was between them to end this weekend she would have to try harder, get better at sharing with the other woman. It seemed like an insurmountable task, one that seemed so easy for being something so hard.

Micah's thoughts kept circling in her head, winding around her frustration without offering a single answer.

Holding her head in her hands, Micah groaned as she felt everything spinning out of control.

Picking up her knife from where it lay on the counter, Micah felt comforted by the heft of the handle, the dull gleam of the metal flashing at her as she examined the edge. She could feel the pressure building inside her, begging for a different type of release than the one she enjoyed this afternoon. Absently twirling the razor sharp blade in her hands, she mentally sifted through her options. She could opt for a new tattoo. Since she was still healing from the road rash, her artist wouldn't be able to work on the shoulder and she wasn't sure if she wanted her working on the other area right now. Possibly a piercing? She had toyed with the idea after talking to a couple of other girls at work. Either would satisfy the urge she was feeling, at least for now.

"Micah, what are you doing?" Olivia took one look at the knife in Micah's hand and panicked. Her voice was shrill with fear, but it failed to get through to the other woman. Micah's hazel eyes were unfocused, staring at some unseen point in the distance. Her expression was odd, almost dreamlike.

"Hmmm?" It took her a moment to respond to Olivia's question. "Sorry, I was just thinking," she muttered, roughly sheathing the knife and setting it on the counter behind her.

"What were you going to do with that?"

"Nothing," Micah muttered, going on the defensive. "Olivia, you can't think I am going to cut myself every time I have a knife in my hand. I mean, give me some credit here. I would never do that with you in the cabin." With hot anger fueling her words, she didn't even realize how much she had just revealed to her lover.

"Does that mean you would if I wasn't here?" Olivia demanded.

Micah cursed under her breath. The woman was too intuitive by far. Micah felt herself edge past cold reason, slamming the knife down on the counter she felt herself shut down completely.

"Enough! I am done talking about this." Striding past Olivia, she escaped to the living room, then flipped the stereo on and turned the music up as high as she could stand. Collapsing onto the couch, Micah laid across the length of it, her long legs stretched out across the cushions.

She wasn't in the mood for sharing anymore. *Hell, she hadn't even asked Olivia to come up here in the first place.*

Olivia crossed over to the stereo and turned down the deafening music. Micah smirked, picked up the remote and turned it back up.

Olivia didn't want to have another argument with Micah. The day had been a rollercoaster ride of emotions. It was hard to believe that so much had happened between them in just a few hours. From this morning, when she had been a witness to Micah's pain, to when they had finally made love. Having Micah make love to her had been mind-blowing. Not being able to reciprocate had left her frustrated, making her push for more answers, which only led to hard feelings between them. She had returned to the kitchen intending to apologize to Micah, only to find her standing there with the knife in her hand.

Seeing Micah with that knife had scared the hell out of her and she reacted before thinking. Now she truly understood what Jonathan had been trying to tell her. Pushing Micah didn't work, nor was it wise on her part, not if she had any chance of a future with the other woman.

She walked over to the couch and stood, staring down at Micah. There wasn't any room for her on the couch, which Olivia was sure was by design. It didn't matter; she was used to standing and was pretty damn good at looming when she wanted to get a point across.

Micah tried her damnedest to ignore the woman standing over her. All she wanted to do was find some solace in her music. She needed to quiet the inner voice that was so insistently clamoring for her attention, the voice that begged her to stop before she got hurt or she hurt herself. It wasn't working. Sighing, she turned off the loud music, waiting to hear what Olivia had to say. She could always turn the stereo back on.

"I'm sorry, Micah. I overreacted."

The unexpected apology took a moment to digest. Reassessing the situation, Micah sat up and moved her legs off the couch. Patting the cushion beside her, she invited Olivia to sit down next to her. She took Olivia's soft hand in her own slightly rougher one and planted a light kiss along the smooth knuckles. "Thank you."

"You don't have to," Olivia murmured, lightly brushing her fingers through Micah's tousled mane, reveling in the soft hair gliding between her fingertips. Cupping the younger woman's head in her hand, she gently guided Micah's head, bringing her in for an undemanding kiss.

"I do love you, Olivia," Micah whispered against her lips.

"I love you, too, Sweetheart. We will figure all this out together." Olivia promised, wondering how long it would take for those words to lose the subtle undertones of fear and pain.

"What time do we need to leave in the morning?" Micah asked. The sweetness of the moment was almost too much for her after the intense up and downs of the day. It was easier to focus on more practical subjects.

"Around nine? Regina will be back from her father's tomorrow night."

"That will work." Micah nodded. *That will give me enough time to do one more thing before leaving.*

Chapter Sixteen

The next morning Olivia woke up at her usual time. It was only six-thirty in the morning and she was alone. The blankets had been straightened up and tucked around her. Lacking the warmth of her lover in the bed, she appreciated the gesture.

Stretching languorously, she smiled when sore muscles protested in response. The mild ache was a pleasant reminder of yesterday's lovemaking. Micah might not allow her to reciprocate yet, but the young woman was definitely very skillful and generous in bed.

She had finally given up on Micah feeding her, so she commandeered the kitchen for a quick, but at least, hot meal they shared in front of the fireplace. Neither of them broached any subject more controversial than the weather and before long, they both found themselves nodding off on the couch and she suggested calling it a night. The last thing she remembered was Micah gathering her up in her strong arms and kissing her hair softly before breathing a quiet "Good night, love." Sleep followed closely on the heels of those treasured words as her mind tumbled into darkness.

She woke to sun streaming through the window, with no memory of the time between. If this was one of those lesbian romance novels her assistant Amanda loved to read, she would be lying there thinking about the marathon sex she and her lover had all night long. Instead, they had simply fallen asleep, exhausted by the events of the day. Somehow, that made the night more special to Olivia.

*Coffee...*her thoughts strayed back to her morning necessity. The desire to have caffeine running through her veins was motivation enough to pull herself out of bed. *Please let there be more coffee.*

The cabin was empty; so was the back deck. Her next thought was that Micah had gotten up early to start getting ready for them to leave. Olivia stepped out onto the front porch, hoping to find her out by the truck. The small yard was empty, and so was the truck bed. She cursed when she realized what that meant. Micah's bloody bike was missing.

***

Micah flew down the road on her cross comp bike, her lips curled back in a ridiculous grin at the insane amount of distance she had managed to cover. She had almost forgotten how much she loved the freedom that the backroads gave her, so different from riding in the city. *This is what I came up here to do*, she thought, taking in huge lungful's of pristine country air. She had come up here to ride and she wasn't leaving without getting at least one in.

Up at sunrise, she had snuck out of the cabin as quietly as possible and walked her bike to the road before climbing on for a wild ride. The outbound trip was mostly downhill, but once she headed back to her cabin, the steep uphill climbs really started to put a strain on her injured hip and knee.

Pushing hard, she worked through the pain. With any luck, she would get back and have the bike loaded on her Toyota before Olivia woke up and noticed she was gone, then they would be on their way and back in the city by nightfall. That thought slowed her down until she pushed it away. Micah didn't care about any of that right now. Right now, she was living in the moment and she was happy.

She tilted her face up towards the sun and watched the dizzying pattern of backlit leaves and tree branches blur into one incredibly awesome living canvas.

It was a beautiful day. The crisp early morning air made her skin tingle as she sped down the road. Coming up around the last hill, she sped down the last bit towards her cabin, a quick downhill run that she pedaled hard into, getting up some decent speed as she turned into her driveway.

Crap.

Olivia was waiting for her on the front porch, and she did not look happy at all. Every line of her body spoke volumes—none of it good—and Micah saw her morning quickly going to shit. Stiff legging the pedals, she hit her hand brakes and twisted her bike at the same time, ending her ride with a long slide-out through the fine gravel. She slid to a stop just short of her truck. Aware that Olivia was watching her every move, she dismounted quickly, hopping lightly into the back of her truck and securing her bike. There was no way in hell she was going to show any weakness in front of that disapproving glare. Pulling off her gloves, she sauntered up to the porch. She made sure she didn't limp and even managed to maintain a slight swagger in her walk. Trying to figure out how to play this, she decided cool and calm was probably the best way to proceed.

Olivia stood on the porch with her arms crossed, effectively blocking the doorway.

"Beautiful morning," Micah called out, trying to bluff her way into the cabin without any confrontation. Offering her most rakish grin, she smiled innocently at the irate woman. She wasn't ready to give up the adrenaline buzz of her early morning ride.

"Hmmph." That was it. Olivia wouldn't even speak to her.

Okay, well. That was actually worse than being yelled at.

"I'm just going to go shower." Micah sidled past Olivia and into the shadowed interior of the cabin. It was cool outside and she was too sweaty to stand there and have a one sided conversation. She headed straight for the bathroom to start the shower, hoping to get a good amount of steam going. Then, as nonchalantly as possible, she headed for the kitchen for a couple of Aleve and a soda. She popped the Aleve and opened the refrigerator to grab a cold Coke, trying not to taste the bitterness on her tongue until she could wash them down. The soothing sting of caffeine and carbonation almost washed away the aftertaste of the pills, but not quite.

When she closed the refrigerator door, she almost jumped out of her skin. Olivia was leaning against the doorframe, silently watching her. The cold sensation of soda on an empty stomach turned to ice. She had just been caught.

"Yeah, okay. I'm just going to get that shower now," she continued, glibly ignoring Olivia's silent treatment. *What did she want, an apology?*

The kitchen doorway was a tight fit for two people. Micah tried to stroke Olivia's shoulder as she slid past her, a sort of unspoken apology. Olivia twisted her body away from her and pressed her back against the doorframe, purposefully avoiding Micah's touch. *Oh, boy. She is royally pissed,* Micah thought with a resigned sigh.

"Sorry, I know I'm really sweaty and gross," Micah apologized, then disappeared into the other room.

Olivia glared at the back of Micah's head, unsure of who she was angrier at. It was bad enough she had to wake up alone in the cabin, but Micah was not supposed to be riding her bike right now. It infuriated her that Micah had gone for a ride this morning without telling her. She was sure that Micah had planned it that way, even if she would never admit it, and even more upset that she managed to pretend nothing was wrong.

She went through the motions of making her own coffee while pondering her reactions to Micah's absence. After a few minutes reflection, she found that she was more upset about waking up alone. That she did it to ride her bike only added fuel to the fire. There was only one explanation: she wanted Micah to be there when she woke up, and not for just a day, but every day.

When Micah came out of the bathroom, Olivia was waiting for her, curled up quite comfortably beneath the comforters with a heavenly smelling cup of coffee in her hands.

"Was it worth it?"

"Yes," Micah said, suddenly wishing for a continuation of the silent treatment. Turning her back, she pulled out a fresh t-shirt and slipped it over her head, covering the tattoo that graced most of her shoulder and flank. Using her towel as a cover, she managed to get dressed without giving Olivia too much of a show. Her movements were jerky, rough, broadcasting her irritation at having an audience.

"Turn around, Micah. I really don't appreciate talking to your back." Olivia spoke quietly, but in that understated way that still made it a command. Micah's back stiffened but she didn't turn around. Looking at Olivia seemed like a bad idea right now. Olivia was really letting her temper roam freely, and Micah surely wasn't in the mood for head games. The way she was feeling, they would either end up having one hell of an argument, or she would end up making love to Olivia again—or both.

Even as angry as she was, or perhaps because of it, Micah wanted to finish what she had started the day before. An intense, unbidden image flashed behind her eyes, bringing with it a sudden and powerful surge of desire. *Her long fingers entering Olivia, thrusting deeply, over and over. Tight muscles grasping and holding her inside as Olivia came, an inarticulate scream pushing past begging gasps that sent shivers down her spine like an orgasmic symphony.*

Micah's body threatened to betray her as the thrill of arousal rushed through her. She felt herself clench and spasm deep inside, a flood of moisture leaving her feeling slick and swollen in response to the images.

Damn it, why did this have to be so difficult?

"Just let me finish getting dressed, and then we can talk," Micah muttered. She had to sit down to get her socks on. She chose a spot at the edge of the bed as far away from Olivia as possible. There was a very thin barrier between her fantasy and reality, one barely held together by her need for control. Keeping space between them was a part of that barrier.

Micah didn't think Olivia would really appreciate being taken like that, admitting to herself that her fantasies skirted the edges of what society would consider "rough sex". Micah had very much enjoyed making love to Olivia, but she couldn't see asking her to participate in some of the darker thoughts that ran through her mind. What she envisioned was straight up fucking—hard, nasty, and aggressive—and it turned her on just thinking about it.

Oh yeah, it was going to be a long drive back to New York.

"Okay, so let's talk." Olivia was way too close to her. Micah could smell her perfume, she was that close. When she laid a hand on her shoulder, Micah launched off of the bed.

"Don't touch me."

The words were torn from her throat, as rough and violent sounding as her thoughts.

Olivia recoiled, snatching her hand away and holding it close to her body as if burned.

"What's wrong? Micah? What's going on? Why are you acting like this?"

"I'm sorry, Olivia. Please, just don't touch me right now, okay?" Micah asked, still struggling with her emotions. Olivia stared at her for a long moment, then nodded.

"Okay Micah. I won't."

"I said we'd talk, and we will...I just need a few minutes," Micah promised. Frustrated and confused, Micah grabbed their bags and threw them in the backseat of her truck, leaving the intimate setting before she lost control and succumbed to her baser instincts.

Olivia came out a few minutes later, climbed into the passenger seat, and sat quietly...her eyes firmly planted on the view out of the windshield.

Micah drove for about two hours with the music blasting, singing the lyrics to every song that came on.

She had put a rocking sound system in her truck last summer, and she rarely got the chance to enjoy it since her poor beast of a truck was stuck in the parking garage more often than not. When she did get out, it was usually for road trips like this, which gave her an excuse to play her music as loud and for as long as she wanted. The music wasn't going to fix anything, but at least it kept her mind occupied. She certainly didn't need it wandering around today.

Risking a quick glance over at her silent passenger, Micah found it hard not to look at Olivia for longer than was safe at freeway speeds. The woman was gorgeous, even in profile as she looked out the window. The muted sunlight that managed to penetrate the tinted windows softly haloed her light blonde hair. She looked more contemplative than angry—a definite improvement from this morning.

The last few minutes in her cabin were too tense, the air swirling around them with mixed emotions and barely-contained desires. The tension between them had dissipated a bit, dialing down to a slow simmer that didn't make Micah's blood boil. The music had helped, but it was just a temporary fix. She had promised they would talk and now she felt like she was just putting it off and using the music to delay the inevitable.

During the extending silence between them, Olivia listened to Micah sing. Even as upset as she was at her, she had to admit Micah had a beautiful voice. Her taste in music was very eclectic—hard, pounding songs interspersed with softer ballads. Her voice was haunting. Some of the lyrics were sung with such meaning it made Olivia wonder what importance they held.

When Micah stopped singing, the absence was profound enough to bring Olivia's attention away from her self-accusing reflections. Micah had a death grip on the steering wheel, her knuckles pale against the black leather. She looked stiff, tense, and decidedly uncomfortable. Olivia could see Micah's jaw muscles work beneath pale cheekbones; she could practically hear teeth grinding against each other.

"Are you okay?" she asked.

"Fine," Micah gritted out, subtly shifting in her seat.

Olivia wasn't convinced. "Are you in pain?"

"Yeah, a little," Micah reluctantly admitted, waiting for the lecture that she was sure to come.

"Oh, Sweetheart, why didn't you tell me sooner?"

"Um, I didn't want to complain, and I am pretty sure I already know what you think."

"Do you...really?" Olivia asked, drawing out her words as a different sort of anger flared. "Are you so sure of that?" *Of all the damnable assumptions!* Olivia thought, unable to keep the sarcasm from putting a sharp edge on her response. A sign caught her eye—they were coming up on a truck stop advertising a store and restaurant as well as gas. "Pull over. We need a break."

"Fine, I need to get out and stretch some, anyway." Micah obliged Olivia by pulling off at the very next exit then grimaced at their choice of stops. They had found one of those greasy places that dotted the highways along the lonelier areas of the country. It was a place you could get cheap gas and cheaper food, and truckers could stop and rest for a while and take a shower.

"Stick close, this place looks kind of skeevy."

"I'm sure we'll be fine," Olivia said, falling back a little so she could watch Micah limp into the truck stop. Obviously, the silent treatment didn't work on her; Micah was just too stubborn. She didn't think yelling would work either. Looking at her watch, Olivia estimated that she had approximately four hours to figure out how to broach the subject of this morning's disagreement without it sounding like she was interrogating Micah. She DEFINITELY knew that would not work. Maybe it was time to be the one to compromise and step up to the table first.

Following the other woman through the flyer dotted glass doors, she spotted Micah in front of the cooler, checking out the drink selection. Walking up to her, she took her hand, lacing their fingers together. Bringing their clasped hands up to her lips, she placed a feather-light kiss on Micah's knuckles.

"Are you okay?" This time Olivia meant it to include more than just the pain in her hip.

"I am now," Micah said, gazing deeply into Olivia's sky blue eyes. Whatever she was looking for there she must have found because she relaxed a bit. "I'm sorry about this morning, Olivia."

"It's okay. Like I said yesterday, we will figure it out together. I am sorry, too. I seem to overreact a lot when it comes to you," Olivia apologized, remembering the hurt look on Micah's face when she had turned away from her touch at the cabin. *No wonder Micah didn't want me to touch her after that*, she thought, feeling the sting of rejection from both sides.

The admission from the normally prickly attorney meant a lot to Micah. She offered her a tentative smile, then squeezed her hand once in reassurance before letting it go.

"Um, Olivia, please don't take this the wrong way, but this isn't New York," she murmured, a worried expression on her face. Turning to follow Micah's gaze,

Olivia noticed a few locals staring at the two of them a little too intensely.

"Ah, yes, I do see your concern. I don't believe I have ever had the pleasure of stopping at a place like this before. You do seem to create opportunities for new experiences for me, don't you?"

Micah's nervous smile widened into something closer to her normal grin. "Yes, I do, don't I?" Despite her reassuring grin, Micah thought it would be better just to get their stuff and go. She hadn't expected Olivia to be the PDA sort, but she had surprised her before. She stepped away, putting a bit of space between them, just in case.

Honestly, Micah wasn't personally worried about offending the local population, but she had Olivia to consider. It wasn't that everyone outside of the bigger cities was intolerant, but there were enough roughnecks around who felt a lot like her father did about gay people. Normally, it hadn't been a problem since she always flew solo when she visited her cabin. Having Olivia join her had added a dimension to her trips that she hadn't had to consider before. Luckily, it was daylight out and no one was drunk or feeling especially opinionated, yet.

"Do you want anything?" Micah asked, pulling out a couple of cold sodas from the case in front of her.

"Do you think the coffee is safe?" Olivia asked hesitantly, grimacing at the thought of what they might call coffee.

"Let's find out, then I need to find something to eat. I'm starving."

"Did you eat at all this morning?"

"No."

"Why not?" Olivia asked.

"I can't eat when I'm upset," Micah answered frankly. She had meant to make breakfast before they left, but the way things fell out, leaving the intimacy of the cabin had become a more urgent matter than feeding an empty stomach. Add that to the energy she had spent on her early morning ride, and she was famished. Catching the eye of the waitress at the restaurant's checkout counter, she ordered a burger and fries to go. She didn't realize that Olivia hadn't joined her, so she missed the contrite look that shadowed the other woman's face in response to her offhand comment.

There was a reason that Micah usually didn't stop at truck stops unless she absolutely had to, but it wasn't because of the food. When the waitress returned, she handed Micah a Styrofoam container with a fake smile that quickly disappeared once she paid and took her change back. Ignoring the woman's dour expression, she smiled sweetly and thanked her. The smells coming from the container, on the other hand, smelled heavenly, grease and all.

She found Olivia standing where she had left her and looking a bit forlorn. Deciding on taking a to-hell-with-it attitude, Micah strolled over to Olivia and boldly took her hand, leading the older woman out of the building and into the warm sunlight. She even managed to do it cockily, adding enough jaunt to her step to mask the limp, if not the pain in her leg.

***

Olivia took over the driver's seat despite Micah's insistence that she could drive and eat at the same time. Once back on the road, Micah took advantage of the

197

extra legroom the passenger seat provided to stretch out, propping her feet on the dashboard.

"Really, Micah?" Olivia exclaimed, mortified at the act of putting dirty boots on the clean dashboard.

"My truck, Olivia," she reminded her, taking a huge bite out of her hamburger.

"That's true, but still...try not to get ketchup everywhere, okay?" Olivia returned the smile, then innocently reached over the center console. She stole a French fry from Micah's to-go container, earning an amused snort.

"What?" Olivia asked.

"You."

"What about me?" Olivia asked as she tried to swipe another fry.

"Well, let's see," Micah started, counting off on her fingers. "Ms. New York here is driving a pickup truck through the countryside, staring down truck drivers, braving bad coffee, and of course, slumming around with the likes of me." Laughing at her own words, Micah continued gleefully. "I hardly think anyone would believe it...and me without a camera!"

Olivia sputtered, unsure where to go with that particular list of offences against her socialite status.

"Well, the coffee was quite bad," she finally admitted. "But I am enjoying driving. It's been a while."

"I can tell," Micah, teased, holding onto the grab bar for dear life. Olivia chuckled. When Micah let herself relax and enjoy herself, she was quite the delightful driving companion—even if she did enjoy mocking Olivia's driving skills. The easy laughter was a welcome addition to their trip. They continued to chat amicably about the most mundane things while the blue truck ate up the miles towards New York, the promise to speak about that morning all but forgotten.

A few hours later the familiar skyline, complete with the gray haze of industry surrounding it, sprang into view.

"Will you come home with me tonight?" Olivia asked. The question was spontaneous, and left an awkward pause in their conversation as it sat in the air between them for a moment. Olivia held her breath and her tongue, afraid that after blurting out that unexpected request, she would ruin everything by following it up with something equally ridiculous.

"Seriously, you're not tired of me yet?" Micah asked in return. Her joking response was forced, masking her insecurity.

"No, quite the opposite in fact. Plus, I would really like to have the pleasure of waking up with you still in bed," Olivia continued. *Okay now stop*, she told herself, then ignored her own advice. "Since you cheated me of that this morning, you owe me." *What is wrong with me?*

"Is that why you were mad?" Micah asked, ignoring the other woman's gibe.

"One of the reasons. So, yes or no?"

"Sure, sounds good." Micah clasped her hands behind her head, her eyes narrowing as she replayed Olivia's words. "You said 'one of.'"

"Yes."

"Well?" She took her feet off the dash and turned to look at Olivia, waiting for more. Olivia studiously kept her eyes glued on the road in front of her, but she couldn't stop the heat from crawling up her cheeks.

"Okay, then. I didn't like waking up alone in a strange place and it really pissed me off that you left me to go ride your infernal bike. Especially when two different doctors—two, Micah!—have told you to take time off!" Olivia's voice rose an octave with each sentence, reflecting the frustration, anger, and concern behind the words. Olivia sucked in a deep breath when she finished. She had been afraid she would be interrupted before she could get it all out.

"I'm sorry, I guess I didn't think that through. I was so caught up in what I wanted that I didn't take into consideration how you would feel," Micah apologized, sounding genuinely contrite at causing her new lover such distress. "Are you really sure you want me to stay tonight? You still seem upset."

"I'm very sure." Olivia reached across the seat blindly, keeping her eyes on the road ahead of her.

"I am still upset, but I am not mad anymore. Let me have a good night's sleep and the pleasure of waking up in your arms and I won't have any reason to stay upset." It was blackmail, pure and simple. Squeezing Micah's hand, she paused for a moment before adding, "And for God's sake, stay off your bike for a while."

"Yes, dear," Micah said, smiling at Olivia's attempt to take charge. She would concede this time, as much for Olivia's sake as her own, but mostly because this morning's ride was making her hip hurt like a bitch.

Chapter Seventeen

Early Monday morning arrived far too soon. Olivia woke up well rested and smiling like a kitten after a bowl of cream. She could definitely get used to the comforting sensation of Micah's warm body pressed up against her back every morning. She yawned but resisted the urge to stretch, enjoying the feel of Micah's strong arm wrapped around her middle too much to give it up just yet. Having the younger woman in her bed was dangerous, doubly dangerous. Her desire to stay in bed and enjoy a lazy morning with Micah was engaging in a serious internal competition with her everyday routine of getting up early and heading into the office. Moreover, there was Regina to consider.

While her daughter had been thrilled to see Micah again, the two women hadn't been very good company. Olivia had sent her daughter to bed early, citing school the next morning when she looked like she was going to argue about it. They weren't that far behind her.

Holding back a groan, she slipped out of the warm bed to start her morning routine. As much as she wanted to stay put, Olivia still needed to get Regina up and out the door before the bus came. Micah continued to sleep on, oblivious and probably still exhausted after the long drive and even longer weekend.

She found her daughter already downstairs, independently eating her breakfast while she waited for the school bus.

"Good morning, Regina," Olivia said, greeting her daughter with a quick peck on the top of her head. She pretended to not see the pre-teen scowl Regina gave her for acting so mom-like.

"Hi, Mom!" Regina quickly spooned up the last bit of her cereal, then enthusiastically jumped up out of her seat. "Can I go say hi to Micah before I go?"

"She's still sleeping."

Regina's face fell. Olivia then spent the next ten minutes convincing Regina that it wasn't a good idea to go up and say good morning to Micah. Olivia sighed in relief when the bus pulled up soon afterwards; her daughter could be quite adamant when she wanted something. A quality she was well acquainted with, she thought ruefully.

"Off with you, now." She pushed Regina towards the door.

Regina gave her a quick hug, then admonishing her to give Micah a hug from her as well.

"I will, I promise," she said, and then her daughter and all that whirlwind energy was out the door.

Now that Regina was off to school, it was her turn to get ready for work. She went back upstairs to check on Micah and leave her a surprise. Before heading out, she stopped at the bed once more just to look. She knew it was silly, but she wanted to make sure Micah was really there.

Irrational jealousy surfaced against the feather pillow Micah cradled, her tan arms contrasting darkly against the pale cream pillowcase. Olivia wished with all her heart that it wasn't Monday. She carefully leaned over the bed to brush one soft kiss on Micah's cheek before quietly leaving the room. Scribbling a quick note on her signature parchment paper, she left it where Micah was sure to see it upon waking.

***

Micah blinked against the sunlight streaming through the bedroom and groaned. Mornings were not her favorite time of day. Memories of last night filtered through the cobwebs in her brain, reminding her that she was at Olivia's home, in Olivia's bed. It was surreal. She looked at the time.

Almost nine, Olivia must be long gone by now, she thought. There was no way the work driven woman would go in to work late, especially not on a Monday. What she had thought was a half-dream must have been reality. She rubbed her cheek; the memory of Olivia kissing her before leaving that morning lacked a visual. She could only remember the soft touch of lips tickling against her skin before falling back into the void. Sitting up, she saw a note folded and leaning against a can of Coke. The can was still cold, covered in beads of sweat that had dripped along its sides, only to be captured by a sandstone coaster she recognized from the kitchen. She chuckled; that was so Olivia. Popping open the can, she offered up a silent salute to her considerate lover then picked up the note.

A single brass key tumbled out of the thick parchment paper, the scent of Olivia's perfume wafting up to greet her. Breathing in deeply, Micah noted that while still pleasing to the senses, the expensive scent lost something in the translation. She couldn't quite put her finger on it, but somehow Olivia's skin transformed it into something a bit more heady and provocative. She set the key aside so she could read the elegant scrawl.

Thank you for the pleasure of waking up with your arms around me. Call me when you wake up.
  Love, Olivia

Micah's smile broadened; she could definitely get used to this sweet Olivia. She took a few more sips before grabbing her cell phone.

"Micah, good morning!" the husky voice greeted her almost on the first ring.

"Morning Love, thanks for the soda."

"Yes, well, I remember that being your morning routine at Jonathan's."

"So, how's your morning going?" Micah asked, her thoughts moving away from the common banalities of their little conversation.

"Busy like normal. Would you like to come meet me for lunch?"

"Sure, where?" Micah asked. The smell of Olivia's perfume wafting up from the parchment paper was distracting her.

"Here, say noon?"

"Sounds like a plan." Micah grinned. *That would be just perfect.*

"Just lock up when you leave."

"Okay, will do." She picked up the key, twirling it in her fingers idly. *Hmmm,* Micah thought to herself. *I wonder...*

"Olivia?"

"Yes?"

"Thanks for giving me some space yesterday, I know I can be a bear sometimes."

"Of course," Olivia murmured after a brief pause. "Oh, and Micah? Be safe getting here."

Micah sat there for another few moments, her eyes half closed in contemplation. Last night had been odd for her. Not only because she had spent the entire night in another woman's bed, but also because they had done nothing but sleep. The weekend trip to the cabin had wiped her out emotionally, and after her little snit she was surprised that Olivia had let her hold her. She wasn't sure if she could have been so forgiving.

***

A few minutes before noon, Micah strolled into Olivia's office. The door was wide open and she didn't bother knocking. Olivia looked up, surprised that someone would just walk into her office unannounced, but instantly forgot the sharp retort forming on the tip of her tongue when she saw who it was.

She had been so involved in her work, she hadn't noticed how much time had gone by. It wasn't that she had forgotten their lunch date; on the contrary, she found herself so distracted by the anticipation that she had to dive full force into her work in order to get anything done at all. Her irritation at being interrupted dissolved instantly, replaced by an inviting smile.

Olivia liked everything she saw. The memory of Micah's warm body wrapped around her last night, her breath soft against her neck as they slept together was still fresh in her mind. It made her want to feel those arms around her again.

"Hey, Love," Micah said.

Olivia put her hand up, silencing her with a gesture.

"Amanda, why don't you go ahead and take lunch now?"

Olivia waited for the telltale sounds of Amanda gathering up her purse then waited another few seconds for the sound of the elevator opening up in the main hall before dropping her hand.

"Close the door and lock it so we won't be disturbed, Sweetheart." Micah did as Olivia commanded. "Good, now come kiss me."

Micah cocked one eyebrow at her lover in amusement as she sauntered over to Olivia's desk. Evidently, Olivia in her own environment felt like she should still be in charge. *Well, that's not going to happen, not if I have anything to say about it.*

"Someone is bossy." She smirked. Leaning her hip against the front of the desk, she crossed her arms, showing off well-defined biceps and forearms. "YOU come kiss ME."

Olivia stood slowly. Taking the challenge seriously, she made the walk around her desk painfully slow, sliding her fingers along the smooth planes of the desktop until she stood in front of Micah. Leaning back against the desk, Olivia silently appraised Micah's lean form. She assumed a power pose that looked deceptively relaxed, her hands grasping the edge of the desk. If it were anyone else in any other situation, alarm bells would be sounding inside their heads. It was the pose Olivia often held while listening to someone talk themselves into a corner before pouncing and tearing them apart.

"Really?" Olivia drawled, forcing herself to stand stock-still. She wanted to pounce all right, her urges felt downright feral in response to the hooded gaze Micah was leveling at her.

In the end, neither of them gave in. Neither would ever admit to being the first to kiss the other. It was more that they seemed to come together due to an irresistible force, a force that drew them together of its own volition. Word play was lost when their lips met. Micah demanded and sought dominance, kissing Olivia feverishly, her tongue seeking entrance to Olivia's mouth and finding her eager to join in their ongoing mock battle.

Micah's muscles flexed as she stiff-armed the desk behind Olivia, forcing her to lean back as denim-clad legs slid between Olivia's thighs. Micah grunted in frustration. Olivia's skirt was too tight, preventing her from bringing her thigh closer to her goal.

A battle of give and take began between the two strong-willed women. Olivia shifted, bringing her arms up and around Micah's neck until her forearms rested on muscular shoulders. Drawing Micah closer, she leaned into her, feeling the strong arms that were starting to represent safety wrap around her possessively.

Micah stroked Olivia's tongue with her own while her hands stayed busy, openly roaming the smaller woman's body. Exploring fingers danced along Olivia's back and shoulders before sliding along her ribs and finding her breasts. Eager thumbs easily found her nipples, already hard and pushing against the thin silk blouse. The offending material was in the way of direct contact. Micah fought the urge to grasp the expensive cloth and tear the delicate fabric away from her goal, then lost. The now buttonless shirt lay open, exposing deliciously pale skin framed by a black lace bra. Breaking away from their kiss, Micah looked down. Olivia flushed a gorgeous shade of pink beneath her gaze, her breathing turning quick and shallow.

"God, Olivia, you're so fucking sexy." Micah breathed. Fucking was the operative word. The buzz in Micah's head grew stronger until all she could think about was how to get the overly dressed woman naked and wrapped around her hips as soon as possible. The desk behind her was cold and hard. It didn't suit her purpose at all. Besides, fucking on the boss's desk was so cliché it offended her sensibilities.

The couch, on the other hand, was soft and inviting, much like the woman in her arms. A quick flashback to another couch they had shared only a day ago drew a low groan from her, almost a growl that started low in her throat and escaped between clenched teeth.

Unwilling to wait a second longer, Micah proved her strength by picking Olivia up and carrying her over to the couch. Laying her down on the cushions, Micah delighted in the vision of the enticingly disheveled woman laid out before her, her blouse open and untucked from her skirt, her long legs still ending in those sexy ass high heels. Micah had to admit that the look did it for her. It wasn't just the look, though, it was also the expression on Olivia's face. Passion and excitement showed in the flush of her face, her lips full and bruised looking. Olivia's eyes glowed with need, intense and full of fire. But underlying all that heat and passion, there was also a cool undercurrent of patience and trust. Olivia trusted and loved her, and that thought made her freeze.

She couldn't afford to lose control. Not once. Not ever.

"What's wrong, Micah?"

"Nothing," Micah whispered. She couldn't tell her why she had stopped, or what she was thinking.

Micah hesitated beneath that questioning gaze, hating herself for asking but having to find some reason Olivia would believe for her hesitation. "Has anyone ever made love to you here before?"

"Oh, God, Micah...No. Do you really need to ask?" Olivia whimpered, her body aching for the touch of Micah's hands on her body. "I need to feel you. Please, Micah!"

"Good," Micah stated, not caring how possessive she sounded, then grunted in surprise when her roaming hands discovered two things: one, Olivia wasn't wearing any pantyhose, and two, she was so very ready for her.

"No hose?" Micah moaned as her fingers slid unimpeded along the thin strip of silk between Olivia's thighs. "Someone would think that you might have been planning this."

The soaked fabric gave way without any effort. She ran her fingertips along lips full and swollen with arousal, then parted those silken lips gently to glide her fingers along the slick wetness, pausing at the hard ridge of nerves that blossomed beneath her touch. Micah didn't give Olivia a chance to answer her question. Without warning, she slid long fingers into the welcoming heat, reveling in the sensation of finally being inside Olivia.

"Ah!" Olivia gasped, clutching Micah's upper arm in an iron grip. Her skirt was ruined, crumpled around her waist in Micah's haste to get to her. She had already written off the silk blouse, but she could care less. Her entire universe was focused on the feeling of her lover's hand on her, in her. She had been ready for Micah since she flipped the lock on her door, the sound of the latch clicking shut unlocking the passion she had kept locked away all morning.

Micah crouched above her, their legs tangled together on the couch. She was managing to keep most of her weight off of her by balancing on one elbow, which allowed Olivia enough room to let her own hands wander. Running her fingers along Micah's other arm, Olivia could feel the muscles in her forearm working, the movement echoing deep inside her. It was too hot, feeling those muscles clench and tighten, mirroring her own rhythm as she brought her hips up to meet her lovers thrusts. Squeezing Micah's arm impatiently, she rolled her hips in an unspoken plea. She wanted more but was unsure how to ask. Another finger entered her, blinding her for a moment as white hot waves of pleasure sent sparks of electricity shooting up her spine.

"Oh, yes!"

Olivia's hands needed something to do. They kneaded and massaged their way along Micah's back. Desperate to touch hot flesh, they sought the soft skin at the base of Micah's spine.

"More?" Half question, half demand, Olivia's voice was strained with need. Drawing her knees up to give Micah more room, she begged, "Please, Micah?"

"Ah, Gods, Olivia!" Micah panted, "You are so wet, so hot, you burn me." Micah lowered her head to capture one hard nipple between her teeth, her breath hot against the rough fabric between her lips and its prize. She pulled out her fingers, slowly, gently, earning a low moan from the woman beneath her. She circled Olivia's center with her fingers, coating their length with the abundant moisture then stopped.

"Olivia?" She breathed, making sure Olivia was okay with this. She felt a quick tightening and release beneath her fingers, the subtle spasm of muscles seeking to draw her in. Tucking her fingers together, she pushed back inside slowly, watching Olivia's face carefully for any sign of discomfort. She was tight, incredibly tight against her invading digits. Olivia's eyes screwed shut for a moment, her back arching as she sought more contact. A flood of wetness met Micah's careful fingers, velvet muscles clenched around her then loosened enough to give her room to move, encouraging Micah to resume her prior rhythm. Cool fingers slid beneath Micah's jeans, finding the firm flesh of her ass cheeks, pulling her down until her forearm and wrist was caught between them. Olivia writhed and moaned beneath her, bucking her hips onto Micah's fingers, riding them faster and harder with each desperate thrust.

Micah took Olivia's breast back into her mouth, sucking hard against the damp fabric, rolling the rigid flesh between her teeth. Her rhythm becoming frantic beneath her.

"You're so close," she groaned.

"Yes, oh, yes." Olivia tossed her head back and clawed at the couch's padded arm.

Micah took over, meeting Olivia's thrusts with her own more controlled movements. In the heat of the moment, Olivia was practically enveloping her, pushing herself against Micah's hand until she could feel her straining against her knuckles. Even as wet and open as she was, Micah wasn't sure she was ready for that and held back, her imagination taking her where she couldn't physically go. At least not yet, and definitely not in the office. She moaned, her arousal almost overwhelming as she watched Olivia's face, ecstasy transforming her cold features into something that burned white hot in her arms.

Olivia wasn't as eager to give up control to Micah as she had seemed. The sharp sting of nails digging into her skin drove her, encouraging Micah to continue, to not stop what she was doing.

"Oh, I'm gonna..." Olivia was reduced to panting between desperate appeals for release.

"Ahhhhhhhh." The long low moan grew louder, too loud. Remembering where they were, Micah covered Olivia's mouth firmly with her own, tasting Olivia's desire on her lips as she swallowed the sounds of her passion.

When Olivia finally quieted down, Micah twisted to take her weight off of Olivia and rested, holding Olivia protectively in her arms. She had fallen into a relaxed half-sleep when she felt fingers fumbling with the button on her jeans. Micah grabbed Olivia's hand, stilling its movement. She wanted what Olivia was offering, but she couldn't do it. It didn't help that Micah could smell her. Olivia's essence coated her fingers, the heady aroma of sex and perfume hung heavily around them. The combination made her head swim.

"Micah?" The question was tentative, but it was still there. Regret filled her heart. Micah couldn't deny what making love to Olivia did to her—what it made her want to do. Ignoring her own arousal, she climbed off the couch. Trying to temper the hurt look in Olivia's face, Micah gallantly offered her a hand, pulling the disheveled woman up to join her in a quick embrace.

"I'm good for now, this was about you," she said, kissing Olivia almost chastely.

"Um, I think I sort of ruined your clothes." She gestured at Olivia's ruined look, trying to change the subject. "I really hope you still keep a spare in the bathroom," she added, knowing that Olivia generally kept a spare outfit there just in case she had to stay late or go to an evening meeting out in town.

She stooped and picked up a couple of stray buttons from beneath her feet. Handing them to her lover with a crooked and somewhat apologetic smile, she watched as Olivia headed somewhat unsteadily into her private bathroom to clean up.

"Do we still have time for lunch?" Micah called out, thankful for the time it took Olivia to get herself together. She needed a few minutes of alone time to calm down. Yes, she wanted Olivia, but this out of control sexual collision was not like her. Olivia had a way of challenging her that made it difficult to resist. It was almost as if she was doing it on purpose, trying to entice her at every opportunity.

"Yes, I cleared two hours for us. Turned out to be a good thing too." Olivia's amused drawl floated out from her private bathroom.

Olivia stood in front of the mirror and grinned, punch drunk on the sex and trying not to blush. She had come a long way from blindly following her father's rules about fraternizing to letting Micah take her on that self-same couch she used to sit on while he lectured her on proper behavior. She was two parts exhilarated and one part petrified at her boldness, a combination more intoxicating than fine liquor and just as addicting.

It still stung that Micah wouldn't let her reciprocate yet, but all in good time. For once, she was going to practice her seldom-used patience. Pulling out her makeup bag, she made up her face with practiced flourishes. Her ruined outfit lay in a discarded heap on the floor. The skirt could probably be dry-cleaned, but the blouse was completely ruined. *But, oh, so worth it.* She had trouble putting on her lipstick. The only part of her that wasn't shaky was her smile, one, now that she was all alone, reshaped itself into something worthy of the Mona Lisa. A quick glance behind her confirmed what she already knew. A freshly pressed suit hung in one corner, sent up from the cleaners this morning.

Olivia reappeared a few minutes later, freshened up and looking like nothing had happened.

"Do we need to order still? I'm starving," Micah asked, then took a closer look at Olivia's new outfit. "I see you have pantyhose on this time." Olivia blushed. Her freshly applied makeup might have hid the pink tinge from her face, but not her ears. They suddenly turned a lovely shade of red. Micah crossed her arms in front of her, then chuckled evilly.

"Uh, huh. I thought so."

Olivia ignored Micah's obvious attempt at luring her into an admission of guilt and returned to the safety of her corporate chair.

A quick phone call later, along with the promise of a large tip, resulted in lunch arriving in record time. It helped that Olivia ordered from the local Chinese restaurant frequently and they were loath to upset her. After the food arrived, they sat and talked amicably about everything and nothing, just simply enjoying one another's company. The Chinese food was quite good, although Olivia avoided the soy sauce. She didn't have another spare outfit to ruin. Micah, on the other hand, was tucking into the food as if it was her last meal. She ate enthusiastically, and Olivia watched in fascination as her nimble fingers manipulated the chopsticks with casual ease. Olivia had never gotten the hang of the things herself and declined the offered utensils with barely concealed envy.

"So, will you be going back to my house?" Olivia asked, keeping her tone casual. Taking in the surprised look on Micah's face, she felt the need to explain. She cleared her throat and set down her fork. "That's why I gave you the key, so you can come and go as you please," Olivia added, then held her tongue. She really wanted Micah to say yes but any more explanation and it would seem like she was pushing her own agenda. It was up to Micah to decide.

Micah took a drink before answering.

"Actually, I was going to go back home and get some work done on the graphics I am doing."

Swallowing disappointment, Olivia pushed away her plate. Placing her elbows on the desk, she laced her fingers together before resting her chin on them.

"How is that going, by the way?"

"Pretty good. The storyline is complete, and I have a good majority of the panels done. It is mostly editing now, making sure that the dialogue is in sync with the artwork."

"Well, that's good. I remember you saying something about working on a graphic novel. I think you also said you were working on something of your own as well?"

"I did, but it's nothing really. I've been trying my hand at writing again, but it's been a while. It's more for me than anyone else." Micah leaned back in her chair, stretching against the fullness of her stomach.

Olivia got the feeling that there was more to it than that, but held her tongue. Micah didn't seem all that enthusiastic about sharing her writing with her.

They continued chatting for a bit, not so much running out of things to say as running out of steam. What had happened between them earlier was avoided, and both women were distracted from having to tiptoe around it. The mundane conversation faltered several times, usually when one of them glanced over towards the couch. Olivia doubted she could ever look at it again without remembering Micah hovering above her.

Olivia shook her head to clear the erotic images newly ingrained there. She couldn't think logically otherwise. She was still in shock that she had let, no begged, Micah to take her on the couch. In her office. At work. It was all so unlike her.

"Will you at least come over for dinner?" Olivia asked. She really wasn't interested in sharing more food, she just wanted the young woman's company. *No. Be honest,* she chided herself, *you want a repeat performance.*

"I'd like to, but I really do need to get this last bit done," Micah replied regretfully, standing up to leave after checking the time. "I'm already behind as it is. Besides, I think our time is almost up." Micah gathered up the remains of their lunch and dropped the empty containers into the trashcan by the door. "And, I should really let you get back to work as well," she said, the playful glint in her eye matching an equally wicked grin. Walking back to Olivia, she leaned down and softly kissed her on the lips. "Thanks for lunch, Love."

Micah's hand had barely closed on the brass door handle to leave when Olivia called out to her.

"Micah, you forgot to say I love you."

A broad smile graced Micah's face, her teeth flashing white against her tan skin. "I love you, too. Call me tonight." Then she twisted the knob and walked out, leaving the door open behind her.

Olivia sat behind her desk, outwardly composed and pretending nothing had just happened behind her locked door. However, it was hard to ignore the heavy sensation between her thighs, the residual moisture that slid across sensitive skin with every little movement.

Micah stopped at Amanda's desk and casually chatted with her for a bit. She was amazed at how cool and collected she could act after their lunch together. She almost fainted when Micah turned one last time towards her and waved casually, then brought her fingertips up to her lips in a subtle salute and smiled hazily before turning to leave.

Her ears straining, she swore she could hear the ding of the elevator door as it closed. She heard someone clear their throat and she turned towards the sound; Amanda was watching her from her desk. Olivia realized she had just been sitting there, following Micah's departure with both her eyes and her mind.

"Amanda. Let me know when my next appointment is here, will you?" Olivia closed the door between them and retreated back into her office.

"Yes, ma'am." Amanda's voice, crisp and professional, brought a sense of normalcy back to her day.

Chapter Eighteen

Micah practically jumped out of her skin when her cell phone went off, vibrating loudly against the hard surface beneath her elbows. She dropped her pencil and caught the thing a second before it skittered across her art table. With her other hand, she ripped out the page in her sketch book and crumpled it into a tiny little ball of hate. None of her sketches were turning out today, and she took Olivia's call as a sign to just quit while she was ahead.

Micah pushed away from the table and stood up painfully, her muscles stiff and refusing to move smoothly after being still for so long.

"Hey, Babe!" Micah limped out of her room, turning off the blaring stereo on her way to the kitchen. Her knee screamed with each step, so she grabbed her bottle of ibuprofen too.

Balancing the phone on one shoulder, Micah rummaged through the fridge for a fresh Coke, her head cocked at an awkward angle so she could keep her hands free to open the childproof cap on her ibuprofen.

"Micah, how is your work going?"

"Oh, you know, fine." It really wasn't. She was having issues with focusing. Her vague response, however, didn't fool the observant woman on the other end of the line.

"Micah, I told you not to lie to me," Olivia chuckled. "What gives?"

"Well, it was more of a fib than a lie," Micah admitted sheepishly. Olivia was getting too good at reading her. She could practically hear the woman tisking at her over the phone.

"Un-huh."

"I'm just having issues with the last chapter." Why she felt the need to explain herself, she had no idea. When it came to Olivia, how she normally responded and acted seemed to fly out the window.

Micah's leg felt a lot better after getting up and moving about. All she had to do was wait for the ibuprofen to kick in and maybe she could get back to work. Micah was headed back to her room when she heard a knock at the front door.

"Hey Olivia, there's someone at the door. Can you give me a sec?" Micah unlocked the door, only to find Olivia standing there with a pleased smile gracing her lips.

"Is it anyone you know?" Olivia asked, her phone still at her ear.

Always up to a game, she lifted her phone back to her ear and grinned. "Um, Olivia? Can I call you back? There's a hot chick at the door and she's insisting on coming in."

The shocked expression on Olivia's face was priceless.

"Hot, huh?" Olivia managed to look down her nose at Micah in a most delightfully snooty way, mostly because that sort of thing didn't work on her...it just made her want to laugh.

"That's what I've heard." Micah stepped to the side so the other woman could enter. "Come on in."

"Micah, I find myself with an issue." Olivia waited until she joined her in the living room to speak. The ominous tone set off alarm bells in Micah's head.

"What? Is something wrong? Is everything okay with Reggie?"

"She's fine," Olivia assured her, dramatically pausing before continuing. "I went home early today."

Micah's eyebrows shot to the ceiling at that. "Oh?"

"Yes, I have been trying to be home in time for dinner lately."

That revelation secretly pleased Micah. She schooled her face to mild interest, waiting to see where Olivia was going with this. She knew that it was more common than not for Olivia to work past eight most nights, but it wouldn't do any good pointing out her prior absences in her daughter's life. It was good to hear that she was spending more time with Regina.

"So, I sit down to eat with Regina, who then sits down with her iPhone...awful inventions, those," Olivia stated, sounding bemused. "Anyway, after managing to remove my daughter from her phone and actually having a conversation with her, I found that my dinner was lacking something, or someone else to make it complete." Olivia paused so Micah could catch up and let that sink in. She didn't tell her that Regina hadn't been shy about asking after Micah, and that had made it all the more obvious. "Is it weak to admit that I missed you terribly? I found myself not just wanting you there. I needed you there." She took a deep breath, her forehead creasing as if struggling over a riddle she couldn't solve. "But, you weren't there."

"After dinner, I left Regina with the sitter and a movie and came over here. I had to," Olivia admitted, feeling foolish for pouring her heart out like this.

Micah didn't say a thing. Everything Olivia said was a little too close to her own internal battles. They were drawn to each other, both apparently powerless to stop seeking out the other. The strength of that attraction was frightening.

Except that tonight, it was Olivia who needed her, who had succumbed to that inexplicable attraction. Pulling Olivia close, Micah wrapped her arms around her protectively. Olivia immediately settled in to the curve of Micah's shoulder, her head resting on her chest.

Olivia needs me, she kept silently repeating to herself. The mantra echoed deeply within her, reaching a place in her heart that had felt cold for a long time. Ignoring the reflexive twinge of fear that threatened this peaceful moment, she brushed a gentle kiss along the soft mass of blond hair.

"How long can you stay?"

"Only a couple of hours," Olivia murmured.

Micah didn't mind. Reggie would worry if her mom didn't come home. Micah wouldn't burden her like that. She could only offer this brief respite from their shared loneliness.

"It's okay, we can just rest here. Together. Jonathan is out for the night with Adam so he won't disturb us." Shifting her body so they could lie on the couch more comfortably, she lay half-propped up in the corner of the overstuffed couch. Micah didn't fall asleep; she was enjoying the feel of Olivia curled up in her arms too much to give in to sleep. Olivia did fall asleep, eventually, the regular beat of her heart marking off their time together.

Two hours later Micah walked Olivia to the front door, softly closing it behind her after sharing a sweet goodnight kiss. Micah leaned heavily against the door for a moment. Olivia's presence was starting to bring a deep sense of peace and stillness that calmed her in a way that both frightened and exhilarated her. Micah was starting to crave that sensation. What would she do if it went away—if she lost it?

Padding back into her room, she picked up her abandoned sketchpad. Closing her eyes, she found the picture in her mind she needed to put down on paper. Micah sat down and started on a fresh sheet, the lines coming easily, the image practically leaping from her mind to her hand. She didn't stop until the sketch was complete and her hand cramped from the effort. Nodding in approval, Micah covered her work with a clean sheet of paper. It was unique and beautiful and unlike anything she had done before. Inspiration had poured out of her freely and now she was exhausted. Emptied of the vision that had been troubling her, she managed to crawl into bed, falling asleep almost immediately.

***

Tuesday morning was bright and shiny and in direct opposition to Olivia's foul mood. She hadn't slept well at all, at least not after she got home. What she had wanted was to wake up with her lover beside her, but she already felt so damn needy after going over to Micah's last night that she couldn't bring herself to ask if she would come home with her. She was afraid of what Micah's answer would be and afraid of what her own reaction would be if Micah said no.

Rubbing her temples in an attempt to relieve an impending migraine, Olivia sighed in frustration. A quick review of her schedule made her curse under her breath; she was going to be out of the office all day in meetings.

She wouldn't see Micah today, not even for lunch. Resigning herself to the rest of her day and expecting an equally desolate evening, she embraced her foul mood. It suited the day she was expecting.

"Amanda? Can you have Robert come around in twenty?" Olivia stuffed needed files into her leather attaché. It was too early, but she might as well grab a cup of good coffee from across the street before Robert showed up.

***

Micah had a good day. She stayed busy on her computer for a good part of the morning, and then headed out to the gym for some much-needed physical therapy. Before lunch, Micah had called Olivia's office to see if she had time for a lunch date, but Amanda had told her that Olivia was at some meeting across town.

After a quick shower, she hit the art desk and kicked out quite a few rough sketches for a new project. Time flew by unnoticed, and she probably would have forgotten dinner if Jon hadn't come home from a date with one of those silly aluminum swans in hand...the doggy bag of the well-heeled, which he promptly plopped down in front of her with an admonition to eat.

Steak and wonderfully yeasty rolls made for an impromptu hoagie she could eat with her off hand while she continued to draw. By the time her food and her wrist gave out it was almost 9pm. It was time to call it quits.

Her cell phone started to ring the second she stood up to throw away her trash. Micah smiled. There was only one person who would call her that late at night.

"Olivia, how are you?"

"I'm exhausted, Sweetheart, it was a long day." Olivia's voice sounded strained, a muted yawn interrupting her response. "I just wanted to hear your voice before heading to bed."

"Okay. Sleep well, I love you," Micah said. She might not always be comfortable with herself, but she was getting more comfortable with telling Olivia she loved her.

"I love you, too. Goodnight, Micah," Olivia said, then hung up. Micah stared at her phone.

How odd, Micah thought, wondering what was going on with Olivia today. She said she was tired and she definitely sounded it, but that didn't explain why Olivia sounded so choked up when she said goodbye.

Chapter Nineteen

By Wednesday, Olivia was fit to be tied. Once again, she had been stuck in meetings outside of the office, and to make matters worse, the rest of the week didn't look much better.

She had been incredibly short-tempered all day. Her willingness to negotiate was not bountiful, much to the dismay of everyone around her. Olivia felt a little guilty—Micah wasn't answering her phone and her irritation at the universe just flared out of control.

Finally able to relax in the back of her car, she left it to Robert to find their way back to the office. Their normal chitchat was absent. She wasn't in the mood for casual conversation. Checking her phone for the umpteenth time, she felt the tension rising again, a tightness in her face and neck that threatened to turn into a migraine. Not one call, message, or text from Micah all day. She had called several times already and left messages to call her back twice. The second message went straight to voicemail, which meant that she wasn't checking her messages. That could be a good thing. It wasn't that Micah hadn't listened to her messages and ignored them—she simply hadn't listened to her messages yet.

The voice inside her head that she was trying to ignore, the one that felt much less reassured by that bit of knowledge, left her with a deep sense of unease that would not go away. The last time Micah didn't answer her phone, it was because she had left to go to her cabin in Maryland. Alone in the back of the town car, Olivia had plenty of time to review the events of the last few weeks while her driver fought through rush hour traffic, and that meant her thoughts were full of the one change in her life that mattered...Micah.

Running into Micah again was a much-needed second chance. She had seen her riding that bike like a demon possessed, but wasn't sure it was truly her until she called out to someone. Olivia had almost given herself whiplash, following the bike's quick movements as she wove wildly through the heavy traffic. She was barely able to turn in time to catch the name of the bike messenger company plastered on the back of Micah's t-shirt. Knowing what she knew now, she was lucky to have spotted Micah at all. She rarely wore the company logo, preferring her own tight-fitting bike shirts or rash guards. It was sheer luck that she was on that street at that specific time and wearing the company logo.

She wanted to ask her what was different that day, what had made her wear the ugly company shirt on that specific day, but she daren't. Micah didn't know that she had spotted her before their supposedly random meeting.

Olivia shifted nervously in her seat. She wasn't sure how Micah would react if she ever found out that Olivia had orchestrated their first meeting. She hadn't exactly lied to Micah, since she had never asked her about it, but it felt like a lie. That bothered Olivia...a lot, especially after she had demanded complete honesty from Micah.

It didn't take long for her to realize that Micah wasn't the same woman who had left her firm a year ago. Olivia had two versions of the younger woman stuck in her head. The intern she had known and the woman who had walked back into her life. The old Micah had been charming, accommodating, and ready to please Olivia. The new Micah was still charming, but she definitely wasn't as accommodating. She was tougher, more assured of herself, and definitely had no intentions of letting Olivia be in control of their relationship.

She challenged Olivia, almost daily, her stubbornness matching Olivia's inch for inch. Honestly, she had been unprepared for how intense her reaction to Micah's new persona had been. The younger woman was sexy as hell, but it was her devil-may-care attitude that excited and intrigued Olivia, leaving her breathless and willing to do things she had never imagined.

Olivia pressed her head against the tinted glass and stared out the window. In the seclusion of her most private thoughts, she could admit it. She didn't know what the hell she was doing.

So much had happened since that day. Finding out that Jonathan not only knew where Micah was all that time, but that they had become roommates? That had seriously upset her. Finding out how she had ended up living with Jonathan in the first place was devastating.

When Micah ran back to her cabin, Olivia could have repeated history and lost the woman she loved—for good this time. She didn't, and the price she paid for her earlier failure was learning the truth. Micah's admission floored her, forcing her to re-examine her life and her motives. The depth of Micah's pain was almost too much to bear, a pain that she was partially to blame for. Self-accusing anger flared into something stern and hard when she thought about what Micah had gone through alone. Her parents had treated her atrociously; the emotional scars she carried ran so much deeper than the ones she wore on her body.

Robert's deep voice interrupted her chaotic thoughts. "We're here, Olivia."

Momentarily disoriented, she peered out the window to find the town car pulled up in front of her office building. Her musings had been leading her...somewhere. A stray thought sat at the edge of her mind, unwilling to shake itself loose. Pursing her lips in frustration, Olivia let it go for now. There would be no epiphany, no flash of brilliance that would fix everything in one shot today. All she had to know was that Micah loved her, and she loved Micah. Olivia told her that they would work it out, and she meant it. Anything worth having was worth pursuing, and Micah was definitely worth having.

Olivia walked back into her office and stopped in the middle of the room, trying to decide whether to sit down or leave. It was still early, and there was a mound of paperwork on her desk that needed attending too. That didn't seem to matter. All she knew was that she was done with today. Turning on her heels, she headed back for the elevators, running into Jonathan on the way out.

"Leaving, Jonathan?" she asked, startling the preoccupied man. He hadn't expected her to be there today.

"Oh, hello, Olivia. I was heading across the street for a late lunch," Jonathan greeted his boss, pressing the elevator button for the first floor. The metal doors slid open with a small ding. Jonathan stepped forward, holding the doors open and gesturing for Olivia to enter first.

Olivia entered the small confines of the elevator, her reflection greeting her on three sides until Jonathan joined her. Her eyes lit up, and she smiled for the first time that day. Running into Jonathan had given her both an idea and an excuse. Micah's roommate looked over at her nervously, as if he could sense she was up to something.

"Jonathan, I hope you don't mind, but I haven't seen Micah in over a day and I can't seem to get a hold of her."

Ah, there it is. Jonathan smiled. "She's gone incognito, has she? When I left this morning she was in the zone, already up and working on her art. Actually, I'm not sure if she wasn't up all night and hadn't gone to bed yet."

"I see. Would you like to take an early day and walk with me to your apartment? I was hoping to see Micah today."

"Not at all. I don't have any clients scheduled this afternoon," he agreed, then added, "I am sure she just has her music turned up so loud she can't hear the phone."

I hope he's right, Olivia thought.

Olivia made it to the front doors in record time. She practically ejected from the building, moving so fast that the door threatened to close on Jonathan as he followed behind her, struggling to keep up with her quick pace.

"Where's Robert?" Jonathan asked. Olivia's black Town Car was nowhere to be seen.

"I texted him in the elevator, he's heading home for the night," she said. "I feel like walking."

"Oh." Jonathan grimaced. How she was able to keep up such a breakneck speed in those heels was beyond him. By the time they made it to his building, he was out of breath and struggling to keep up with Olivia.

"Geez, I need to get back into the gym," Jonathan muttered, sliding his key into the lock. The doorknob vibrated in his palm and he could hear the thump of bass knocking at the door. Inviting Olivia in first, he tried to focus on the lyrics of the song blasting through the apartment. What she chose to listen to was usually a good indicator of what kind of mood Micah was in.

Micah was singing, her voice was clear and pure, in contrast with the husky quality of the voice coming through the speakers. Jonathan held a finger to his lips for silence. Caught up in the moment, he gestured for Olivia to join him.

Micah was lying on the couch, her long legs stretched out in front of her and a sketchpad in hand. She was wearing comfortable-looking jeans with worn-out knees, the denim fabric faded almost white. A frayed sleeveless flannel shirt hung loosely on her frame. It was unbuttoned, revealing what appeared to be a sports bra beneath the open shirt and exposing her sculpted stomach. But it was her singing that captured Olivia's heart.

This world's a lovely place
But it's dark inside my soul
Most times I do just fine but
Sometimes I lose control

I have, I give
I laugh and I live
I hope, I choose
I accept and I lose
But I'm confused

Olivia's breath caught in her throat at the haunting lyrics. Micah's guard was down, her armor against the world put aside for once. She seemed at ease with herself in the privacy of her home, enough to express herself so openly. Olivia wanted this. She wanted Micah to feel this way when they were together. The desire was so strong it made her heart ache.

***

Blissfully unaware of her audience, Micah was lost in the music.

It was one of her favorite songs; it spoke to her. A lot of her life could be summed up in that one song, and she often went back to listen to it when she was alone and needed reminding. Today, she played it for a different reason and found some new meanings in it. As always, song and lyrics spoke to her in a secret language that went beyond just the words. Today, the song included not only her past, but the present and the future as well. She heard hope and possibility, the chance for a new beginning and a way to heal herself.

The apartment was all hers until Jon came home, so she had taken advantage of the privacy to hang out, literally, leaving her sports bra on and just throwing on her favorite flannel to listen to her music. The music helped keep her mind from wandering around dusty hallways that were best left un-tread—hallways that would take her places she didn't want to go.

She had just gotten up the energy to move when the music turned off suddenly.

"Jonathan, you scared the shit out of me. I didn't expect you home yet." Her heart racing, Micah jumped up from the couch and started buttoning up her shirt.

231

Even though Jon had seen the damage first hand, she still felt self-conscious about her scars.

"Man, I have got to get back on the bike soon. This is killing me, not being able to ride," she babbled nervously then stuttered to a stop. Something wasn't right. Jon was usually much chattier. Her shirt half buttoned up, she turned to see what was wrong and froze. Jonathan hadn't turned off the stereo...Olivia had. Her heart froze.

The flannel shirt was buttoned up enough to hide her stomach, but it didn't matter, she still felt exposed and betrayed. Micah turned and fled to her bedroom with Olivia close on her heels. *Leave it to Olivia to keep pushing,* Micah thought, angrier than she had been in a long time. *How much had Olivia seen? How long had she stood there, observing her without announcing her presence?*

She stopped in front of her dresser, bracing herself on the smooth wooden edge. The haunted face staring back at her was too much. Micah hung her head—she couldn't look at herself. Self-loathing rose up in her throat, bitter and sour, threatening to choke her. She had thought that telling Olivia her story, showing her the scars, would have changed things. The problem wasn't just the scars, though, the damage ran so much deeper. *How do you heal wounds that don't bleed? How do you cover up scars that mark your soul?*

"You have a beautiful voice," Olivia said, closing the door behind her.

"Thanks," Micah bit out.

Olivia was getting tired of watching Micah torture herself. Yes, she was physically here with her, but she was still running away.

"Turn around. Please?" Olivia's hands were insistent. Micah let Olivia turn her around until they were facing each other. Micah's hands were clenched at her sides, her downturned face hidden beneath the shaggy cut of her hair. It was getting long again and Olivia wondered if she was going to cut it soon. She had to stop herself from brushing the hair out of Micah eyes. *Let her hide this way, I have other plans.*

She started unbuttoning Micah's shirt, swatting away the hands that tried to do the buttons back up. "Don't."

She kneeled gracefully before Micah. Pushing aside the open confines of the flannel shirt, she explored the hard muscles of Micah's stomach, muscles that clenched and fluttered beneath her fingertips. She neither avoided nor focused on the scars. They didn't matter, and she had to show Micah that she was beautiful to her. Wrapping her arms around Micah's waist, she drew her into an embrace, calmly stroking the long muscles along her spine. Micah jumped when Olivia's lips replaced the wandering fingertips, planting soft kisses down her stomach. She kissed along the scars to show that they didn't bother her, and that she accepted them.

Olivia inhaled Micah's scent, feeling somewhat intoxicated and slightly dizzy at her small victory. Olivia was doubly encouraged when Micah threaded her fingers into her hair, a low moan escaping from her throat. She felt Micah sway slightly in her arms just as her lips met an obstruction; Micah's faded jeans prevented her from continuing her exploration. She brought her hands back around, intent on unbuttoning Micah's jeans. The button gave way easily, but just as she was starting to lower the zipper, Micah shifted and moved away. "I'm sorry, Olivia, but I just...I can't." Micah helped Olivia to stand before buttoning up, studiously ignoring Olivia's confused face.

"Micah, don't you want me?" Olivia asked, searching Micah's face for an answer.

"Gods yes, I just need some time," Micah said, dragging her fingers through her hair a few times before giving up and pacing the length of the room. She stopped and stared out the window, somewhere between Olivia arriving and now it had started raining. Neon lights streaked across the panes like a melted painting, accentuated by the occasional horn blasting its irritation. She rocked back on her heels then spun around to face Olivia.

Going on the offensive wasn't the best way to handle the situation, but she needed Olivia to back off a little. She didn't think that Olivia understood just how far she had gone to letting her in. Her touch had felt so good. She wanted what Olivia offered so much, what she promised with those soft lips, that she almost let Olivia go down on her. Even though her body still ached for the promised release, she still couldn't let her guard down enough to let it happen. *So broken.*

"What do you want from me, Olivia?"

"Just you." The simple answer created such a look of panic on Micah's face that Olivia felt compelled to expand on her answer. "Your presence. Nothing else. Will you come home with me tonight? I could use a good night's sleep."

Olivia was learning a bit about pushing Micah. Admitting a weakness was not easy for her, even when it was the truth, but it gave Micah something else to focus on. If nothing else, it wakened the gallant nature of the other woman. Olivia didn't think Micah would ever back down from protecting someone else.

"Nothing else?"

Olivia shook her head, "Nothing, just sleep."

"Yeah, I can do that. Just let me grab my bag."

"Bring clothes you don't mind leaving, will you? In fact, bring a few sets with you," Olivia piped up as Micah rummaged through her dresser.

"What?" Micah stopped what she was doing.

"That way you will have clothes when you stay at the house," Olivia explained practically, as if it should be obvious. She had a plan to move Micah in a little at a time, until she didn't feel the need to leave.

"Um, okay. Could you grab my chargers from over there?" Micah asked, flustered at Olivia's request, but not seeing a way to argue with the practical suggestion. "The top drawer has my cords."

Micah was staring at her notebook, waiting for it to shut down so she could bring it with her when Olivia gasped. She turned to find Olivia standing motionless in front of the open drawer, her hand at her throat.

Oh shit, the knife.

Micah strode over to Olivia and shut the drawer, rather forcefully, then stuffed the rest of her clothes into the bag. She retrieved the chargers from the other drawer, the drawer Olivia was supposed to open, and dropped them into her messenger bag along with the laptop.

Olivia hadn't said anything yet. Her silence smacked of judgment, so Micah went on the defensive.

"Look Olivia, this is a fact of my life. I work every day not to give into the urges, to look for that endorphin rush. But if you can't deal with it..." Micah paused, not wanting to continue, but forcing it out anyway. "It's all good, we can say that we tried."

When Olivia didn't respond immediately, Micah tossed her bag on the bed and started unpacking. *It's better this way,* she tried to convince herself. *Better that this happened sooner rather than later.*

"No!" That single word rang out in the silent room. Olivia hadn't meant to raise her voice. "No," she repeated quietly, watching resignation and disappointment dull the gold flecks in Micah's eyes. She cleared her throat, waiting to find the right answer to make things all better and found a question instead.

"How do you handle it?" Olivia asked, struggling to keep her voice from trembling.

"When I need to, I get work done on my tat or get a new one. At least that way I get cool artwork out of the pain and the rush is spectacular," Micah answered as honestly as possible, then shrugged, "Riding my bike helps too, as well as uh, other activities."

Olivia simply blinked, once, then nodded. "I know I asked before, but I have to ask again. If you feel stressed out enough to want to use that..." She gestured at the closed drawer behind her. "Can you promise to come to me first? To try and talk to me?"

"I'll try, but I have to be honest. I'm not used to talking about this with anyone. Not since my grandmother died." *Please, please let it go for now,* Micah thought, realizing that her unexpected candidness might open up a new can of worms. Micah didn't like where this was going. Olivia didn't seem to realize what she was asking her to do, or that she might be setting both of them up for disappointment.

"Micah, was last year...was that the first time this happened?"

"No." Micah grimaced. "I can't seem to be able to keep anything from you, can I?" Olivia didn't get where she was without being overly perceptive and astute. Micah smiled humorlessly at the other woman. "I guess you could say this," Micah gestured at her stomach, "was a relapse."

Micah sat down. What she had to say was too heavy to speak standing up, then looked up at Olivia, expecting to see pity or regret in those cobalt-blue eyes. She was surprised when Olivia stuck around after the first round of this story at the cabin, maybe she needed to hear this, too.

"My grandmother found out what was happening, what I was doing to deal with my father's abuse when I was younger. She made sure I was away from home as much as possible. Whenever there was a holiday or school break, she brought me up to the cabin to stay with her. She bought me a bike and encouraged me to ride as much as possible. That helped a lot. It gave me a way to escape when things got too bad at home."

Micah's voice held the soft Irish lilt that Olivia often noticed when she was angry or upset. Tonight, it held nothing but sadness and the memories of her grandmother, which seemed to bring Micah's accent out even more. Olivia could hear the echo of her grandmother's voice as Micah spoke.

"I wish I had been able to meet your grandmother. She sounds like an amazing woman, and someone who loved you very much," Olivia said. She owed a lot to Micah's grandmother, not only for her efforts to protect her, but also for giving her something to work with. If Micah's grandmother had found a way to understand and channel Micah's darker urges, so could she.

"Yeah, she was." Micah swallowed hard, caught somewhere in the emotional backlash of love, pain, and loss.

Olivia watched her fight with those emotions, and gained some insight into why Micah still kept that knife with her. "Micah..." Olivia started, and then discarded what she was going to say. She started again. "I'm sorry."

"What?"

"I'm sorry. I can't seem to stop pushing, even when I know I should." Olivia shrugged. "Old habits."

"Now that's something we do have in common," Micah said, smiling ruefully.

Their conversation had reached that emotional point where you both drowned in the backlash of the tension and angst, or you flipped 180 degrees and gave in to your instincts, resorting to humor and the illusion of normalcy. Olivia took one last look at the drawer and then turned her attention back to Micah, mirroring Micah's rueful grin. "I guess I would have to agree with that."

Micah pulled Olivia into her arms. They laughed at each other, mostly because the alternative would have been crying.

"Would you take the CD you were listening to earlier? It sounded interesting," Olivia asked as soon as they had calmed down.

"Yeah, sure, I can do that." Micah grabbed her bags and went to retrieve her CD from the Bose stereo. Jonathan was sitting on the couch, nursing a large brandy and looking mightily guilty. Micah walked over to Jonathan and gave him a hug, playfully kissing the top of his head so he knew she had forgiven him. "Night, Jon, see ya' later."

"Later Sweetheart, don't do anything I wouldn't," he said with a playful wink.

"Oh please! That is so limiting. You and Adam are so vanilla." Micah laughed.

"Ha, just because we don't get kinky like you…"

"Leather is not kinky, it's fucking hot!" Micah argued. "Why don't you ask Adam to wear his leather pants? He totally rocks them."

"So do you, and that's not what I am talking about," Jonathan managed to get out before Olivia dragged Micah out of the apartment, still laughing at Jonathan's repartee.

"Really, Micah?" Olivia had to ask. "Kinky?"

"I guess that depends on your definition of kink," she replied with a secretive smile.

"Do you really have leather pants?"

"Oh, yeah!" Micah responded enthusiastically, "And Jonathan is right, I do rock them," she added with her trademark cocky grin.

"I'm sure you do," Olivia murmured, occupied with trying to envision Micah in leather pants, and finding it not that hard to do. It was also getting quite uncomfortable in the elevator. She was sure it was getting hotter by the minute.

Micah had to ask twice before Olivia responded to her question.

"Olivia, where are we going?" Micah asked. The elevator had continued past the lobby and was heading for the garage levels.

"Oh, we need to take your truck. I sent Robert home since I walked over with Jonathan…unless you want to take a cab?" Olivia asked, hoping Micah wouldn't opt for the cab. "I would hate to have to call him back now."

"No, my truck sounds good."

Chapter Twenty

Micah's shiny blue 4x4 stuck out like a sore thumb in Olivia's driveway, a bright spot of color breaking the monotony of all the silver and black Land Rovers and Escalades scattered throughout the upscale neighborhood. Once inside, Micah carried her bag up to the bedroom before joining Olivia and Reggie at the dinner table. Micah smiled at the lone can of soda sitting in front of her plate. Regina eyed it enviously, but Olivia was adamant about her not drinking anything caffeinated at her age, so that was as far as that went.

"Wine?" Olivia asked, pouring herself a glass.

"Um, no thanks, I'm good with this," she said, indicating her Coke. "Everything smells wonderful."

"You'll have to thank Uncle Vinnie's...best Italian take-out in town." Olivia gave a nod towards the pile of aluminum containers sitting on the kitchen counter.

"Hey, what's up, Reggie?" Regina was being very quiet, especially considering that she normally talked Micah's ear off.

"Bad day at school," Regina stopped nibbling at a piece of garlic toast to answer her. "They are making me play basketball this year and I suck at it."

"Regina, language," Olivia automatically responded

"That's not a problem. I love basketball and would be more than happy to help you." Micah grinned at Reggie.

"You would?" Reggie's sullen attitude evaporated in an instant.

"Sure. You know what? Let me make a quick phone call."

She had an idea, but didn't want to break the no phone rule for dinner. Micah got up to retrieve her phone from the den. Olivia followed behind her, curious to see what she was up too. She winked at her, then hit the speed-dial.

"Hey Adam, I need a favor," Micah said, and then winced at his overly enthusiastic greeting. She had forgotten how loud he could be. *Some day he will realize a phone is not two cans tied together by a string.* "Yeah, can you bring your old hoop over to Olivia's, please? I'll owe you big time."

Micah rolled her eyes at the ceiling. "Yes, you can borrow my truck next weekend. Oh, and dude, don't forget a drill and the basketball." Micah hung up the phone and turned around.

Olivia was leaning against the doorframe, a strange expression on her face.

"That was very sweet of you." She held out her hand and Micah took it, then leaned in for a quick kiss.

"Mmm, you taste like wine," Micah murmured.

"I thought you didn't drink wine?"

"I usually don't, but it tastes sweeter on your lips."

"Micah! Stop teasing," Olivia said, reminding Micah that they weren't alone.

"Sorry."

"Micah." Olivia's voice was soft but it stopped Micah in her tracks. "Thank you for thinking of Regina."

Raising her voice, Olivia called out to her daughter. "Regina, get your homework done; Micah has a surprise for you later." Regina squealed and immediately ran up the stairs, making an incredible amount of noise for one little girl.

Olivia laced her fingers in Micah's and led her into the living room. They curled up on the couch together, taking advantage of the quiet time while Reggie studied.

Micah was reminded of the other night at the apartment, when Olivia came over and they just cuddled together. She had to admit that the view was better here. A row of ceiling to floor windows overlooked the deck and a small garden. Everything was in full bloom and exploding with color. The landscaped back yard gave the illusion of being in the countryside; the tall trees and bushes hid the back fence and offered complete privacy from the other houses. It was beautiful, and Micah found herself dozing off as she watched the bees flirting with the rose bushes.

"Hey, where are you?" Olivia asked, running her fingers along the fine jaw line. "You look far away."

Micah's gaze shifted, focusing on the woman in her arms. "Oh, not so far away as all that, Love." Smiling, she found Olivia's lips with her own, kissing her gently. "See, not so far at all, and here I am back with you," Micah continued, the cadence of her words sounding not at all odd with that soft Irish lilt. Olivia returned Micah's smile, enjoying the warmth found in those words.

Their brief respite was short lived as the doorbell chimed loudly, signaling their return to the outside world. Olivia reluctantly left the warmth of Micah's arms to answer the persistent ringing.

When Olivia opened the door, the handsome young man standing in her doorway surprised her. He was taller than Micah. Dark-haired and athletic looking, he sported an easy smile that Olivia could tell was absolutely genuine. She liked him instantly.

"Adam!" Micah called out, "Thanks for coming." Slipping past Olivia, Micah found herself enveloped in a

242

huge bear hug, her feet dangling as Adam tried to squeeze the stuffing out of her. Letting Micah go, Adam subjected Olivia to the same treatment, and she was unable to resist the young man's infectious enthusiasm.

Olivia's scandalized expression almost brought Micah to tears, she was laughing so hard. "Olivia, this is Adam, my best friend since fifth grade," she wheezed when she could finally breathe again.

"This is Adam, as in Jonathan's Adam? I remember you telling me that you introduced them," Olivia exclaimed, finally making the connection. She gave Adam a quick once-over and grinned. *Way to go, Jonathan.*

"Yup, one and the same," Micah answered, playfully punching Adam in the stomach. He pretended to be mortally wounded by the blow, then laughed.

"Hey, lay off there stud, will ya?" he asked, holding his stomach as if it still hurt to breathe. "You been working out?"

"Always." Micah grinned, winking at Olivia. Olivia's face turned bright red and Adam hooted loudly, clapping Micah on the back.

Micah clapped her hands together.

"We need to get busy, or we won't get done before it gets dark," Micah said, bringing the subject back to the task at hand. Bantering with Adam was always fun, but she could never guarantee what might fly out of his mouth at any given time. That was what made him fun.

"Hey, where's your car?" Micah asked, looking around her. The backboard and basket leaned against the garage door, but the only vehicle in the driveway was her   Toyota.

"You mean Jonathan's baby?" Adam asked, making quotation marks in the air to emphasize baby. "He almost had a cow when I told him I needed the car to take this thing with me. I had to take a cab. I had better luck arguing with the cabdriver than Jon." Adam grinned. "The driver wasn't too happy about that, but he got over it."

"Damn, Adam. I'm sorry. If I had known you were going to take a cab I would have picked you up."

"Nah, no biggie," Adam said, waving off Micah's apology. "It was kind of fun."

"Now, all we need is a ladder."

"That I do have," Olivia piped up, thrilled to contribute.

"Garage?" Adam asked. Olivia nodded and pointed them in the right direction.

"Let's do this. We're burning daylight."

Olivia kept a watchful eye on the pair, since it was Micah on the ladder installing the basketball hoop. She had to chuckle as she listened to them heckle each other with a familiarity that spoke of years of friendship.

"Dude, stop shaking the ladder!" Micah yelled, and not without cause.

Adam was waiting until Micah wasn't watching, just so he could jiggle the ladder. Apparently, it was a fun game.

"Wow, Micah your ass looks great in those jeans." Micah was balanced on the top rung, trying to bolt on the backboard.

"Adam, you have a boyfriend, admire his ass," Micah growled, trying to balance the backboard, the drill, and herself on the ladder. Olivia smirked at that comment; someone else was getting a taste of smartass Micah.

"Yeah, but yours is nicer," he joked.

"Dude, seriously, I don't swing that way. Hey, stop feeling me up, you perv," she said, trying to climb down the ladder while also trying to kick his tickling fingers away.

"You should try it, it's fun," Adam insisted, unwilling to let the joke go just yet.

"How do you know I haven't?" she shot back, waving at Adam to pull the ladder down.

"With her?" he joked, indicating Olivia.

"Children, I can hear you," Olivia drawled, getting used to Adam's unique form of humor. The two of them together were hilarious.

"I just want to know why everyone wants to talk about my sex life all of a sudden," Micah groused, picking up her end of the ladder and moving it into the garage.

"Uh, huh…'cause your sex life is more interesting, Micah. Has she seen you in your leathers yet?" He added, ignoring Micah's death glare.

"Hush, Adam. You're going to scare her away." She was serious now. She loved Adam to death, but sometimes he didn't know when to stop.

"I can still hear you and no, he won't," Olivia sang out, joining the pair beneath the newly installed basketball hoop. "Regina is going to love this!"

Wow, this is weird. She now had a basketball hoop on her house. She could easily imagine coming home from work to find Micah and Regina playing basketball in the driveway. She had thought that type of domestic bliss wasn't for her, but now she wasn't too sure.

The sound of the basketball bouncing near her broke her out of her reverie. Evidently, they couldn't wait to try out the newly installed backboard. Adam was bouncing the basketball lazily, daring Micah to engage him. Adam was taller, but Micah was faster, making for a very physical game. She saw her cue to move out of the way, happy to maintain her spectator status.

When Micah elbowed Adam in the stomach in order to steal the ball, she knew that this was not going to be a polite game. Then Adam roughly nudged Micah aside in order to take a wild shot; unfortunately, he bumped her injured hip.

"Ow, shit!" Micah yelled, instantly dropping to her good knee. Adam was by her side in a flash, as was Olivia.

"I'm sorry, Sweetie," Adam apologized, brushing the hair out of Micah's face.

"It's okay, you didn't know."

The sound of the door slamming shut didn't give Micah much warning. Regina must have finished her homework and had heard them playing. When Micah heard young footsteps heading for the driveway, she pushed Adam away. Closing her eyes for a quick moment, she stood up as if absolutely nothing was wrong. It wasn't that the pain was gone; Micah simply refused to acknowledge it.

So that's how she does it, Olivia thought to herself.

"Come on, Reggie, we'll practice some basic shooting today," Micah said, bouncing the ball from one hand to the other. She focused on Reggie and the game, studiously ignoring Olivia's inquiring glances.

Adam stayed for about an hour, helping Micah teach Reggie some basics. Olivia was more than happy to stay in the background and just observe the two friends with her daughter. When it started to get dark, Olivia called a halt to the lesson.

Adam handed Micah the ball, swooping to pick up his jacket before heading out.

"Thanks Adam, I really appreciate you coming over this evening."

"No problem. See you on Sunday, birthday girl," he called out, ignoring her frantic hand motion for him to shut up.

Adam intercepted Olivia on his way out to the taxi, giving her a quick, but gentler hug this time. He threw a nervous glance in Micah's direction before speaking.

"Olivia, I am going to tell you something because I know how much Micah loves you. I know she is a bit of a control freak so just be patient with her, she's worth it."

Serious Adam lasted for exactly 2.6 seconds. Grinning broadly, Adam winked at Olivia before adding, "Oh, and her birthday is on Sunday. See you later, have a good night." Adam climbed into the waiting cab, waving at them as they drove away.

"All right, Reggie. That was an awesome beginning, but it's time to get cleaned up now," Micah said.

Olivia was immensely surprised and more than a little pleased by how both Micah and Adam had gone out of their way to spend time with her daughter. She had also been given an opportunity to see an entirely different side of this complex woman. Micah never got cross with Regina, even when she had accidently hit her with the ball instead of getting it anywhere near the hoop. Olivia smiled as she replayed the last couple of hours in her head. Micah had just laughed and made it a point to take a step away each time Regina tried shooting the ball. She was so caught up in her musings that she didn't hear Micah come up.

"Um, Olivia, you know how you want me to be honest and share if I am having a problem?"

Olivia just nodded, unsure where this was going.

"Well, the thing is, my hip and knee are really hurting." Micah hated admitting it, but she was really having a hard time. She needed to get inside and get off her leg.

Touched by the admission, Olivia pushed down the impulse to scold the stubborn woman for continuing to play while she was in pain. She was coming to realize that she couldn't force Micah to stop pushing herself. All she could do was try to make sure she took care of herself afterwards, and of course, be there to help.

"Go ahead and go upstairs, Sweetheart. I'll make sure Regina gets ready for bed."

Micah nodded silently, grateful for the respite. Turning to leave, she couldn't hide the obvious limp from Olivia's observant gaze.

Olivia went up to check on her daughter. Surprisingly, she was already in bed after taking a quick shower. The two of them had a nice mother-daughter chat, with Regina excitedly babbling about how cool her basketball practice had been. Olivia kissed her goodnight before heading for the door.

"Good night, Sweetie." She was about to turn out the light and close the door when Regina spoke up.

"Mom, I'm really glad Micah is back."

"Me too, Regina." Olivia couldn't agree more.

"Will she be coming around more?"

"Yes, hopefully a lot more. Is that okay with you?" Olivia asked, smiling gently at her daughter's curiosity.

"Absolutely! I missed her a lot." Regina practically bounced out from under the covers.

"And, I know you missed her, too," Regina spoke thoughtfully, her young face reflecting a tiny hint of the intuitive young woman she was becoming. "I like it better when she's here, you're happier too."

"So you're okay with us, you know, spending time together?" Olivia asked quietly, unsure if her daughter would completely understand what dating Micah meant.

"You mean like girlfriends?" Regina asked, her face screwing up in that familiar pre-teen look that meant they were starting to talk about something icky.

"Yes, like that."

"Oh, mom...that would be great. Then Micah would be here all the time, right?" Regina exclaimed, bouncing back into her normal mode.

"Let's see, okay? But, right now, it's time for you to go to bed. I love you, Regina."

"Love you too, mom. Tell Micah I said goodnight."

Olivia closed the door and stood there for a moment, her forehead pressed against the cool wood. At that moment in time, she couldn't have been happier. She knew that Regina loved having Micah around, but now she knew that Regina accepted the idea of the two of them as a couple.

Entering the room, she found Micah sprawled out in a chair, waiting for her. She looked apprehensive when Olivia entered. She did not like seeing that look on Micah's face. She would have preferred cocky Micah to the one looking at her right now.

"Oh, don't worry, Sweetheart. I'm not going to scold you for getting carried away while having fun. I am going to draw you a hot bath, though." Micah's sigh of relief urged Olivia on. She decided to make her concession on one condition, just because she wanted to see if she could.

"But, you have to come into work with me tomorrow. I have been out of the office so much that I've missed seeing you. Maybe you could help me get everything caught up, poor Amanda has been doing double duty trying to keep up with me. We could ride in together and have lunch as well?"

"Fine." Micah agreed to the terms with a groan. She hated mornings...and she hated early mornings even more.

Olivia filled the deep tub with hot water, poured sandalwood scented bath oils into the steaming water, then went back to the bedroom to check on Micah. She had already undressed and stolen one of Olivia's silk robes.

"You don't mind, do you?" Micah asked, running her hands along the cool silk.

"Not at all," Olivia murmured.

Leading Micah into the bathroom, Olivia reached around her waist from behind, quickly untying the robe before Micah could even think about what she was doing. Sweeping the robe off Micah's well-defined shoulders, Olivia let it fall to the floor beneath them, a dark pool of cool silk laying between them on the smooth marble surface. She tried not to stare because she knew it made the younger woman uncomfortable, but it was incredibly difficult.

Micah was gorgeous. The unfinished tattoo that travelled across her back twisted along one hip before twisting back on itself again across her thigh.

"This is so beautiful," Olivia murmured, running her fingertips along the bold lines. She leaned in to kiss Micah's shoulder, her breath quickening at the touch of warm skin against her lips.

"Thank you." Micah's inner wars raged even as she stood there, feeling the hot trail of Olivia's fingertips trace the outline of her tattoo. She didn't think Olivia knew how sensitive the inked skin was. She wanted Olivia's touch. She craved it. Her body ached with desire every time Olivia laid hands on her. She was okay with Olivia exploring the lines of her tattoo, but she was dirty and tired and in a lot of pain and she just wanted a bath. When she had felt Olivia's breath on her skin, her hands exploring her back and then her hips, she should have moved away. When Olivia's lips touched her bare skin, a sharp spike of desire flashed through her that was so intense, it made her tremble with need.

"But not as beautiful as you." Olivia's lips found that spot at the base of her neck that made her crazy.

"Stop. Please, Olivia. You promised, remember?" Letting Olivia make love to her meant that Micah would have to lay aside her last bit of hard-earned armor. That armor had kept her sane, had saved her when she was at her most self-destructive. Micah knew it would break her if she let Olivia completely past her guard and it became too much for the other woman. Or, worse yet, those blue eyes would look at her with pity or even loathing. That, most of all, would kill her.

"May I join you in the bath, at least?" Olivia's voice poured over her skin like warm honey.

"Olivia, I can't, I'm sorry," Micah choked out, her voice thick with regret. She stepped away, feeling the loss of Olivia's presence like it was a part of her. It hurt, a lot, but she knew what would happen if they kept on like this.

She left Olivia standing in the middle of the room, staring at her back as she slipped into the hot bath alone.

"I'm sorry, too," Olivia stated flatly, leaving the bathroom before she said something she would regret. Every time she thought they were getting somewhere, Micah shut down, closing her out. *Control, it's all about control.* That was what Adam had told her. If he was

251

right, she had the key; she just needed to know how to unlock the right door.

Micah curled up in the tub, unable to enjoy the scented water that Olivia had so lovingly prepared for her. Her misery was overwhelming. She knew she was losing it. This relationship with Olivia was almost too intense. How many times could she push Olivia away before she gave up on her? Invisible tendrils of anger and self-loathing rose up in her, much like the steam curling around her half-submerged body, threatening to choke her with its toxicity. Unlike the steam, though, there was nowhere for it to go.

Micah could feel the pressure mounting inside of her rising to dangerous levels. Olivia kept pushing, always pushing for something she was trying to give. She had told Olivia this afternoon that she needed time, and she had thought Olivia had understood that. Especially after her apology.

Micah climbed out of the tub to make a phone call. She couldn't relax anyways and was wasting her time trying. She had upset Olivia, and she didn't know what to do about that either. Micah was doubly frustrated; this evening certainly wasn't going as she had planned. She dried her hands off before grabbing her phone then hit number four on her speed dial. Idly, she wondered how many people kept their tattoo artist on speed dial.

"Hey Cassandra, it's Micah, I really need some work done." After listening for a minute to the voice on the other end, Micah sighed in relief.

"Friday at 8pm. Thanks. I really need this. Yeah, I'll be okay until then. Don't worry."

Micah couldn't do anything else tonight; she would have to wait until Friday. She went out into the bedroom to talk to Olivia, only to find the room empty. Olivia must have gone back downstairs to do some work. Evidently, asking Olivia to back down meant backing all the way down. Micah's mood was too volatile tonight; she tossed disappointment out of her heart and let anger reign. *Fine. Two can play at that game.*

The muscles in Micah's jaw worked hard, her jaw clenching so tightly her teeth hurt. She couldn't cry now, not when Olivia might walk through that door any minute. Her throat felt tight, and it hurt to swallow. A sharp pain in her chest rapidly overshadowed the throbbing pain in her leg, making the injury inconsequential. Ignoring it all, Micah threw on a change of clothes and grabbed her laptop bag. She couldn't do this tonight. She needed to get some control back. On her own terms, come hell or high water.

Olivia didn't know Micah had left the bathroom, let alone the house until she heard the truck start and pull out of her driveway.

Goddammit, Micah! Olivia's hand clenched and twisted in her robe, her knuckles white against the silk gathered at her throat. She couldn't even go after her since she didn't have a sitter tonight. Micah knew that, too.

Why am I blaming her? It's my fault. I promised not to push tonight and that's exactly what I did.

***

Micah set her alarm for zero-dark-thirty. She knew she had to be up and out of the apartment as early as possible just in case Olivia decided to show up. At 5:30am, Micah was up, dressed, and ready to go. She grabbed her messenger bag and her bike, then quietly left the apartment so she wouldn't wake up Jonathan.

Micah rolled up to the coffeehouse just before dawn, the night sky lightening into the dull grey of early morning while she rode. Foregoing her usual Coke, she ordered a double latte, intending on nursing it until it was time to head across the street.

She yawned, her jaws cracking in opposition to the early hour. She hadn't slept very well last night, and running away again had made Micah re-evaluate her motives. That re-evaluation had stolen her sleep along with the solace it offered. *Risks and Rewards*. The tattoo on her arm should burn with her hypocrisy. She had told Olivia what it meant to her, even while lying to herself. Any risk was worth the right reward. Anything worth having was worth a fight. Her grandmother had told her that, and she had shamefully forgotten.

Micah had nothing else to do but wait, so she pulled out her laptop. Maybe she could write something, since her art seemed to be suffering again. Pulling up a blank document, she tapped her fingers lightly against the keys, her thoughts wandering around in her head, trying to find her creativity. Unfortunately, her thoughts kept circling back to last night.

She took another sip of her coffee then decided to try an old trick she knew that helped break writer's block. As an artist, Micah had used this concept many times, letting the graphite or pencil travel across the paper unimpeded by thought or vision. Clearing her mind, she let her eyes lose focus, turning her thoughts inward. Her fingers travelled along the keyboard, typing without thinking.

It is an unfortunate truth that people are destined to repeat the same patterns in their life over and over again, unless something happens to wake you up, makes you open your eyes to new possibilities. It is also true that it is easier to see these patterns in others, while remaining blind to your own.

Micah read her paragraph.

Holy crap. Where did that come from?

Micah had read dozens of stories that involved characters so wrapped up in themselves, it took something major in their lives to shake them up, to make them re-evaluate their past choices, forcing them to make a conscious decision to change. It was almost embarrassing that she had fallen into the same trap.

She was hurting Olivia, and in doing so, she was hurting herself and their relationship. It was ironic. Olivia kept pushing her, but at least it was because she was trying to get closer. Every time Olivia got closer, Micah had pushed back, caught up in her own issues. If they continued the way they were going, there would be no relationship to worry about. Micah shook her head. It was a difficult pill to swallow, discovering that you have been your own worst enemy.

Closing her laptop, Micah looked out the window. The early morning light had found its way back into the city, chasing the shadows away for another day. It was time for her to make a conscious decision to change. This was her story; it was up to her to decide if it was to have a happy ending.

Chapter Twenty-One

Olivia had a bad night. After calling and texting her errant lover to no avail, she had finally given up and gone to bed. She might as well have given up on sleeping, however, since she spent most of the night tossing and turning and staring up at the ceiling. More than once she questioned the volatility of her emotions and wondered what Micah saw in her. This game of push me-pull me was getting tiring and yet she couldn't seem to stop making stupid mistakes.

Guilt ridden and pissed at herself, she hadn't been able to bring herself to call Micah this morning, but a quick text to Jonathan had at least stilled her fears that Micah had not run off to her cabin again. That news had given her hope. She had Robert swing by in the morning, only to find out that Micah had gotten up early and left with her bike before Jonathan woke up. All she could do was wait and see what might happen, and that did not sit well with her at all.

Olivia had barely settled in behind her desk when a soft noise at her right shoulder intruded on her thoughts. The invigorating smell of good coffee hit her nose at the same time. Looking up to see who would enter her office unannounced, let alone bring her coffee, Olivia fell into a maelstrom of confusing and conflicting emotions that stormed across her heart. Feelings of relief and irritation battled for dominance.

Micah stood in front of her, her mouth set in a lopsided grin as she carefully set the steaming cup down in front of Olivia. A troubling sense of deja-vu hit Olivia hard. Micah was dressed in her signature cargo shorts and biking shirt, the form-fitting fabric displayed familiar lines, much like that first day.

Setting down her pen, Olivia slowly leaned back in her chair and glared at Micah. *How dare she avoid me like that? Micah hated mornings, everyone knew that. She had purposefully left her apartment early enough to avoid me, so what is she doing here now?*

She had been worried, very worried, and it didn't help her temper at all that she had been left alone all night to do nothing but think about their relationship.

She had told Micah she loved her, but the reality of what that meant didn't sink in until she heard the squeal of truck tires when Micah gunned it out of her driveway. The pain in her heart was a physical thing that made her want to collapse right there on the sidewalk. It took everything she had to turn her back on the receding taillights and go back inside. She had Regina to think about. She couldn't just run out of the house any old time and leave her alone.

Olivia had unwillingly dragged herself back up the stairs towards her bedroom. It used to be her refuge, but now it seemed to be lacking despite its opulence. The huge bed was cold and lonely without Micah's warm form disturbing the shape of her coverlets. Wandering into the bathroom, she had found the bath still full from when she had drawn it earlier. Running her fingers through the warm, scented liquid, she found it hadn't had time to cool yet. Plunging her bare arm into the warmth, she pulled the plug. The sound of the water as it drained out of the tub had been discomforting.

Olivia couldn't sleep in her bed alone. She ended up sleeping in the guestroom, unable to endure returning to a bed she only wanted to share with Micah.

The awkward silence stretched out between them long enough to make Micah second guess her decision to come in.

"What are you doing here?" Olivia's voice sounded as cold and hard as iron.

Well, that was something, Micah thought. Direct and to the point as always. She knew she had been shitty, leaving like that, but she planned to fix that today, if Olivia would let her.

"Showing up for work."

"No, you are not." Olivia's tone was flat, absolute. Unfortunately for Olivia, Micah wasn't backing down either.

"I beg to differ, I'm here and ready to work, so give me something to do."

Two very different faces suddenly held very similar expressions. Micah felt her jaw tighten, the muscles working along her jaw line as she tried to hold her tongue.

She had hoped casual would work. She needed it to work since she wasn't in the mood to fight anymore. She was hoping they could just start fresh this morning; the coffee and offer to work was her way of apologizing for last night. *Unfortunately,* she thought ruefully, *things rarely stayed casual between them.*

Olivia wasn't going for the "let's pretend nothing happened last night" ploy that Micah was trying to throw at her.

"I don't want you here right now." Olivia spoke up first, perhaps unwisely. Micah stilled, like a snake waiting to strike. Her grin faded. The corners of her mouth reset themselves, her full lips becoming stern and flat. The originally playful challenge in her eyes faded beneath gathered brows. A harsh expression extinguished the golden sparks their argument had generated, as if all the oxygen had been sucked out of the room, taking the prospect of flames with it.

"Are you sure about that? Think very carefully." The warning tone in her voice brought Olivia up short. Slowly, comprehension dawned on her as she replayed her words in her head.

Micah had won, yet she found no solace in that knowledge. Olivia looked dumbstruck for a moment. Caught off guard, Micah had witnessed a rare and fleeting view into Olivia's soul during that one raw, exposed moment. *Is it possible that Olivia is as scared and off balance as I am?*

"Fine, go pick up a packet from here," Olivia relented. She scribbled an address on a Post-it and handed it to Micah.

"As my lady commands," Micah drawled, bowing chivalrously before turning on her heal, striding out of Olivia's office.

Olivia waited until Micah disappeared from sight before bowing her head, hiding her face in her hands. *Micah was so, so...*she searched her mind for the right word: *exasperating. Yes, that was the right word.* Her behavior was so damned confusing. Why would she avoid her all night just to show up this morning expecting to work as if nothing had happened? It was so damn hard sometimes, trying to keep up with her moods.

Shaking her head, Olivia gave up trying to figure out what was going on and focused back on her work. It was a welcome distraction. The briefs she read were organized, logical, and held none of the chaos her relationship with Micah did.

Thirty minutes later Micah walked back in, her cheeks flushed red from the brisk morning air, and handed Olivia an envelope. Her scent greeted Olivia, fresh and spicy, and she found herself inhaling greedily. She smelled so good, so alive and vibrant. Her personality was almost too big for the somber walls of Olivia's office.

Before Micah could even sit down, Olivia had another address ready for her. Micah didn't complain, she just looked at the address and left with a bow of her head and her infamous smirk in place. She sent Micah out on two more runs before lunch time. Honestly, Olivia wasn't sure if she was trying to punish Micah or if she was just trying to avoid their earlier confrontation.

Either way, her questionable motives backfired on her as she watched Micah return with another package, her limp even more pronounced as she strode into the room. She tried to hide it, but a barely concealed wince as she sat down in front of Olivia's desk gave her away.

Stupid, stupid woman, Olivia berated herself. She knew Micah rarely admitted weakness. She also knew that she would keep working through pain even if she ultimately injured herself. Olivia had let her pride and anger fuel her behavior this morning. There was no doubt now. She was punishing Micah for last night, and Micah, for some inexplicable reason, was letting her.

"Micah, take a break, okay? It's almost time for lunch, so why don't you stretch out on the couch for a while." She tried to keep her voice light and practical, while on the inside she was mentally kicking herself for being an ass.

Micah nodded and headed for the couch. Stretching out her long legs in front of her, she relaxed into the overstuffed cushions. Her sore hip was screaming for attention after this morning's exertion. Glancing at Olivia behind her desk, she waited a moment before putting in her earbuds and laying down. Olivia didn't look up. She was busy at her computer, the sounds of the keyboard clicking rapidly beneath her fingertips. Micah closed her eyes, evidently content to wait until Olivia called for her again.

Olivia wasn't ignoring Micah—she was stalling. First, she ordered lunch online for the both of them, then she checked her schedule to make sure she wasn't going to be interrupted for a while. She looked up from her computer. Micah was stretched out on the couch, her head resting on the padded arm.

Subtle hints suggested Micah wasn't as relaxed as she was letting on. A slight tensing around the lips and eyes and a certain stiffness in her posture gave away how much pain she was actually in. A wave of guilt hit her hard and fast, her stomach clenching in response to the imaginary blow. She had been such a royal bitch this morning.

She left her office for a moment to talk with Amanda, not wanting to disturb Micah's rest.

"Amanda, I just ordered lunch. Do you think you can run out and get it for us?" She ignored Amanda's shocked expression. That expression quickly turned sly, containing more understanding than Olivia was comfortable with.

"Sure, Olivia. Where did you order from?"

***

Micah opened her eyes when she felt the cushion beneath her thigh dip. Olivia sat down next to her, balancing precariously on the edge of the couch. She pulled out her earbuds, shifting over slightly so Olivia could sit on the cushion without risking falling off the edge.

"I ordered lunch," Olivia said.

"Okay?" Olivia had the oddest expression on her face, one that Micah couldn't easily decipher. If she had to guess, she would say self-conscious, an expression totally at odds with the power suit she was wearing.

"It has, ah, come to my attention that I have been behaving deplorably, and I want to apologize." The unexpected confession left Micah searching Olivia's face closely. Her makeup was good, but it didn't hide the telltale signs of a woman trying not to cry.

What the hell?

Olivia grabbed Micah's hand, kissing the palm before bringing her hand up to her face. Micah felt moisture greet her palm.

"We are not over; I am not letting you go. Not when I finally got you back," Olivia choked out, almost a sob. Olivia's eyes were wide, practically wild with fear.

Micah's heart started to gallop at a dangerous pace. This was not what she expected. She couldn't even fathom what was going on in her lover's mind to bring her to this conclusion.

"Oh, Olivia of course we aren't. I love you, you know that." She paused for a moment, gently removing her hand from Olivia's grasp. Using just her fingertips, she brought Olivia's face up so she could look into her eyes. Micah had seen Olivia's eyes change with emotion, brightest blue with anger, dark with passion, and now, they were a dark blue-grey of a violent summer storm.

Whatever emotions ruled that color was purely for and because of her.

"You do know that, right?" Micah's voice was gentle, questioning. When Olivia didn't answer right away, her heart sped faster, fueled by a sudden rush of fear-driven adrenaline. A sick feeling deep down in the pit of her stomach twisted itself around her gut, leaving Micah feeling dizzy and lightheaded. The silence ran out between them to the time of her beating heart, until a jagged, guttural noise that spoke of base fear and desolation broke through.

"You left. You left, Micah, and then you were gone this morning," Olivia choked out. Taking in a ragged breath, Olivia continued in a mere whisper, "You were gone, and wouldn't answer your phone. All I could think of was that damn knife, that you might be somewhere, hurt." All of her bottled up anguish poured out of her at once. Her body went limp, exhausted from the effort. Micah caught her in her arms, gathering the woman she loved in a tight embrace.

"No, baby, no... I didn't mean to make you worry." Micah's heart was breaking...she didn't know, she hadn't thought. How could she have been so careless?

"I'll be honest, Love. I was just scared." The excuse sounded pat, even to her own ears. How could she explain her insecurities to Olivia? Her admission led to the one question she dreaded most, the one she had been trying to avoid.

"What are you afraid of?"

Micah looked away. *Such an easy question to ask, but a much more difficult one to answer.*

A muffled thump interrupted their conversation. Both women turned their heads at the same time and stared at the closed door. Amanda must have returned with their food. Micah smiled in nervous relief at Amanda's overly loud entrance, a smile that widened into a sympathetic grin when she noticed Olivia's similar expression.

Micah's stomach growled. The noise was a much needed and unexpected source of comic relief, and if the laughter was a bit constrained or forced, both women chose to ignore it.

"Uh, can we discuss this later?"

"Will you actually talk to me?" For once, there was no challenge in her question, only a need for reassurance.

"Yes, I promise." Somehow, they had arrived at the place Micah had been trying to get to all day.

"Tonight then." Olivia gathered herself together, dabbing her face gingerly with a tissue before standing up. "I need to freshen up, Micah. Do you think you could get our lunch from Amanda?"

"Of course, Olivia," Micah replied, waiting for Olivia to vanish into the bathroom before heading for the office door. *It was one thing to fall apart in front of the woman you loved, quite another to let your staff see you red eyed and puffy from crying.*

***

After a quick lunch, Micah sat on the couch for a good thirty minutes before the forced inactivity started getting to her. She pulled out her notebook, intending to get some work done, but she just couldn't concentrate. Nervous energy ate at her patience, demanding more activity than she could accomplish sitting on a couch.

"Come on, Olivia you have got to have something for me to do," Micah pleaded.

"No, just sit there and be quiet."

Micah groaned. Olivia had extracted a promise from her during lunch. She wanted Micah to rest and didn't trust her to stay off her hip if left to her own devices. At least, that was Olivia's excuse. Micah had an idea that Olivia was motivated by personal greed, more than anything else. She wanted Micah there, with her. If the amount of times Olivia looked up from her desk were proof of her hypothesis, Micah would have to bet she was spot on. Olivia looked up quite often.

Another hour passed, and Micah was getting quite impatient. "Seriously, anything?" she asked when she caught Olivia looking up at her again.

"Nothing at all."

Micah swore she saw Olivia smirk. She didn't have to wonder where she learned that from. This was a game, she realized. Olivia was enjoying screwing with her. The friendly banter was refreshing, natural. *Comfortable.*

"Come on, I'm sorry I left last night." *Maybe petulance would work.* Micah doubted it, but she thought she would try.

"I know that already, but you can still sit there. Think of it as a time out." Olivia's droll response as she looked up at Micah over the top of her reading glasses gave Micah the image of Olivia as a schoolteacher scolding her in class. Micah laughed, earning her another scolding look. Micah laughed harder.

A few minutes later, she found herself staring at the ceiling, counting the dots on the ceiling tiles.

"For how long?" she asked again. This time she just wanted to annoy Olivia, interrupting her work for fun. Idly, she wondered if she could still get a pencil to stick in the tiles, like she used to do in high school.

"Until five." This time, Olivia didn't look up from her work.

"Aw man, fine." Micah sat back, resigned to her fate. She pulled out her drawing pad and pencils, contemplated the ceiling and her pencils, then decided against her decidedly adolescent temptation. Besides, her drawing pencils were expensive.

She pulled her MP3 player out next. It had a lot more music on it than her phone. Tucking her earbuds in, she found a good song and turned it up. Humming to the music, she leaned against the arm of her couch, bringing her knees up to use as a convenient easel.

She became lost in the music and her art, tuning out Olivia, the office, and everything else around her completely.

***

It took Olivia a while, but eventually she realized that it had gotten overly quiet. She looked up from her work to discover that Micah had gotten lost in her own little world. *Ah, so that's why she hasn't complained in a while*, she thought. Their little game of one-upmanship had been fun when she was winning. Now, Micah was winning by being able to ignore her, and that was unacceptable. Resting her pen on the desk, Olivia resolved to change that right away. Olivia grinned wickedly at her unsuspecting target. Micah challenged her like no one else would dare, and it fascinated her. The woman sitting and ignoring her so studiously somehow made her behave in ways that were completely out of character. She found that she liked the changes more than she thought she would.

***

Micah wasn't as preoccupied as Olivia thought. When she saw Olivia approaching her, she slid a quick glance over towards the door, making sure it was still closed. *Good.*

When Olivia's shadow fell across her art pad, Micah looked up, feigning innocence and surprise. She tucked the art pad next to her, moving it out of the reach of Olivia's grasp. When Olivia leaned forward to take away her player, Micah lunged forward, grasping Olivia's hips and dragging the lawyer onto her lap. The unexpected movement earned her a gratifying gasp from Olivia. Yanking her earbuds out with one hand, she kept the other firmly around Olivia's waist.

Smiling evilly, Micah pulled Olivia closer until their lips were almost touching. She could feel Olivia's hot breath whispering across her skin. Olivia's lips parted, waiting for the kiss.

Not yet. Not yet. The silent whisper skittered across Micah's brain. She wanted Olivia to come to her, to bridge that small gap between them. She could tell that Olivia was fighting it, fighting her, and she was enjoying the battle of wills between them. She waited, completely tuned in to the other woman's body language. A simple shift, a softening in her spine gave Olivia away. That was all Micah needed, she would give this gift to her lover: the illusion of winning this round between them.

"You win, now kiss me," Micah whispered against the softness of Olivia's lips. Olivia didn't have to be told twice. Their lips met, tasting, teasing, until Olivia let her tongue slip between her lips, seeking access to Micah's mouth. Olivia pulled back first.

"What did I win?"

"Me, if you want." The unexpected answer left Olivia breathless. So did Micah's mouth, which had found new things to explore, kissing along Olivia's neck. Olivia moaned softly when Micah's lips found the soft hollow above her collarbone, her pulse beating rapidly in response to the insistent nuzzling. This was threatening to get out of hand quickly.

"Oh, I definitely want—but we can't do this right now." Olivia threaded her fingers through Micah's hair, encouraging her to pull back when what she really wanted was just the opposite. Olivia's grip tightened, sending sparks of sharp pain through her scalp.

"Gods, Olivia, don't do that. Not if you ever want to get off this couch." Micah exhaled, trying to control herself. She managed to catch Olivia's lips again, kissing her deeply before letting Olivia pull her away again.

"Come home with me tonight?" Olivia asked when she could breathe again, then added, "I'm not asking you to come over just to talk. I'm asking you to stay the night with me."

Micah held her breath, searching her heart and choosing her desires. Olivia's offer held such promise, but they had to make it through their talk first. The night could go so many ways, she could either run again or honor the promise she had made to herself early this morning.

"Okay. I just need to ask Jonathan if he'll take my bike home tonight." Disentangling herself from Olivia, Micah reached for her phone to text Jonathan. Before she could, her phone vibrated suddenly in her hand. Micah's sudden curse exploded in the air, startling Olivia. Grimacing, Micah answered the phone with a level of hostility in her voice that Olivia had never heard before.

"Yeah, what?" Micah leveled a rueful look at Olivia. It was her office, and she shouldn't have to put up with this. The only reason she answered at all was because she knew they would keep calling until she did. Gesturing apologetically, she wandered into the bathroom. She hoped Olivia wouldn't mind her taking over like that, but there was a good chance it was about to get loud.

"No, I haven't." *Jesus, the same old shit again.* She listened impatiently for a while before interrupting the tirade. "No, absolutely not!"

She had heard enough. There was really no reason to continue this conversation.

"That's enough, okay? I won't hear another word on this," Micah practically spat out. "Oh, and mom? Tell Dad thanks, I really loved having surgery because of him. Yeah, and to you, too."

Micah hung up abruptly and emerged from the bathroom agitated and unable to stand still. She reminded Olivia of one of those wild cats she had seen at the zoo. The big cat had paced restlessly in front of the enclosure, back and forth, its tail thrashing angrily at being stuck in an enclosed space.

"Olivia, I need some air," Micah announced suddenly. She practically vibrated with the need to do something.

Briefly, Olivia entertained the idea of finding her another run for her to do, but she didn't think that was what Micah needed. As much as she wanted to find out what was going on, Olivia held her tongue. Tonight was too important for them. If Micah's family ruined it with that damnable phone call, they would have hell to pay from her. Olivia's dislike of Micah's family dialed up another notch.

"Okay. Will you be back by the time we are supposed to leave or do you want me to pick you up?" The question was purposefully worded. She wanted Micah to know without a doubt that, one way or the other, she wanted her home with her tonight.

"No, um, I don't know. You know what; just meet me at the apartment...if that's okay?" Micah replied. Her thoughts were scattered all over the place. "I'm not going anywhere; I just can't be here right now."

She looked down at her hands. "Please, Olivia, I just need to blow off some steam."

Olivia exhaled in relief; she had thought Micah was cancelling on her. "What are you going to do?"

"I'm just going to ride my bike for a while then drop by the apartment to get cleaned up."

"Okay, Sweetheart, be safe. I can come get you after work, say around five?"

"I will. Five it is."

***

Micah was so pissed. She hadn't talked to her parents in almost a year and that was by choice. Now, her mom was calling her to see if she was still, as she put it, "continuing with that nonsense about being a lesbian."

Her mother had a lot of nerve, offering to let her come home for her own birthday on Sunday if she would apologize to her father and deny who she was. What was she supposed to do, formally renounce her sexual orientation in the living room while the congregation raised their arms and sung hallelujahs? Well, that was never going to happen. She had Olivia and her friends and that was enough family for her.

Micah felt a little guilty for lying to Olivia. She didn't actually go for a bike ride after leaving, instead, she went straight to her apartment. She placated herself with the idea that it was only a half lie; she didn't say how long she was going to ride her bike and she did ride home. In her present mood, she would be dangerous out on the streets. She needed a better way to burn off all that negative energy and a bike ride simply wasn't going to do it. She had her appointment with Cassandra but that wasn't until tomorrow; she hoped the anticipation would hold her until then. There was one thing she could do that might help.

Micah grabbed her gloves and headed for the basement gym. Hitting the heavy bag sounded like just the thing to keep her mind off her family. After her workout, Micah took a quick shower to clean up. It really surprised her that the always-impeccable attorney seemed to have no issue with Micah when she was filthy and sweaty. She always went out of her way to let Micah know she was beautiful, with no reservations or conditions attached to her opinion. *Unlike my parents, who used every opportunity to tear me down.*

Micah wanted to scream in frustration. Her parents kept intruding on her thoughts when all she wanted to do was focus on tonight. She had enough to think about without them adding their own practiced brand of homophobia to the mix.

After her shower, she rummaged around in her closet for a while, trying to find something to wear tonight. Nothing seemed appropriate. Flipping through the hangers, her hand brushed against soft leather. Her leathers hung in the back of the closet, black, sleek, and begging to be touched. She pulled them out, laying the pants and vest out on the bed.

She knew it might seem an odd thing to do, but she went ahead and put on her leather pants. She always felt better when she wore them. They gave her a sense of security and control, and after her mom calling her, she needed that sense of control back. Besides, she looked good in her leather pants, thanks to all those hours spent on the bike and in the gym. She pulled on her heavy boots and looked at herself in the mirror.

Oh yeah, she looked good. After all the teasing and forced inactivity today, maybe she should show up like this, just to return the favor. The idea had merit, especially since she had promised herself that she would be more open and honest with Olivia. Well, Olivia hadn't met this Micah yet, maybe it was time to test the waters.

She pulled off her tank top and found her black lace bra, the one that didn't show under her leather vest. The vest went on next, sliding intimately across her shoulders, butter-soft and unrelieved in absolute black. The only break from the solid black was the steel buckles on her boots and the buckle at her waist. She ran her hands along the smooth leather, admiring how it felt, how it made her feel.

The past tumbled free from the locks she had put on it, throwing her back to the first time she had put leather on.

It wasn't long after Jon had found her, broken and bruised, and brought her home with him. She had locked herself in her room, refusing to go out, refusing to do anything at all, until Jon had it out with her. She was going out with them to the club, no excuses accepted. He had been adamant, even going so far as to start digging around in his own closet for something nice for her to wear. He threw a pair of leather pants and a matching black shirt on her bed, then gave her ten minutes to meet him in the living room. Micah didn't bother asking where they came from, it didn't matter. Not much did.

When she showed up at the club in her unrelieved black, the leather outfit felt like armor against her skin, protecting her from prying eyes and hiding her scars from the world. Jonathan introduced her to a friend of his. Peter had almost fainted at the sight of her. He insisted that she come by his shop to get measured for a custom set of leathers. It took her a week to find the energy to get out of the apartment and follow up on that offer, and another two weeks before he called her back in for a final fitting. When she put on the outfit he had made for her, she felt like she had come home.

The workmanship was exquisite. She had offered to pay him, but he had refused to accept her money. "Just be my model, Micah…you will more than pay for this one outfit by showing up in it at the club," he had told her, offering homage to her transformation.

Needless to say, her next trip to the bar created new opportunities for her, ones that satisfied her needs and woke something up in her that she had kept hidden from everyone, including herself, for a very long time.

Micah owed a lot to Peter. He had recognized a kindred spirit in Micah, and he wasn't shy about explaining how things worked at the club. Looking at herself now, she had to admit he had been right. The cut of the vest accentuated her muscular frame, without completely sacrificing her more feminine attributes. The lazy smirk everyone was so familiar with fit her to a tee. The attitude and the outfit were a matching set. She slicked back her hair, her high cheekbones and strong jawline creating an edgy profile that defied gender boundaries.

There was something about wearing her leathers that made her feel powerful, and that kind of power had its own appeal. She missed how this felt, it wouldn't hurt to soak up the attitude for a while. What harm would it cause to keep them on for a while?

Chapter Twenty-Two

Shortly after Micah left, Amanda knocked on Olivia's door. She stood in the doorway, waiting for permission to enter. "I'm sorry to interrupt, Olivia, but I had a quick question for you, one that involves Micah."

"Really? Do come in, Amanda." Olivia's voice sounded cool and level and held none of the real concern she was feeling inside.

"Did you know Micah's birthday is Sunday?"

"Yes, Adam told me the other day," Olivia answered, relaxing instantly when Amanda mentioned Micah's birthday.

"Well, she is forbidding any of us from doing anything for her."

"When you say us, I assume you mean yourself and Jonathan?" she asked, wondering when Jonathan was planning to tell her that Micah's birthday was this weekend.

"Yes, she doesn't want anybody to make a big deal of it, and we really wanted to do something for her, and I thought you might like to know. Just in case," Amanda answered almost too carefully. Evidently, Amanda saw her as someone with a little bit more influence than her friends. Olivia almost laughed aloud. No one really influenced Micah, not really, and definitely not if she didn't want them to.

"I see, and you think there is something I might be able to do about it?" Olivia asked, watching Amanda's reaction carefully. She saw relief and anticipation, but not an ounce of judgment or discomfort.

"Yes, I, um… we thought you might know where Micah would be this weekend." Amanda did stutter over that bit, especially when Olivia's eyebrows started to climb up her forehead.

"I'll take care of it," Olivia replied drolly.

"Okay, just let us know. We really want to spend it with her."

"Of course," Olivia replied, already making plans in her head. "Amanda, do I have any meetings scheduled tomorrow?"

"Nothing that can't be moved to next week."

"Not a client?" Olivia gave her a sharp look.

"No. Mostly in house stuff."

Olivia nodded. "Good enough. I'm going to work from home tomorrow. You can reach me by cell if you need anything."

A quick glance up revealed Amanda still standing in her doorway. "Don't worry, I will let you know what I come up with."

When Amanda hesitated a second too long, she shooed her from her doorway. She had a lot to do before Sunday.

"Go, Amanda, I've got work to do, and so do you."

"Yes, Olivia," Amanda said, then disappeared from the doorway.

***

Micah considered changing out of her leathers and getting ready for Olivia to come pick her up, but she was reluctant to remove the black leather just yet. She still had an hour left before Olivia was due to come by. That was an hour she could relax and soak up the attitude that came with wearing her leathers, an attitude that was actually a big part of who she was, and someone that Olivia had not met yet. She briefly wondered how Olivia would react if she showed up at work dressed like this, then dismissed that fantasy. Casting one more glance at herself in the mirror, Micah sighed and turned away.

Olivia was a highly regarded attorney, a strong woman and powerful in her own right. That in itself was a turn on for Micah, but not for the reasons some people would think. Olivia challenged her, and Micah's dominant heart found that fascinating. She hadn't worn her leathers or gone to the club since that day she walked into Olivia's office. She hadn't realized how much she missed wearing them until today, but she didn't miss going out to the club, not really. She couldn't even begin to compare her adventures there with what she had going on with Olivia, but still...

The sound of the doorbell ringing intruded on her thoughts. She spent less than a second deciding whether to ignore the person on the other side, change and answer the door, or just answer the door in her leathers. Then she shrugged. Everyone in the building knew her and how she dressed when she left to go out at night, so it wouldn't be a surprise. If it was someone she didn't know and they got offended, it wouldn't matter because they were disturbing her, and frankly, she didn't give a damn.

The problem was, when she opened the door, neither type of person stood in her doorway.

"Hey, Olivia. You're early."

Olivia turned around. Her mouth hung open for a full ten seconds before she remembered to close it.

Micah stood in the doorway, wearing an outfit that seemed designed to cause Olivia a heart attack. Her high cheekbones were more pronounced with her thick black hair slicked back away from her face. A few tendrils still managed to escape, but that just added to the rakish look. If she hadn't seen Micah's womanly attributes before, she would have had trouble imagining them under the tightly laced leather vest that graced her leanly muscled upper body. A wide leather belt sat low on slim hips covered in supple black leather pants. But that wasn't all. She wore heavy black motorcycle boots, the silver buckles at each ankle winking at her when Micah pushed off from the doorframe.

Micah stepped aside, leaving enough room for Olivia to pass by. Her invitation to enter was a smoky smile and a casual toss of the head that made her shiver. Micah led the way into the living room, her arms swinging easily as she strode across the floor. Olivia's attention fell on leather-wrapped wrists as she followed her into the apartment, then travelled south.

God, that's sexy as hell. Olivia could barely think. Hell, she could barely breathe as Micah stalked into the living room, the black leather outfit matching her stride in its natural aggressiveness.

"You look, ah, different," Olivia stuttered.

"I do?" Micah grinned. Olivia at a loss for words was a rare treat. She couldn't resist teasing.

"Where on earth were you going, dressed like that?" Olivia asked.

"Nowhere, I just felt the need to put this on."

"Hmmm."

Just hmm? She looks like she wants to say a lot more than that.

278

"Why don't you have a seat? I'll just change and we can be on our way," Micah said, turning towards her bedroom.

"No, wait." Olivia held out her hand, stopping Micah with a gesture. "You don't have to change; Regina is with her father until Sunday. Please, join me."

She waited until Micah sat down on the couch next to her before asking her next question. "Can I ask you a question?"

"Yes."

"Are these the leathers that Jonathan was referring to?"

"Yes," Micah replied.

"And, where would you go dressed like that? I mean, normally. If I wasn't here?"

Micah blew out her breath, relieved that Olivia asked a where question rather than a what question. She wasn't sure Olivia was ready to find out what she did when she wore her leathers. Where was a safer question, but not by much.

"The club."

"Ah, I see," Olivia said. "Well, seeing as how we have the whole night to ourselves, why don't you take me to this club? That way you don't have to change. Besides, it would be a shame to waste that outfit."

Olivia eyed Micah's appearance appreciatively. She would be a liar if she said that seeing Micah in the skintight leather wasn't a turn on. She looked absolutely wild, dangerous even, and that made her all the more delicious to look at.

"Are you sure?" The catchphrase made Olivia pause. Micah had used that warning question before, usually when she wanted to make absolutely sure that she understood the importance of what she was saying, or in this case, asking.

"Yes, I want to see this...club?" She also wanted to see Micah in her natural habitat. The elusive young woman had so many facets to her, she was hoping to gain a little more insight into who she really was. Finding Micah dressed this way had spiked her curiosity, and she wanted to learn more about the woman sitting next to her wearing nothing but leather.

What followed in the next few minutes had to be one of the strangest conversations she could ever remember having. Micah in black leather and Olivia still dressed in her power suit, sitting together on a pristine white couch and chatting amicably about innocuous things while an entire world of questions and experiences sat between them.

Olivia took advantage of the conversation to observe Micah. Her initial impression had been on the spot. Micah did look different, but it wasn't just the outfit. Micah appeared more relaxed, more assured of herself. She radiated calm, but not in the passive way of a still pond. No, this calm was deeper, and called up images of a deep well or a dark cave where to remain calm you had to be completely comfortable in the blackest of shadows. This hint of darkness in Micah's persona held an element of danger that Olivia found inexplicably attractive. This surprised her so much she stopped talking and just stared, wondering what that meant.

"Are you okay?" Micah asked. No answer, just a blank stare.

"Olivia?" Micah called out gently, reaching out and stroking the other woman's jaw line. Olivia jumped, and then closed her eyes for a moment before looking directly at Micah.

"Yes, sorry, Micah...where were we?" Olivia asked, an odd catch in her throat.

Micah felt like something had just subtly shifted between them, but she couldn't put her finger on it. "You wanted to go to the club, right?"

Olivia nodded.

"Good enough, just wait for me here, okay? I need to finish getting ready."

Micah left Olivia waiting for her in the living room. After locking the door behind her, Micah stood alone in her room for a moment. *This was going to be fun*, Micah thought. *But, was it going to be fun in a good way or a bad way?* She trusted her instincts, and from the look that Olivia had just given her, she had a feeling she wasn't going to be wrong tonight. She started unbuckling her belt. It was time to find out.

When Micah re-emerged from her bedroom, there was something subtly different in how she carried herself, in how she walked.

Olivia tried to figure out what it could be. All she knew was that watching Micah stalk across the room towards her, looking so dark and dangerous, Olivia knew she wanted her...badly.

Micah held her hand out, barely giving Olivia time to grasp her fingers before pulling her up into a leather-clad embrace. Micah's cologne enveloped Olivia, its spicy scent bringing more of her senses into play.

"Micah?" Olivia whispered hazily. She brought her arms around Micah's neck and attempted to kiss her.

"No." Micah stopped her, her voice firm, commanding.

"Not tonight, Love." Micah looked for any sign of refusal from the older woman. Seeing none, she smiled broadly before tipping her head down, capturing Olivia's mouth with her own. A quick twist of her hips rewarded Micah with the sound of a muffled gasp.

"What?" A bulge tucked along Micah's thigh ground delicately against Olivia's mound. Her arousal skyrocketed and she felt her clit tingle and jump when the leather-wrapped package rubbed intimately against her.

"I told you I had to finish getting ready. This is what I wear to the club. This is who I am." Micah threw her words out like a challenge. "Do you still want to go?"

"Oh, yes." Olivia sounded breathless.

"Good. But we have to have an understanding before we go anywhere. Tonight I'm in charge." There was no room for negotiation, Olivia had to understand that before this evening went any farther.

Olivia clung to Micah's neck, trembling with desire. Without Micah's support, Olivia feared her own legs wouldn't hold her.

"Yes," Olivia murmured in agreement.

Micah shook her head in disappointment. It wasn't enough. Olivia had to feel that one word and everything it meant. It had to caress something deep inside her. Micah held Olivia at bay, not letting her close the millimeter of distance between them.

"Say it, tell me what I want to hear," Micah whispered, her breath caressing Olivia's cheek, their lips so close she could taste her breath. Micah had let her need for control out to play and Olivia had joined her, but it was up to Olivia now to seal the deal. She could always say no.

"Micah, please," she begged. Olivia's body softened against her then, her lips parting slightly.

Micah's nostrils flared. She could smell Olivia's arousal; could feel her need, hot and electric, dance across her skin. It was both intoxicating and dangerous, because it made Micah want to forget this game they were playing. This very real and intense game that she had lived and breathed for so long, but never with such a worthy partner.

"Yes." The word rang out clear and strong between them. Olivia spoke clearly, she didn't beg or cry. Micah exhaled, pride and relief in her eyes. Olivia didn't have to wait long after that to feel Micah's lips on hers.

Chapter Twenty-Three

Olivia was playing along much better than Micah had ever expected, and considering the number of heavy looks and envious stares she was receiving, Olivia was doing quite well. Micah had met more women at the club than she cared to count, some of them had even joined her upstairs, but she had never actually arrived with a woman in tow. Curious looks followed them as she tried to find a relatively private corner to relax in. Olivia followed quietly and close behind her. Her normally assertive manner was absent, dropping away like a shed skin after only a few minutes of quiet observation.

Micah didn't drink, but Olivia did. It was incredibly busy, so she ended up running to the bar rather than wait for one of the overworked barmaids to find them. Unfortunately, her absence emboldened another to approach her lover. The desperate glance she received on her return sent her into a cold rage.

When Olivia launched out of her seat to seek the safety of Micah's embrace, Micah let her, wrapping one protective arm around her shoulders.

"Hello, Micah. Long time no see." The other woman greeted Micah.

"Yeah, so what's going on here?" Micah spoke coldly, her eyes flashing angrily.

"I was chatting with your friend here. She looked like she could use a drink." That comment brought Micah's hackles up; the insult was clear and she didn't care for the other woman's attitude one bit.

"Well, as you can see, she has a drink," Micah replied, pulling Olivia in closer. She was not going to make a scene, not with Olivia watching. She forced her body to relax; studied insolence was always so much more effective than anger. Anger didn't suit her mood tonight, and in this case, it wasn't necessary. The woman was a poacher, no doubt, but she also knew better than to compete with Micah for something she had already laid claim to.

"And as for my friend here, she is mine." Micah bared her teeth into a semblance of a smile. "And has absolutely no desire to chat with you. Isn't that right, Olivia?"

"Yes, Micah," Olivia responded, her voice suspiciously submissive considering the pleased smile she hid against Micah's vest.

After the other woman stalked away, Micah lifted Olivia's jaw with a single fingertip, her thumb tracing the full line of her lower lip.

"That was perfect, Olivia. I'm sorry you were approached that way, I really didn't think anyone would try." Micah complemented Olivia and apologized in the same breath. Her eyes darkened with desire when Olivia closed hers against the caress, her lips parting slightly and nipping gently at Micah's thumb.

"Well, now, aren't you naughty," Micah murmured, a sharp gasp escaping from Olivia when she tightened her embrace, pressing the bulge along her thigh against Olivia's pelvis. A gasp that ended suddenly when Micah's lips captured hers, kissing her possessively. Micah knew they had an audience, she could practically feel the heat on her back from a dozen jealous stares, but she didn't care.

As the kiss continued, Micah felt her arousal rise to almost painful levels. The urge to take Olivia somewhere else, somewhere dark, private, and conveniently close was growing by the minute.

"This was a mistake," she said, ignoring the pounding beat of the music and the scent of liquor and excited bodies flooding the room. "You don't belong in a place like this."

"What?" Olivia gasped; she hadn't quite recovered from Micah's demanding kiss.

"Never mind. It doesn't matter." The gold flecks in Micah's eyes practically glowed, a slow shudder passing through her body that Olivia felt but couldn't see. "We need to go now."

Olivia didn't ask what was wrong, she just took her lead from Micah. Once they were back on the street and away from the noise and crowd, she took one look at Micah's face and pulled out her cellphone.

"I'll call Robert."

***

They arrived at the house in record time. Olivia practically launched out of the back seat, intent on getting inside as soon as possible. Micah slid carefully across the seat; leather on leather wasn't always cooperative. She caught Robert's face reflected in the rear view mirror.

"Thanks, Robert," she said, offering a lopsided smile as she glanced at Olivia's rapidly retreating form.

"You're welcome, Micah," he replied, and then broke out into a wide grin. "You girls have fun now, you hear?"

Olivia had left the front door open. When Micah turned to close the door, she felt Olivia's presence behind her. She was trying to hide her impatience and handling it poorly now that they were in the privacy of her home.

"Come here and kiss me," Micah commanded, enjoying Olivia's internal struggle but loving her too much to torture her for no reason.

She let herself enjoy the hungry kisses, her own appetite flaring awake in response to Olivia's passion. When those soft lips abandoned hers to travel along her neck, nipping delicately at the sensitive skin, Micah shivered delicately. *So good.*

"Stop, Love." Micah saw disappointment flash across Olivia's face when she pulled away. She took Olivia's face in her hands, kissing her gently to reassure her, a mere brushing of their lips that promised more.

"Slow down, we have time right?" She reminded her lover, brushing the pale hair away from even paler blue eyes. Her fingertips traced a path along smooth skin, caressing her cheek and jaw line. It was entirely too convenient that Olivia had ensured their privacy for the entire weekend.

She had thought she was going to have to play nice tonight, but with the house empty, Micah could only think of all the fun they could have. They wouldn't even have to be quiet. That thought manifested in a slow grin that could only be described as devilish at best.

"Let's go to the bedroom," Micah suggested, taking Olivia's hand in hers and leading her towards the stairs. At the landing, Micah turned around, her trademark smirk in place.

"Enjoying the view?" she drawled, drawing Olivia into a firm embrace. It was only one floor up to Olivia's bedroom, but first she had to taste those soft lips again.

Opening her mouth, she snaked her tongue out playfully, inviting Olivia to join her. Olivia moaned, long and low, the sound vibrating along their joined lips. Micah stepped away again, inviting Olivia to go up the flight of stairs first

"Turnabout is fair play, Olivia." Micah's playful grin was entirely at odds with the arousal-fueled endorphin rush coursing through her veins.

Both women were breathing hard when they arrived at the bedroom, but it wasn't from climbing the stairs.

"I need a shower first," Olivia said.

"Go ahead. I'll be waiting right here for you," Micah said, stretching out on the bed and tucking her hands behind her head.

Olivia emerged from the bathroom a few minutes later, naked except for a towel wrapped around her middle, her hair still wet and slicked back from her face. Micah sat straight up, then stood at the edge of the bed.

"Come here," she commanded, and Olivia came to her.

Micah slowly unwrapped the towel from Olivia's body, taking a moment to admire the flawless skin before she let the towel fall to the floor. She let her hands wander down Olivia's body, reverently skimming along skin that was still hot and damp from the shower. Tucking one stray strand of hair behind her ear, she grasped the back of Olivia's head to bring her closer. Gathering her in a one armed embrace, she drew Olivia in for a hot, wet kiss. Micah felt Olivia's hands, still trapped against her body, seek a way past her leathers. Nimble fingers undid the laces along the front of her vest, then sought the warm flesh beneath. Micah's back arched at the sensation of nails scratching along her ribs before finding and cupping her breasts. Her breath quickened when Olivia rubbed her thumbs across the rough lace of her bra, finding her nipples taut and straining against the thin fabric. A sharp pain travelled from her breast to her groin, her passion igniting like a hot flame when Olivia rolled and pinched a nipple between her thumb and forefinger.

Micah moaned, her hips jerking forward in reaction to the sudden pain, reminding Olivia of the hard thickness hidden along Micah's thigh. Olivia gasped, breaking their kiss and bringing the two women up for some much-needed air. Micah reached up between them, cupping Olivia's hand in her own before bringing it down, pressing her palm against the bulge in her pants. Watching Olivia's face intently, Micah held her breath, waiting to see her reaction after a night's worth of teasing.

"Oohhh, Micah." Olivia breathed, her pupils dilating until only a thin circle of blue remained. She chose that time to roll Micah's other nipple beneath her thumb, sending a second wave of pleasure crashing through her. She threw her head back, arching into Olivia's hand, begging for more contact. "Fuck, Olivia!" she cursed, Olivia's hands at her breast and groin were a double tease that made it hard to think.

Olivia paused for a moment, then ran curious fingertips along the soft leather. Wrapping her hand over the hard bulge beneath her fingertips, she worked her palm against Micah's groin. Micah's breathing became ragged, regressing into a low growl, guttural and utterly animalistic in nature. Before she could discover how much power she had over Micah, Olivia found herself suddenly lifted into the air, effectively removing her teasing hands from the devilish play.

Laying Olivia on her back, Micah kneeled above her. Bending her head down towards the perfect breasts of her lover, she ran her tongue along the pebbled flesh. Without warning, Micah sucked a hard nipple into the warmth of her mouth, running a rough tongue over the swollen flesh. It was Olivia's turn to arch and beg for contact. Micah shuddered as a wave of arousal coursed through her. *The sounds Olivia made, Gods above, they were enough to drive anyone wild.*

Micah felt desperate fingers threading through her hair, urging her to suck harder. She obliged, taking care not to pass that threshold between pleasure and pain. Olivia tightened her grip in Micah's hair, trying to direct her head. She let Olivia guide her mouth to the other breast, offering it the same lavish attention. Holding herself up by one arm, Micah's free hand wandered along the smooth lines of Olivia's body, tracing her ribs and following the hollowed curve of her hips before finding soft curls. Cupping Olivia's sex, she slid one finger between the soaked lips, parting her folds delicately before exploring further. She let her fingers play in the abundant wetness there, running her fingertips over the hard ridge of nerves. Micah backed off each time she felt Olivia's clit swell and harden beneath her, denying her the impending orgasm.

She did this again and again, until Olivia squirmed, her hips rolling frantically against her unrelenting fingers. More wetness coated Micah's fingers as she circled Olivia's opening. Sliding two fingers deep into the silken heat of Olivia's center, she was rewarded with a long moan. Moving up alongside Olivia's body, she captured her lips with her own, her tongue forcing its way into her mouth. She kissed her less than gently as she began to thrust her fingers deeper, the swollen flesh tight against her, fighting her movement. She worked Olivia hard, her fingers opening her for what was to come next.

Olivia was lost in her own world, her hands twisting violently in the sheets as Micah's fingers found their rhythm. Each thrust brought her closer, closer to oblivion. Straining against the need to finish, she met Micah, thrust for thrust, her vision a red-tinged haze of lust and arousal. Just as she was about to reach that precipice, that edge-of-the-cliff moment when you can't stop your orgasm from erupting, everything stopped. Micah's sudden absence shocked her out of that steady climb. She groaned in disappointment and opened her eyes to find Micah moving down, positioning herself between her legs.

Micah kneeled between Olivia's legs then waited until she looked at her. She unbuttoned her leather pants with one quick jerk, the buttons giving way easily. She had to work the pants down a little to make room for her cock to escape the tight confines. Bracing herself on one arm, Micah lowered herself over Olivia's body, kissing her gently as she lowered her hips. She used her other hand to guide the dildo gently into Olivia's sex. She pushed slowly, the thick shaft sliding in inch by tight inch while she watched Olivia's face.

When she was fully inside, she lay still, allowing Olivia to adjust to the girth.

"Are you okay?" she asked. Olivia was so incredibly tight. She could feel her muscles fighting against her, trying to push her back out. The base of the dildo pressed firmly against Micah's swollen clit, making it hard not to move.

"God, yes," Olivia moaned. She slid her hands beneath Micah's leather pants, kneading the firm flesh of her ass until she found the leather straps hung low on her hips. Wrapping her fingers around the soft leather, she pulled Micah into her as deep as she could go.

"Fuck," Micah squeezed her eyes shut against the sudden pressure on her clit, but she got the hint. Hips rocking, the base of the dildo slipped against Micah's swollen clit with every push, teasing and tormenting her mercilessly.

Olivia could barely think. Micah's back muscles bunched and flexed beneath her hands with every thrust. The friction from the dildo was exquisite. She felt full, stretched to her limits yet still wanting more. Olivia moved against Micah, urging her to speed up her rhythm. Digging her nails into Micah's back, she was rewarded with a violent thrust that sent shivers up her spine, her eyes rolling back in her head at the sudden intense wave of pleasure that immediately followed.

"Oh God, Micah...feels so good."

Micah stopped suddenly. All Olivia wanted was for her to speed up. She started to protest when she felt Micah shift, gathering her close to her.

"Don't worry, Love, we aren't done." She rolled onto her back, pulling Olivia around with her.

Olivia found herself, suddenly, on top. Raising herself up so she was on her knees straddling Micah, she gasped as the change in angle buried Micah's cock deeper inside her; she practically sobbed, the sensation was so intense. Micah rolled her hips, the slight movement more than enough to regain her attention. Olivia looked down.

Micah's body was laid out before her, inviting her to see, to touch, and to taste, except for where they were joined together. The shock of seeing Micah half-naked and open to her gaze stilled her movements and made her heart sing. Everything she was feeling doubled in intensity when she saw the love and trust in Micah's lust-darkened eyes. This was more than sex, and it would always be more than just sex between them. Micah had bared her soul to her by exposing her scars, and Olivia almost cried tears of joy.

"Move, Olivia. This is your show." Micah's words might have come off as cocky, but Olivia knew her too well. Micah was offering her control, an unexpected gift tonight. Well, she would take it, then, whenever and however it was offered.

Olivia found she liked being on top as she began working her hips over Micah's cock. Olivia experimented with her movement, finding that when she braced herself against Micah she could rise up off of the dildo, feeling the length of it slide along her core and hitting her G-spot with every thrust. When she sat up, her knees wrapped tight against Micah's hips, she found she enjoyed having her hands free to roam along Micah's body.

Olivia discovered that Micah's breasts were incredibly sensitive, especially her nipples. They seemed to demand harsh treatment, preferring rough pinching over a lighter touch.

Holy hells, she's a fast learner.

Micah's body screamed for release. Between the visual stimulation of watching Olivia riding her, and the harness grinding into her with every thrust, she was hard as stone. Olivia had had her fun but it was time to take over again. She reached down between them, enjoying the feel of the thick cock sliding into the woman above her. She pressed her thumb against Olivia's swollen clit, letting their rhythm slide the rough pad across already sensitive nerves. Olivia rocked into the pressure, letting out a choked scream before coming suddenly, her nails digging into Micah's biceps as she wantonly rode out her orgasm. The frantic movements brought Micah close to the edge. She dug her heels into the bed, giving her the purchase to thrust her hips up as Olivia ground down on her. The base of the dildo slammed into her clit, over and over, until she felt a familiar tingling start at the base of her spine and spread. Her world exploded into blinding white light as she followed Olivia into ecstasy.

Micah drew out Olivia's orgasm as long as possible before letting Olivia come to a rest on top of her. She withdrew carefully; twisting away and tucking everything back in before buttoning partially up. Tired and satiated, she just lay there for a minute, content to hold Olivia in her arms. She would have to get up soon and clean up, but she was hesitant to end this moment. Olivia hadn't spoken since they finished, which started to worry Micah.

"Olivia, is everything okay?" she asked. Not getting a response, Micah shifted, brushing damp hair away from Olivia's face so she could see her. Olivia had fallen asleep in her arms. She mumbled something unintelligible before curling up as best she could under the tangled bed sheets. Micah gently disentangled her arms and pulled a blanket over her exhausted lover before crawling out of bed. She limped to the bathroom to run a bath, leaving Olivia to sleep. She had pushed herself too hard today and now she was paying for it. *Not that it wasn't worth it,* Micah thought as she peeled off her leathers.

***

Olivia didn't so much wake up as return to consciousness. She was alone in the bed. She refused to freak out, and forced her voice to normalcy before calling out.

"Micah?"

"In the bath," came the muffled reply, the sound of running water ending abruptly.

Olivia had a little difficulty crawling out of bed. She wasn't really sore, but she did feel well used, in a good way. Getting her legs to work again, she walked into the steam-filled bathroom. Micah was relaxing in the hot water, her head resting against the back of the tub. She had found bubble bath somewhere, and only her arms and upper chest showed above the thick white foam scenting the air. She would have looked totally relaxed and content if it weren't for the slightly clenched jaw and a tenseness around her lips.

"Is everything all right, Sweetheart?" Olivia asked, concerned.

"Yeah, I'm just soaking the kinks out of my muscles," Micah answered without opening her eyes. "Care to join me?"

Olivia was climbing into the tub before Micah could even finish the question. The offer was so unexpected; she wasn't going to give Micah time to reconsider. She settled in front of her, snuggling between her legs so she could lie against Micah's solid frame. She could feel soft curls against her backside; there was nothing between them now. Micah made a small noise in her throat, shifting slightly behind Olivia until there was a small amount of space between them.

"Ah, still sensitive, Love."

Olivia resisted the urge to wiggle; she wasn't ready for round two yet either. Even so, she didn't mind it a bit when Micah wrapped her arms around her, planting a line of soft kisses along her shoulder.

"Mm. Nice," Olivia murmured, resting her head on Micah's shoulder.

"Did you enjoy your nap?" Micah asked mischievously, sounding suspiciously proud of herself.

"It's your fault. You wore me out."

"It's all good. It was pretty intense," Micah replied casually.

"What about you? Are you okay? You said you had some kinks."

Micah snorted. She doubted Olivia caught that little play on words, but yeah...she would say she had some kinks.

"Well, I guess I pissed my boss off today, so she made me pay. It was my fault though. I pushed, she pushed back."

"Oh, really? How about if your boss makes it up to you?" Olivia stretched, arching her back against Micah. The action brought her body partially out of the bubbly water, exposing her breasts to the cold air.

Micah inhaled sharply. She tipped her head down to kiss Olivia lightly along the back of her neck, tasting both salt and sweet against her lips. Her arms slid around Olivia's middle, cupping her breasts above the bath bubbles.

"And how would she do that?" Micah asked her voice husky and low in Olivia's ear.

"A massage to make you feel better?" The offer hung in the air, heavy like the steam circling around them. "Although I am not sure if you aren't the one who owes me one."

"Olivia, it's okay. I deserved it. I shouldn't have left last night without talking to you."

"That's true, you shouldn't have left, and we will talk about your habit of running away later. But, right now I'd like to take care of you, please?" Olivia slipped out of the bath then held her hand out for Micah to join her.

Micah took Olivia's hand as she climbed out of the tub. She let Olivia lead her back into the bedroom, pausing just long enough for Olivia to grab some scented body oil. Micah felt her old fears surface. She felt exposed and vulnerable walking around naked, but she had made the decision to let this night happen. She was going to trust that Olivia wouldn't hurt her. She wasn't afraid of her physically, but emotionally, Olivia had the power to rip her to shreds.

Motioning for Micah to sit down on the bed, Olivia climbed in behind her, resting her weight on her knees as she poured a generous amount of oil in her hands. Spreading the oil across Micah's shoulders and back, she inhaled deeply. The scent of sandalwood and amber on Micah's skin was intoxicating. Rubbing gently, Olivia was surprised at how tense Micah was. The firm muscles felt like iron bands under her hands, and she realized this might be more work than she expected.

"Micah, you have got to relax, I can't give you a massage if you aren't going to relax."

"I'm sorry, Olivia. This is hard for me."

"What is hard?"

"Letting you touch me, letting you in." The words came out almost a whisper, as if speaking her fears aloud would make them come true.

"You can trust me, Micah, you have to believe me."

"Gods, Olivia, I want to, I really do."

"Then what's stopping you?"

"Fear." It was such a small word for being so difficult to speak aloud. Fear made you weak, vulnerable—two things Micah vowed she would never be again.

"It hasn't gone well in the past, you know, when I've been honest and open about my life. My parents hate my guts—hate who I am and what I do. How do I know that there isn't something about me you can't accept, that will make you change your mind and just walk away?"

Olivia was shocked. How incredibly awful it must feel, to have the two people in the world who are supposed to love you unconditionally place conditions you can't meet in order to earn their love and acceptance. No wonder Micah didn't trust easily. Olivia felt her heart breaking over the inner pain Micah felt she had to carry alone. She held her tightly, offering what strength she had to the woman she loved.

"Listen to me very carefully, Micah Connolly. I am not going to leave you or change my mind or any of the other things you are worrying yourself to death about. As for letting me in, you already have, can't you see? Whether you ever let me make love to you or not, you have already let me into your heart. I am there every hour of every day, for the rest of your life."

Placing her hand on Micah's chest, Olivia could feel her heart beating wildly against her palm.

"Do you love me, Micah?"

"Gods, yes, you know I do."

"Can you trust me?"

Can you, not do you. Micah focused on the wording. It was up to her to trust or not. And, Olivia was right about the other thing too. She had let her into her heart, so why couldn't she offer the rest of her?

Nodding once, Micah relaxed into Olivia's touch. She could practically feel the self-imposed shackles of her past loosen, giving her room to let Olivia in all the way.

Olivia kissed her, gently at first then more earnestly, until she felt Micah's passion rise again. Then she let her lips wander, leaving trails of kisses along Micah's collarbone. Taking one firm breast into her mouth, she reveled in the taste of Micah's skin against her tongue, her nipple hardening between her teeth as she bit lightly, eliciting a low moan from the otherwise silent woman.

Her hands kept busy as well, first at Micah's other breast then travelling down along her stomach, tracing the line of muscles running along her stomach. When her seeking fingers reached soft curls, she stopped.

"Are you okay with this?" Olivia asked quietly, her fingers tangling in the short curls but waiting for Micah's okay before straying further.

"Yes." Micah gave her permission. That was all that she needed. Gliding her fingers down, she felt Micah shudder beneath her as she found her center.

"God, Micah, you are so hot." Her fingers found Micah's swollen clit, the slick bundle of nerves jumping beneath her touch.

"Yessssssss," Micah hissed, stomach muscles bunching as she moved beneath Olivia's fingers.

She continued to explore Micah's wet folds, learning what she liked and disliked. Micah was incredibly responsive to her touch, her clit almost too sensitive for her fingertips. Abandoning the over-sensitized bundle of nerves, she dipped lower, finding the source of so much heat. She circled her opening with her fingers, coating them in the copious fluid.

"Micah, love?" she asked. "Can I go inside? I want to go inside." *Please, Micah, let me in*...she begged silently.

"Yes, do it...I want to feel you inside me."

Olivia slid one slim finger within slick walls that contracted and pushed against her. "Oh, Micah. You are so beautiful...I have wanted this for so long, wanted you to feel this..."

She was babbling, she knew it but couldn't stop herself—she could barely think past the fact that she was finally making love to Micah.

"Oh, Gods, Olivia, I never thought...you feel so damn good." Micah captured Olivia's lips with her own, forcing her tongue into Olivia's mouth, demanding her attention.

Olivia let her tongue dance alongside Micah's, not fighting her need for dominance in this domain. She felt Micah open up to her, rocking against her. She carefully added a second finger, curling them forward as she pumped into her. Micah's arms tensed against her, gathering her in an almost painful embrace. Tucking her face into the soft curve of Micah's neck, she kissed along her pulse line, urging her on. Micah's body arched against her, bucking wildly as she came. The force of Micah's orgasm trapped her fingers as she spasmed and pulsed around her. Olivia stilled her movements, waiting for Micah to come back to her.

While Micah struggled to take control of her breathing, Olivia propped herself up on her elbow so she could look down at her lover.

"Um, Sweetheart...you kind of need to let me go." She didn't want to just pull out; she could still feel aftershocks grabbing at her fingers, squeezing them tightly. She wiggled her fingers in emphasis.

"Jeez, Love, don't do that..." Micah groaned, her body jerking in response to the intense sensation. She had just gotten her vision back; she wasn't ready to head down that path again just yet. She forced herself to relax, gasping when Olivia slid her fingers out.

Micah started to drift, sliding into sleep as the long day finally caught up with her. The last thing she remembered was soft blankets being pulled up around her and then a soft arm draping itself across her stomach, holding onto her tightly.

Chapter Twenty-Four

The sensation of Micah's warm body curled up behind her, one proprietary hand draping loosely across her hip, felt absolutely decadent. It was the first Friday in a long time where the law office wasn't the controlling force in her morning routine, but that didn't mean there wasn't things needing to be done.

As much as she would love to continue lying there, Olivia regretfully crawled out of the warm bed. She had some personal phone calls she needed to get out of the way. A quick glance at the time told her that it was just before eight. Since she was awake, sort of, she decided to get up and spare Micah from the alarm.

Her plan to let Micah continue sleeping didn't quite work out the way she planned. After their night together, Olivia's tired muscles weren't moving as quickly as she would have liked. She didn't make it to the alarm before it went off.

"I'm sorry. I've got it." Trying to make sleep-numbed hands work, she attempted to silence the annoying noise right away, but she wasn't coordinated enough just yet.

Micah groaned and sat up at the edge of the bed. Rumpled and shaggy-haired, eyes screwed shut against the morning sunlight pouring in through the bedroom window and trying to rub the sleep out of her eyes, Olivia thought she was the most beautiful creature she had ever seen.

"Good morning, Sweetheart," Olivia purred.

"Morning," Micah grumbled. One eye popped open, balefully scanning the room before shutting it again. "Arggh, there's no stereo in here. I need some noise in here if I'm going to wake up."

"What did you do the other morning?" Olivia asked.

Micah usually started her day with music. Olivia preferred quiet in the morning to offset the hectic and horn-laden ride into the city. They would have to find a compromise on that one. She honestly didn't know if music was a substitute for caffeine or something Micah used to relax. Perhaps both. All she knew was that music was important to Micah and that she absolutely loved listening to it. If they could just work on the decibel level a little, maybe they could work something out.

"Huh, what do you mean?" Micah's brain wasn't quite awake yet so she was a little foggy.

"What did you use for music the other day?"

"Used my cell, but it's dead. I didn't charge it yesterday and I forgot my charger at the apartment."

Olivia shook her head then kissed Micah on the cheek before handing over her phone. "Download what you need, okay?"

"Thanks, Love," Micah replied distractedly, her fingers moving rapidly as she searched for a website. She downloaded her internet radio account and signed in, flashing a bright smile at Olivia before hitting the play button.

Olivia shook her head, amused at how simple that was. Micah was so adorable in the morning. She was so grumpy it was actually endearing. Kind of like how cute bulldogs were, wrinkles and all. Somehow, Olivia didn't think it was wise to tell her that, though. What she did need to do is get up and get ready for the day. She left Micah to her music while she went about her business.

When Olivia emerged from the bathroom, she couldn't hear music anymore. Micah had found her earbuds and was blissfully enjoying her music without subjecting Olivia to the loud noise so early in the morning. She was however, waiting impatiently for her turn.

Micah nimbly avoided Olivia's attempt to kiss her on the way to the bathroom, although she did take advantage of the close quarters at the bathroom door. She let her hands wander along Olivia's flank, cupping her full breast for a quick second before slipping past her lover.

"Let me clean up first, Love. Morning breath," she apologized before disappearing into the bathroom.

Micah finally started feeling human again after washing her face and brushing her teeth. She ran her fingers through the unruly dark hair, even trying to wet it down a bit, but it was getting too long to control. Looking at her image in the mirror, she found she liked the shaggy look, but made a mental note to plan on a haircut soon.

Sometime in the middle of the night, she had woken up and slipped on a t-shirt. She had lain there for a long while afterwards, watching Olivia sleep peacefully next to her. She hadn't been able to fall back asleep right away, not with so many things in her head demanding her attention. They had made love and Micah had finally let her guard down enough to let Olivia see her, to let her touch her. That in itself amazed her, but then she had fallen asleep, exhausted, satiated, and still naked. She rarely slept naked even when she was at home and alone. It wasn't something she was comfortable doing very often and something she had never done with someone else. She felt guilty pulling her t-shirt back on in the dim moonlight streaming through the room, as if she was somehow going to disappoint Olivia by doing so.

Running her palm across her stomach, she could feel the hard lines of her scars beneath the thin fabric. Even after last night, she wasn't comfortable having her scars exposed, not in the light of day and not to casual observation. Micah shrugged at the image staring back at her in the mirror and went back to brushing her teeth. There was nothing she could do about how she felt. Olivia would just have to understand.

Olivia was waiting for her when she emerged from the bathroom. She wasn't up to conversation yet, and hoped that Olivia wasn't going to be a huge morning conversation person. Her expression must have given her away, because Olivia simply looked at her and laughed, then handed her a can of her favorite beverage.

"Thank you." Micah took the can in both hands like a precious offering. Sometimes she wondered if she could live on caffeine and bubbles alone.

"Come down for breakfast whenever you're ready. There's no rush." Olivia kissed Micah on the cheek and left the room.

Micah found a charger sitting on the bedside table. Olivia must have found it for her. She made sure to plug her phone in before going through her choices in clothes for the day. There really wasn't much, just a pair of old faded jeans and a couple of black t-shirts.

Olivia's early morning energy was infectious. She felt more alert and alive this morning than she ever had and she so wasn't a morning person, but waking up with Olivia in her arms might change her mind about that. She still couldn't figure out what Olivia saw in her, but after last night, it didn't seem to matter as much.

Padding downstairs in her bare feet, Micah found Olivia in the kitchen standing in front of the stove in her silk robe. Her stomach growled. Whatever Olivia was fixing for breakfast, it smelled heavenly.

Despite Micah's silent approach, Olivia knew when she had entered the kitchen…she always seemed to know when Micah was near.

"Hungry?" Olivia asked, keeping her eyes on the pan in front of her.

"Starving. What time do you have to go into work today?" Micah crowded behind Olivia, trying to see what she was making. "Aren't you late?"

"No," she answered, shooing Micah away from the stove. Olivia scolded her. "Now go, sit. Breakfast will be ready soon."

"But it's daylight outside, and unless I missed a day, it's still Friday?" Micah asked. *Fat chance of that, its tattoo day.*

Olivia turned back to the stove. "You didn't miss anything. I won't be going into work today. One of the perks of being the boss that I've decided to exercise."

Since Olivia was still facing the stove, she didn't see the shocked expression that crossed Micah's face. *How about that?*

Basically told to sit down and wait, Micah found herself with nothing to do but think. Usually not a good idea, except this time what was going on in her head didn't involve anything remotely close to deep thoughts.

Olivia's silk robe hid very little and promised quite a bit. Micah's stomach growled loudly, interrupting her daydreaming and reminding her that she had missed dinner last night. She would have to wait until after breakfast to find out what Olivia had on under her robe. She seriously hoped it was nothing. A war of appetites was starting to brew...but she couldn't help herself. Olivia was sexy as hell, and she was a greedy woman.

"Is that walnut syrup?" Micah asked, surprised when the familiar aroma reached her nose.

"Yes," Olivia replied, setting a huge stack of pancakes down in front of her.

"How did you know?" Micah asked, speaking around a mouthful of pancake and syrup. She grinned apologetically then tucked back into her food like a lumberjack.

"Jonathan told me this is your favorite breakfast, but that you don't get it very often."

"Did he also tell you I can't cook?" Micah asked, laughing gaily at her own inadequacies.

"I figured as much since all you made at the cabin was cereal." Olivia sat down to join her after making a cup of coffee.

"I don't make time for breakfast very often either," Olivia admitted, her expression wistful. Micah stopped eating and looked at Olivia. The Olivia she had known before lived and breathed for her work—for the office. Now she was playing hooky from work just to fix her breakfast. Micah grinned. That was her ego speaking, but it was a nice enough fantasy.

"This is delicious, Love. Thank you," Micah said, reaching out and lovingly squeezing Olivia's hand. Olivia beamed back at her, returning the squeeze with equal affection. Micah felt warmth spread through her chest. It was times like this, when they could simply relax around each other, that Micah truly felt privileged to be the object of this amazing woman's affections.

Once breakfast was finished, Olivia took their dishes into the kitchen. Micah offered to help but Olivia waved at her to sit back down. Micah followed anyway;

she never was very good at following orders. Besides, she really wanted to know what Olivia had or didn't have on under that robe, especially after Olivia stood up to leave and had to retie her sash. The silky material seemed prone to slipping open more frequently than not, revealing a tempting bit of cleavage.

Olivia was at the sink, rinsing the sticky syrup mess off their dishes when Micah snuck up behind her. She turned off the water when Micah's breath, hot against her skin, heralded a trail of soft kisses down her neck. "Micah! The dishes," Olivia protested.

"I don't think the dishes are going to get done anytime soon, Love. Let me show you how much I appreciated breakfast," Micah whispered against her ear, making her shudder deliciously. Turning Olivia around to face her, Micah eagerly captured her lips, the sugary sweet taste of walnut syrup competing with the more familiar taste that was uniquely Olivia. She untied the silk robe slowly, allowing the smooth fabric to fall open beneath her fingertips. The loose fabric framed the exquisitely pale body in that tempting way partial nudity held the mind's eye.

A woman's naked body held infinite delight for Micah, but there was just something about a woman whose attributes lay partially hidden from her sight, whether it was a tousled sheet or the line of an open robe that left a teasing view of skin to follow with her eyes, it just did it for her.

She slid her hands inside Olivia's robe, moving down and around to grasp Olivia's backside, cupping her firm cheeks and pulling her body closely against her.

She dropped to her knees in front of Olivia. Her fingers kneaded soft flesh, travelling along her hip and thigh until they found the soft curls above Olivia's sex.

Running her fingertips along her center, she found wetness waiting for her. She brought her face closer, opening the smooth folds with her tongue, lapping gently. Her splayed fingers held her in place, and she could feel Olivia's abdomen clenching and twitching beneath her as she teased her with her mouth and tongue.

When Micah's tongue touched her clit, Olivia's hips jerked violently. Leaning back against the countertop, she parted her legs slightly to give Micah more access. The wider stance allowed her to move her hips against Micah's teasing mouth.

Micah loved the feel of Olivia grinding against her shamelessly as she sucked and licked against her clit. The sweet taste of her arousal lay on her tongue and lips, encouraging her to tease her more. She eased her hand up between Olivia's legs, pressing her fingers against the source of the copious wetness. A deep shudder passed through Olivia's body when Micah pressed her fingers inside, teasing Olivia's entrance until the slick wet of her arousal coated her fingers.

Olivia moaned and grasped at her, threading her fingers through Micah's hair until they were tangled in the morning mess. She didn't stay long. She slid her fingers back, hearing Olivia gasp when her fingers slid over another entrance, one that held its own source of pleasure. Lightly caressing, she spread the wetness against her tight hole, feeling the strong muscles contract and spasm in response to the unexpected exploration.

"Oh my God, Micah, no one has ever..." Olivia panted, her breath coming in ragged gasps as she struggled to remain standing, grasping the hard countertop to stay upright.

"Is this okay?" Micah asked, tipping her head back to gaze up at the woman towering above her. Olivia was magnificent from this angle—leaning back against the counter, her back arching in response to Micah's teasing, her breasts bare and heaving with every ragged breath. She had thrown back her head, her long neck flushed and straining against the need to come. Keeping up the lightly teasing caress with her soaked fingers, Micah schooled herself to patience. She was offering Olivia a new type of pleasure, but it was up to her to accept her offering.

Olivia looked down at Micah kneeling on the floor, her lips still wet from her juices. Micah continued caressing her gently, waiting for her to answer. The sight alone was almost enough to make her come.

"God, yes! Please, just don't stop!" Olivia found her voice only to have it stolen away as Micah ran her fingers along her ass, gliding forward to gather more moisture on her fingers. Returning to her other opening, she pushed more insistently against the tight muscle, pressing two fingers against her, encouraging Olivia to relax into the shallow intrusion.

"You feel so good, Love," Micah whispered reverently, watching Olivia's face carefully for any sign of discomfort with what she was doing.

Olivia was breathing hard, her body motionless, her eyes closed as if concentrating on what Micah was doing to her. Satisfied, Micah brought her lips against Olivia's center, sucking her clit into her mouth. She started a rhythm that would quickly be her lover's undoing, her tongue lapping against the sensitive bundle of nerves in time with her teasing fingers. She had to struggle to keep contact as Olivia came, her hips thrusting against her mouth. Olivia's low voice rose into a loud keening wail that ended in a begging plea to stop.

Micah stood up. Olivia quivered and shook in her arms, as weak as a kitten after her orgasm. Micah picked her up and carried her over to the couch, sitting down with Olivia cradled on her lap.

"Micah?" Olivia's voice begged a question. She had been lying so still that Micah had thought she was falling asleep in her arms. Instead, Olivia moved restlessly against her, soft lips nuzzling insistently against her neck.

"Hmm?" Olivia's lips were very distracting. The satiated woman suddenly became quite active in her lap, turning until she straddled Micah.

"I want to make love to you." Olivia gazed at her greedily. Her voice was insistent, demanding, and Micah couldn't find any good excuse for saying no. Making love to Olivia had set her on fire; she could feel the wetness between her thighs, driving her crazy with even the slightest movement. Insatiable in her appetite, Micah was constantly amazed at how the other woman had matched her, passion for passion when they made love.

"What's stopping you?"

"You have too many clothes on," Olivia said, opening the top button on Micah's jeans only to find more. "Button fly?"

Olivia struggled with her jeans, growing increasingly frustrated with the unfamiliar buttons.

"Let me." Micah took over with a quick flick of her wrist, the row of buttons undone in one swift motion to the muffled staccato sound of brass sliding against denim.

"Impressive," Olivia said. One eyebrow rose high in response to the smooth movement, so much easier than her clumsy fumbling.

"Practice," Micah said, her cocky response raising a few unwanted questions that almost derailed Olivia's single-minded goal...she wanted those jeans off. Questions that were quickly forgotten when Micah pulled her shirt and bra off in one swift motion, rising up into a half sit-up to accomplish the task. The sight of Micah naked from the waist up, her jeans unbuttoned and open at the waist was so incredibly erotic it made her groan in anticipation.

If Micah had hesitated for one short second, if her normally smooth movements had faltered just the slightest bit as if she had suffered a silent moment of uncertainty, Olivia made sure not to let on.

"Up," Olivia commanded, impatiently tapping Micah's hip. Micah lifted her hips off the couch so Olivia could pull off her jeans.

"Oh, God, Micah, you have really got to warn a girl," Olivia moaned. Micah wasn't wearing any underwear.

Olivia crawled back up until she straddled her lap, leaning in to kiss her soundly. Micah pulled off Olivia's robe the rest of the way, not wanting any clothes in the way of their skin touching.

"Holy shit, Olivia!" Micah yelped when Olivia reached down and cupped her sex.

"You are very wet, my dear," Olivia purred into Micah's ear, lightly nibbling on her earlobe. When she began leaving hot kisses along the lines of Micah's body, she stilled. When Olivia boldly continued, finally reaching the sculpted planes of her abdomen, Micah stopped her.

"You don't have to do that," Micah protested.

"But I want to," Olivia insisted. Then, taking a hint from earlier, she stopped and looked directly into her eyes.

"I want to, but it is up to you."

Olivia looked at her with such love and longing, yet she waited for Micah to decide. Micah knew in her heart that if she said no, Olivia would be disappointed but she would stop. That knowledge was enough to help her make a decision.

Nodding once, Micah gave her permission.

At the first swipe of Olivia's tongue, Micah lost the ability to think coherently. She heard and felt Olivia moan into her, the vibration adding to the sensation of Olivia's lips drawing her in, sucking her gently before moving farther down. Olivia's tongue entered her, lapping up her arousal before returning her attention to her clit. Back and forth, Olivia didn't let up, nor did she stay in one rhythm long enough to bring her to completion. Instead, Olivia teased her to greater and greater heights until she couldn't stand it any longer.

"Gods, Olivia, please stop teasing!" Micah didn't care if she was begging, every nerve in her body was screaming for release. As if on cue, Olivia sucked her clit into her mouth, flattening her tongue against the sensitive tissue. Olivia brought her to orgasm quickly, her body already primed from making love to her.

"That was wonderful," Micah whispered.

Olivia curled up next to Micah, resting her head on her chest. Drawing Olivia's face up to hers, she kissed her, tasting herself on Olivia's lips. "I think I could get used to mornings."

Olivia almost fell off the couch, she laughed so hard at the offhand comment.

"Mm, I hate to leave your arms already, Sweetheart, but I do need to run a short errand." Olivia hadn't expected to be mauled after breakfast, and although it was a delightful surprise, she had an appointment she had to keep. She had to leave—now.

"Not a problem, how long do you think you will be?" Micah started gathering her discarded clothes, standing up to pull her jeans back on. She wasn't surprised. She knew that Olivia had said they would have the whole weekend together, but she really didn't expect her to be completely free of work.

"I can't believe you aren't wearing any underwear. That's a horrible tease you know."

"You didn't have anything on under your robe," Micah shot back, giving Olivia a quick but passionate kiss to let her know what that knowledge did to her. "But, just for future knowledge, I very rarely wear underwear." The look of shock and scandal on Olivia's face was so worth it, even if it did turn into a look of calculated speculation far too quickly.

"Now go. The sooner you leave, the sooner you'll be back." Micah handed her the discarded silk robe.

"It should only be an hour or so. What are you going to do?"

"I am just going to relax and work on the computer a bit before my appointment tonight."

"What appointment?"

"Did I forget to tell you?" Of course she had, she'd been more than a little preoccupied. "I have an appointment to get some tat work done."

"What time?"

"Eight tonight, do you want to come with me?"

"Are you sure?" Olivia wasn't sure about going to a tattoo parlor, but she didn't want to stay at home alone, either. She had Micah for the whole weekend, and she wasn't going to stay home while Micah had someone pushing needles into her skin.

"Yes, of course."

Chapter Twenty-Five

Olivia made it to her appointment with only a few minutes to spare. When she found Micah's ring sitting on the bedside table, she seized the opportunity to act on an idea for her birthday present. While a part of her worried about giving Micah a ring as a present so early in their relationship, there was something Micah had said that made it seem like it would be the perfect gift.

Micah's ring was heavier than what a woman usually wore, but it suited her well, so Olivia chose a similar band style of ring for this one.

Convincing the silversmith to commit to the rush job took some wheedling and a lot of extra cash to get it done in time for Micah's birthday, but it was so worth it. Now all she had to do was get back home before Micah realized her ring was missing. She wanted her little surprise to remain just that...a surprise. Luckily, Micah had been so preoccupied with other activities this morning, she hadn't noticed it was missing.

The ride back from the jewelry store gave her some quiet time to think about last night. Micah had come a long way in letting her in and opening up to her, something for which Olivia was eternally grateful.

Making love to Micah had been an amazing experience, the last twenty-four hours holding more firsts for her than the last ten years. Her imagination had prepared her for the physical aspects of their lovemaking, but not how it made her feel, what it made her want to do. She had expected to feel hesitant, self-conscious even, but all she had wanted to do was make Micah feel as good as she made her feel.

Then this morning on the couch, when she had finally been able to taste her lover for the first time, it was intoxicating. Olivia was still in awe at the way Micah had come from having her mouth on her, her tongue eager to lap up the sweetness that proved the extent of her pleasure. She wasn't sure if Micah was aware of how physically naïve she had been before taking her into her bed, or that she was the first woman Olivia had ever made love to. Just thinking about it made her squirm in her seat. She had to stop reminiscing; it was too risky in the heavy traffic to be that distracted.

***

The trip back home took longer than she expected. What was supposed to be a one hour trip had turned into more than two, and she was frantic to get Micah's ring back where it belonged.

"Micah?" Olivia called out the minute she stepped into the house.

"Family room," Micah's voice drifted in from the other room.

"Great! Just let me run upstairs and change." The first thing Olivia did was drop the ring back down where Micah had left it, then reconsidered. She pushed it farther back out of the way until you had to look for it to find it. *There, now it would look like she just missed it this morning.* Pleased with her ingenuity, Olivia hid the other package in the bathroom cabinet, changed and ran back downstairs before Micah came looking for her.

"I wasn't sure you actually watched TV," Olivia commented when she walked into the room. Micah was

317

sitting on the couch with her feet up on the coffee table, watching a movie. The scene flashing across the screen was fast, bloody, and disturbing; certainly nothing she would ever let her daughter watch. Olivia ignored the feet on the table.

"Whatever are you watching?"

"I don't know, some zombie movie," Micah replied, completely engrossed in watching half-eaten zombies attacking and devouring a less fortunate human.

"That's disgusting," Olivia remarked, swallowing hard when the camera zoomed in on a particularly bloody bit.

"But the lead chick is freaking hot, so it's okay," Micah quipped. She loved this type of movie and her enthusiasm showed.

"Micah!" Olivia exclaimed, then gave up. She was right; the lead female was very attractive.

Olivia plopped down and cuddled up next to Micah. When Micah put her arm around her and pulled her in, Olivia took advantage to burrow in closer.

"Do you want me to change the channel?"

"No, go ahead and finish it." Olivia yawned, she could care less about the movie but she was too comfortable to move.

Micah turned off the TV when the movie credits started to roll. Olivia had fallen asleep on Micah's lap, her body heavy and boneless against her.

"Olivia, Love?"

"Hm?" Olivia mumbled. She didn't want to wake up. She was perfectly content to remain where she was.

"I need to get my computer so I can get a little work done before tonight." She had already played hooky for too long by watching a movie when she should have been working. She was way too easily distracted today, and she was pretty sure she had used up her quota of hot sex with Olivia. She was running out of options to keep herself occupied until her appointment. A little creative writing might be just the thing to keep her busy until then.

"Did you get your last chapter done?"

"Yeah, but now they want me to expand on one of the scenes, since they decided to add more dialogue." Micah sighed, hating the reminder that she was behind. The thing was, she didn't want to work on it today. She had something else stuck in her head that was clamoring to get out.

"Will it bother you if I work on it down here where the stereo is?"

"Of course not, you are welcome to work anywhere you want."

"Even your study?" Micah teased, knowing how particular Olivia was about her personal working space.

"Yes, if you want to work in there that is perfectly fine with me," Olivia replied amicably.

That surprised Micah. *Touché, Olivia.* "I think I'll just stay where the stereo is for now."

"Will you play that CD from the other day?"

"Sure," Micah agreed.

Olivia went into her study to do a few things while Micah worked. She left the door open so she could hear the music, and Micah. When the CD got to the song Micah had been listening to at her apartment, she leaned back in her chair and just listened.

Micah soon found her rhythm and found herself typing away like crazy, before long, she had several pages written. She saved the file and gave it a quick read through, tweaking it in a few spots before nodding, pleased with herself. What she had written was for her and her alone, although she had to admit it did have the makings of a good book or maybe another graphic novel. Even if it wasn't really work, Micah was impressed with what she had done.

She wasn't sure if her inspiration was last night, the impending relief from her tattoo session, or a combination of both. All she knew was that she was really amped up about tonight and whatever writers block she had been suffering from had disappeared in a flurry of activity.

A couple of hours later and she was done. She checked her clock for what was probably the umpteenth time that day and let out a huge sigh of relief. She stood up and stretched, leaving her computer on the coffee table as she made her way to Olivia's study.

"Hey, Love, I'm gonna go get ready," Micah said, keeping her voice low. She had been leaning against the doorway waiting for Olivia to get off the phone, but when it didn't look like the call was going to end anytime soon, Micah became impatient and risked interrupting her. Olivia looked up and nodded that she had heard her before turning back to her phone call. Micah blew her a playful kiss before heading upstairs, practically sprinting up the stairwell in her excitement.

***

Olivia finished her call and wandered into the living room. She could hear Micah moving around upstairs and headed that way herself, then stopped. Micah's computer was still up and running, and curiosity got the best of her.

What have you been working on so diligently, hmm?" Olivia slipped over to the couch and took a closer look. The document file she had been working on was still open. From the looks of it, the document didn't have anything to do with the graphic novel. *Someone has been playing hooky again.*

Micah had said something about dabbling in writing for herself, but she had been incredibly secretive about it. She glanced up the stairs, then sat down in the same spot that Micah had just vacated, pulled the computer closer to the edge of the coffee table and started reading.

> *Fear settled deep within Alex, a hard lump of cold despair sitting low in her belly, burning with the sour taste of bile up into her chest. Swallowing hard against a sudden wave of nausea, she realized that the woman before her, the one she loved more than her own life, was slowly dying before her. Too much of who she was had been damaged by Bellaria's spell. Covering her face in her hands, Alex pushed back the tears that threatened to come, pressing her palms firmly against eyes reddened by sleepless nights. The cool, firm edge of her leather bracer pressed hard against her cheek, and she breathed in deeply. The soothing smell of leather and smoke spoke to her, reminding her of the forge, but even those familiar scents held no solace for her.*
>
> *A flash of lightning and the sudden roll of thunder announced the beginning of another summer storm. She could hear the heavy patter of rain starting to ping rhythmically from the metal roof above her and thought it fitting to her mood. Another lightning strike crashed closer, blinding in its*

intensity. Another furious roll of thunder that shook the timbers of the house around her followed it.

Olivia cast another nervous glance over her shoulder to make sure Micah wasn't headed back downstairs. She really wanted to know where the scene was going, but she felt guilty as hell, peeking at Micah's personal writing without asking first.

Turning back to the computer, she continued to scroll down, her eyes widening as the story developed into something a bit more visceral.

Alex towered gracefully above Rohanna's trembling form, her leather encased legs braced at shoulder width. Her arm, sleekly muscled and solid from hours working at her anvil, barely felt the weight of the leather flogger hanging loosely from her left hand. A soft pink glow was growing slowly across Rohanna's smooth back and firm bottom, evidence of Alex's art with the soft leather. Able to caress with kisses as soft as a butterfly's touch, it could also lash out like a scorpion's sting, laying flesh open in long angry welts.

Alex looked down, her eyes resting on skin beautiful in its complementary pattern of pale white and subtle red. Rohanna's skin glowed brightly, much like the steel Alex forged in the adjoining room. She admired her work, knowing that like that glowing metal, Rohanna could now be shaped by the power of the fire she contained within her, without fear. What Alex sought was not pain for pain's sake, but pain for pleasure's sake. She wanted Rohanna to sink into the pleasure of the stinging pain she rained down upon her, to soften into the caresses of leather and submission. Too much would break her, and Alex wanted the softly moaning woman before her to lay pliable before her. The night was still young and there was, oh so much more she wanted to do.

Alex placed the flogger down. Rohanna's hair was soaked with perspiration. The salty fluid dripped from her brow, dampening her face before travelling down her neck to trail like a boiling stream between her breasts. Her chest heaved, the rapidly drawn breaths disturbing the rivulets and creating new pathways as they followed the curve of her body. Head thrown back, eyes closed and lips parted slightly, the long line of Rohanna's throat begging to be kissed. Alex's hot gaze took in Rohanna's firm breasts thrust out proudly before her. Her flushed nipples were hard and swollen, waiting eagerly for the feel of Alex's mouth, to be lovingly sucked and fondled roughly. Aware of her own ragged breaths, Alex fought herself for control of her barely contained arousal. This was all for Rohanna, she reminded herself, and silenced her own body's demands for satisfaction.

Olivia paused. Even within Micah's writing, she emphasized the need for control. Olivia knew she shouldn't be reading into the characters, but she couldn't help wondering how much of Micah was hidden in this Alex character.

From the moment Alex had buckled the wrist restraints on Rohanna, the proud woman had refrained from uttering a word. Now, given leave to ask, Rohanna found herself begging. Her need was so great, and she had held her voice for so long, that her words came out as a choking sob.

"Please, Alex, please...I want..."

Another whispered command breathed softly against Ro's burning skin. "Tell me, tell me what you want!" Urgent, demanding, the voice was reinforced by two slick fingers gliding shallowly into Ro's depths, and then withdrawing. The empty ache that filled Ro's heart and mind for so long now centered between her legs. Ro wanted so much to be filled, to feel the ache of fullness that Alex's fingers promised. She didn't want to feel empty any longer. Reality shrunk around Ro's fevered mind, until it contained only her and the woman pressed against her, nothing else mattered except heat, and wet, and need.

Olivia was caught up in it now, her pulse jumping as she continued, unable to stop her eyes from rapidly following the scene progression. Despite the heavy sexual content, there was a solid storyline that made it something more than plain smut. Olivia's mind focused on titillating details that offered her ideas and presented concepts she really had little experience in, let alone ever considered. If this was what Micah knew and liked, she had been holding back, a lot. *If she's been holding back, I could be in deep trouble,* she thought. A slow, speculative smile crossed her lips. Micah certainly had quite an imagination. Caught up in the final paragraphs, she didn't even notice Micah standing behind her until she heard her voice. She didn't sound very happy, either.

"Like what you see?"

"Um." Olivia looked up at Micah. The hot flush rushing across her cheeks was more from her response to what she had just read than embarrassment at being caught. She was quite sure there were other bits of her just as flushed and red as her cheeks felt. *And hot, don't forget hot.* She had all sorts of excuses lined up for her intrusion into Micah's computer, but unfortunately, they remained unspoken in a shock-induced silence. Her mind was too busy trying to wrap itself around her physical response to Micah's words. It was so unexpected, so intense, and so damned exciting. How could she explain to Micah that she was utterly and completely turned on by what she had just read?

Micah, of course, misinterpreted Olivia's silence. Her face darkened, reshaping itself into something stern and closed off as she took in Olivia's blushing cheeks, her wide eyes.

"Yeah, that's what I thought. That's why you weren't supposed to read it."

"No, no, it's not that." Feeling flustered and having a hard time articulating, Olivia hoped that Micah wouldn't jump to all the wrong conclusions before she could find the words to explain.

"Are you into that? Is that what you like?" she asked, waving her hand towards the computer screen. *Jesus, I sound like an idiot.*

Micah slammed the offending laptop closed, closing her secrets away from prying eyes.

"Not to that extreme, no. I have no desire to cause pain like that, but a little rougher sometimes, yes. But don't worry, Olivia, I would never ask that of you."

And with that, Micah stalked out of the room.

"Wait, Micah..." Olivia cried out. She had screwed up royally, invading Micah's private writing and then quizzing her on what she found. She needed to apologize before things got out of hand. She found Micah standing in the middle of the kitchen, staring out the window, her arms tight across her chest. "Micah, please don't be angry with me. I'm sorry I read your story, I really am."

"Jeez, Olivia, you think that's what I'm upset about?" Micah's eyes flashed, dark and full of unrestrained fury.

"I thought..." Olivia tried to touch her arm but Micah stepped away, putting space between them. Confused and hurt, she dropped her hand. "Okay? Then tell me what you are upset about."

"I saw your reaction to the scene," Micah said, then clamped her lips shut. She shook her head violently, then gave Olivia a look she would never forget. Conflicting emotions stormed through her eyes, flickering in and out of focus like an old movie. Fear was one of them, along with desire, hope, and something else that looked like regret but tasted like resignation. None of it made sense to her. Olivia mentally rewound their conversation, looking for clues. A bright sliver of understanding broke free from her clouded mind. She had seen that look before, right before Micah announced it was time to leave the bar. She cursed, loudly.

That got Micah's attention.

"Look, Micah, I need you to not to jump to conclusions so easily. Your scene didn't upset me. It just surprised me, Sweetheart."

"Really, Olivia, you're not just saying that to make me feel better? I thought you were turned off by it." Micah's voice was hopeful.

"On the contrary—it turned me on, more than I want to admit." This time when she reached out for Micah, she didn't move away. She closed her eyes and swayed in Micah's arms. *This is what her touch does to me.*

"Are you okay?" Micah asked.

"I'm not sure," Olivia answered. She looked into Micah's eyes, so concerned and full of love for her. "Micah, I have to know..." Olivia paused, "have you been holding back when we are together?"

"Yes," Micah said. "A bit."

Did Olivia know what she was saying? What it meant that she admitted to being affected that way by what she had written? She had thought Olivia's behavior in the club had been a fluke or a deliberate attempt to fit in, but now she wasn't so sure. Perhaps that imaginary gulf between them wasn't as large as she had thought. Perhaps they had more in common than Micah had considered. Micah practically vibrated with conflicting desires. She wanted to continue exploring this unexpected development, but she NEEDED this tattoo, and it couldn't wait and neither could she.

"I see," Olivia said, completely intrigued by what Micah's definition of "a bit" might be.

Micah threw her head back and laughed. "You are the queen of understatement."

"What does that mean?"

"That means we have a lot to talk about...later. Right now, we need to get going. I'm starving and you are going to take me out to dinner before my tattoo."

"I am?" Olivia asked, finally noticing Micah's outfit. Micah was wearing leather pants, this pair slightly different from the ones she wore yesterday. She wasn't wearing her vest; instead, she had on a plain black t-shirt that somehow dressed down the pants to acceptable daily wear, at least on Micah. She looked like an artist, or a musician, not the dangerous woman in full leathers she had taken home from the club the night before.

"What are you looking at?"

"Your outfit." Olivia grinned. "How many pairs of leather pants do you have?"

"Two. I had to have Adam bring these over this morning, since my other pair need to be cleaned after last night." Micah smirked.

"God, I love you in leather. Who would have guessed?" Olivia asked, her eyes drinking in Micah's image. Micah's trademark smirk widened into a decidedly wolfish grin that let Olivia know just how much she appreciated that comment.

"Honestly? Not me. Come on, let's go," Micah said, unable to contain her excitement any longer. It was tattoo night.

Chapter Twenty-Six

Olivia nervously tapped the steering wheel of her Porsche. It had been months since she had an excuse to take the sleek sports car out for a drive and now she had the opportunity to drive it twice in one day.

Olivia had never been to a tattoo parlor and didn't know what to expect. Oh, she had examples from movies and television, most of which gave her the impression that she was going somewhere a little rougher around the edges than she was used to, but Micah had assured her that both her and her baby would be safe.

Olivia had been so intent on following the GPS directions that she hadn't noticed her surroundings until they stopped. She had been delightfully surprised when they pulled up to a large converted industrial building in the arts district and her GPS announced their arrival. The sign above the door was metal, smooth and polished, the lettering spelling out the name. *Missing Ink*. It was a nice play on words.

A stylized chain wound its way around the sign, with a broken link separating the two words. The glass door and windows were tinted to the point of being reflective, preventing anyone from seeing inside the shop. She would have never guessed it was a tattoo studio, not in passing.

The inside of the tattoo studio looked more like an art gallery with an industrial bent. Framed paintings and drawings covered the walls, a lot of it quite good. She read a couple of the small cards taped below each frame.

Apparently, everything was the work of various local artists.

The place was a lot bigger than she expected. There was another doorway at the back of the room, separating them from the rest of the studio with a 60s style beaded door hanging. She got a feeling that was where all the work happened. The place was neat and clean and altogether not what Olivia had expected, but she still felt out of her element. Micah, in her tight leather pants and unrelieved black, matched the décor—artistic, dark, and somewhat dangerous looking.

Olivia turned away from examining a painting that had caught her eye and towards the sound of a woman's voice calling out from the back of the shop.

"Is that you, Micah?"

"Yes," Micah called out, her boots striking dully against the finished concrete floor.

A tattooed young woman with unnaturally bright red hair flaming down her back and dressed all in black like Micah, popped through the beaded doorway and grinned. "Hey, Micah, I'll be right with you. I'm just getting the room set up."

"Sure thing, Cassandra, no rush."

"Yeah, right, Micah. When are you not in a hurry to get started?" Cassandra shot back.

The way the two women easily bantered back and forth spoke of their familiarity with each other.

"Uh, hello?" Cassandra looked over, finally realizing there was someone else in the room with Micah.

"She's with me, Cass," Micah said.

Cass raised one reddish blonde eyebrow and shifted her gaze from Micah to Olivia and back again. Micah chuckled. Her surprise was well founded. Micah never brought anyone with her...ever. To her credit, she didn't make a big deal of it. She just shook her head and smiled at Olivia.

"Sure, Micah." She winked at Olivia. "Welcome to my shop. Come on back, I'm all ready for you."

It didn't take long after that for Micah to hear the bad news. Even if she was half expecting it, it still didn't make her happy.

"I'm sorry, Micah. I can't work on this yet. The skin is still too new," Cassandra said. She was examining Micah's shoulder, carefully running her finger along the smooth skin with a practiced, almost clinical touch.

"You were lucky. It looks like most of the outline is still intact, so at least you didn't damage my work completely," she continued, then shook her head when she found a spot where the once clean line faltered. "It could have been worse."

Cassandra rolled her chair over to the light box, examining the pattern illuminated on top of it. The transfer copy of Micah's tattoo rolled and twisted along the thin paper, a complex and intricate pattern that had challenged even her skills. Cassandra was good at what she did, she was the best tattoo artist in the city. Her work was fast and clean, but she never hurried her art and that meant she decided when and what was done. Her reputation was solid, and that meant her shop didn't even have to advertise but relied purely on word-of-mouth for clientele.

Cassandra's eyes followed the familiar lines, mapping out in her mind what she wanted to work on today. She had planned on working on the upper back and shoulder, but Micah's road rash had changed that.

"Hmmm. Well, Micah I have to tell you, unless you want to start another tattoo, we're going to need to work on the other part." Cassandra flashed an apologetic look at her friend. There was only one other area needing attention, and Cassandra was unsure if Micah would be game for it. The enigmatic young woman had never brought anyone with her before. Micah prized her privacy during their sessions, so much so that Cassandra made sure to clear the shop and lock the door before they started.

"Yeah, I had thought of that, too," Micah replied, "But, I really wanted to finish this up first."

"Okay. Then I think we should work on the legs," Cassandra suggested, rummaging through her memory of Micah's completed work. The lower legs of the dragon ran along Micah's waist and abdomen, an area that her client had been avoiding. If Micah would let her do it today, it would go a long way towards completing the tattoo. Her machines were already set up, one for lining and one for shading, all she needed to do was put on her gloves. She turned her attention towards the table behind her and finished setting up, but when she turned back around, she found Micah still sitting at the edge of the table, her leather clad legs swinging anxiously.

"Um, Micah, you're going to have to lay down for me to do this." Cassandra shifted her gaze to the right, where Micah's guest was watching their interplay carefully.

Was Micah going to do this with an audience? Recalling how stressed out Micah sounded on the phone earlier this week, she knew how much Micah needed this tattoo work done. That was another reason she was so surprised that Micah had brought someone with her. It made her wonder if this woman had played a part in her unexpected phone call and request. She glanced over at Micah's companion. Such an unusual woman for Micah to be with. So proper and well dressed, she screamed vanilla with corporate sprinkles on top, not the sort of woman she usually associated with Micah's type. Cassandra was sure that the woman had never seen the inside of a tattoo parlor before, but the two obviously knew each other. Quite well, if she was not mistaken.

Micah remained silent. Cassandra blew out her breath and counted to three. "Okay...I see we need a little time to think about this."

Cassandra decided it was a good time to introduce herself to Micah's companion.

"Hey, I'm Cassandra." She stood up and offered her hand. Micah's guest oozed self-assurance and power, and managed to pull it off casually. Another surprise, since this was definitely not the type of woman she expected to find Micah with. Perhaps she had been wrong about how well they knew each other or what their relationship might be.

The movement caught Micah's attention, shaking her out of her "zone." She had been so intent on the pending ink work and all that it entailed that she had forgotten her manners.

"Damn, Cass, I'm sorry," she apologized. "Cass, this is Olivia, my, my..." Micah faltered. *How should she introduce Olivia to her friends? She didn't want to assume that Olivia was okay with discussing their relationship with a stranger, but "friend" always sounded so crappy when she heard others say it.*

Rising gracefully from her chair, Olivia took Cassandra's hand. Cassandra had expected a tepid grip; Blonde and petite, Olivia seemed positively delicate in contrast to the darkly handsome Micah. The firm handshake surprised her, as well as the direct and appraising look that peered out from beneath equally pale eyebrows.

"Lover," Olivia finished Micah's sentence for her, her cultured tones matching her casually elegant appearance. "I believe that was the word she was looking for."

Micah's eyebrows shot up in shock. *Damn, I didn't expect that.* The possessive tone was obvious, too. Cassandra flashed Micah an amused grin in return, letting her know that she hadn't missed that little nuance either.

"Well, then." Cassandra coughed and turned away, missing the look passing between the two women. Micah asked an unspoken question with a twist of her head. Olivia schooled herself to passive innocence before leaning forward and offering an unspoken answer. She took Micah's hand and brought it to her lips, planting a soft kiss along the knuckles. She squeezed gently, trying to project support and understanding. This was hard for Micah, and she didn't want to make it any harder.

Micah returned the squeeze before pulling her hand away. Swinging her long legs up on the padded table, she pulled her black shirt up over her head in one swift motion to expose her midriff, then lowered herself onto the padded table.

Olivia tried to suppress her reaction to Micah's controlled movement. It was too close to what they had done earlier that morning. Luckily, for her, Cassandra turned around at the same moment, whistling sharply at Micah's physique. The sound masked Olivia's gasp, and gave her time to recover from the unexpected rush that made her heart beat hard and fast within her chest.

"Jesus, Micah, how much time have you been spending at the gym?" Cassandra exclaimed eyeing Micah's leather clad form appreciatively.

"Some," Micah replied, grinning at her friend's reaction.

"I see," Cassandra spoke drolly. Even for Micah, that was an extreme form of understatement. Cassandra let the sound of the tattoo needle accent her next comment. Micah might have the body, but she was the one who got to decorate it, the next few hours were hers.

"Are we ready?"

"Oh, yeah, let's do this!"

The next hour was filled with the intermittent buzz of the needle. Olivia watched the orchestrated dance of needle on skin, wipe, turn and dip, repeat. There was more to it than that, but she was too busy watching Micah's face half the time and missed things.

"So, are you going to the art show next weekend?" Cassandra asked, spreading a bit of Vaseline on a new section.

"Yeah, I was planning on it," she responded, then turned to look at Olivia. "Would you want to go with me?"

"What is it?" Olivia asked, instantly distracted when Micah turned to look directly at her. Her pupils were huge, making her hazel eyes look almost black— except for the small gold flecks trapped between the inky pools and the thin ring of dark green circling her irises. Excitement and lust swam in those deep pools. Olivia had to know...was all of that intense emotion in direct response to the pain of the needle travelling across her skin?

She sat up straighter, sure that she was on to something. Olivia could practically visualize the key she needed to unlock the knowledge trapped in her head. Maybe then, she could fully appreciate what this experience might mean to Micah.

Micah spoke over the sound of the tattoo machine buzzing around them, her voice tight and mildly clipped as the needle passed along her skin. "It's a very eclectic collection. It's not necessarily mainstream, but there are many talented artists, most of them still starving but quite good, all waiting and hoping for their big break. Some friends of mine host it, and it brings in a ton of potential buyers. The artists appreciate it, since they often make enough sales to keep afloat until the next show. There is pretty much everything there from paintings and drawings to sculptures, with some metal work thrown in for the hell of it."

"Are you going to be showing anything this time around?" Cassandra piped in, putting down her gun to wipe the ink off Micah's abdomen.

"Um no, not this time."

"What does she normally show?" Olivia asked Cassandra, caught up in the conversation now.

"Drawings mostly, pen and ink and some pencil." Cassandra had resumed tattooing, so her responses came out as short bursts between lines.

"I didn't know that you showed your work?"

"I dabble." Micah smiled at her depreciatively.

"Hah! She drew the dragon that I am working on," Cassandra gleefully tattled on her friend. Dipping the needle into the small capful of ink on her table, she snuck a quick glance at Olivia over Micah's prone body. "Just having Micah's name on the list of artists would boost our attendance, her work is always popular."

"Why don't you have anything ready?" Olivia asked, intrigued at the direction their conversation was taking.

"I've been busy working on Tristan's graphic novel, and—other things."

Olivia tried very hard not to read into the slight pause. Tristan must be the friend that had asked Micah to illustrate for him. Micah hadn't really gone into much detail about their arrangement, only that the graphic novel was almost complete.

Cassandra's tattoo machine continued to dance along Micah's skin while they chatted. After a while, Cassandra put her machine down to inspect her work more closely. After cleaning the area, she spread Vaseline over her work and removed her gloves with a loud snap.

"Okay, are you ready for a break?" Cassandra asked. She stood, stretching her back until her spine cracked. She pulled out a pack of smokes, taking out a cigarette then passing the pack over to Micah, who quickly took the offering and lit up.

"Cokes are in the fridge in the back."

"Thanks," Micah said, taking a deep drag before wandering down the hall.

"She looks happy," Cassandra spoke as soon as Micah was out of earshot. Her unlit cigarette sat loosely between her forefinger and middle finger, apparently forgotten.

"I sincerely hope so," Olivia replied, wondering about the tattoo artist's sudden interest.

"Aren't you going to smoke?" she asked, nodding at the unlit cigarette.

"Nah, I just take one so Micah will, otherwise she won't accept one from me and she always forgets to bring her own," Cassandra explained. "She's quirky that way."

"Yes, she is," Olivia agreed.

"I'm glad she came in. I have to tell you, I am surprised to see her here with someone else. Micah is usually a very private person." Cassandra peeked over her shoulder to make sure they were still alone, then cleared her throat. "You know, I was worried when she called me up earlier this week that she was going to do something bad. I am so glad to see that she didn't."

She nervously lit her cigarette and took a drag, then made a face. "Dammit. Almost made it three months."

"When was this?" Olivia whispered, a feeling of dread creeping up her spine.

"Wednesday night, I could tell she was crying and seemed frantic but she seems fine now." Blowing the smoke out of the corner of her mouth, Cass stood there silently, waiting for Olivia's response.

"I, uh...I didn't know. Thank you, Cassandra, for telling me. You are a good friend." Cassandra's relieved smile told Olivia that she had said the right thing. On the inside she was kicking herself for being so incredibly dense about the other night. She had no idea that Micah had been that upset.

Micah returned before they could continue their conversation. At first, she hung back in the doorway so that the cigarette smoke wouldn't bother Olivia. It was a sweet gesture, but Olivia found that she really didn't care.

"You don't have to stay out there, Micah," Olivia said, holding her hand out for Micah to join them. Cassandra displayed her own lit cigarette, looking a bit embarrassed as she did so. Olivia pulled Micah against her so she could slide her arm around Micah's waist, demanding the semi-intimate contact and getting it.

Micah looked down at Olivia then shot a curious glance towards Cassandra, trying to figure out what had changed while she was gone. Cass just shot her a warning look, and then pushed off from the wall. "I'll give you two some privacy," she said, crushing the rest of her cigarette out before walking away. "Besides, I think I'll grab one of those Cokes before we start up again. Do you want anything, Olivia?"

"No, thank you, Cassandra. I'm good," Olivia said, offering a polite smile to the other woman.

"You two seemed to have hit it off," Micah said, pulling Olivia away from the door so they could have some privacy.

"I guess so. Cassandra seems like a nice person, and she is quite talented." Olivia's response sounded less than enthusiastic, even to her own ears. She was still processing the information that Cassandra had given her. Micah stiffened up next to her, reacting to Olivia's tone of voice rather than her words.

"Are you okay with this? If it's bothering you to watch me get a tattoo, you can always come back later and get me. I understand it disturbs some people."

"No, it's fine, I want to be here with you." Olivia squeezed Micah's bicep in reassurance, running her hand along the hard muscle. Cassandra was right about one thing, Micah spent a lot of time at the gym.

"All right, but if it starts to get to you just let me know. I won't be upset if you need to take a break. You could go get some coffee or something and come back after I am done," Micah offered. She didn't want Olivia to be uncomfortable.

"Really, Micah, I'm fine," Olivia reassured her lover. "I promise I will let you know."

"Okay, as long as you promise," Micah pushed.

"I promise."

"Ready to start again?" Cassandra called out from inside her room, interrupting their private conversation.

"Yep," Micah called out, her eyes glowing with excitement. There was no doubt that she was more than ready to get started again.

***

"Okay, Micah, I'm done up here," Cassandra announced, wiping the upper leg and claw wrapped around Micah's ribs down with a wet paper towel, then spreading a good bit of Vaseline on the fresh ink. "Are you still good to keep going?" she asked. Cassandra examined her work, making sure that the dark lines and shading were clean and even.

"Yeah, I am, let's get this done," Micah said. When she didn't hear the tattoo machine start up again, Micah looked up to see what was holding things up.

"Um, Micah—the tat is a little low. You're gonna have to unbutton your pants so I have room to work," Cassandra explained, holding a small towel in her hand. Micah reached down and unsnapped the top two buttons of her leather pants with one hand, then pushed the soft leather down off her hip.

Olivia inhaled sharply, following the deceptively casual movement of Micah's hand. The movement was not so casual to her, not with last night still fresh in her mind. The black leather now rode low on Micah's hip, revealing only smooth skin, and nothing else underneath. Even last night, the leather had remained a barrier between them, and while Micah's "surprise" had been an exciting and new experience, she had longed to touch what had remained hidden from her. It wasn't until later that night that Micah had finally trusted her enough, allowing her to act on that desire. Finally shedding her second skin, you might say, and letting her in. A spike of jealousy forced its way past her inappropriate thoughts as Cassandra's fingers slipped under that smooth leather to tuck a protective cloth into Micah's pants. Gloves or no, that was closer than Olivia liked. She had to forcibly push down the inner voice that growled *MINE.*

Olivia moved closer to the table. It was fascinating, watching Micah's pale skin transform under the needlework. She had to admit that the woman had an artist's eye that went beyond technical proficiency. She had laid the design out so that it complemented Micah's lines and muscle movement. When it was done, the dragon wouldn't just be something that graced the surface of Micah's skin, it would become a part of her, moving and shifting as she did. With the new ink filling in the middle of the design, the dragon was coming alive, becoming a part of her.

Cassandra had inked the dragon's claws to rest along the linear scars on Micah's abdomen, making it look like they were the result of some battle fought and won in order to earn the right to nestle against Micah's skin. Despite what Micah had told her, she had thought it was just another form of armor, a way to hide away from the world. Now, she was wondering if she was wrong and that Micah's tattoos were more healing in nature.

"You're really enjoying this, aren't you?" Olivia whispered, taking Micah's hand in hers. Her palm was hot against hers, her pulse beating strongly beneath Olivia's fingers.

"You have no idea," Micah answered, gazing directly into Olivia's eyes for a moment before closing them again. Her expression was almost ecstatic as she accepted the pain from the needle. Micah's hazel eyes had been dark, bordering on feverish. The high-pitched buzz of the tattoo needle deepened each time it touched her, sounding more like a million wasps singing in concert than anything else. Micah's hand gripped Olivia's tightly each time the needle travelled along her skin. A subtle flutter of eyelids betrayed her. Evidently, Micah wasn't immune to the pain; she just seemed to enjoy it...a lot. Olivia's heart sped up.

Their earlier conversation surfaced, adding context to her response. *Are you into that? Is that what you like?* She had asked. *I have no desire to cause pain like that,* Micah had responded. Closing her eyes, she flipped through memories of their times together. Images of nails raking down Micah's back, her hands clawing for purchase along Micah's forearms, Micah's back arching, her voice a low growl, encouraging her. They all had one thing in common.

Pain. Micah's pain.

Opening her eyes, she twisted her grip on Micah's hand. Short, semi-circular gouges, half healed and scabbed over, dotted the underside of Micah's forearm. Olivia knew that if she looked, she would find a similar pattern on her other forearm. Things that had been sitting at the edge of her consciousness coalesced into one blinding flash of comprehension.

Olivia continued the motion of her hand, not wanting Micah to realize she had seen the scratches. She had to know if she was right. Olivia brushed her lips against Micah's knuckles, kissing along them before gently opening Micah's hand, exposing her palm. Bringing her lips down again, she let her tongue slip along the warm flesh of Micah's palm, tasting salt and heat. Olivia could sense Micah forcing herself to stillness.

She looked up to see Micah staring at her, her gaze intense, unreadable. Good, she had her attention.

Rolling her eyes up so she could watch Micah's expression, she continued to tease her lips down the meaty flesh of Micah's thumb until she could feel the steady thrum of her pulse. She nipped gently. Her reward was a quick intake of breath. Encouraged, Olivia nipped more aggressively, sealing her lips against Micah's wrist and sucking the salty flesh against her tongue, hard.

"Christ!" Micah yelled, jerking her hand away from Olivia's grasp, her hips arching off the table in response to the unexpected pain.

"Goddammit, Micah!" Cassandra bitched, the hand holding the tattoo gun flying up and away from Micah's skin. Caught up in tattooing the intricate pattern, she hadn't been prepared for the sudden movement. Reaching for a fresh paper towel, she angrily sprayed green soap on it before turning to wipe away the overflow of ink.

"I know you are a better canvas than this Micah, what the hell?" Her tirade stopped suddenly, taking in the view of the two women staring each other down. It took a quick moment to realize that what she was witnessing wasn't a fight. Oh, the emotions were running high, that was for sure, but it was anything but anger.

"I swear, Micah, if you fucked up this tat," she continued, evidently the only one in the room who was angry. Micah never, ever moved during their sessions—it was a given. She had never seen anyone sit for so long or endure the pain as well as she did. She pressed the cold, wet paper towel against Micah's skin, wiping the skin down in firm, angry strokes.

That got Micah's attention.

"Shit, Cassandra, that's cold." Swinging her head around, Micah focused the full force of her gaze on Cassandra.

Cassandra froze under that intense gaze. She knew Micah got off on the pain; most of her customers did to some extent. But this was something else. This was passion and violence and pain all rolled up into one exquisite emotion. It rolled off Micah's skin in bright waves, in stark contrast to the dark nature of its origins.

"Um, Micah?" Cassandra's voice pierced through the sound of thunder pounding in Micah's ears. Micah took in a couple of deep breaths, forcing herself into some semblance of calm.

"I'm sorry, Cass."

"That's okay, Micah, but I really think we are done here." She stood up slowly and stretched, stiff after sitting in one position for so long. "It's a lucky thing I had been finishing up on a bit of shading instead of any heavy line work."

Micah nodded, accepting her friends scolding without any argument. She avoided making eye contact with Olivia while she buttoned up her leather pants, carefully avoiding displacing the dressing then slipped her shirt back on with quick, jerky movements.

"How much do I owe you?" Micah asked, reaching for her wallet.

"Just catch up with me next time, okay?" Cassandra asked, busying herself with her machine. She felt awkward and more than a little overheated. Her hands shook slightly as she performed her cleaning routine with a lot more attention than the familiar task required. Micah just nodded and headed out the door. Olivia followed close behind, casting an apologetic glance her way.

***

They barely made it home and back into the house before Micah turned and pinned Olivia to the front door. Thrusting her tongue into Olivia's mouth, she kissed her roughly, self-control the last thing on her mind.

Her insistent lips and tongue roamed along Olivia's jawline and neck, biting and sucking along her pulse line, leaving red marks in their wake. Olivia's hips rolled against hers, the demanding rhythm meeting Micah's rising passion with her own. She moaned loudly, the desperate sound swallowed by Micah's mouth as it returned to devour swollen lips, sucking the tender flesh between her teeth before kissing the mild pain away. A low growl vibrated deep within Micah's chest, escaping between clenched teeth when Olivia found her skin. She raked blunt nails down Micah's back, the sharp pain sending waves of pleasure down her spine. Her body arched in response to the rough play, bringing her groin firmly into contact with the front of Olivia's soft body.

Olivia felt the moment that Micah backed down, seeking to regain control. She drew fresh air into her lungs with great ragged draughts as she buried her face against Olivia's neck.

"No," Micah said; the strain of trying to shackle her passion turned that one word into something harsh. *This couldn't be what Olivia wanted, not now, not ever.*

"Micah. Let go, it's okay," Olivia begged her lover, her voice jagged with need.

Micah looked up, searching those clear blue eyes for any signs of hesitation. She had to know if Olivia truly understood what she was asking.

"You sure?" she whispered painfully, feeling the weight of her self-imposed restraint more profoundly than she ever had before.

"Yes, I trust you. I know you have been holding back, Micah. I don't want you to. I want to know your passion—all of it," Olivia spoke ardently, the desire in her eyes flashing like lightning to Micah's thunder. "Please, Micah, I'm begging you," Olivia whispered, her body trembling in Micah's embrace.

Those words, spoken so desperately, quickened the fire burning deep within Micah. Grasping Olivia's hands together, Micah held them above her head against the door, preventing Olivia from touching her. Her free hand found the buttons at Olivia's waist, opening the front of her slacks and giving her room to thrust her hand beneath the thin panties. Her fingers found Olivia already soaked, her folds open and wet beneath her questing fingers. Without warning, she slid three fingers deep inside her lover's slick walls, the muscles clamping down around her. She didn't wait for her to accommodate to the sudden intrusion. Instead, she began to work her fingers in and out, her hand cupping Olivia's sex, working her swollen clit against her palm. The visual impact of Olivia pressed against the hard wood of the door, her hands captured above her head as Micah's forearm worked against her partially clothed body sent Micah perilously close to her own orgasm.

Olivia had thrown her head back as far as the door behind her would allow, her eyes closed against the pleasure, her skin flushing bright red along her neckline as she fought for air. Each breath came in ragged time to the deep stroke of Micah's fingers. Micah held Olivia's wrists tightly against any attempts to move. She could feel Olivia's hands claw and flex against her stronger grip as her hips bucked and thrust against her other hand. Olivia started to babble, calling out her name as Micah's fingers fought to maintain her rhythm within Olivia's silken core. Her muscular walls clenched tightly around her fingers until Micah was forced to still her movement as Olivia came in one long shudder, her body convulsing around her trapped fingers in one violent aftershock after another.

Before Olivia could recover, Micah picked her up and carried her upstairs to the bedroom. Olivia knew Micah was strong, but she didn't realize just how strong she really was until she carried her all the way up to the second floor. It was then that she realized just how careful Micah had been with her.

Once in the bedroom, Micah laid Olivia down on the soft bed, intent on removing the rest of her clothes so she could finish what they had started downstairs. However, as she leaned in to kiss her lover, Olivia placed a halting hand to her chest.

"What's wrong?" Micah asked, instantly alarmed. Had she gone too far?

"Not a thing is wrong, Sweetheart, everything is so very right," Olivia replied huskily, her voice raw from calling out. She drew Micah down into a tender kiss, her fingers threading through the thick black hair in order to pull Micah deeper into the kiss, demanding more. Without warning, Olivia gathered all of her strength and twisted, flipping Micah onto her back beneath her. Olivia had to laugh at Micah's shocked expression, her throaty chuckle promising more surprises to come.

She pulled Micah's shirt and bra off in one quick motion, using the movement to mask her true intent. Her mouth found Micah's breast, gathering the pebbled flesh into her mouth. She sucked hard on her nipple, letting her teeth play along the swollen nub and eliciting a startled gasp out of Micah. Olivia started unbuttoning Micah's leather pants, knowing that she wore nothing on beneath them. Once she got them unbuttoned, she switched to the other nipple and gave it the same treatment, until both nipples were firm and swollen, flushing deep red beneath her tongue. Pushing the leather pants down the well-muscled thighs, she helped Micah kick them away, her abdominal muscles clenching and bunching as she curled her body up to accomplish the task. The dragon danced across her smooth skin, coming to life with every movement, joining their dance and promising fire.

Sliding her body down and careful to avoid the fresh tattoo, she kneeled between Micah's legs. She pressed her lips against the long length of muscle running along Micah's inner thigh until she reached the soft black curls shining damply at her apex. Running her tongue along Micah's slit, the silken folds opened and spread for her inspection. Olivia didn't give Micah any warning before she pressed her tongue flat against her swollen clit, lapping up the sweet wetness gathering at her center.

"Oh shit, Olivia. I'm not gonna last long," Micah moaned. Making love to Olivia had primed her; her sex ached for the attention she was receiving from Olivia's mouth. The coverlet beneath her felt abrasive, rubbing roughly against the parallel lines of burning pain along her back where Olivia had dug her fingernails in. She shuddered at the remembered pain.

When Olivia slid two fingers inside her, Micah moaned low and deep. Her hands clenched, needing something tangible to grasp. She threaded guiding fingers into Olivia's soft hair, holding her tightly as she ground her hips against the teasing tongue and fingers. When she came, her hips jerked off the bed as she dug her heels in, the much-needed release overtaking her and igniting bright flashes of light that danced inside her skull.

Olivia chuckled in satisfaction as Micah collapsed on the bed, breathing hard and fast as she tried to recover from her orgasm.

"We will have to do that again." Olivia's pleased voice penetrated Micah's post-coital exhaustion. Snuggling into Micah's side, she tucked her face into Micah's neck, breathing in her unique scent.

"Sure, anytime," Micah mumbled.

"Were you still holding back?" Olivia asked suddenly, forcing Micah back from semi-consciousness.

"No."

"Good, now go to sleep."

Micah had no problem following that command since she was already crashing from her earlier endorphin rush. She had ridden that rush as she made love to Olivia, even before Olivia surprised her by taking over, intent on giving as much as she had received. She had expended herself, and felt nothing but the heavy sensation of exhaustion within her tired limbs. She barely noticed Olivia pulling the covers over them and cuddling up to her side before they both fell into the waiting arms of Morpheus.

Chapter Twenty-Seven

Olivia woke up late the next morning to an empty bed and the smell of good coffee. Stretching across the bed, she spent a few glorious moments reveling in the memories of last night's lovemaking. Running her hand along her stomach, Olivia closed her eyes against the morning sunlight, squirming a little when a memory-inspired residual threatened to blossom into full-blown arousal. She was still exquisitely sensitive wherever Micah had touched her.

Last night she had given Micah free rein to do as she pleased. She had to admit that she had never expected to enjoy being taken like that. The feeling of Micah's arm pumping against her stomach as she filled her, Micah's other hand restraining her arms above her head was absolutely the most arousing and intense sexual experience she ever had.

Micah walked in, taking in the languorous posture and lazy smile on her lover's face. Olivia flushed at the knowing grin that quickly spread to Micah's eyes, brighter and more awake this morning than usual.

"Good morning, Love." Micah grinned at the normally up and running attorney lounging so decadently across the tossed bed sheets. She was carrying a steaming cup of coffee in one hand and a Coke in the other. Smiling at the morning ritual, Olivia accepted her coffee with a quick kiss on the cheek and a murmured "I love you".

Micah meandered into the bathroom to brush her teeth and ready herself for the morning while Olivia enjoyed her first coffee of the day. When she returned, Olivia was wide-awake and ready to talk. Micah sighed. Olivia was still so much more of a morning person than she was.

"So what would you like to do today?" Olivia asked, smiling at the jaw-cracking yawn Micah was trying to hide behind one hand as she rifled through her depleted duffle bag. All she had left was a pair of jeans and a t-shirt, just enough to get her through the day.

"Well, I need to go home and get some clean clothes." She picked up her now empty duffle bag and turned it upside down.

"No, I have you for the whole weekend."

"You do?" Micah asked, cocking her head at Olivia. "I don't remember making that promise."

"Ah, see, I asked you to come home with me...I never said for how long," Olivia answered slyly.

"Okay..." Micah drew out the word. "I will give you that, but then I really do need to go home and pick up more clothes."

Olivia's sly grin turned into something more salacious; she had no doubts that the two of them could manage a whole weekend without needing a change of clothes.

"No, you don't," Olivia said, earning another quizzical look from Micah before dropping her idea on her. "We could go shopping."

"Yeah, right. It would be easier for me to just run back home and pick up a few things."

"Or, we could go shopping," Olivia repeated, taking a sip of her coffee to hide the sly grin behind the porcelain lip of her coffee cup. She purposefully ignored Micah's reaction to her suggestion, which by the rise of one dark eyebrow was one of incredulous dismay.

"Or, I could just do some laundry," Micah countered, sliding into her jeans before crawling back into the warm bed to sit cross-legged next to Olivia, managing to balance her Coke during the entire maneuver without spilling a drop.

Briefly, Micah considered forgetting about leaving the bed altogether today. Olivia was still in her silk pajamas. *It shouldn't take much convincing to either keep her in them, or out of them,* she thought. Either choice was a good one. She really didn't want to go shopping, not when there was more interesting things they could do.

"Or, we could go shopping," Olivia repeated again, letting Micah kiss her before placing a hand on Micah's chest.

"Or we could go shopping." Micah groaned, sitting back on the bed with a dejected slouch. *Shopping with Olivia, that should be interesting.*

***

"Olivia, I want these," Micah repeated herself, holding up the button-fly Levi's she had picked out. Hell, she had even compromised, going with black jeans that could be dressed up instead of her standard stonewashed, AND she had stayed away from cargo anything. What more did Olivia want?

"Why can't you just try these on?" Olivia asked, holding up a pair of dress slacks that probably looked good in the boardroom or even a dinner party, but were something that Micah had no interest in. She didn't need dress pants for either situation, because she avoided both places like the plague.

"Because I like these," Micah said, then sighed. Pitting yourself against Olivia Holden on objects of fashion and clothing was exhausting.

"You're being ridiculous! Think, Micah. You can't wear jeans every time we're out together. What if I wanted to go out to a nice restaurant, or a play? People I know might be there, I do have a reputation to keep." The minute the words came out of her mouth, Olivia realized she had made a huge mistake.

"You know what you can do with your reputation, Olivia Holden?" Micah hissed, the fierce whisper pitched too low to create a public scene. "You knew who I was and what I was like when you pursued me."

"Micah, that came out all wrong."

"Yeah, you think? There's something you aren't telling me. All this stuff about shows or dinner, that's bullshit. Why are you pushing fancy clothes on me all of a sudden, Olivia?" Micah took a step away. She really was done shopping for the day if this was how it was going to be.

"I love you, Sweetheart. I spoke without thinking." Olivia looked appalled and embarrassed, two emotions she did not wear easily.

Micah waited to see what else Olivia had to say.

"But, you will have to dress up a little when we go out, you have to know that," Olivia tried again. *Why does she have to be so stubborn?*

"So, you want me to dress up so we can go out without me embarrassing you? Is that what you are saying?"

"No, of course not. It's just that eventually we will have to have dinner with my father."

"Your father?" Micah rocked back on her heels, the unexpected answer sparking an anger that always bubbled dangerously close to the surface.

"You mean the man that had so many rules that you couldn't even admit that you liked me, the man with such a hold on you that you were more worried about what was proper than admit to me that you wanted me?"

The senior Holden was a stodgy old bastard who didn't care if Olivia was happy as long as she played by his rules. His rules had sent Micah running home, believing that she had made a huge mistake. It didn't even matter that she knew better now. Hell, Micah could even forgive Olivia for letting her father sway her, but she didn't think she could say the same about her father. God knows she had let her own father rule her for many years, despite the damage it had done, how could she continue blaming Olivia for doing the same?

"Let me get this straight, you want your father to know we're a couple?" Micah asked, gesturing between them. She wanted to make sure she had heard Olivia right.

"Yes, I've already told him about you, and he has invited you to join us for dinner sometime."

"But, I thought he didn't want us together," Micah protested, her mind reeling over the entire notion.

"No, Micah. It was never about us. It was because you were an intern. You know, Micah, he's not that bad of a guy. He doesn't care that I'm a lesbian, and he has nothing against you."

Micah just looked at her. She wanted to believe Olivia but there was just so much bad history standing in the way. *How much of that history is mine? How much of my father am I projecting on Olivia's?*

"Are you okay with meeting him for dinner sometime? Is that a problem?" Olivia asked gently.

"No, no problem at all," Micah murmured, trying to wrap her head around it all. *She sees us as a couple.* It seemed incredulous to Micah, but there it was. *And, she doesn't mind other people seeing us together as a couple.* Micah found any traces of anger melting away as she absorbed the implications of Olivia's statement.

For the most part, their relationship had been private—just between the two of them. Oh, Amanda and Jonathan were aware, and no one she knew really gave a damn—but Olivia knew people, a lot of important people. That Olivia was willing to be "out" in her own circles for her, for them... this was huge. No wonder Olivia was complaining about her penchant for jeans. Olivia's mistake was trying to bull her way through to what she wanted, rather than explain things. Which was why Micah was still going to buy those jeans.

"Just so you know, I'm still getting these." Micah held up the offending jeans, letting Olivia know that she would not be manipulated into giving up her comfortable clothes. When Olivia was about to protest, Micah put up her hand to forestall any renewed argument. "Look, Love...when the time comes, I promise that you won't be disappointed, but it has to be something I'm comfortable with. Can we just let it go for today?"

"That sounds reasonable."

Micah just smiled at her, and then made her an offer she thought Olivia would like. "Well, I do need, um, under things if you want to help me pick those out?"

"Ah, I thought you dispensed with most of that," Olivia said, following Micah's lead.

"This is true, but I still need bras and stuff."

355

Olivia proceeded to pick out something made of lace and silk that Micah knew was solely for her visual enjoyment.

"Uh huh." Micah's response made Olivia laugh aloud, the delighted sound sweet in her ears. Picking out a few items a little more appropriate to her needs, Micah turned a blind eye to Olivia's attempt to hide the frilly things between some other items. She wasn't completely opposed to sexy things; she just didn't have that much of a need for them, not unless Olivia planned on wearing them for her.

"You do realize at some point I am going to have to do laundry. I can't keep buying new clothes," Micah informed Olivia as they stood in line to pay for their items. The women held two very different bundles of clothes.

"I know, I just wanted this weekend with you without anything else getting in the way."

"Greedy, huh?" Micah asked, grinning lasciviously.

"Mm. Maybe just a little," Olivia admitted.

Just as they were leaving the store, Micah's cell went off. She shuffled her bags around to take the call, then frowned angrily before declining it.

"I'm going to have to get their number blocked, this is getting out of control," Micah muttered. She really didn't want to deal with her mom, especially not this weekend. Her parents had ruined one too many birthdays for her, and always for the same old thing.

"She's been calling you a lot." It was a statement, not a question, but Micah's tight nod confirmed Olivia's assumption.

"I thought it was an ex harassing you."

"What?" Micah stopped dead in her tracks. She had no idea what Olivia was talking about.

"I figured you must have a few ex-girlfriends out there," Olivia teased. Micah was gorgeous, smart, strong, and great in bed, the probability was highly likely. Tucking her arm behind Micah's elbow, she got Micah moving and guided her towards the exit.

"Olivia, I haven't had a relationship with anyone in well over two years," Micah responded seriously. Irritation at her parents put a sharp edge to her voice that hadn't been there a few minutes ago.

Olivia brought them to a stop on the busy sidewalk to let traffic pass. The mood had gone serious. Olivia nervously wet her lips with her tongue before asking, "What did you do before, after you got a tattoo? I saw what that does to you."

That was an understatement, Olivia thought. She hadn't just seen it; she had felt it all the way down to the tips of her toes and then back up again.

"Seriously, you want to talk about that now?" Micah's eyes widened at the incredulous question, gesturing broadly at all the people around them. This was so not a great time for someone to develop a case of jealousy. She uttered a silent curse at her parents; even from another state, they could manage to fuck up her day. If they hadn't called, this conversation wouldn't be happening.

"Fine, if you must know, I went to the club and blew off some steam. If you know what I mean?" She knew she sounded cruel, but Olivia's question had hit a sore spot.

"Jonathan said you never went home with anyone." Olivia pulled back as if she had just suffered a physical blow.

Why would it matter if she had taken anyone home? She was so tired of people judging her, first her parents, and now—Gods, she was tired of this conversation. Micah stepped away from Olivia, turning her body away for a moment before looking back over her shoulder. "I didn't have to leave the club to have a quick fuck, Olivia. But he was right, I never left with anyone."

"Oh." Olivia's flat response only served to reinforce Micah's beliefs. She should have never taken Olivia to the club. Olivia wasn't stupid or naïve, she had to know what was happening, what it meant when she had seen people pair off and head for the dark corners of the club.

"That night at the club, you wanted me."

"Oh, Gods yes, Olivia...and everyone at the club knew it," Micah choked out. "But, Olivia, you have to know, that would have never happened with you."

"Why?" The thought of Micah possessing some stranger in a dark hallway, not thinking past her need for release, made Olivia uncomfortable. "Why did you act differently with me?

"Because Olivia, you weren't a casual fuck," Micah practically growled. "You could never be that to me."

Olivia was right, she had wanted her badly that night. She had thought Olivia's behavior in the club had been a fluke or a deliberate attempt to fit in, some kind of game...but not anymore. Not after Olivia admitted to being turned on by things Micah hadn't considered a possibility. Then after the tattoo, she had given her free rein, begging Micah not to hold back anything. To Micah's delight, Olivia's passion had risen as hot and demanding as her own. Olivia had marked her last night. She could still feel the stinging burn of a dual set of nail marks dug into her back, instinctively giving her exactly what she had wanted.

"Did any of these women, you know...reciprocate?" Olivia asked, stuttering over the words.

"No, Olivia, you are the first person I've let touch me in a very long time." The incredible sadness in Micah's voice was made all the more poignant by Olivia's knowledge of why this was so.

"I am such an idiot sometimes," Olivia muttered, barely loud enough for Micah to hear. "I am so sorry, Micah. I got jealous and couldn't stop myself from asking. You are so beautiful, so strong; I still don't understand why you want to be with me."

Micah turned around then, staring out towards the parking lot over Olivia's head.

"Look, Olivia, I'm not proud of everything I've done in the past. But you have to understand, that was all I had to give, all I could stand to offer for a very long time." Micah lifted Olivia's chin so she would look at her; she had to make sure Olivia understood how important this was. "This is a part of who I am, but don't you see? With you, I want it to be more. I don't want to be the person no one can touch." Micah paused then, waiting for Olivia to process everything she just said before speaking again. "You know, someday we will stop doing this."

"Stop what?" Olivia asked.

"The whole putting the foot in your mouth thing— someday we will stop making these mistakes and get onto something more important." Micah gathered Olivia's hands in her own, noting how cold they were.

"Wha–what's more important?" Olivia stuttered.

"Us."

"Oh!"

The breathless response made Micah grin, breaking the spell between them. They were still standing on the sidewalk while other shoppers walked around them. That they were having this life-changing moment while the mass of humanity trudged around them in blissful ignorance, unaware of any of it was too hilarious.

"We should go," Micah suggested.

Olivia thought that was a wonderful idea. They stepped out from under the shaded entrance into the bright summer sun that beat down on them and reflected sharply off the concrete

"What's wrong, Sweetheart?" she asked, hearing Micah curse lightly under her breath.

"I need new sunglasses; it's really bright out here," Micah replied. Her eyes had always been photosensitive, hence the ever present and now trademark shades, but with everything going on lately she kept forgetting to go buy a pair.

"That's easy; we can go get some now." Olivia took advantage of their joined hands to drag Micah back into the mall. She laughed when Micah groaned; she had been so close to escaping.

"Oh, and Micah, no more anonymous sex, okay? You have me now," Olivia deadpanned, raising one elegant eyebrow that was in direct conflict with the leering grin she was sporting. She wanted to make sure Micah knew exactly what she was talking about.

"I know, and I would never do that to you." Bringing Olivia's hand to her lips, Micah pressed a quick kiss along her knuckles.

"Good, let's keep it that way," Olivia, responded imperiously, patting Micah's hand.

"Yes, Olivia." Micah tried to sound meek, but failed miserably. It just wasn't in her genetic makeup.

***

Olivia was working very hard to remain patient while Micah tried on several different pairs of Ray-Bans, trying to find just the right ones. *How hard was it to choose a pair of sunglasses?* Still, it was her own fault. She had dragged Micah back into the mall, and this was her penance for her enthusiasm.

"Olivia, I really need to get back to work. Are you okay with me starting again on Monday? What do you think of these?" Micah was bouncing from one subject to another almost seamlessly while trying on a pair of dark mirrored wraparounds that looked identical to the ones she used to have.

"Those are fine," Olivia replied absently. She had a feeling that needing to get back to work really meant, "I need to get outside and ride my bike."

"Will you take it easy if you come back?" Olivia asked. Micah wasn't the only one that could hold two conversations at once.

"I don't want just fine. Do I get to decide what easy is?"

"Those look good on you; they flatter your face well. We just need to agree on easy."

The clerk was having trouble tracking their conversation and it showed. He couldn't get a word in edgewise, which was fine with her. She hated the hard sell tactics that the kiosks often resorted to. The smirk on Micah's face was revealing. She knew what they were doing to the poor man, and she was enjoying it as much as Olivia was.

"I'll take these." Micah took off the glasses and handed them to the thankful clerk. Before she could pull out her wallet, Olivia stepped forward and offered him her Visa.

Micah waited until they were back outside before looking sideways at Olivia.

"You know, I could have bought my own sunglasses."

"I know. Just say thank you."

"Olivia, you don't have to buy stuff for me. I can afford my own things."

"I wanted to get them for you. What's the use of having money if you can't spend it on the people you love?" Olivia asked, confused by Micah's reluctance to accept a gift from her. She had wanted to do something nice and it was backfiring on her. "Why is this bothering you so much?"

The hurt question hung between them for a second. Micah closed her eyes and took a deep breath before answering. "I'm sorry, Love—I'm not going to make an excuse for being an ass. It's just that, well, just that my family would use money to manipulate me when I was younger. If I did something they didn't like..." Micah shook head. "Never mind, it doesn't matter. I know you aren't like that."

Micah's smile didn't quite reach her eyes. The shadow of painful memories lurked there, memories that seemed to find their way to the surface at the oddest moments. Olivia frowned. She was developing an intense dislike for the people who had done this to her. It was no wonder that Micah's eyes were so sensitive to the light; she had been living in the dark for too long. Olivia's heart ached for her lover. She so wanted to be the one to chase those shadows away.

As if sensing the direction of Olivia's thoughts, Micah ran her fingertips along Olivia's jawline and brushed away a stray strand of hair, willing the melancholy thoughts away.

"Why don't we just consider this an early birthday present, then?" Olivia suggested, giving Micah an out.

"Thank you, Love. They are very nice." Micah smiled, graciously accepting Olivia's gift. "You know, if we weren't in public right now, Olivia Holden, I would kiss you right here to show you my appreciation for such a lovely gift." Micah's voice cracked with emotion. Olivia swallowed hard. Micah was looking at her with the strangest expression on her face. Olivia had the distinct impression that Micah wasn't kidding. She was going to be kissed, in public, and quite thoroughly.

"Kiss me anyways. It's New York, no one cares," Olivia said, shocking herself with her own sense of abandon. Her heart soared as Micah cupped her face in gentle hands, her vision narrowing until her world was reduced to the gold flecks in Micah's soft hazel eyes and the feeling of soft lips brushing against her own. For a moment, the mass of humanity swirling past them meant nothing to her. As long as that river continued to split and flow around them, she was content to stand apart from the flow with Micah's arms wrapped firmly around her.

"All right beautiful, let's go home." Micah wrapped her arm around Olivia's slim waist. The two women walked arm in arm through the mall, ignoring the ignorant stares of a few intolerant souls. It didn't matter, they didn't matter. All that mattered was Micah leaning against her as they walked back to the Porsche. Olivia was overjoyed. Micah wanted to go home, her home. A mad giggle threatened to rise up, unbidden, in Olivia's throat. Being with Micah could be such an emotional roller coaster, she thought to herself. Another quickly followed that thought.

It was so worth the ride.

Micah's phone rang again the minute they climbed back into the Porsche. This time, Micah just hit the decline button without saying a word. Olivia had a pretty good idea who was calling again; Micah was right, it really was getting quite ridiculous. She watched Micah's jaw twitch against the tension she was holding in.

"Sweetheart, I hate to ask, but why do your parents keep calling? It's obvious that it's upsetting you. Is there anything I can do?"

"No Olivia, there's nothing you can do." She looked out the window for a moment then down at her hands.

"Ah, hell. They want me to fix something, something I can't fix," she muttered, her voice almost lost in the roar of the engine as Olivia's Porsche came to life.

"I don't understand, what do they want you to fix?"

"Me." It was only one word, but it held a lot of weight and history behind it.

Olivia's jaw practically dropped to her chest as her fury ignited as loud and powerful as the engine in her car. She threw the Porsche back into park with a well-deserved curse for Micah's parents on her tongue. *Of all the ridiculous nonsense. What the hell is wrong with those two?*

"Look at me, Micah," she demanded. "I will only say this once. There. Is. Nothing. Nothing about you that requires fixing!" She emphasized each word to make sure that Micah understood her. "Do you understand?"

When Micah didn't respond, Olivia grabbed her hand and squeezed hard, pressing her fingers together almost painfully. Micah's head shot up at that unexpected maneuver, opening her mouth to protest. Olivia shook her head once, forcefully; "I will not allow you to continue with this ridiculous belief that you are somehow broken. You are not broken. Bent a little, maybe, but what woman isn't that's had to deal with everything you've been through. You are strong, Micah. Stronger than anyone else I've ever met, and if the way you've built up that strength isn't necessarily socially acceptable, who cares. It worked for you, you being here with me right now proves that."

Olivia had to stop. Tricked into thinking she was in some kind of danger, her heart pounded wildly in her chest, that's how furious she was.

"Do you understand?" she repeated, her voice softer this time.

"I do now, Love," Micah spoke even softer. "I think I really do, now."

"Good, now let's go home." Olivia was loath to let go of Micah's hand, but she had to drive and the Porsche couldn't shift itself. Ripping through the gears, Olivia flew out of the parking lot and onto the freeway. She was pushing the engine, changing gears expertly just before the engine screamed past it's redline. Olivia never abused her Porsche, but today she expected it to perform, driving more aggressively than Micah had ever seen her do.

It was oddly gratifying.

***

Olivia made room in her closet for Micah's new clothes. Actually, she made more room than the current amount of clothes required. When she walked out of the closet to find Micah waiting for her, the humorous symbolism wasn't lost on her.

"What are you doing?"

"Putting your clothes away where they belong," Chuckling to herself, she walked over to Micah and wrapped her in a warm embrace.

"Where they belong?" Micah peered inside the closet. "I have a feeling this has been your evil plan all along."

"You caught me." Olivia chuckled. "A couple of pairs of jeans now, a few shirts...and soon you won't have any excuses to ever leave."

Olivia's hands snaked beneath her shirt, intent on distracting her.

Micah let her, enjoying the sensation of soft fingertips running along her back. When she flexed her fingers and started skimming along her ribs with her fingernails, Micah made a noise in her throat somewhere between a purr and a hum. She nuzzled against Olivia's neck, breathing in her unique scent. She felt Olivia's pulse quicken beneath her lips, a soft moan brushing against her ear as Olivia leaned into her. The delightful sensation of nails against her skin turned to sharp pain as the blunt edges scraped across her lower abdomen. Micah hissed and pulled away. Olivia had just run her nails across her new tattoo.

"I'm sorry, Sweetheart. I forgot!"

"It's okay." Micah pulled her back into her arms before she could move too far away. "I love your touch; you know that, just no nails on my stomach for now. At least not until the tattoo heals. I really didn't mind the pain, but I couldn't bear telling Cassandra that she had to do a touchup because we'd gotten overly amorous."

Micah bent down and kissed away Olivia's fears.

"Jesus, you are good at that," Olivia whispered, earning a second kiss, this one deeper and more demanding.

"What would you like to do with the rest of our day?"

Micah responded with a heated look and a suggestive shift of her hips.

"Other than that, Sweetheart." Olivia smiled, her palm resting on Micah's cheek in apology before extricating herself from Micah's embrace. "It's not that I don't want to, but we have plenty of sunlight left before tonight and there are other things that we can do until then."

"It's your fault," Micah joked. When Olivia held steady against her advances, she gave up on the game and held her hands up in surrender. "Okay, fine. How about we just watch another movie? I know it's rare for you to be able to just sit back and relax."

"That sounds wonderful. Why don't you go downstairs and see what's available while I get changed?"

"Sure, babe." Micah sauntered off, feeling Olivia's eyes on her backside as she walked out of the bedroom.

The effort wasn't lost on Olivia—as much as she hated seeing Micah leave, watching her leave was a totally different thing.

After she was sure that Micah was out of earshot, Olivia pulled out her cell phone.

"Olivia?" Amanda's voice sounded thin over the phone. "What can I do for you?"

She didn't sound too excited to hear from her boss on a Saturday until she told her why she was calling, then she perked up considerably.

"I need you pick something up for me. At five." Olivia gave her the address where she was to go. "Just leave it on my desk in the study; you know where the key is. Also, I've planned a small get together tomorrow night at 6pm; you'll find the instructions on my desk as well." Olivia held the phone away from her ear as a loud squeal of excitement screeched through the small speaker.

When things quieted down, she continued. "Will you let Jonathan know? Thank you, Amanda."

After calling Regina and checking in on her, she changed into something she knew would shock Micah, and ran downstairs.

"All done. I just had to check up on Regina."

Micah looked up. Her jaw dropped when she saw what the fashion-conscious lawyer was wearing. "You have jeans?"

"Yes, I have jeans. Don't act so surprised, Micah." Olivia tried for haughty but it just came off as amused. Probably because she couldn't stop laughing at Micah's expression.

"Sorry, I just didn't think you wore jeans." Then Micah noticed what else Olivia had on. "Is that one of my t-shirts, Olivia?"

"Yes. It's quite comfortable," she admitted.

"You look beautiful." Micah wrapped Olivia in a tight hug. "I like how you look in a t-shirt." Micah grinned when she found something hanging from Olivia's belt loop. She wrapped her fingers around the offending tag, then pulled...hard and fast.

"If this is the reaction I get, maybe I should wear your shirts more often," Olivia joked, her pleased smile transforming into a mortified expression when Micah held up her prize.

"Jeans, huh? Don't be surprised, huh?" Micah was grinning in the most evil way, catching Olivia in the lie, but secretly thrilled that she had gone outside of her fashion box to buy a pair of jeans.

"You can borrow my t-shirts any time you want, Love. This IS one of mine, right? I don't have to check for another tag, hmm?" Micah danced her fingertips along Olivia's ribs, where she was most ticklish.

It was only after Olivia begged her to stop that she stepped away, eyes bright from laughter. "Come on, let's go watch that movie. Maybe by the time it's over you'll be hungry again. I know I will be."

Chapter Twenty-Eight

Sunday morning. No drama, no expectations, definitely no work, and nothing to do but relax and enjoy the summer sunlight. That was the idea except for one minor detail: it was Micah's birthday today.

Olivia woke up early and snuck downstairs to her home office where she spent the next hour doing what she did best: organizing and planning—all the way down to the last detail.

This was Micah's first birthday with her. Olivia wanted it to be perfect and that meant personally ensuring that everything was done right the first time. She suppressed a jaw cracking yawn as she furiously texted everyone that needed contacting; there was no coffee for her this morning...not if she wanted to get this done before Micah woke up.

With the computer up and running, her phone pulling double duty as she checked emails and waded through confirmations, it sure looked a lot like what she did on a day-to-day basis. Work. Only this time she didn't have to play the hard-ass and no one was walking away from the table a loser. Not to mention, she probably wouldn't be negotiating in her PJ's. She amused herself with the thought that all this unusual behavior on her part was probably creating a different sort of stress in all those unfortunate souls who didn't know how to handle her being in a good mood. Olivia checked her watch after shooting off the last text of the morning and headed for the kitchen. Regina would be home soon. The three of them would celebrate Micah's birthday today before the adult's only dinner later that night.

Now all she needed to do was brew a little coffee and Micah wouldn't even realize she'd been up for almost an hour.

***

"Hmm," Micah croaked, opening one stubborn eye and stared blankly at the ceiling. If she lay perfectly still and listened hard, she could almost hear Olivia moving around downstairs—the familiar smell of freshly brewed coffee was a dead giveaway. Groaning against the need to get out of bed, Micah made an effort to move, working her bad knee to get the kinks out of it before even trying to go vertical. She winced at the grating noises coming from the stiff joint, followed by a solid wet pop as she rotated her knee. Grabbing her phone, she realized that she had forgotten to charge it, again. The charge was too low to play her music, not without leaving it plugged in on the table.

Although her phone was useless as an MP3 player, it didn't mind giving her the time. "Nine? Damn, Olivia let me sleep in late." She yawned, then noticed the date next to the time. *Crap, it's my birthday.*

Running her fingers through her hair, she massaged her scalp for a minute, trying to wake up and face the day. She even contemplated crawling back into the still warm covers and hiding but she knew that Reggie would be disappointed. That thought alone was motivating enough to get her out of bed and moving.

Micah managed to get her jeans on and was working on her t-shirt when Olivia breezed back into the room, wide awake and ready for the day. To Micah's delight, she was dressed casually in a tight pair of black designer jeans and a t-shirt.

"Good morning, Sweetheart. I was just coming to wake you." Olivia's voice was as bright and airy as the morning sun streaming through the bedroom window. She handed Micah her customary morning soda, smiling at a routine she would be thrilled to perform every day of the week—if Micah would let her.

"Thanks, babe. I smelled coffee but this works just fine." Micah scooped Olivia into a quick one-armed hug before popping open the can. She took a long swallow to wash away the worst of her morning breath before commenting on Olivia's outfit.

"Is this one of mine?"

"Yes," Olivia said without a hint of guilt.

"I guess it's a good thing I bought a bunch of those yesterday." She smirked, running her fingertips along the hem of the stolen shirt.

"Well, you do seem to like seeing me in them," Olivia responded, leaning in to brush a quick kiss on her cheek.

"I do, I like how relaxed you look—once you get a chance to escape all those confining suits." She also didn't mind how her other, ah—assets looked in those jeans, but she wisely didn't comment on that. She didn't think Olivia would appreciate knowing how much eye-candy she was going to be for her all day.

"Hmm." Olivia didn't know how to respond to that, but it was a great example of why she loved Micah so much. Her lover could tell she was more relaxed, but was totally oblivious that it was her presence that let her feel that way. Micah never expected anything from Olivia, never imposed or demanded something she could not give. Micah was simply there for her when she needed it.

How do you explain to someone that not having any demands put on you in your personal life is what is letting you relax? It was so nice to know that when she simply wanted to cuddle or relax, all she would have to do was lean on Micah and she would automatically put an arm around her.

Micah never made her feel that she was being weak or needy. Olivia didn't have to control every aspect of her life, or be in charge all of the time. She found that she could leave that part of herself at work and let Micah take over...especially in the bedroom. In that realm, her lover was demanding—dominating her easily and taking her places she never knew she wanted to go.

"Are you ready?" Micah asked, fully dressed now in faded blue jeans, boots, and a sleeveless muscle shirt that accentuated her deltoids nicely. Olivia couldn't help herself; she ran her fingers down Micah's arm, tracing the lines of her muscles.

"Do I need to change? The tattoo shows on my arm and Reggie will be able to see it."

"No, Micah. She will find out sooner or later, and it is a part of you. You shouldn't have to hide." The casual strength in Micah's wrist and hand were gentle as their fingers threaded together. It seemed the most natural thing in the world—their hands intertwined together, their eyes locked on each other as if nothing else existed in the world.

Micah brought their joined hands up to her lips to lightly kiss Olivia's knuckles, then smiled broadly. Her eyes glowed brightly as she spoke the words that Olivia would never tire of. "I love you, Olivia."

"Oh, Sweetheart, I love you too," Olivia said, wishing they had more time alone before their day had to start. Her thoughts must have been transparent or else

Micah was developing a talent as a mind reader because she followed up with a very similar suggestion.

"I'm sorry, but I will have to take a rain check. Regina will be here soon and will be expecting breakfast." Olivia patted Micah's cheek in apology before turning to go downstairs.

She screamed, just a little, when Micah's strong arms suddenly wrapped around her middle from behind, gathering her close enough to bring soft lips against her hairline. Olivia felt the fine hairs at the nape of her neck rise in response to the hot breath against her neck. The teasing lips and sharp teeth left a trail of goose bumps along her arms and a tingling sensation inside her skull that travelled down her spine to spread low between her hips. *God, we're insatiable together.*

"I mean it, Micah," Olivia warned, weakly trying to wriggle out of Micah's arms.

Micah stepped away just as quickly as she had embraced her, acting as if nothing had ever happened. If it wasn't for the naughty grin Micah couldn't completely wipe from her face, Olivia would be hard pressed to believe that she hadn't just imagined the whole thing. Of course, the heat and moisture radiating between her thighs, as well as the throbbing pulse nestled there, was a great reminder.

"I know, Love. I just wanted you to think about that today. Think of it as a promise, if you will. Or, a present—a very special birthday present." Micah's grin widened as she wagged her eyebrows at Olivia wickedly, her teeth showing as she laughed at Olivia's reaction. It was always fun to render Olivia speechless.

"Ah...yes, as to that." Olivia cleared her throat before continuing in a more controlled voice. "Um. How did you know I knew?"

"Because you've been acting very strangely, and I know how meddling Jon can be. Or was it Amanda? You've been very adamant about me not going home this weekend."

Damn, and I thought I was being so careful. Olivia jutted her jaw out, determined not to wilt in front of Micah and spill all her plans for the day.

"Perhaps. I'll never tell." Olivia's tone turned speculative. "Now, what was that about a birthday present? How many years is it this year, hmm? When was the last time you had a good Birthday spanking?" It was Micah's turn to be speechless, which gratified Olivia to no end. She managed to keep a poker face long enough to watch worry creep into Micah's face before bursting into laughter.

"Touché, Love." Micah tipped her fingers at Olivia, saluting her for the well-earned win. "Now, let's get downstairs and get that breakfast started."

***

"Micah!" Reggie abandoned her mother the minute she spied Micah.

"Hey, Reggie," Micah greeted the young girl and gave her a quick hug, smiling at Regina's youthful enthusiasm.

"Should I be jealous?" Olivia asked, relegated to closing and locking the front door and moving her daughter's overnight bag to the stairwell.

"Never mind. I don't want to know. Regina, breakfast is almost ready, why don't you help Micah pour the orange juice?"

"Come on, kiddo, I think your mom made pancakes." Micah had just enough time to mouth "I love you" and then she was gone, dragged off to the kitchen by a very small dynamo with a lot to say.

Olivia's daughter could talk even faster than her mother. She followed her rapid-fire greetings with a quick list of the weekend's activities that she was all too thrilled to impart on her mother and Micah. Micah made a wry face and Olivia just took it all in stride as Regina bounced between the two of them.

"What would you like to do today?" Micah asked Reggie as they served up pancakes with whipped cream and strawberries.

With a sudden switch from hyper to pseudo-serious, Regina glanced at her mother almost shyly before whispering a suggestion in Micah's ear.

"Really? That's what you want?" Micah glanced over at Olivia. She looked like she was going to explode if someone didn't tell her what was going on soon. Micah was tempted to drag out the suspense, especially since that conversation was going to rule the next few hours of their day's activities, but knew that would be cruel.

Micah's toothy grin was worthy of any of the predators they would be visiting today.

"The zoo it is," she announced, then laughed at the pained expression on Olivia's face, sure evidence of the groan she barely managed to suppress. At least she let out all the air she had been holding. Micah wasn't sure just how close Olivia had come to self-combusting.

"Just think of it as a thank you for taking me shopping yesterday."

***

Olivia sat on a wooden bench, resting her sore feet and watching her two favorite people in the world watch the seals show off inside their enclosure. From their clown-like actions, it was obvious that the playful creatures were hoping for treats and had learned exactly what to do to get the humans to throw them food. It was crowded and noisy, so Olivia was grateful that Micah kept a close eye on Regina's safety, making sure her energetic daughter stayed close. Olivia stopped a vendor as they walked by with their rolling cart, buying everyone something to drink and grabbing Regina a couple of sugary snacks she knew would be devoured almost immediately.

Regina magically appeared in front of her mother the minute the forbidden treats hit Olivia's hands, dragging Micah behind her. Handing out the drinks and snacks, Olivia let Regina find her own bench close by where she could enjoy her snack without spreading powdered sugar all over the adults.

"Make sure you stay where we can see you," Olivia called out. Micah joined Olivia on her bench, sighing in relief when she was able to stretch out her leg in front of her. She was still limping when she got tired, and the limp was coming back after several hours at the zoo.

"Regina really likes having you around," Olivia said.

"Yeah, she's great."

"And a handful at times. Don't let her run you ragged."

"Humph! Like mother like daughter. But really, I don't mind. I'm having a great time, and she's having the time of her life."

Olivia fell silent after that, happy to just sit and watch her child be happy. It seemed so natural, the two of them enjoying a sunny day on a quiet bench at the zoo. Her daughter was a handful, but she was also the most important thing in her life. Micah was so good with her, and it was obvious that Regina thought Micah was, as she put it "awesome".

"Have you ever thought of having children?" Olivia blurted out.

Unfortunately, Micah had just taken a swallow from her soda when she asked that. Micah ended up choking on the carbonated beverage, gasping and coughing as the burning sensation hit her nose and throat. She glared at Olivia for her timing.

"Are you trying to tell me something?" Micah looked pointedly at Olivia's flat stomach. "You're definitely not showing," Micah's teasing continued, then wavered when she saw the look on Olivia's face.

"I'm just joking Olivia. But no, I don't want a baby."

"You're so good with Regina, I didn't know," Olivia said. Secretly, she was relieved. Regina and Micah were more than enough for her. She didn't want to share them with anyone else, and she didn't care if that sounded selfish, either. At the same time, she felt a bit sad at the thought that there would never be a little Micah running around.

"Well, yeah. But you already trained her," Micah replied awkwardly. "I've never considered myself prime parenting material." Micah went silent, as if contemplating the odd idea. "She's a good kid," Micah said, nodding towards the now sugar coated child happily slurping down her soda. "And, you're a great mom."

Olivia smiled at the compliment, and then offered her own. "Don't sell yourself short, Sweetheart. I think Regina loves you as much as I do."

The offhand compliment affected Micah more than Olivia expected. She looked away, scanning the crowd around them as if taking note of every family that passed. Parents and their children, oblivious to their own happy lives, marched by in a sea of normalcy without a clue that what they had was something special.

Olivia watched Micah's face transform into something wistful and holding more peace and happiness than she had ever witnessed. This window into the gentler side of Micah was as rare and beautiful as the leopards in their enclosure. Even those magnificent and dangerous creatures showed the utmost caring and tenderness to their young. It didn't detract from their fierceness, just as it didn't detract from Micah's. She knew some might argue the point, but Olivia was quickly discovering that people could be a lot more complicated than they appeared on the surface.

Threading her fingers into Micah's waiting hand, she simply absorbed the moment, accepting it for what it was. She didn't notice Regina snapping a picture of the two of them with her cell phone. In that moment, she only had eyes for Micah, the woman she loved more than she could ever have imagined.

***

When they finally got home, Regina ran off in a sugar-induced sprint up to her bedroom, leaving Olivia and Micah to wonder what she was up to. Olivia was rethinking her ill thought of decision to give her daughter that much junk food at the zoo. The ride home was a non-stop diatribe of babble, at first amusing but slowly sinking into verbal overload until Micah had the bright idea of turning on some music that both she and Regina could sing along with.

Micah's clear voice carried the notes beautifully, encouraging Regina to sing along with her. She discovered that her daughter had quite a good voice. Olivia made a mental note to see if Regina would be interested in taking vocal lessons. She could still hear the excited babble flowing down the stairs, even with the door closed. She was probably filling her father or one of her friends in on her day at the zoo. "That sugar crash they talk about couldn't happen soon enough," Olivia said, praying that her little devil would calm down soon.

"It's okay, she had fun today."

"I know, and it was nice of you to take her to the zoo, even though it's your birthday." Olivia pulled Micah into her study. "I wanted to give you something before the party tonight."

"Um, what party, Olivia?"

"Just a small get together, nothing fancy...I promise." Olivia kept her tone nonchalant, as if it was truly nothing big. "It's just a few close friends."

Micah eyed her lover suspiciously. "Uh-huh. And not a one of these close friends told you about my no party rule?"

"Duly noted for next year, Micah. Now, will you just open this, please?" Olivia held out a small package. Micah huffed once in irritation and then gave up, holding her hand out to accept Olivia's gift.

Micah opened the box to find a beautiful white gold ring embedded in dark blue velvet. It was obviously custom made and, she found, quite heavy. Somehow, Olivia had found someone to make her a ring designed to look like a stylized master link for a bicycle chain. Where the two posts would be, two pale green stones lay embedded, their rounded edges catching the light as she held it up for inspection.

"How?"

"I sized it off of your other ring, so it should fit. The stones are green amber. Please, try it on, Sweetheart." Olivia felt like she was babbling, but she wanted to know if Micah loved her present.

Micah slid the unique ring onto her middle finger— it fit perfectly.

"Thank you, it's beautiful," Micah said, amazed that Olivia had thought of this gift. "I've seen amber before, but never this color."

"So, you like it?" Olivia could have chosen a precious stone, but the green amber held all the colors of Micah's eyes when she was happy, all the way down to the gold flecks.

"It's an incredible piece of artwork."

"It's engraved, you know." Olivia tapped the band; she had one more surprise for Micah.

Micah pulled off the ring and looked inside the band.

You let me in and love followed.

"That's very true," Micah said, incredibly touched by the gift and in awe of the woman standing before her. Her chest felt tight from holding her emotions in. It wouldn't do to break down and cry, not when she wanted to laugh at the same time. All of that emotion had to go somewhere, so Micah bent down and kissed Olivia. She kissed her hard and deep, pouring her joy and love into something more direct and a lot more physical.

Kissing Olivia like that was not without its risks. As the kiss intensified, Micah had to fight the urge to pick her lover up and onto her desk for easier access. Pulling herself away from those soft lips caused an almost physical pain as they separated, but they were not alone in the house. "So, what time is this party?" Micah asked, running her fingers through her hair. She had to keep her hands busy or they would be all over Olivia in one hot minute.

"It's at six, but the good news is, it's completely casual. No dressing up," Olivia said, trying to butter Micah up.

Micah glanced at her watch. It was after four.

"Great." Micah sounded more resigned then happy about tonight.

"The sitter will be here soon. Why we don't we go see what Regina is up to?" Olivia suggested, concerned about Micah's less than enthusiastic response. Olivia knew she had pushed her on this, but she really wanted Micah to have a good birthday. Besides, Micah hadn't told her NOT to have a party. The distinction was minimal at best, but it gave Olivia the excuse she had needed. Now she was starting to second-guess her decision. Maybe she should have told Micah yesterday instead of an hour before they were supposed to leave. Worrying her lower lip with her teeth, Olivia's concern switched to a more immediate problem. Regina was being too quiet, and that never boded well.

***

They found Regina in the family room, happily watching television. When the two adults walked in, she launched out of her chair to meet them and handed Micah a folder.

"Hey, mom. Hey, Micah. I took this today. Happy birthday, Micah, thanks for going to the zoo." Regina's words tumbled out, almost overlapping each other in her

382

excitement. Micah opened up the folder and took out a photograph. It was of her and Olivia at the zoo, sitting on a bench. They were smiling at each other and it was very easy to see the connection between them.

"I love it. Thank you, Reggie," Micah said, accepting another enthusiastic hug. "I'll need to get a frame."

"We'll get one tomorrow, I have just the spot for it on the dresser," Olivia said. "But right now, I need to go get ready." Olivia wrinkled her nose in an affected grimace as she pulled her zoo scented t-shirt away from her body.

"That's actually a good idea, I'll do the same," Micah offered. Seeing that picture had dampened her irritation. It also made her realize something. That picture was a memory, a happy memory that couldn't be taken away and could be the start of a thousand other happy memories. She could use that in her life...memories that didn't make her cringe or wish she could carve them out of her head. Olivia didn't plan this party to punish her or subject her to something unpleasant. Olivia wanted to celebrate her birthday because it was important to her to participate in Micah's life, and she couldn't blame her for that. She resolved to make the best of the situation and keep the past where it belonged.

In the bedroom, Micah changed into a fresh pair of jeans, picking out the new black ones she had bought yesterday. She was beginning to button them up when Olivia stopped her, placing her hand on Micah's chest just over her heart.

"May I?" Olivia swept her other hand down suggestively.

Micah moved her hands away so Olivia could take over the task. Her breath caught in her throat when Olivia's fingers brushed lightly along her skin as she did up the buttons, one at a time. Slowly.

"Decided to go without underwear tonight, I see," Olivia murmured.

"Um, isn't this a little backwards, Olivia? Shouldn't you be undoing them instead?" Micah was hard pressed to think of anything witty to say, what with all of the blood draining from her brain to travel south, following the trail of Olivia's teasing fingers.

"That will come later tonight, if you are good." Olivia finished with the last button and kissed Micah before turning around to put on the outfit she had selected for the night, a black pantsuit Micah enjoyed seeing her in, since it—as she had put it before—"showcased her butt."

"Olivia, if I'm good you will be the one coming later tonight." The double entendre was obvious and meant to be that way.

"Of that, I have no doubt. Now shoo! I need to get dressed."

"If you don't mind, I'll just sit here and watch. Don't worry, I'll behave." Micah sat on the edge of the bed while Olivia got dressed. It was a different sort of intimacy, this casual comfortableness with each other they were developing, despite the hooded glances cast at each other that held a sharper edge of promise. The subtle nuances of their relationship was like a living thing, shaping itself around their needs while leaving room for new experiences, and there was so many places they still had to go. Of all those places, she had to admit...a party was not one of them.

"Are you sure you want to go to the party? We could always stay here and you could let me have my way with you," Micah suggested, trying one last time.

"Nope, you are going to wait until later. Anticipation makes it better." Olivia smirked. "And you are being bad. You promised to behave."

"I did, didn't I?" Caught by her own promise, Micah had to admit defeat.

"Let's face it, Sweetheart, you might as well go and enjoy yourself. Regina is going to be up for hours yet. Even if we wanted to, we'd have to wait until she's asleep." Olivia slipped on her heels as she spoke. "At the very least, the party will keep you busy until we can come back here."

Micah's outlook brightened considerably, but she couldn't resist playing the martyr. "You're right. I'll suffer through this cruel foreplay you've planned, but only because I know I'll get the prize at the end of the night."

"It is your birthday, after all." Olivia conceded. She touched up her lipstick in the mirror then headed for the door. "I'm ready to go."

Micah launched off the bed.

"Okay, let's do this."

Chapter Twenty-Nine

It was a beautiful night. Robert dropped them off at the park a couple of blocks away so they could walk the rest of the way home. They decided to cut through the park rather than walk around it since it was late and they had the path to themselves. A full moon lit the still waters of the small man-made lake sitting in the middle of the park. The occasional light breeze distorted and softened the reflection dancing along the surface of the inky black water. The only thing breaking the late night silence was the muted honking of domesticated geese across the water as mates called out to reassure one another. Other than that, they walked in comfortable silence. Olivia accepted Micah's offered arm as they breathed in the midnight air, still warm from the day but holding just enough crisp to add flavor and bite.

Neither of them seemed interested in talking. It was too quiet and too perfect of a night for chatter, and after all the party noise, it was a welcome respite for abused ears.

"Did you have a good time?" Olivia only had one question of importance and once she asked it, she fell silent again, pleased with the answer.

"Surprisingly, yes," Micah admitted. It had been a nice evening, even when Adam had decided to get drunk and tease her.

"Sooo, Olivia?" Adam slurred, leaning heavily across Micah's shoulders while balancing what was obviously not his first gin and tonic of the night. Despite his obviously inebriated state, he managed to lower his

normally exuberant tones to a more conspiratorial whisper so he could talk to Olivia without everyone else in the room overhearing.

"Have you unwrapped Micah's package yet?" he asked with a sloppy grin. Micah groaned in embarrassment while she extricated herself from her best friend's awkward embrace. He was freaking heavy and was leaning way too much on her to be comfortable.

"Jesus, Adam, get the hell off of me, how much have you had to drink anyways?" Micah demanded as Olivia's face turned beet red in response to the not so subtle innuendo.

Great, Micah thought, all I need is for Olivia to start thinking about how often my package and I went out to play. It's a damn good thing we already had that conversation, but it still wasn't cool. No one needs to be reminded of past deeds like that.

Openly grasping Olivia's hand, Micah squeezed her fingers sympathetically before offering Adam a scathing glare.

"Don't worry Olivia, he's just jealous because mine is bigger and I last longer than Mister Speedy Gonzales over here." Micah emphasized her words with a quick jab at Adam's ribs, resulting in a gratifying grunt as she made heavier contact than she would ever admit she intended. Adam grunted in pain, then stumbled off to aggravate some other poor fool, thankfully leaving the two women alone at their table.

"I'm starting to wonder if I need to get you two a romper room." Olivia's voice practically dripped with sarcasm.

"Naw, we like bouncy castles," Micah joked back, her childish humor fast forwarding back to grown up land then racing straight on to rated "M" for mature audiences

when Olivia's fingers danced against her thigh under the tablecloth. She inhaled sharply when those travelling fingers found the seam of her jeans and played along them until she reached the apex of her thighs, fingering the buttons on her jeans under the tablecloth.

Olivia's laughter washed over her. Micah knew she was struggling to keep a poker face as her seemingly innocent dinner date took a sip of her wine with her other hand. She lost the fight when Olivia once again began feeling her up underneath the table, requiring her to take Olivia's hidden hand firmly in hers. Blunt nails scraped against her wrists in one last bid to tease.

"Don't worry. I know no one else is playing with your package. It's mine now." Olivia smiled sweetly at Micah before giving up her game.

They paused at the front door. The darkened entryway practically begged for the sweet kiss that they shared before the light blinked on, blinding them and making them laugh. It was too funny, getting caught making out on the porch like nervous teenagers on a first date.

After sending the sitter off for the night, Micah followed Olivia upstairs but begged out when Olivia stopped in front of Regina's door.

"Meet me in the shower," Micah whispered then sauntered away, swaying her hips just enough to get Olivia's attention before disappearing into the master bedroom.

Oh, yeah...this was going to be fun tonight.

Olivia peeked in to Regina's room. Her daughter was fast asleep, curled up in a little ball under her blankets. The stuffed animals Regina claimed she was too old to need any more stood guard along the headboard, holding court above the small blonde head.

There was no reason to wake her up, and every reason to leave her soundly sleeping. Closing the door behind her carefully, Olivia whispered a quick good night and headed for her bedroom.

Micah was already in the shower when Olivia slid the glass door open. When she stepped through the heat and steam like some ethereal creature stepping out of the mists, Micah's breath caught in her throat, just as it always did whenever they were together. Pulling Olivia in under the showerhead, Micah kissed her deeply as the spray ran down between them, gathering between their joined bodies.

"Hello, Love. Thank you again for a wonderful birthday." Micah breathed in the hot steam when they finally separated, noting how cool it felt in comparison to the heat of their kiss. Soapy hands slipped along smooth skin as she took liberties with offering to wash Olivia's back.

"It's not over yet, birthday-girl's choice for the rest of the night," Olivia promised, having difficulty concentrating when Micah's wandering hands moved away from her back to cup her ass.

"Hmm—so many options," Micah murmured, forcing Olivia back until she was pressed firmly against the shower wall. Olivia's head dropped back against the cool tiles behind her, exposing her neck to the waiting woman. She moaned loudly when Micah's mouth descended onto her offered flesh, full lips and an insistent tongue tasting the skin along her collarbone and licking along her neckline.

"Control, Love—for what I have planned tonight, I want control." Micah's low voice carried with it promises best kept in the dark, an exotic menu laid out for her approval in such a way that she couldn't speak, couldn't think. Olivia licked her lips in anticipation. The flood of wetness pooling between her thighs had nothing to do with the water beating down on her, and everything to do with what Micah was offering her. It was, simply put—a promise of something exquisitely naughty that Olivia found overwhelmingly enticing.

Micah's lips found her ear. "Most of all, I want to continue what we started in the kitchen the other morning."

Olivia felt her body tighten in response to Micah's suggestion, the memory of gentle fingers touching her in other places, teasing but never exploring fully. Micah watched her now, feverishly waiting for her permission, for her to answer yes or no. This was the last thing between them. With a simple yes, Micah would own her body, all of it...without reservation.

"God, yes, I want that, too." The admission came easier than she expected. "Anything, Micah."

Her words freed Micah. She dropped to one knee, her elbows against the tiles behind Olivia, locking her in place, then started at her abdomen. Soft kisses rained down on her, tracing the concave line of her hip until Micah reached her center. Micah rolled her eyes up at Olivia, making sure that she was watching before snaking her tongue out, parting wet lips to find her ready for her.

Olivia's eyes slammed shut at the intense sensations. She blindly sought out and found Micah's short hair, tangling her grasping fingers into the wet tresses as she sought even more contact with Micah's teasing mouth.

When Olivia was close, her body tensing in anticipation of the impending orgasm, Micah stood up. Gracefully unfolding herself from the floor of the shower,

Micah looked down at the flushed face and closed eyes of the woman she had just brought to the edge of oblivion and licked her lips. *So sweet, but not yet.*

"Micah, what...?" Olivia moaned. Confused and aroused, her body was on fire and Micah had left the flames licking along her thighs unquenched. Micah's mischievous gaze wavered in front of her, watching her intently before bringing her lips close to her ear.

"That was for teasing me all night. Meet me in the bedroom after you finish in here." Micah opened the glass shower door and stepped out, letting another rush of cool air in to disturb the steam swirling around them. Before closing the door, she gave her a promising grin before adding, "Oh, and Olivia, no cheating."

***

Olivia took the quickest shower of her life. The intensity and heat in Micah's voice as she described what she wanted to do to her had sent her into a frenzy of arousal. Olivia rubbed the towel across her skin roughly, not willing to wait any longer than necessary and taking Micah's warning seriously.

How Micah had teased her on Friday morning was like nothing she had ever experienced before. She found herself wanting Micah to touch her like that again—and she needed her to finish what they had started in the shower.

Hurrying into the bedroom, she came to an abrupt halt as she took in the view of her lover lying on the bed, completely naked. She wasn't used to seeing Micah flaunt her body so boldly, even though she had artfully covered part of her torso with the bedsheet, it didn't matter. She had this lioness of a woman waiting for her in bed.

It seemed ridiculous that she had wasted time drying off after her shower when she was so wet in other places. As she sauntered over to the bed, Olivia noticed the bottle of lube sitting on the bedside table, the one she had bought the other day when she was ordering Micah's ring. She must have found it earlier and didn't bother telling her.

Micah caught the direction of Olivia's stare and glanced over at the innocuous-looking bottle before turning the full weight of her gaze back on the woman standing there, so prettily blushing in embarrassment.

She invited Olivia to join her with a look and an outstretched hand, thinking she would have to take the lead again to get things moving. Instead, Olivia surprised her by boldly crawling into the bed and up her body until she crouched above her.

"I owe you for all that teasing, Sweetheart; let me make it up to you," she offered.

"By all means." Micah remained perfectly still, keeping her hands clasped behind her head as she watched Olivia do what she wanted.

Olivia kissed her way down Micah's taut body until her head lay between her legs, her breath hot against soft curls damp with arousal. She gently cupped Micah's sex before sliding her fingers into the heat and wetness, spreading her lips to expose the delicate bundle of nerves hidden there

Micah struggled to keep still, but when Olivia caressed and then pinched her swollen lips, Micah couldn't keep her hands idle anymore. She threaded her fingers in Olivia's soft hair, her grip tightening at the first touch of her lover's tongue on her. Olivia alternated between licking along her folds and teasing her entrance before taking Micah's swollen clit into her mouth and sucking lightly. When Olivia slid two fingers inside, Micah let out a low keening sound.

"Get up here, now!" Micah commanded, and Olivia rushed to obey.

"Kiss me."

Micah tasted herself on Olivia's lips, while her own tongue still carried the sweet flavor of Olivia's essence.

"Do you like how you taste?" she asked. "How we taste together?"

Olivia growled. The question worked as Micah had intended. Sharp teeth found her neck, then her breast while Olivia continued to plunge her fingers inside her.

"Harder, suck harder." Micah's hand tightened in Olivia's hair, the small pain there reminding Olivia of what she liked, what she needed.

The webbing of Olivia's fingers strained with each deep thrust. She locked passion glazed eyes onto Micah's face before adding a third digit to work the writhing woman beneath her. She had abandoned her breast to watch, she had too, but that didn't mean she couldn't give Micah what she wanted. Cruel fingertips tugged and twisted nipples that seemed to crave even more than she was willing to give.

"Fuck!" Micah called out, arching off of the bed beneath her, pumping her hips against Olivia's hand. Her arm muscles burned and trembled from the effort but she didn't stop until Micah told her to. They both collapsed after that, breathing hard and too tired to speak.

"My God, Olivia, are you sure I'm the only woman you've been with?"

"Yes, I'm very sure. I think I would remember ever doing this before." It was Olivia's turn to sound cocky. How could you not after feeling your lover's muscles clenching and pulsing around your fingers as they came—hard? She would never forget the sound of Micah's moans escalating, the sound of her name on Micah's lips as she found release with just her touch.

"You are definitely a natural." Micah wasn't being shy with the compliments at all and Olivia was pleased with the high praise. She remained tightly wrapped against Micah's neck, content to listen to Micah's heartbeat as it slowed down to something close to normal.

Olivia didn't expect Micah to recover so quickly.

Without warning, Micah flipped her over, capturing Olivia's breast between her lips, lashing the pebbled flesh with her tongue. When the nipple stood at proud attention, she moved to the other one, while her hands found more interesting places to explore

Olivia was still sensitive from Micah's earlier tongue play, she jumped when Micah's fingers brushed against her clit. She avoided the swollen bundle of nerves at first, concentrating on the slick folds and swollen lips that soon glowed from her light pinches. She teased her, backing off when she thought Olivia was too close to finishing, then bringing her back to the edge again without letting her tumble over it. She brought her to that precipice several times before withdrawing her hand.

"Turn over," Micah murmured. She was impressed with Olivia, other than the occasional muffled moan, she never gave in to begging. Micah was done teasing, now it was time to reward Olivia for her patience.

Olivia was eager to comply with the mild command. She was so turned on from making love to

Micah and the anticipation of what was to come, she thought she would burst from the need to orgasm.

While Olivia was situating herself on her stomach, Micah grabbed the lube and set it beside her. It was Olivia's first time doing this, and she wanted her to enjoy it. Running her fingers down Olivia's back, she lightly massaged the perfect ass cheeks she always admired, dipping down occasionally to tease her much like she had the other morning.

Her lips and tongue followed along the same path her fingers had just taken, licking and nipping the pale flesh as she tasted her skin over and over. A soft touch encouraged Olivia to open her legs, giving her more access to her. She coated her fingers with the lube, rubbing them together to warm the sticky fluid before running her fingers along the puckered opening between Olivia's firm cheeks. Micah concentrated on her lover's reaction to the unusual stimulation, waiting for the tight muscle beneath her fingertips to relax into her touch. Micah moved up alongside her lover's body, resting the weight of her body on her elbow so she could view Olivia's entire body. Olivia grasped at her blindly, seeking some sort of contact. She took her hand, lacing their fingers together above her head, and bent down to kiss her shoulder. "I'm right here," she said, "Do you trust me?"

"Yes."

"Spread your legs more."

Without hesitation, Olivia shifted her hips to bring herself in line with Micah's touch, bending her knee to give Micah more room.

"I love you, Olivia." Micah breathed against Olivia's neck as she slowly inserted one lubed finger into the tight opening, waiting for the tight muscle to relax into the intrusion. The transformation was immediate.

"Oh, my God, I love you Micah," Olivia moaned, her fingers clamped down around Micah's. Her other hand found the bed-sheets, twisting her fist into the thin fabric. A slow shudder passed through her followed by a choked sob. "So good."

Olivia moved restlessly against her, slowly fucking herself on Micah's finger. Micah took the hint and met each hip roll with her own movement, pushing into her and withdrawing past the resistance until she felt her open up. When Olivia was ready she withdrew completely, only to press against the tight opening again, slipping two fingers back inside the now slick opening. The woman beneath her moaned and writhed against her, but her position didn't allow for much more movement than that.

"Roll over, Love," Micah commanded, gently removing her fingers so Olivia could lie on her back. "Touch yourself; show me how you do it."

Olivia's eyes were glazed over with need and unrelieved arousal, but she couldn't help feeling a surge of embarrassment at performing such a personal act in front of her lover. From the amount of moisture that lay slick and hot between her thighs at just the thought of having Micah watch her come this way, Olivia's body betrayed her unvoiced lie. She wanted to do this, and she wanted to watch Micah watch her do it.

Micah waited while Olivia hesitantly moved her hand down her body. She waited until her fingertips dipped down between her thighs and she found her rhythm.

"Beautiful," Micah whispered, repositioning herself between Olivia's legs so she could watch her pleasure herself. She ran her fingers back along Olivia's puckered orifice, slipping back inside her while Olivia played with herself.

A deep shudder passed through Olivia's body. Her eye's snapped shut so she could focus on every sensation. Her breathing reduced to ragged gasps, she felt herself open up, accepting the intruding fingers with abandon. She drew her knees up and out, leaving her even more exposed. She rocked against Micah, silently begging her to speed up her thrusts. She was so close, the pleasure so intense, she could barely stand it. Micah's arm pumped rapidly, pushing deep inside her before almost withdrawing completely, matching her stroke for stroke until Olivia let out a strangled cry.

"Yes!" Triumphant, Micah felt Olivia's orgasm overtake her, the familiar rhythmic spasm grasping her fingers as Olivia stroked herself relentlessly. Micah stilled her movements as the woman beneath her bucked and clawed—letting Olivia ride out her orgasm on her own terms, waiting until her movement became less frenetic before pulling out carefully.

God, she's beautiful when she comes. It was a cheesy thought and Micah knew it, but it was also absolutely true. She was so incredibly lucky to have found this amazing woman, someone who could meet her passion for passion as an equal.

She murmured a sweet "I love you" before heading into the bathroom to get cleaned up. By the time she returned, Olivia had fallen into a deep sleep. Micah crawled into bed and gathered the exhausted woman into her arms, spooning against her lover's naked body.

Best birthday ever.

Chapter Thirty

Olivia's alarm clock disturbed the early morning quiet with a blatantly annoying repetitive buzzing sound. She smacked the snooze bar on the clock with awkwardly numb digits, trying to stop the incessant noise before it woke Micah.

Damn, it's Monday.

Olivia drifted back into that half sleep of semi-awareness that often occurred after hitting a snooze alarm, then jumped in surprise as the alarm went off again. Olivia reluctantly crawled out of bed and turned off the alarm. *It's amazing how quickly ten minutes can go by when you want to experience every one of them.* Olivia was sure that if she had been doing something even mildly unpleasant those ten minutes would have felt like an hour instead of thirty seconds.

What happened to her vaunted work ethic? The arrival of Monday morning just didn't hold the same anticipation it used to have, not when it meant being away from Micah and her daughter. Her thoughts left her mildly unsettled. Was she such a workaholic that the last three days were such a treat for her? Yes, she had to answer truthfully. She had patterned her career and her work schedule after her father, patterns she was starting to realize were not conducive to having a good relationship. She wanted more time with Micah, more time with her family. This weekend had shown her that.

She turned to find Micah surprisingly vertical and sitting at the edge of the bed, stretching her arms up and circling them gently until she heard a solid pop in each shoulder joint. Olivia took a moment to admire the play of muscles along her lover's back and shoulders as she stretched and twisted her torso. Micah's musculature was cut just enough that you couldn't quite describe her as sleek. There was an obvious hardness to her that didn't detract from her femininity, but spoke in great lengths of her strength—both physical and mental. You didn't get a body like hers without a huge amount of discipline. Micah finished stretching and stood up, awkwardly grabbing a black silk robe from the chair closest to her side of the bed.

For the most part, early morning was the only time Micah moved that stiffly, unless she really overdid it physically. It was an unwelcome reminder that Micah, although younger than she was, had suffered more injuries in her life. Her lack of joy at greeting the morning seemed to be more a reluctance to reacquaint herself with her past each time she woke up than anything else.

"Morning, Sweetheart."

"Morning," Micah mumbled.

Olivia smiled. The woman was practically non-verbal until her first caffeine fix. Olivia headed for the bathroom. She wasn't going to get anything close to a conversation this early on, so she might as well get ready for work.

Olivia was in the middle of putting on her makeup when Micah walked into the bathroom, the stiffness in her leg already worked out with just the hint of a limp giving it away. Olivia's hand paused in mid-stroke as she watched Micah's reflection approach in the mirror. Her hair was wildly tangled from sleeping; the short, wavy locks pressed down on the sides so it looked like she was sporting a faux-hawk.

Micah joined Olivia in front of the mirrored vanity, completing her morning routine in relative silence while she brushed her teeth and splashed water on her untamed mane, trying to finger-comb the unruly locks into something halfway respectable. Micah put her earbuds in so she could listen to her music without subjecting Olivia to the early morning racket, as she brushed her teeth with single-minded determination, humming around her toothbrush with eyes half-closed against the harsh bathroom lights.

Olivia had never heard someone actually hum while they brushed their teeth, but surprisingly, the melodic noise didn't bother her. She was overly pleased that they could share the same space in the morning without getting in each other's way. Micah was a comforting presence that lent a domestic quality to her morning—a quality that she found she had been missing.

"Awake now, Sweetheart?" Olivia asked, teasing gently.

Micah grinned and walked over to where Olivia was sitting, her arm raised but unmoving, her makeup ritual forgotten as she watched Micah stalk towards her. Turning Olivia around in her chair, Micah leaned over, catching Olivia's chin in one crooked finger and tilting her face up to meet hers in order to plant a firm kiss on her coral pink lips. When Olivia reached up to capture the back of Micah's head, she didn't resist. Instead, she just deepened the kiss until Olivia melted into her, her mouth sweet against hers with undertones of mint.

"Good morning, Love." Micah smirked, her lazy smile a pale imitation of the hazy, heavy-lidded look Olivia was giving her. "Your lipstick is smeared."

Olivia turned back to the mirror. She looked like a woman who had just been thoroughly and properly kissed good morning, down to the smeared lipstick that Micah didn't seem the least bit guilty about ruining. "Micah!" Olivia threw a towel at the unrepentant woman before grabbing some tissues.

"I'll meet you downstairs." Micah laughed, then tossed the caught towel in the laundry basket before leaving Olivia alone in front of her mirror.

Olivia stared at her reflection in the mirror, taking in the bruised lips and smeared makeup, her overly bright eyes and flushed cheeks. Her pulse bounded at her wrists, and her hands shook from the sudden surge of adrenaline. She felt shell-shocked from her lover's enthusiastic morning greeting. Willing her heart and mind to focus on the job at hand, Olivia set herself back to the task of fixing her face then finished dressing. It was time to go see what trouble Micah and her daughter were getting into.

When she arrived downstairs, she found the two of them eating cereal together at the kitchen table. The rich smell of coffee greeted her as she entered the room, leading her to a fresh cup of coffee and a third bowl of cereal waiting for her. Taking the coffee, she sipped delicately, finding it just to her taste. She pushed the bowl of cereal away from her as she sat down. When Micah pushed the bowl back towards her, she declined automatically. "I don't feel like breakfast this morning, Micah." She rarely had the time or inclination in the morning to wait around long enough to eat breakfast.

"It's good for you," Micah insisted. Micah ignored Olivia's baleful expression, meeting it with her own stubborn gaze, challenging her right to refuse breakfast. Reinforcing that steady gaze was another set of bright blue eyes as Regina looked from Micah to her mother.

"Yes, because you're such an expert about taking care of yourself, Micah. You don't even care about causing yourself pain." The instantly-regretted words came out without thought. Olivia saw the flash of hurt and betrayal darken Micah's countenance, her eyes narrowing in response to Olivia's ill-conceived statement. Olivia was feeling peevish about having to go in to work, and it had felt like Micah was scolding her in front of her daughter.

"Do what you want, Olivia." Micah's voice wasn't exactly cold, but it was decidedly neutral and held none of the warmth Olivia had grown used to. "Excuse me, Reggie. I need to call Jonathan."

Olivia shivered; it was like taking away the heat of the sun.

"Micah?" Olivia tried to call her back. She knew she had made a huge mistake, but Micah ignored her as she walked away.

***

Micah didn't exactly run from the sting of truth in Olivia's accusation, but she wasn't about to have a fight in front of Reggie, either. Running upstairs to retrieve her phone from the charger, she dug a pack of smokes out of her messenger bag before heading back downstairs and detoured out the front door. She needed a smoke, and that meant going outside. She didn't want Reggie to see her smoking when she left for school, so she wandered around to the side of the house where there was a small bench surrounded by a few shrubs. Pulling out a cigarette, she lit up and took a deep drag before dialing Jonathan. The calming effects of the nicotine couldn't come soon enough, and she held the burning smoke in her lungs as long as she could, exhaling only after Jonathan answered the phone.

"Hey Jon, can you bring me some work clothes and my bike this morning?" Micah asked, distracting herself by watching the grey smoke billow around her before the morning breeze pulled it up and away from where she sat.

"Does Olivia know you are planning on working today?" Jonathan asked almost hesitantly. "You know I hate to ask, but it helps to know what I'm walking into before I come into work."

"Yes, she does, Jonathan, not that it should matter. The last I checked I was a fucking adult and could make my own decisions." The strain in her voice exploded into full-blown stress out mode. She didn't want her relationship with Olivia to affect Jonathan; that he was worried just added to her stress.

"Okay, what happened?" Jonathan questioned gently. "Everything seemed fine last night at the party, so..."

"That's the thing, Jon, I really don't know." Feeling exposed, she brought her feet up onto the bench, tucking her knees close to her chest before lighting up another smoke. She was chain-smoking. Not a good sign, but she really didn't care right now. "All I did was try and get her to eat breakfast."

"Well, you know she doesn't eat breakfast that often, Micah," Jonathan responded, trying to sound reasonable.

"Yes, and by lunch she's a royal pain in the ass and feels like crap. I was just trying to take care of her and I get shit for it."

"What did she say?"

"She basically reminded me that I suck at taking care of myself. She was throwing my past in my face, Jonathan! I know I've screwed up before, but I am doing better." Micah had to stop for a moment—she could feel her stress rising to an unacceptable level. She rubbed her temple against the headache she could feel starting behind her eyes.

"I am trying to do better," she repeated in almost a whisper, her throat raw and burning with emotion and cigarette smoke.

Micah hadn't expected Olivia to throw her past actions in her face like that. She had been getting more comfortable around her, maybe too comfortable. The woman had gotten under her skin and beneath her armor, and this morning was a good example of just how vulnerable that made her. Micah had given Olivia the power to hurt her with just a sentence.

Micah jumped when she felt a soft hand touch her shoulder. She instantly knew Olivia's touch. *How can one person's touch make you feel so complete while leaving you feeling so exposed at the same time?*

"Jonathan, I need to go. Just bring my bike in today." She ended her call, but continued to stare at the blank screen. She couldn't look up at the woman she had fallen in love with—the woman who just used the knowledge of her past to cause her pain.

"Micah, Regina is getting ready to leave for school and wants to say goodbye to you."

"Yeah, sure," Micah responded dully, picking up her discarded butts and shoving them in her pocket.

"Hey Reggie, have a good day today, okay?" Micah managed to infuse a fair imitation of enthusiasm into her voice.

"Bye Micah! Will I see you later?" Regina asked. Her enthusiasm and genuine affection made it difficult to hold it together.

"Of course." Hugging Reggie goodbye, she left Olivia to see her off to school. Running back into the house, she grabbed her messenger bag and prepared to leave. When she turned around, she came face to face with Olivia.

"Sweetheart, can we talk?"

"Now isn't a good time, Olivia." Micah brushed past Olivia, intent on leaving the house.

"Where are you going?" Olivia's voice changed as Micah walked towards the door. She sounded panicked and almost terrified that Micah was willing to walk away from her.

"Why does it matter?"

"It matters! Micah, wait."

Micah paused with her hand still on the doorknob, silently waiting to hear what Olivia had to say for herself.

"I know I acted like a bitch this morning. My only excuse is that for the first time in a very long time I—" Olivia took a deep breath in and blew it out slowly before continuing. "I don't want to go into the office."

Micah turned around at that bit of news, letting her hand fall away from the door handle. Olivia lived and breathed her father's law firm—her firm now, Micah amended.

"I wanted to stay here with you, I wanted more time. I overreacted at breakfast and I have absolutely no excuse."

Micah moved away from the door, striding back through the foyer to stand in front of Olivia. She had wanted to stare her down, to force the confession and apology from her before rescinding her anger and hurt.

She wanted to stand there with her arms crossed, waiting for Olivia to explain why she felt it was okay to cut her with her words while berating her for doing the same with a blade. She had wanted to do all that, yet all she could do was watch silently as Olivia struggled to explain herself, and control her desire to take her into her arms and tell her it was okay.

"I—I spoke without thinking. What I said—I was referring to your hip, how you keep trying to ride through the pain. I saw how stiff and sore you were when you first woke up. I NEVER—EVER—meant to make you think I was talking about your past," Olivia stuttered through her explanation, motioning towards Micah's stomach with her hand as she spoke. "What happened in your past–God, Micah, I can't even imagine what you went through. I'll be honest, I can't pretend to fully understand all of it, I may never be able to, but," Olivia drew a ragged breath. "You offered me your trust, Micah. You shared your pain and suffering with me regardless of how much it frightened you to do so. I would never violate that trust."

"It's okay, Olivia." Micah did the only thing she could think of that didn't require more words. She pulled Olivia in for a heartfelt embrace Olivia tucked her face into the crook of her neck, the soft press of her lips not meant to arouse but to reassure. Gently brushing a few tear-dampened strands of hair away from Olivia's forehead, Micah tucked the errant strands behind her ear before lightly kissing the top of her head. Olivia sighed, closing her eyes at the loving touch before tucking herself even closer.

"Better?" Micah asked.

"Yes, much," Olivia mumbled.

Micah took a deep breath in then let it out, allowing the anger and hurt drain from her body. It didn't matter, the whole crazy argument didn't matter anymore. Micah shivered, feeling Olivia's hot breath against her neck turn to something more than simple reassurance when Olivia's lips parted, capturing the flesh along her pulse line between sharp teeth as she sucked gently against the sensitive skin. Micah inhaled sharply, her thoughts heading south in quick pursuit of the flash of pleasure Olivia's teeth and lips sparked. Ignoring the familiar tingling sensation sliding down her spine, she tried to stay on point. She couldn't let Olivia distract her, not when she had to go into work.

"Not now, Olivia." Not wanting to do something and not doing it were two different things. "As much as I enjoy our time together, you have responsibilities, responsibilities you can't just blow off because we're distracted by the newness of all of this. I know that sucks, and I understand how you feel, but we can't keep taking it out on each other, okay?"

"Okay."

"Will you eat at the office?"

"Yes, I promise."

"Good enough," Micah replied agreeably. She pulled away from her lover, tipping her head down to place a chaste kiss on Olivia's lips, back in control of her body and the situation. She grabbed Olivia's bag, looped her messenger bag around her neck, and walked out the door, turning around and holding her hand out for Olivia to join her. Robert was at the curbside, waiting for them. After they settled in and the privacy screen was up, Olivia scooted close to her.

"Micah, can I ask you a question?" Olivia had taken Micah's hand in hers and was idly playing with her fingers.

"Of course you can."

"I won't be upset by the answer; I just want to know something." Olivia sounded apprehensive, her small white teeth worrying her bottom lip as she hesitated. "But, I won't ask if it will upset you."

Okay, now Micah was nervous. Olivia was still playing with her fingers and she was procrastinating. It was fidgety behavior, and Olivia did not fidget.

"What do you want to know?"

"Um, that night you went out with Jonathan—after you waltzed back into my life, did you have sex at the club?"

"Nope, I didn't even go out that night."

"Really?"

"Really," Micah repeated drolly. She hadn't expected that question. "I couldn't, not after seeing you again. What happened in your office, the way you looked at me, it was all too fresh in my mind for me to even consider going out. So, I just stayed home and hit the gym."

"Oh."

"That's it? Just oh? What's really going on, Olivia?"

Olivia broke their eye contact, unsure how to best answer that question. Worrying her lower lip with her teeth as she thought about it, she decided honesty was the best way to go.

"I worry that I don't have enough experience to satisfy you completely." Olivia finally whispered, voicing a fear that sounded silly even to her own ears.

Micah chuckled, not meanly, but still amused. "Oh, Sweetheart, after everything we've done this weekend, you still feel that way?"

When Olivia didn't smile at her joking answer, Micah realized that it was time for a more serious approach. She had never considered how insecure Olivia might be feeling over everything that was happening between them. It explained a lot. "Listen to me; you are an amazing woman, both in and out of the bedroom. To tell you the truth, you have surprised me each and every time we have been together. I have never found someone who could match me, passion for passion, as you have done. There is no way that I will give that up, ever. Not for as long as you want me."

"Oh." Olivia turned her face away before asking another question. "Would you do it again?"

"Do what?"

"Go back to the club...for sex, I mean?" Olivia stuttered through the question. She wasn't used to being so bold, but it was something she couldn't stop thinking about.

"I told you, I was done with that." Micah frowned at her.

"Even if it was with me?" Olivia asked, glancing at Micah out of the corner of her eye.

This time it was Micah who squirmed. "Uh, I..." she swallowed and started over again. "I think that's something we should talk about later, much later."

Olivia wasn't fooled. Micah had liked the idea, she had liked it more than she would admit.

"That's okay, I'm a patient woman." She pulled Micah's lips down to meet hers for a very thorough kiss.

"Now you need to fix your lipstick again," Micah quipped.

"I don't care, it was worth it," Olivia said, but she did hurry and wipe the smears away before Robert pulled up in front of their building.

Micah's bike was locked to the bike rack just outside the front door. Jonathan must have made it in before they did, and that meant Olivia was later than usual. Micah stopped to check on her bike, running her fingers along the brake lines and checking her tires when she heard Olivia's honey-tinged voice directly behind her, colored with her own personal brand of sarcastic wit.

"Would you two like some privacy?"

"Very funny, Olivia." Micah laughed. "After you, my lady," Micah added, making a sweeping gesture with her arm as she bowed towards the glass doors.

"Am I?" Olivia asked as they walked into the open elevator.

"Are you what?" Micah asked, pressing the button to their floor before looking over at her lover.

"Your lady."

"Yes, I believe you are. Is that okay?"

"I believe so, yes."

"I'm glad that's settled."

They walked past Amanda's desk and into Olivia's office together. Jonathan had already been there and left Micah's work clothes sitting on the couch. She took them into the bathroom so she could change while Olivia settled in behind her desk.

***

Olivia sat back in her chair and stretched her tight back muscles. *This is what playing hooky gets you*, she thought, sighing at the amount of work left. She had already separated the pile into what should have been

410

left to her and what could go elsewhere, but the remaining pile was still impressive.

She looked at her watch and cursed, choosing a favorite of Micah's to utter under her breath. It was almost lunch and the mountain of paperwork didn't even look dented. To make matters worse, one of her rare but debilitating migraines was threatening to come on. She had to stop frequently to rest her eyes.

Olivia pushed her chair away from her desk and tried to rub the tension out of her temples with her fingertips.

When unseen hands suddenly slid across her shoulders to massage her neck gently, Olivia purred in delight. She knew the feel of those hands, and no one else would have dared to sneak up on her.

"Do you have a headache?" Micah asked as she continued to massage Olivia's neck, working along the base of her skull where all the tension seemed to build up. Olivia's stress-bound muscles relaxed instantly at her lover's touch, releasing tension that had been building up since Micah left that morning.

"Yes. Oh, that feels wonderful." Micah's fingers seemed to hone in and locate the worst points, the firm digits breaking down the stiffness in her neck and releasing the band of pain wrapping around her head like a crown.

"Can you take a break?"

"For you, yes." It was close enough to lunchtime that she could afford to start a little early.

Micah shut her office door to give them some privacy.

"Lay down, Love, let me massage your neck."

Olivia couldn't hold in the small moans and sounds of pleasure that escaped her lips when Micah started working out the kinks in her neck and shoulders with expert precision. The relief was almost immediate. Her headaches could get quite bad if left long enough, but somehow Micah had managed to chase it away before it became unbearable.

"How's that?" Micah asked after a while.

"Better, thank you."

Micah helped Olivia turn over on her back, grabbing a pillow for Olivia to lay her head on. Micah cocked her head and just looked at her before leaning down and kissing Olivia on the forehead. "You do look better. It must have been a bad one, for me to sneak up on you like that. You're still pale, though. Why don't you lie there and relax while I order us some lunch?"

Olivia threw an arm over her eyes to shade them against the bright glare of the fluorescent lights. "Yes, but nothing spicy if you don't mind."

I could really get used to this, Olivia thought to herself. It was amazing. There were so many sides to Micah, and she loved each and everyone one of them.

"Sure."

"Oh, and Micah? Thank you for taking care of me like this."

"Of course."

Olivia peeked out from under her sleeve. Micah sat behind her desk so she could use her computer and order some food for them. Micah looked completely comfortable behind her executive desk, her clear eyes and sharp features radiating both power and intelligence as she typed away. That Micah could pull off that kind of attitude wearing just a t-shirt and cargo shorts made Olivia think. Micah would never pass as a secretary or assistant to anyone; how she had hidden that dominant nature from her during her tenure as an intern—Olivia had no idea. Olivia experienced a strange shift in reality. Micah wore a frown so similar to her own when she was in that seat that it felt almost surreal. Olivia found that she didn't care for that frown, and was suddenly and immensely glad that Micah had chosen a different path and given up law. She wouldn't have been happy.

***

Lunch was a great idea. Olivia's headache faded to a survivable ache and Micah told her that her color was back to normal. On the other hand, Micah was limping again. Olivia had hoped that Micah would let her know when she started to hurt. If she had, she would have stopped sending her out. She sighed at the intractable stubbornness of the woman. That limp meant one important thing: her time with Micah at the office was over for today.

"Sweetheart, go home. I can see you are in pain." As much as she enjoyed her lover's presence at work, she couldn't keep her here for personal massages and companionship. She also had more meetings to go to today, so as far as she was concerned, the day was a bust anyway. It would be better for Micah to go home and rest up her knee so they could enjoy their evening together.

"Um, okay," Micah's responded dully. Micah gathered her things to go, then looked over at Olivia before leaving.

Olivia was intently reading something on her desk. She wasn't prepared for her two o'clock meeting and was so caught up in reading the brief that she didn't see the look of disappointment Micah gave her.

"See you later then," Micah murmured, then slipped out the door.

"Micah?" Olivia looked up distractedly, surprised to find her office empty and her lover already gone.

Oh, she's gone. Oh well, I can talk to her tonight. Olivia was determined to get her work done so she could have dinner with her small family. Micah and Regina. Just the thought of the two of them waiting at home for her brought a smile to her face. Looking down at the pile of paperwork again, Olivia vowed to find a way to change the way things were going—she couldn't remain a workaholic all her life. The amount of paperwork shunted to her was intolerable; she had a life just as much as the people who worked for her. For the first time in her life since she started working as an attorney, she questioned whether her job was worth the time spent away from her family. A family that now included one very important dark-haired woman who had captured her heart.

***

Micah sat in bed and doodled in her sketchpad. She had piled about a dozen pillows behind her back and made herself a comfortable little nest of the blankets, but she still was having trouble getting her ideas down on paper. Her sketches were unenthusiastic and uninspired and she couldn't seem to finish any of them. Her sketches reflected her mood, angry little doodles that ended in sharp edges and heavy shading.

She had already taken a hot bath to soak out the kinks in her muscles, but she still couldn't relax. She considered pulling out her computer and getting some writing done, but her heart just wasn't in it tonight. Usually when she couldn't draw, she would write until her inspiration warmed up to something. Tonight, her creativity sat cold and congealed, lying heavy in the pit of her stomach like a bad meal.

It was close to six when her cell phone rang. Micah's phone danced across the bed a second before Olivia's ringtone sounded. Her mood lightened immediately at the chance to hear her lover's voice, even if only over the phone.

"Where are you?" Olivia demanded before Micah could even offer a greeting.

"At home?" Micah was confused. Olivia had told her to go home.

"I just thought—never mind. I'll see you tomorrow." Olivia hung up before Micah could say a thing.

What the hell was that about? She told me to go home and then wonders where I am.

"Oh, crap. You're an idiot, Micah." She could have smacked herself square between the eyes. She had made a major error in judgment, assuming she knew what Olivia meant. Micah stuffed some necessities into her messenger bag, packed up her computer, grabbed her bike, and headed for the basement and her truck.

She was going home.

***

Micah almost knocked at the door, then changed her mind and just let herself into the house. Opening the door with the key Olivia had given her suddenly held special significance to her. She felt like she wasn't just opening the door into Olivia's house, she was also turning the page onto a totally new chapter in her life. The hairs on the back of her neck rose as she stepped through the doorway. She couldn't shake the feeling that something changed when she crossed that threshold.

Following the sounds coming from farther within the house, Micah found Reggie first, doing homework in the family room. The TV was on and the sound turned down low. When she walked in, a guilty face whipped around to stare at her. That guilty face quickly reshaped itself into one of relief when she saw Micah standing there instead of her mom.

"Hey Reggie, where is your mom?"

"In her bedroom. She said she had a headache," she told her, rolling a nervous eye towards the staircase. "Did you guys have a fight?"

"No, Reggie, not really. Just a misunderstanding." *A misunderstanding I intend to fix.*

"You won't tell her I was watching TV?"

"I won't if you get your homework done, how's that?" Micah offered.

"Okay, deal," Reggie turned off the television and picked her schoolbook back up. She didn't look happy, but it was better than getting into trouble.

Micah practically vaulted up the stairs, dropping off her bags at the doorway before hesitating at the door. She wasn't sure if she should knock or just go right in. Opening the bedroom door quietly, she saw Olivia stretched out on her side of the bed. It sounded like she was crying. Micah softly closed the door, locked it behind her and crawled into bed beside Olivia.

"I'm here Love. Don't cry, I'm right here."

"Micah?"

"Yes. I didn't realize—I'm sorry."

Olivia turned over to face Micah, her smile brilliant and beautiful to Micah regardless of, or perhaps because of the tears staining her cheeks. A slight twist of guilt nagged at Micah's gut because she knew that she was the one to cause those tears. No one had ever cried for her, not because she was gone. Except Olivia.

"I should have asked. I just assumed you would know I wanted you here." Olivia flung her arms around her young lover, squeezing her hard enough to know she wasn't just a dream.

It was an amazing feeling for Micah, this fervent embrace that had nothing to do with sex or passion or lust, but was simply and unabashedly an extension of the love they held for each other.

"I learned in my life never to assume. I really wanted to be here with you. I was totally bummed when you didn't ask me to come back over. I couldn't even get any work done," Micah admitted, trying to explain her actions. It was true—she would never assume she was invited, she would never intrude or push or demand what was not freely given to her.

"Well, so there are no more misunderstandings in the future, I want you to stay here with me, with us, as often as you want. You don't need to ask me if it's okay."

"Why, Olivia Holden! Are you asking me to move in with you?" Micah affected a pretty convincing southern drawl.

"Micah!"

"Okay, okay! I'm joking. But I really need a stereo in here if you want me to get up in the mornings."

"We can do that; I can always get earplugs or those noise reduction headphones."

Something caught Micah's eye and she turned to look over Olivia's shoulder. "Hey, when did you get a frame?" Micah had noticed a new picture on the dresser; the photo was of the two of them at the zoo. The one that Reggie had given her.

"On the way home."

"I like the sound of that."

"What?"

"Home," Micah said. She was trying to unbutton Olivia's shirt but the little buttons were being annoyingly uncooperative.

"Micah, we can't right now. We need to eat dinner with Regina." Olivia's voice held a scandalous tone. "But, tonight we will celebrate."

"That's a promise." Olivia pulled Micah into her arms and sealed the deal with a kiss that left her breathless.

"I love you, Olivia."

"I love you, too."

Chapter Thirty-One

Olivia stopped working for a moment to watch Micah stare out the large picture window in her office. Micah never seemed to tire of the view, but today her profile held a touch of melancholy that shouldn't be there. That worried her.

Looking back at the last couple of weeks since Micah had moved into her home, she had to say that everything had been wonderful between the two of them. Surprisingly, there had only been a few small disagreements while they adjusted to living together. The biggest point of contention had been Micah's need to play music to wake up in the morning—but they had learned to compromise. Micah would keep the stereo down low until Olivia left the room, then she was free to turn it up. They also agreed that Micah could have free rein over the weekends without any complaint from Olivia. She smiled at that. Although Micah wouldn't admit to it, it was obvious that some of her music choices had changed to something a little less jarring on Olivia's ears for the morning hours. For someone who didn't wake up easily, Micah's hearing certainly could take a lot of abuse in the early hours of the day. Conversely, Olivia woke easily but she craved silence until it was absolutely necessary.

Her workday didn't officially start until she consumed at least one cup of coffee, accepting the responsibilities of the day more by the ritual than the need for caffeine...unlike Micah. Micah seemed to need the jolt of caffeine to stimulate her brain awake, but only after it was primed by music. It was an odd and quirky ritual, but it was a small price to pay for the pleasure of waking up each morning wrapped in the arms of the woman she loved...the same woman who was now gazing so pensively out the window.

Olivia frowned. It was generally against Micah's nature to be so somber in her presence. In fact, Micah usually brought Olivia out of her workday funks with her quick smile and sharp wit. That wasn't to say that Micah couldn't be temperamental, but that was the point. She usually bounced back and forth, and this dark mood had lasted the better part of an hour.

Ever since she had come back from her last run.

It couldn't be their living situation that was bothering her lover; Micah had joined her little family so seamlessly it felt like she had always been there. Regina simply adored her, and the feelings seemed mutual, with Micah helping with her homework and taking her out to play basketball afterwards. *So, what was wrong?*

"Micah?" Olivia called out, trying to get her attention but getting zero response. *That's disturbing.*

"Sweetheart?" She tried again. Micah didn't acknowledge her, she didn't even twitch. Whatever had captured Micah's attention, it had placed her thoughts and mind far away from where she was physically. Olivia got up from her chair, the creaking of the suspension loud in the silence. Even that high-pitched and intrusive sound failed to penetrate Micah's silent contemplation of the cityscape beneath her. Olivia approached her unnoticed; even touching her shoulder didn't get her attention.

"Micah?" she asked again. The rounded muscle of Micah's deltoid was as rigid as banded iron beneath her fingertips. She squeezed the tense muscle lightly, feeling the muscles twitch under her hand in response.

"Yeah?" Micah responded automatically. She blinked but did not turn towards Olivia, despite the subtle pressure of her fingers. Micah finally relaxed, if only a small bit, beneath her touch as Olivia continued to knead the tense muscles.

Micah's hand came up to capture Olivia's, the slight roughness of her palm scratching across her knuckles. She flexed her hand over Olivia's, returning the affectionate action. That was something, at least, but Olivia hadn't liked the subdued tone in her voice. It was unlike Micah to be so disengaged—especially with her. Micah's voice sounded listless, lacking its normal color and vibrancy.

"Are you okay?" Olivia asked, touching her face. Micah felt cold—the impression of hard stone flashed through Olivia's thoughts. Micah's walls were up, as if she was purposefully blocking herself off from her emotions, and Olivia felt that wall as an almost physical presence between them. It made her heart ache, seeing Micah like this. She wanted Micah to turn towards her and cast that trademark grin at her—to shed this melancholy mood like an ill-fitting coat.

"Yeah—I just have to figure something out."

Micah's response offered no relief for Olivia's imagination, which was running rampant with possible explanations—none of them good.

Micah hadn't shrugged her off, but she wasn't especially welcoming Olivia's touch either. Normally, she would have put her arm around Olivia and hugged her. What had started as concern was now escalating into something more alarming. She was used to the closeness they usually shared. She hadn't realized how much she had come to expect it, that its sudden loss made her feel like a part of her was missing.

421

Please let this be something I can fix, she silently begged, not caring who was listening, just as long as they were.

"Did I do something to upset you?"

"No, of course not. This has nothing to do with you." Micah woke up a bit with that question. Bringing her head around sharply, Micah's normally clear hazel eyes had dulled to a muddy-looking dark ochre, revealing more than she seemed able or willing to express. Olivia noted the dark circles beneath those expressive eyes—so filled with apprehension and fear that she almost missed the shadow of something dark and heavy simmering just beneath the surface.

"Did something happen?" Olivia felt that if she could just find the right question to ask, it would be the key needed to open Micah back up to her. A surge of frustration welled up as Micah simply stared at her, her normally full lips set in a thin line. When Micah wasn't in the mood to share, it was like pulling teeth to get answers.

"I'll figure it out," Micah said. She seemed to travel from a great distance before coming back to her, actually physically shaking herself out of her thoughts before she warmed to Olivia. Her eyes lost that haunted expression as she smiled down at her lover. The smile held a tinge of sadness that she couldn't seem to completely banish, but she was back, and that was all that mattered.

Micah wrapped her arms around Olivia, pulling her in closely for a solid hug before pressing her lips against Olivia's temple. If the embrace felt desperate, there wasn't anything else Olivia could do except offer her support and empathy. Whatever strength Micah needed from her, she would gladly offer it.

"I just need to work my thoughts out, Love. If you don't need me anymore today, I am going to head out for home. Maybe taking a long ride will help me clear my head some."

Olivia was loath to let her go, but she knew that it wouldn't help and it might actually make things worse if she tried to stop her. She made herself step back, giving Micah the space she needed.

"Be safe. I will be home by six." Olivia had gotten used to the fact that Micah preferred to ride her bike over any other form of transportation. The woman seemed to live, breathe, and eat cycling.

"Micah? I love you." Olivia never let Micah leave her presence without letting her know that. It was sappy and emotional, but it made her happy.

"I love you too. See you in a few."

***

Micah arrived back at the house frustrated and still angry; the ride hadn't done a thing to calm her nerves. She checked the time. She still had several hours of alone time to try to figure things out. Micah didn't know how long she could maintain equilibrium with all of the conflicting emotions coursing through her system, but she knew it wasn't very long.

Grabbing her head, she rocked back and forth on the edge of the couch for a minute before the overwhelming need to do something rose up again inside her, sending her pacing through the house. It was all just too much. She knew one thing that would instantly calm her...but she didn't want to handle it that way.

She could feel the knife where it lay hidden in her bag, the sharp edge calling to her with its hot promise of relief. Instead of going upstairs to their bedroom, Micah turned and headed for her gym to try to work out some of her inner turmoil.

It would be too tempting to fall back on old habits if she went upstairs, and she had promises to keep—both to herself and to Olivia. Entering the largish room, she scanned the various weight machines and dumbbells. The smell of iron greeted her, hard and cold and solid. She needed more than just the strain of muscles against the heavy weights or the feel of her lungs burning to meet the needs of her pumping heart. What she needed was something to keep her mind from touching on darker thoughts, other options for dealing with the stress building up inside her. The heavy bag sat in one corner, suspended from a chain bolted to the ceiling. It was perfect.

It didn't take long for Micah to lose herself in a red haze of pain, caught up in the sound of her fists hitting the bag, each blow reverberating through her arms and into her shoulders as she tried to push her emotional overload into the physical exertion.

***

Olivia walked into an eerily quiet house. Usually, when Micah had the house to herself, she took advantage to play the music as loud as she liked. Olivia had watched Micah typing away on her laptop with the music blaring full blast. That always amazed her. How could she think, let alone be creative with all that noise blasting in her ears?

Coming home to a silent house when she knew Micah was inside alone was disturbing. A nauseating sense of foreboding took up residence in the pit of her stomach.

"Micah?" she called out, dropping her purse and keys off in the foyer and went in search of her. Micah wasn't in the family room or their bedroom. She decided Micah had to be in the one room she herself normally stayed out of.

The home gym was a belated birthday present for Micah, one she discovered soon after she moved in. Everyone left her alone when she was in there—that was Micah's place to hide or get away. She never asked for the privacy, but Olivia gave it to her, anyway. After all, she had thrown Micah into a full family situation by asking her to move in, it was only fair to offer her a place to get some alone time. She had made the gym Micah's space and only her space. Even Regina knew better than to go there and bug her, which the pre-teen was prone to do at any given moment.

When her daughter cried foul for the unfair rule, Olivia was forced to add herself to the list of banned persons, which placated her daughter's simplistic idea of fair and equitable treatment. Micah had just grinned and watched the antics for a while before silently slipping away to her new gym and closing the door. The argument had dwindled away quickly once that happened, since the two of them were left listening to the steady clink of iron on iron as Micah tried out her new equipment in privacy.

Today she was going to break her own rule. She opened the door and found Micah taking her troubles out on the heavy bag. The muffled thud of strike after strike on the canvas could be felt as a tremor travelling along the ceiling beam, the heavy bag swaying against the impact of her blows.

"Micah, stop," Olivia commanded, her voice loud and resounding in the open space as she stood horrified in the doorway.

Micah paused and turned, looking up in surprise at the unexpected voice.

"What's wrong? Is everything okay?" Micah asked, confusion lacing her eyebrows together even as the sweat poured out of her. Olivia never interrupted her when she was working out.

"Look at your hands."

Micah looked down at her bare hands, taking in the raw redness and swelling, the bleeding knuckles, then looked back at the red streaks marring the white surface of the heavy bag. Comprehension dawned in her eyes as she realized what she had been doing. She forced her fists to unclench, then spread and flexed her fingers stiffly, looking down at them as if they were somehow disconnected from the rest of her. Her hands started to shake. She let them drop to her sides, then looked up at Olivia.

The whole scene disturbed Olivia, but what really bothered her most was the blank expression, the lack of understanding that what she was doing was dangerous. She looked at Olivia as if the wounds on her hands didn't matter. This was another side of her lover that she had to learn to accept. Micah was simply wired differently than other people.

"Come with me." Olivia grabbed Micah by the arm and pulled her through the house to their bedroom and into the bathroom. She held Micah's hands under the cold water so she could get a better look at the damage. Sighing, she made a mental note to grab some ice and make sure Micah used it. The bleeding had stopped but the abrasions were extensive, they would take a while to heal. Thankfully, it didn't look like anything was broken.

"You're going to ruin your towel." Micah tried to pull her hand away.

"I don't give a damn about the towel, Micah. I think I have some ointment in the cabinet that will help the worst of this," she said, trying not to lose it while she cleaned out Micah's wounds...her self-inflicted wounds. Olivia ground her teeth together. She had to ask. God help her, she didn't want to hear the answer but she had to ask. "Why?"

"I forgot to put on my gloves, and then it just didn't seem to matter." Micah was calming down and she was starting to think more clearly. It was an accident, she had gotten caught up in her emotions and the pain and she hadn't been careful. Now, Olivia was here, taking care of her hurts and trying to pretend it didn't bother her. She knew Olivia too well to not see the telltale signs that she was holding back tears. Micah wanted to crawl into a corner and hide.

"I'm sorry, I'll be more careful next time."

Olivia was studiously cleaning Micah's knuckles, spreading some ointment carefully against the angry skin. Her touch was gentle, but it still burned where the skin was abraded and torn.

"You promised to talk to me," Olivia whispered, her voice hollow. She held in her tears but couldn't hide her disappointment.

"Look, Olivia. I'm okay. I didn't hurt myself on purpose. I could have, but I didn't." Stung by Olivia's reminder of the promise she had made and wasn't sure if she could always honor, Micah spoke in pained whisper. "I never wanted you to see this side of me."

"I know, Micah. And I appreciate that." Olivia stopped what she was doing and looked at her lover. "Will you tell me what has you so upset? Please, talk to me."

Taking a deep breath to center herself, Micah flexed her sore fingers, contemplating her next words. No matter how long she stared at her battered hands they couldn't give her the answers she needed. Micah finally looked up, meeting Olivia's concerned gaze.

"My father's in town and he's looking for me."

***

Olivia lay awake, staring into the dark well after Micah had fallen into a fitful sleep next to her. She was extremely worried about her. Micah had already told her a lot about her father, and none of it was good. She had never even met the man and she wanted to cause him so much misery and sorrow for everything he had put Micah through, not to mention the limp Micah lived with every day. That knowledge sent her into a red rage every time she thought about it. The man was a menace, and she was sure his visit had nothing to do with fatherly love and concern for Micah's welfare.

Micah still wasn't talking much, but at least she was answering Olivia's questions.

If the responses were monotone and lacking, it was still better than the alternative, which had been overwhelming silence. Each time she withdrew into herself, Olivia would bring her back, encouraging Micah to speak about what was bothering her so much that she would hurt herself without thinking.

From what she could gather, Micah had been on the way back to the office after a routine delivery when

Jordan, her boss from Street Slicks, called. He let her know that her father had stopped by and was looking for her. Jordan was apologetic and a little distressed because he made the mistake of telling him that she was currently loaned out to Olivia's law firm. The man had been insistent. After making a nuisance of himself for several hours, Jordan tried to kick the older man out. Somehow the situation had become verbal and he had just wanted him to leave. As soon as he learned where Micah was, the man's entire demeanor changed. Jordan realized he had been played; the man had made him angry on purpose. After hearing the whole story, Olivia could see why Micah was freaking out. This wasn't a man simply looking for his daughter—this was a very angry and insistent man looking for God knows what. If Jordan's description of the events was accurate, Micah's father hadn't changed one bit from the violent and volatile man that Micah had described.

She had made a lovely meal that had been barely touched. Micah was a woman who appreciated her appetites—she always complimented Olivia on her efforts—but tonight she had to remind Micah simply to eat. Even when she made the attempt, Olivia could tell she was simply going through the motions, barely tasting the food she automatically brought to her mouth before putting her fork down again. The gauze dressing wrapped around her knuckles stood out starkly against the low lighting of the dining room, a painful reminder of finding her lover beating the hell out of the unyielding heavy bag.

She only showed interest in the outside world once, and that was when Olivia was trying to coax her to come downstairs and eat. She had hesitated at the top of stairs, her face pale and drawn beneath the hallway light.

"Where's Reggie?"

"Remember she is with her dad this weekend?"

"Sorry, I forgot."

Olivia let herself cry in the privacy of the darkened room, remembering how it felt when she realized that Micah was injuring herself. That it didn't even seem to faze her was terrifying; the blank expression on her face as she looked down at her hands was a painful reminder of just how broken Micah had been—could still be, if she lost the will to fight.

Since sleep continued to elude her, Olivia turned and silently watched her lover, absently running her hand down Micah's arm in an attempt to calm her. Usually Micah was a deadhead when she slept, rarely moving throughout the night once she found a comfortable position, but tonight she twisted restlessly under the covers. When Micah started to whimper and shrink away from her touch, Olivia sat up, alarmed and unsure what to do. Micah started to fight against the coverlet. Her whimpers turned to desperate moans that Olivia recognized as sleep muffled screams. She had gone through her share of nightmares in life to recognize that Micah was locked into something violent and frightening that she seemed unable to shake.

"Micah, sweetie, wake up," Olivia rubbed her arm, trying to shake her awake.

"Let go!" Micah bellowed, her voice guttural and booming in the darkness of their bedroom. She sat up suddenly, yanking her arm out of Olivia's grasp, her eyes open but still caught up in the vision of her nightmare. Micah's sudden movement was so violent that Olivia had to back away to avoid getting hit.

Bringing both palms up to her face, Micah rubbed her eyes roughly. She shook violently, the images behind her eyelids refusing to give up their hold on her psyche.

Olivia reached out a tentative hand towards Micah, watching her carefully. Micah stared at Olivia's hand suspended between them as if it was a gavel raised and ready to hand down a guilty verdict.

"Fuck, I'm sorry, Olivia." Distraught, her eyes wild as she tore at the tangled bedding, Micah climbed out of their bed and headed for the bathroom, stripping off her sweat-soaked t-shirt on the way.

Olivia gave Micah a few minutes to recover before she went to check on her. She found Micah staring at herself in the mirror, her hands spread wide and clenching the edges of the marble sink as if she could garner strength from the cold stone.

"Are you okay, Sweetheart?" Olivia wanted to gather the younger woman into her arms, to kiss away the pain and suffering she saw in the mirror's reflection. The woman looking back at her wasn't the Micah she knew. The woman looking back at her had shadows in her face that made her cheeks look hollow and bruised— gaunt. Feverish hazel eyes looked back at her, artificially bright against the dark circles under her eyes.

"Am I okay? Christ, Olivia...I should be asking you that," Micah said. "Did I hurt you?"

"No. You frightened me but you didn't hurt me."

"Oh, God, Olivia. I'm so sorry about that." Micah felt sick to her stomach. She had almost, or even may have hit Olivia. "I was caught up in the nightmare; everything was just so jumbled up."

"About your father?" Olivia guessed. It would make sense, considering how much she'd been thinking about him.

"Yes. When my father threw me out of the house, he grabbed my arm. Threw me around like a ragdoll. He couldn't wait for me to leave his house on my own power.

431

He wanted my presence, my stain on his precious reputation... removed from his home," Micah practically snarled that last bit. "I'm lucky he didn't do a number on my shoulder like he did with my knee. As it was, I had to hide a set of very colorful bruises for weeks."

"And I grabbed your arm," Olivia stated simply, making the connection.

"All I saw was my father, I didn't know it was you."

Olivia nodded—Micah had told her about that encounter, but had not gone into all of the details.

"I take it that wasn't the first time."

"No, it wasn't the first time," Micah admitted.

Micah looked ready to bolt, or to be sick. Olivia wasn't sure which one would happen first if she didn't find a way to calm her down.

"It's okay, Sweetheart, I know you wouldn't hurt me, not on purpose. Please, don't berate yourself over something you had no control over."

Micah bowed her head, hiding her face beneath her shaggy black hair. When she raised her head again, tormented hazel eyes locked on hers.

"What do you see when you look at me, Olivia?"

"I see a wonderfully strong young woman who I love more than I ever thought was possible." Olivia didn't get the reaction she had hoped for; if anything, the expression of guilt and pain on Micah's face intensified.

"Do you know why I put on so much muscle?" Micah's stiff armed posture accentuated her question, her gym rat physique plainly apparent in the mirror's reflection.

"I think I have an idea, but why don't you tell me?"

"So I would never be a victim again." Micah's voice came out hoarse, almost ragged as she forced her lips to form her innermost fears into words. "God, I hate even having to say that. I never wanted to claim victim status. That's why I made sure I would never have to again."

"I can understand that."

"But that's what I am doing right now. I am letting him get to me again." Micah's voice hitched, caught somewhere between misery and fury. "He makes me so angry, Olivia, and that scares me to death. My father was always angry, and he used that anger to back up what he really felt...hate. Hate is such an ugly thing, Olivia. It turns on you, twisting and building on itself until all that is left is the hatred. It doesn't leave room for anything else. I have been so careful to avoid this, after seeing what it did to my parents." Micah shuddered. "I used to think that righteous anger was so much cleaner. It was simple and easy and it lent me strength when I needed it most. But, Olivia...I can feel it. I can feel my anger twisting on itself and I can't help myself. God help me, but I hate my father, Olivia. I hate him and I don't want to become like him because of it."

"So what are you going to do?" It was obvious that Micah had been thinking about this a lot, and Olivia was worried that she would do something stupid or hazardous. The man seemed dangerous...deranged, and she wasn't about to let Micah put herself in harm's way if she could help it.

"Face him on my terms." Micah's voice was resolute. "I'm done playing games. It's time to finish this. He has to learn that I'm not a scared child anymore. Hell, I'm not the same person I was a year ago when he did this." Micah shifted her leg, drawing attention to the knee that still bothered her.

"We." Olivia gently corrected Micah's statement. She wasn't about to stand by and let Micah take care of her problems alone. If she could interfere, she would.

"No." Micah didn't want her father anywhere near Olivia. He was too unstable and she couldn't handle it if something happened to Olivia because of him.

"Yes. We are in this together." Olivia ran her fingertips across Micah's jawline, bringing her around to face her directly. "We, Micah, we are in this together." This time the iron wasn't couched in soft words. Olivia was adamant that Micah would not be alone with her father. There was a long moment where the two stubborn women just stared each other down, each trying to force the other to accept the inevitable.

The conversation was getting them nowhere quick, and besides, Micah had already figured out what she was going to do. She didn't want to fight all weekend over it— it wouldn't change the outcome at all. Letting their relationship suffer over her father's presence was another win for him, and she couldn't let him ruin the best thing that had ever happened to her.

Let her think she has won this round, at least.

"Fine. I won't meet him privately."

"Thank you, Micah."

"Let's go back to bed, Love. We still have the weekend to ourselves. Maybe you can help me forget all this drama for a while." It was dissembling at its worst, but when Micah brought her lips down to meet her lover's she found that she wasn't dissembling in the least. Passion flared as she deepened the kiss, her insistent tongue demanding entry past Olivia's lips until she gave in to her.

Olivia wasn't stupid. She knew Micah too well to think that she would just give in this easily. Micah's offer was a calculated attempt to distract her. Even so, she wasn't prepared for the sudden spark of arousal Micah's kiss set off in her. It was as if all the emotional drama of the last twelve hours suddenly poured out of them, emptying them and then refilling them with an equal amount of blinding, irrational and overwhelming passion.

Micah had asked her to help forget her problems for the weekend, and she would honor that request— under her own terms.

Chapter Thirty-Two

Olivia rolled over and stared at the face of the clock on her bedside table. The sky outside her window was still dark but held that odd shade of blue black that would both fade and brighten as the morning sun fought to reach the horizon. As the glowing numbers slowly ticked away, she sighed, not wanting to face this morning's disappointing facts.

The digital face of the clock ticked off another minute. Another minute closer to the alarm going off and starting the day, and one less minute before she would have to drag herself out of bed and away from the warm presence curled up behind her. Olivia couldn't sleep, not when she knew that Micah was up to something. If she hadn't been keeping a close eye on her lover she would have missed the occasional frown as Micah's thoughts travelled somewhere dark, as well as the phone calls she dismissed rapidly—a guilty expression forming and then disappearing before she thought anyone would notice.

Micah was many things—loving, incredibly smart, cocky, great in bed—the list could go on and on but there was one thing she wasn't. Micah wasn't a good liar. Olivia could always tell when she was trying to hide something. Despite everything Micah had been through and all the walls she had thrown up, she retained a core naiveté and lack of guile when it came to deliberate deception.

The red lines of the clock face reshaped themselves into serial numbers as the minutes continued to tick away. Soon the alarm would go off and Micah's solid weight would leave her, the arm wrapped tightly around her would tense and move away.

Micah still hated mornings and probably would every day of her life, but it didn't matter to Olivia. She would rather watch Micah move from her initial and practically comatose state every morning, through her routine of caffeine and joint popping stretches, than wake up to a cold and empty life that did not include the intractable but lovable raven-haired beauty.

Despite herself, she drifted off to sleep, only to be jarred awake by the dreadfully repetitive bleat of the alarm clock she had spent so much time contemplating.

Yawning so hard her jaw cracked, Olivia crawled out of bed in search of caffeine—coffee for her and a Coke for the grumbling woman who was earnestly trying to burrow herself deeper under the blankets rather than get up. Today she had nothing but empathy for Micah's lack of appreciation for the morning hours.

***

Micah's habit of riding into work was a continual source of worry for Olivia. She was relieved to find Micah's bike locked in front of the building when Robert pulled up, but she didn't completely relax until she saw Micah, sitting and happily chatting with Amanda. Micah grinned at her expression, having beaten her to work yet again. The New York traffic didn't keep her from racing through the tangled streets and stop-and-go traffic like Olivia's town car, hence her unease. She knew how crazy Micah was on that bike of hers.

Settling in to her Monday morning routine, she looked up occasionally to find Micah staring at her computer. She wasn't typing much, just making faces and occasionally scrolling down the screen as she read her work. Olivia had a secret. She didn't even need Micah there today, she just wanted to keep her close by so she wouldn't go and do anything stupid. The fact that Micah hadn't complained once about being cooped up in the office with nothing to do was a good indicator that she was up to something—Olivia just didn't know what. Finally, at about ten, Olivia closed the file in front of her and stood up.

"Micah, I have a quick meeting across town with a client. I should be back for a late lunch. Will you be here when I get back? We can have lunch together," Olivia asked casually. She caught the quick flash of interest in Micah's eyes, but only because she was looking for it.

"Yes, of course. I will even order us something for lunch, if you like, so it will be here when you get back." Her response was spot on. Her embrace, while eagerly welcomed by Olivia, was longer and held more strength to it than normal. Her answer also carried a question within it, an obvious attempt to learn when she was coming back.

"That sounds lovely. I will just text you when I am on my way back," she murmured, gathering up her purse and heading out the door. She had already texted Robert to meet her, just not in the way that Micah expected. Unlike Micah, Olivia was practiced in deception, and she had just pulled a big one on the other woman. Setting her up like this was not something she enjoyed doing, but she wasn't about to let her lover get hurt just because she didn't want Olivia to get involved.

She met Robert at the door and they crossed the street together to meet Jonathan at the coffee shop. It hadn't taken long for Olivia to set things up—she knew her lover too well. A well-orchestrated string of emails had accomplished many things this weekend: it had put a non-existent appointment in her schedule book as well as let Jonathan and Robert in on her plans, both designed to make sure that Micah wouldn't be meeting with her father alone.

She had expected Jonathan's response when she had told him what was going on. He was incredibly protective of his young friend and he knew, probably better than she did, how badly Micah's father had hurt her in the past. That Robert insisted on coming along as well was a welcome surprise. Evidently, he had become quite protective of Micah over the last few weeks, including her in Olivia's small little family.

Olivia was thrilled; she figured it wouldn't hurt to have his extra muscle.

"Jonathan, did you manage to do that research I asked for?" Olivia asked by way of greeting.

"Of course." Jonathan smiled grimly, then pulled out a sheaf of papers and handed them to her. "Are you sure Micah is planning on meeting her father?" he asked, shifting his gaze out the window. They had a clear view of the front of their office building from here.

"I'm pretty good at reading her, so I feel pretty confident."

"I really hope so, the sooner this gets done, the better it will be for everyone," Jonathan replied. Micah needed to get this chapter of her life over and done with and Olivia's involvement was exactly what Micah needed to move forward.

Olivia shuffled through the data Jonathan handed her. "Jonathan? Did you read any of this?"

She was pissed, more than pissed at what their PI had found, and it didn't even take long for him to dig out some rather sordid details.

"Yes," Jonathan answered.

"And why hasn't this man," she spat, using the term loosely for such a horrible specimen of humanity. Now she knew why Jonathan looked so grim this morning. "Why hasn't he been thrown in jail already?"

"Small town politics. He's well-known in the community. Influential in his own way, I guess." Jonathan's face hardened. "No one wants to go against the former Sheriff."

"Well, he can't do anything to me." Olivia stuffed the envelope into her purse.

She had what she needed. When the chance presented itself, she would have a few words of her own to share with Micah's father. He would never bother her again, she would see to it.

The three of them sat there and watched the building, the coffees that Jonathan bought them grew cold, wasted and forgotten in their hands. Olivia had enough adrenaline coursing through her body to make caffeine redundant.

They didn't have to wait long, which was a good thing since Olivia's personality was definitely not made for stakeout work. The two men stood just behind her, conversing quietly so as not to disturb Olivia.

Micah walked out five minutes later and leaned casually against her bike, lighting up a cigarette and waiting. Olivia frowned. Micah only needed to smoke when she was stressed out, so she knew that the casual act was just that—an act. She watched Micah pull out her phone and check it then stuff it back into her pocket before pulling out another cigarette. Chain-smoking was another big indicator that Micah was nervous and trying to hide it.

"Dammit." She knew now without a doubt that the younger woman was going to try to deal with her father alone. She knew it was Micah's protective nature that made her do this, but still... *I really hoped I was wrong, I should have known better, but I still had hope.*

Just as she finished that thought, a rather large older man walked up to Micah. She launched away from her bike to confront him on the sidewalk. She couldn't hear anything from her location, but she could read the body language.

"That must be him," she said. He was tall, with the same shock of black hair, although his was peppered with grey. He had approached Micah with that overconfident, fake toothy smile that some men used to intimidate a woman, the kind of smile that was at odds with their intentions. Olivia was already regretting her promise to Jonathan. He wanted to give Micah a chance to deal with this herself...they would only get involved if things deteriorated.

It didn't take long. Micah's father became more animated, gesturing angrily towards the building behind them, then pointing his finger at her. The fake smile slid from his face when Micah shook her head. When he stepped further into Micah's personal space, trying to use his bulk to intimidate her, Olivia cursed.

"Dammit, I told her this was a bad idea." Micah wasn't backing down. Even from where she stood, Olivia could see Micah's jaw tensing, her bandaged hands clenching into tight fists. Every line of her body screamed defiance.

"I think this has gone on long enough," Olivia announced. Her untouched coffee barely made it into the trash before she was through the glass door and heading across the street. Jonathan and Robert were close behind her.

Micah never saw them approaching as she stood there, standing toe to toe with her father, not backing down as he bellowed at her like some crazed street preacher promising the end of the world was on its way.

"I don't want to hear anything about your sick twisted relationship with that woman. I am sure that you wouldn't want your precious lawyer friend to suffer if her clients found out she made it a habit of seducing her interns. Not very ethical of her, is it?" The not so subtle threat was thrown down boldly, a verbal gauntlet intended to create fear and indecision in Micah's heart.

"Ethics? You want to preach to me about ethics? How dare you!" Micah bellowed back. He hadn't heard a thing she had said, and what he had heard had been warped and twisted by his own bias and hatred until it was unrecognizable even to her. "You haven't a clue what ethics are. If Olivia had seduced me, which by the way— SHE DID NOT, it wouldn't be any of your damn business anyway."

"It is my business, Micah. I've always tried to do what was best for you. To keep you straying from the path to God. What you are doing, it's not right. God will punish you for it, and he's punishing me and your mother for not teaching you better."

"You only want what's best for me, huh? Funny, that's what you always said, what you tried to make me believe for all those years. Is that what you thought you were doing every time you laid hands on me? Punishing me because that's what your God wanted? Was that what you were doing when you fucked up my knee? Or, maybe you just liked feeling powerful, taking your anger out on a woman like the coward you are. The doctors are saying I'll probably have this limp for the rest of my life, all because you were trying to do what was best for me. How's that for your precious ethics, huh?"

"Your mother..."

"No, don't bring mom into this. You've got her so whipped she doesn't even have her own opinion. If she thinks I'm going to hell for being gay, it's because you made her believe it." Micah was livid. "I'm done with this charade. You wrote me off a long time ago, there has to be another reason you're here. What the hell do you want from me?"

He drew himself upright and smoothed back his hair before looking down his nose at Micah. This was the man she remembered, self-righteous and full of himself, always ready to point out someone else's sins while conveniently forgetting his own.

"I want what is rightfully mine. That property should have gone to me. The old bat had no right to leave it to you."

Fury erupted inside Micah's brain.

"You mean your mother, right? My grandmother. Even after her death, you have no respect for her, or anyone for that matter. All you care about is your precious reputation, as if money makes you a respectable person. Grandmother knew you too well. She didn't leave you the property because she knew you would destroy everything that our family had built. She understood the importance of keeping the land pristine. You just wanted it for the profit it could bring you."

"I can sue you for it, you know," Micah's father threatened. "I have proof that I spent money, taking care of her...."

Micah felt something deep inside her turn hard and cold at the mention of her grandmother's care. When she spoke again, her voice was cool and controlled, and held a core of iron will that Olivia recognized. Micah had adeptly borrowed Olivia's commanding tones and added her own unique flavor to them.

"Go ahead and try, it won't matter. And as for 'that woman' as you put it, do I need to remind you that she's one of the best attorneys in the state? I doubt you have the money or resources to win against her," Micah spat out, her eyes glowing victoriously. He had lost, she knew it and he knew it. This pathetic attempt at bullying her was just that; he had nothing left to try except to frighten her into giving him the property.

"Oh, and just in case you wanted to know. I am going to ask her to marry me and yes, everyone will know about it." Micah paused, then angrily jabbed her finger at the man she once called father. "But you know what? No one will fucking care. Get with the times, Dad. Your version of the world is sadly out of step with the times. I'm not sick, not evil and I'm certainly not going to Hell because you say so. Just remember, hate is a sin, too. I suggest you go home and think about that."

Micah grinned as her father spluttered and carried on, sounding unsure of himself for the first time since their little argument started. She pressed on, unable to stop herself.

"You just need to go, along with your medieval mentality and holier-than-thou attitude. And since everybody back home knows your business and thinks they have a right to an opinion, it won't take long for everyone to know who and what I am, and just what I am doing here in New York. How's that for your precious reputation?" Micah asked, goading him further. There were people at home who knew she was gay and didn't care. The people who mattered to her father, on the other hand, held the same beliefs he did. It would reflect on him poorly that he had a lesbian daughter.

"What about kids, a family? You would throw it all away just so you can live this—this lifestyle?"

That he had the gall to call on concepts of family and children when he had been such a shitty father sent Micah over the edge.

"Olivia has a child. That means I have a family. The property that grandma left ME will be half hers, and you will never be able to touch it—EVER!"

Micah was royally pissed. For all his supposed concern about her, all he really cared about was the money that her property could generate. It was worth millions in old timber growth and she had the mineral rights to it. Her grandmother knew that she would never have it clear-cut—but she must have known her own son would. That she knew that was a sad testimony to what a terrible person her father had become. How it must have pained her grandmother that her own son would do something so against her wishes. Micah didn't care about the money; she just loved the land for its beauty. In that way, she was a kindred spirit to her grandmother. She would do anything to honor her legacy, which meant not letting her father get his destructive mitts anywhere near it.

As Micah spoke, she watched indecision give way to self-righteous anger, then to white-hot hatred as her father's face transformed into something barely human. His entire body shook as the desire to lash out took over, a familiar enough expression to warn her a second before he raised his hand.

Not again, never again! Her mind screamed even as her body responded to the threat. Before he could make contact, she blocked his wild swing with her arm and stepped close, slamming her palm into his solar plexus so hard the jolt reverberated down her shoulder. She had intended only to knock him away, to keep him from hitting her, but with the adrenaline adding strength to her strike she managed to knock him square on his ass.

The expression on his face was priceless. His hands skidded across the rough concrete sidewalk as he fell, and she hoped he enjoyed the pain that only road rash could offer.

"How does it feel to be the one on the ground, you miserable, selfish prick?" she asked, taking a step back just in case. As she did so, she felt a familiar presence behind her.

"Oh, shit."

"Very articulate, Sweetheart," Olivia drawled.

After watching the confrontation between Micah and her father, Olivia felt incredibly grateful that Micah had not succumbed to the same fate as her father. It would have been so easy to become just as hate-filled as he was, to have let him damage her beyond repair. Instead, she had found strength where she could have embraced weakness, and she had chosen to let love rather than hate rule her life.

Micah had just faced down her demon and sent him reeling. It was her turn now to make sure that this particular demon never came back to haunt her, or them, ever again.

"How much did you hear?" Micah asked.

"Enough, but don't worry." Olivia smiled at her nervous lover. Cupping Micah's face gently with her palm, she drew the surprised woman in for a quick kiss on the lips before gazing directly into her eyes.

"I will wait for you to ask, but just so you know, the answer will be yes," she murmured, kissing her again before breaking contact and turning away.

Olivia uttered her next words in a voice so cold and deadly that it made Micah shudder.

"Right now, I have a few words for your father." Olivia gestured towards Jonathan and Robert. Jon wrapped his arm around Micah's waist and pulled her away. Robert moved closer to her father, his considerable size and obvious strength casting a shadow that engulfed the prostrate man.

"Robert, can you stand him up?" Olivia stepped in front of the miserable excuse of a man, taking his measure. "So, Mr. Connolly, we finally get a chance to meet. I'd rather conduct business in the privacy of my own office, but I guess this will have to do."

"I have nothing to say to you!"

"Oh, but I do have something to say to you." Olivia smiled sweetly then leaned in and whispered something to him in a voice too low for Micah to hear. Whatever she said caused him to pale considerably. His head shot up, casting a sharp look at Micah. There was fear in his eyes, an emotion she had never seen before. He looked away before Olivia caught him. When Olivia finished, she went back to Micah's side and took her hand, planting a light kiss across her damaged knuckles.

"Robert, will you take the trash to the curb?" she asked in a bored voice, then silently watched Robert "help" him walk towards the curb. Perhaps Robert was being too gentle, because Micah's father suddenly found the courage to fight the stronger man, twisting against the hand that held his shirt bunched up at the chest, trying one last time to get to Micah.

"Micah!" he bellowed. "Are you really choosing that woman over your family?"

"Of course not," Micah responded, feeling Olivia stiffen next to her until she heard her next words, "I am choosing MY family over you. Olivia and her daughter are my family now."

Olivia tightened her grip on Micah's waist, feeling tears forming in her eyes. Micah loved her, loved her family, and wanted to be with her...there was nothing more she could ask for in life.

A cab pulled up, the infallible sense they had for a fare making her father's exit a quick and painless one. "Micah?" He held one arm out towards her in one last pitiful attempt to change her mind.

"No. When are you going to learn that blood doesn't make a family? Love does." Micah stood there with Olivia in her arms, the very picture of a loving family. The self-imposed blinders her father wore would never let him see that, see them as a family. His salt-and-pepper hair was the last thing to disappear inside the cab. Robert handed money to the cab driver, ensuring that he would go somewhere, anywhere rather than there. It was over.

She had finally done it. She felt odd, almost giddy. She felt physically awkward after her altercation with her father, her muscles refusing to respond to her commands. So much had happened in a very short time, her mind was having trouble catching up with all the implications. *It's a good thing I already have a ring.* Micah muffled a giggle beneath the palm of her hand. Her sloppy grin slipped and then fell from her face when Olivia turned back towards her.

"I am very upset at you Micah, but also very proud." Olivia's tone lacked any real anger. She had seen what anger and hate could do to a person first hand; it wasn't an emotion worth harboring. Olivia slid her arms around Micah waist. "And, you are right, we are your family."

Micah started trembling. A line of perspiration beaded up on Micah's forehead and she paled noticeably.

"Um, Olivia, I don't feel very well," Micah croaked. Her heart was racing and she felt cold, chilled to the bone against Olivia's warmth. The world spun around her and she held onto consciousness by sheer will alone.

"It's okay, Sweetheart. We just need to get you home." Olivia took charge while Micah clung to her, evidently in shock that it was finally over. "Jonathan, will you take Micah's bike with you when you go home? She can retrieve it later."

Chapter Thirty-Three

Micah felt like shit. Her hands kept shaking, no matter how hard she clamped them together in her lap. She felt like her stomach was going to rebel at any minute, especially when the car turned a corner too fast. As it was, the stop-and-go traffic was already creating a decidedly sickening feeling in her throat, as her innards seemed to lag a few moments behind the repetitive seesaw motion.

"Micah, have you eaten yet today?" Olivia's voice sounded muffled and distorted through the thick fog rolling around in her head. *What the hell is wrong with me?* Micah thought, trying to shake the heavy feeling in her head. She moaned and grasped at her temples when the simple motion made the interior of the car spin and topple around her. She blinked away the darkness that perched at the edge of her vision, almost passing out from the movement.

"Micah, sweetie?" Olivia's voice swirled out of the fog again. *She sounded worried, why does she sound so worried? What had she asked her? Oh yeah, food.* Micah struggled to focus on her lover's voice.

"Ah, no...I didn't eat. I was too wound up."

Olivia grimaced. No wonder she was shaking like a leaf.

"Robert, stop at the closest deli." Robert caught Olivia's eye in the rear view mirror and nodded.

"Sure thing, Olivia. I know just the place."

"Don't worry Sweetheart, you'll feel better after you get something to eat." Olivia turned her attention back on Micah.

The confrontation with her father must have stressed out Micah past her limits. Micah had a terrible habit of forgetting she couldn't exercise absolute control over every emotion. Now, she was suffering from both the physical and psychological repercussions that finally dealing with her father had triggered.

Olivia's hand moved in gentle circles across Micah's back, massaging the tense muscles in her shoulders and neck. Micah's skin felt cool and damp, and every so often, a delicate shiver would vibrate against Olivia's palm. Since Olivia's focus was on Micah, she felt rather than saw when Robert stopped the vehicle.

Olivia hesitated, she didn't want to leave Micah alone in the backseat.

"I'll grab something, Olivia. Just take care of her," Robert offered, accepting the handful of bills Olivia pushed in his hand before disappearing into the deli. He returned in record time with a plain paper bag and a large fountain drink.

"Thank you, Robert. I'm grateful."

Micah ignored the sandwich at first, instead taking the waxed paper cup and drinking thirstily. Olivia watched the carbonated beverage disappear rapidly, the combination of caffeine and sugar bringing the color back into Micah's cheeks almost instantly

"Thanks, Love. Sorry about that."

It seemed too easy of a fix, and Olivia wasn't going to let Micah rely on soda alone to revive her. She opened the paper bag and unwrapped the ham and cheese sandwich Robert had ordered.

"Eat," Olivia commanded.

"I'm not hungry. I don't want it." Micah refused to take the sandwich.

"Stubborn woman," Olivia muttered under her breath.

"This isn't a negotiation, Micah. A soda isn't going to be enough, you need to eat something."

Micah was a determined woman; she would ignore Olivia if she thought she could get away with it. Olivia met Micah's aggravated look with her own steady gaze, refusing to lose in this battle of wills. When Micah finally gave in and started eating, Olivia let out a relieved sigh.

"Feeling better?" Olivia asked after a few minutes.

"Much." Micah sounded a lot more like herself; she no longer looked like she was going to pass out and all the color had returned to her cheeks.

"Are you sure?" Olivia asked, choosing her wording carefully. Olivia had seen Micah ignore pain before, turning it off as easily as flipping a light switch. She needed to know that wasn't the case now.

"I'm sure, Love." She actually felt pretty good, now that she had gotten something to drink and eat.

Going to meet her father on an empty stomach had been a stupid thing to do and she had paid for it. She still couldn't believe it, she had faced down her demons and won the day—*and the girl.* She smiled at the memory of her proud announcement, not caring that the whole world had heard her tell her father of her intentions. She hadn't expected Olivia to overhear her, though. Her smile widened as she replayed Olivia's words. Olivia had said yes, she had said she would wait for her to ask, but it would be yes. Joy washed over her with the soul-warming sensation of the summer sun. She had chosen her family and her love and it felt too damn good to be true—but it was.

"Actually, I think I'm better than I've been in a long time." Micah threw the remains of her sandwich away and pulled Olivia close to her.

"You feel good," Micah murmured, nuzzling Olivia's neck. She would never tire of this, feeling Olivia's body against hers, inhaling the scent that was uniquely Olivia's. It felt like home.

Olivia wrapped her arms around Micah's neck, her fingers finding the soft curls at the base of her hairline, encouraging Micah to continue her tender exploration. Tremors raced along her spine at the feel of Micah's hot breath on her neck, talented lips finding Olivia's pulse point and sucking gently before nibbling along her collarbone. Olivia arched into Micah's touch, then made a small, frustrated sound in her throat and pulled away.

"This is so inappropriate."

"I know. I'm sorry. I don't know what's going on with me." Micah flung herself back in the seat. As much as she wanted Olivia, there was no way she was going to put on a show in the back seat.

"I think I understand what's happening," Olivia said, kissing Micah one more time before retreating to her own corner. It had scared the living daylights out of her to see her lover in danger. Now that it was over, all that emotional upheaval and fear demanded a new outlet.

"We'll be home soon, and we can finish what we started then."

As far as Micah was concerned, they couldn't get home soon enough.

***

Olivia pulled Micah into the house and up the stairs without a word.

She kicked off her shoes and pulled off her suit jacket, dropping the expensive item on the floor without a second thought and earning her a shocked look from Micah. Her eyes darted from the pile of fabric on the floor to Olivia's face, then widened as she recognized the fire burning brightly in Olivia's clear blue eyes. Micah stood stock still, fascinated with this new development and waiting to see what Olivia would do. She didn't disappoint her.

Micah had seen Olivia in many different roles. She was assertive and demanding in her role as a successful attorney. In bed, she was utterly responsive and eager for Micah's touch, but now her flushed face held an air of desperate need. Micah found herself utterly captivated with the prospect of such an aggressive approach by her lover and allowed Olivia to push her down onto the edge of the bed. Olivia stood above her as Micah waited to see what she would do next.

Olivia wrapped her arms around Micah's neck, then proceeded to kiss her. Each kiss was maddeningly gentle, like butterfly wings brushing against her lips.

Micah's hands slid across the softest of silks. Olivia's blouse was in her way and she made quick work of removing that barrier.

Olivia moaned when Micah's wandering hands found her breasts, cupping them gently before running the pads of her thumbs across nipples that strained against her lace bra. She arched into the contact, her breath escaping in a wordless sigh.

She couldn't wait any longer. Olivia crawled up onto the bed, straddling Micah and threading her fingers through thick black hair. This time her kisses weren't tentative. They were waves crashing against the shore, demanding, cresting and falling back in a natural rhythm that echoed the movement of her hips.

Micah took advantage of Olivia's position to shift her hands, cupping the other woman's ass and pulling her closer. Micah could feel the heat coming off her in waves through her slacks. Micah growled in frustration; the thin material was preventing her from exploring her lover more fully.

"Too many clothes," Micah managed to get out, her voice harsh as she tried to express herself past her desire-clouded mind. The kiss had lasted as long as it could. The need to breathe had forced them to stop long enough to replenish their bodies' need for oxygen.

Olivia nodded, not trusting her ability to speak intelligently. Every fiber of her being was attuned to the woman beneath her. She pulled Micah's shirt up and over her head, quickly relieving her of both shirt and bra before reaching for the button on her shorts. Pushing the surprised woman back onto the bed, Olivia bent down and captured one puckered nipple in her mouth. Micah gasped at the sudden pain as Olivia sucked roughly, her tongue rasping across the sensitive nub as she ran her fingernails down her stomach, teasing the fine hair exposed by her unbuttoned shorts. Olivia hummed appreciatively when she found one barrier to her searching hand absent.

The knowledge that Micah wasn't wearing anything under her cargos sent a spasm of need through her. Sliding down Micah's slim muscular body, Olivia slipped off the bed, grasping Micah's shorts as she went and peeling them off her hips and thighs. Olivia looked down at her handiwork. Micah lay before her in all her naked glory, trust and longing darkening her eyes until only the thinnest ring of gold glowed softly around blown pupils.

Micah watched silently as Olivia kneeled before her, planting a teasing kiss along each thigh before flicking her tongue against her center. Micah almost came up off the bed then, half-sitting up before Olivia captured her hips in her arms. Olivia dug blunt fingernails along Micah's flanks, cautioning her not to move.

When Olivia's tongue flicked out again, it was to spread Micah's lips open—delicately exposing the hot, wet folds hidden within. Olivia moaned at the first taste of Micah's arousal, the sweet taste making her thirsty for more. She started in on Micah, teasing her with long, bold strokes of her tongue. Micah's clit swelled and hardened beneath her tongue, demanding her attention. Pressing her lips against the pulsing flesh, she sucked gently. Despite her sharp hold, Micah rolled her hips against her. Scrabbling her blunt nails against Micah's sculpted abdomen, she was rewarded with a low moan as Micah arched her back, pushing her hips against Olivia's hungry mouth.

"Jesus, Olivia—please—just finish me," Micah begged, her hands clawing at the bed sheets as she tossed her head back against the overwhelming sensations spreading from deep inside her. Her pulse pounded loudly in her ears, the familiar tingle that promised the blinding oblivion of ecstasy multiplied a hundred, a thousand times in intensity, and still Olivia continued with her teasing.

Olivia closed her eyes against the sudden rush of arousal that Micah's words brought. Holding onto Micah's writhing body as tightly as she could, Olivia brought her tongue back into play, lashing her lover's clit and letting her teeth graze against the sensitive flesh until Micah moved frantically against her. She felt Micah shudder against her suddenly; the flood of moisture that heralded her orgasm was irresistible. Olivia lowered her mouth to Micah's center, drawing out the sweetness until she begged her to stop.

***

"My turn." Now that Olivia had her fun, Micah was ready to take over. Olivia had way too many clothes on for Micah to be comfortable naked. She quickly rectified that situation, not satisfied until Olivia lay naked beneath her, their legs tangled together and their bodies pressed against each other. Micah gazed down at the woman in her arms.

Whatever need had driven Olivia to ravish her like that, it no longer haunted the corners of her eyes, watchful eyes that had darkened to passion-inspired cobalt. That deeper hue reflected all the promises of the coming hour and all the things people do in the dark and quiet of the evening hours.

She was in no hurry. Micah focused solely on bringing Olivia pleasure, in making sure that through their lovemaking, Olivia would know just how much she meant to her. As a lover, Olivia was a delight to explore. She was more adventurous and accepting than Micah could have ever imagined, even when things became intense or involved a bit of kink. Olivia's body never failed to arouse her, and she had never left their bed unsatisfied.

Today wasn't about any of that. Today was about expressing her love, her hands gentle as she explored her lover's body. When her fingers slipped inside Olivia's wet core, she cried out in unison with Olivia, feeling what she was feeling as they moved together. Her arousal reignited as she felt slick muscles flex and grasp at her with every thrust. When Olivia came undone, she gathered her up in her arms, holding her tightly as Olivia arched and bucked onto her fingers, her face pressed tightly into Micah's neck to muffle her screams.

Neither woman was sated, each fed off the other's arousal, explored each other in turns. Each time was different. Tender moments circled back on themselves after being marked by explosive moments of unadulterated lust where teeth and nails reigned, until they finally exhausted themselves in their eagerness to bring as much pleasure to the other as possible. Olivia felt like an addict and Micah her drug of choice, but Regina would be home soon, and it was that knowledge that had made them finally pull away from each other. They had brought each other to completion several times before time and the rest of the universe caught up with them.

Olivia rested her head on Micah's chest, lightly tracing the lines of the tattoo across her ribs and stomach. The blankets were a lost cause, flung onto the floor at one point and left there in a discarded heap.

Not one to be lulled into the idea of perfect post-coital bliss, Micah could sense that something was still bothering her lover. She had a feeling Olivia was still pissed about how she had chosen to deal with her father. It would be better to just get it out in the open now and let Olivia say what was on her mind than to let it fester. That it was dirty snooker to do it after their sexual marathon didn't bother Micah a bit.

"Olivia, is everything okay?"

"Yes. No—okay, I am still upset," Olivia, admitted.

"Okay."

"We were supposed to deal with him together. You almost got hurt—again."

"Olivia…"

"Because of me." Olivia wasn't going to be deterred.

"Excuse me?" Micah was sure she had misheard.

Olivia pushed herself up and twisted around so she could look at Micah, holding her weight up with one slim arm.

"He threw you out of the house and injured your knee when you told him you were in love with me, and that was before we were even together. What do you think he would have done this time? He could have seriously hurt you." There was no need to explain who "he" was.

"He's a violent man, Olivia. He would have just found another excuse. If it wasn't you, it was because I wouldn't give him what he wanted."

"I was so scared. I was sure something bad was going to happen and we wouldn't get there quick enough to stop him." She sniffed, feeling hot tears gather at the edge of her eyes.

"But he didn't," Micah reminded her. "Just let it go. We're together and we're both safe. That's all that matters."

When Olivia didn't relax into her embrace, Micah turned so she could face her lover. "Spit it out. Something's still bothering you."

"No, I'm okay, just a little tired." Olivia planted a sweet kiss on her lover's lips before yawning.

"It has been a long day." Micah grinned. Content to lie there and listen to the sound of Olivia's steady breathing, Micah started to fall into a relaxed half-sleep.

"You're right," Olivia announced suddenly.

"What?" Micah woke up instantly.

"Micah, there is something I need to tell you." Olivia sat up, then scooted back until her back rested against the headboard.

"Okay?"

"I—uh—I set up our first meeting that day. I saw you before that, on your bike one day—riding like a hellion in all that traffic. You rode right past me and yelled out at someone. When I heard your voice, I knew it was you. I had to see you again so I called your company. I specifically asked for you that day," Olivia rushed through her confession.

"I know." Micah smirked, her lips curling up in amusement.

"How do you know?" Olivia asked, "And why aren't you upset?"

"Jordan told me. When you contracted me to work for you, I wasn't happy. I went to his office and demanded an explanation. He told me everything."

"You never said a thing," Olivia murmured. *How extraordinary.* She felt better, ridding herself of the one secret that had been eating at her for so long.

"Well, at first I was curious what your game was. Then, things happened so quickly between us that I honestly stopped trying to figure out what your motivation might have been."

"I just wanted to see you again. I am so relieved you aren't upset." She had been so afraid that Micah would be angry that she kept worrying at it like a bone, hoping she could find the right time and place to bring it up. Evidently, this was the right time.

"No, I'm not upset at all. I thought it was cute, what you tried to do," Micah teased, earning her a weak slap on the arm. "Kind of like how cute you were today, trying to take charge and seduce me."

"I thought you might need to, you know, blow off some steam after everything that happened today." Olivia gestured at the rumpled bed sheets around them, the sweep of her arm taking in the overall disheveled appearance of their normally immaculate room. It was nothing near the post hurricane disaster they'd manage to pull off during some of their more interesting escapades. "I have to say that I was surprised. I expected something a little more aggressive today."

"It wasn't necessary. I just wanted to feel you." Micah looked at her oddly, but didn't ask her what she meant. "Are you telling me you weren't satisfied?"

"Oh, no. I am very satisfied," Olivia purred.

"Good, now can we move past this and just be happy?"

"Of course, Micah. I am happy. You make me happy." Just when she thought she'd figured Micah out she threw her for a loop.

"Now that that's settled, I have something I'd like to discuss with you."

Oh, my God. Was Micah going to propose now?

"Yes?"

"I'm quitting my job," Micah announced.

"What?" That wasn't quite what Olivia thought Micah was going to say. She tried to contain her disappointment. "What will you do? I know how important riding is to you."

"It is, and I will still ride. Mostly around here...and we can always take more weekend trips to the cabin. But I don't need the messenger work. You and Reggie are more important to me. It's dangerous and I know you worry—besides, I already got something wonderful out of it."

"Yeah?" Olivia lifted one delicate eyebrow.

"You know I did. Don't get me wrong, the risk was definitely worth the reward, but now that I have you, I'll not risk losing you for a bit of joyriding."

"Okay, I'll miss you during the day, of course—but at least I know you will be here when I come home every evening," Olivia gracefully conceded. She was relieved that Micah wouldn't be putting herself at risk anymore out on the busy city streets. "What will you do during the day, then?"

"Cassandra reminded me about the art show coming up. I figured I could spend some of my time getting a few pieces together. That should keep me busy for a while." Then Micah added something that Olivia was thinking but was afraid to ask. "And, I am sure we can think of a few ways to satisfy my need for a little excitement now and then?"

Olivia managed to look scandalized by the suggestion, before a wicked grin spread across her face and gave her true feelings away. "You are terrible, you know that?"

"No, I am very good, actually," Micah shot back before turning serious again. "I do love you, Olivia."

"I love you, too. But it's time to get dressed. Regina will be home soon and she will be expecting you to play basketball."

SWITCHING GEARS

Chapter Thirty-Four

Olivia was enjoying herself immensely, on several levels. What could be better than a night out on the town on the arm of the most handsome woman in the city, a glass of fine wine in hand, and a visual feast of fine art to peruse as she walked through the converted warehouse that now held one of the premier art shows of the year?

The art show was going incredibly well. It was all spectacular, and most of it was from artists she had never heard of but was quite sure would be known soon enough. For now, many of them were starving artists looking for their big break, the big sale that would put them up in paints, brushes, and canvases for a year. Or in some cases, fuel for blowtorches and flux for the more industrial works that climbed high towards the ceiling in a twisted, surreal, but utterly majestic expression of art that demanded your attention.

A single sale by one of the buyers here tonight could elevate an artist's work from three hundred dollars a canvas to three thousand. The artists were easy to pick out, their clothes as colorful and unusual as their inner vision. A good number of visitors that mingled and milled about were either friends or family members of the artists, like Olivia.

The eclectic group of artists and buyers had been joined by a more upscale crowd who had abandoned the pomp and circumstance of the stuffier uptown shows—an odd mixture of in-crowd notables who had discovered this hidden jewel in the heart of the city. They walked

463

around with a secret smile, as if they had discovered this place all on their own. Olivia thought they were funny, thinking that their willingness to travel to the less posh side of town to mingle with the common people and wallow in their art somehow made them special.

Luckily, there were only a few out of the hundreds attending that believed they were adding something to the event by simply attending. That Olivia recognized a couple of those people as clients of hers was a secret source of embarrassment for her. They might have been her peers in the business world, but being with Micah had really opened her eyes. How pretentious she must have seemed in the past!

As they wandered around, she saw more than a few of the patrons admiring Micah, their open appraisal making her sidle closer to the leather-clad woman in an obvious display of ownership. She wasn't jealous at the attention, not really; she knew there was no real threat to their relationship. However, she did enjoy smiling evilly at all the other women who ogled Micah, relishing the knowledge that they harbored a great deal of jealousy towards her.

Olivia didn't think she was imagining the heated looks, either. Micah looked absolutely stunning in her black leathers, tall, tan, and stalking through the gallery like a living example of what would happen if you could embody power and grace in a human canvas and then add a dash of dangerous intention. It was quite delicious and all she could do was lick her lips at the sweetness of it all and think...MINE. It didn't hurt her ego either, when Micah's gaze passed over all the beautiful people in the room with nothing more than polite disinterest. It wasn't until she looked at Olivia that the smile widened and a mischievous glint promised a lifetime of glorious moments to mark their time together. A quick press of warm lips against her knuckles usually followed that mischievous glint. Micah always did know how to get her attention.

"Are you enjoying yourself, Love?" Micah asked, her trademark smirk making the innocuous question seem more intimate.

"I'm having a wonderful time," Olivia said, accepting Micah's offered arm.

Olivia accepted another glass of wine from a server. When she turned back to Micah, she was surprised to find her exchanging pleasantries with another woman. Sipping her wine and finding the vintage surprisingly sweet and well-rounded, she slipped her arm around Micah's waist and waited for an introduction.

"Olivia, you remember Cassandra, from the tattoo parlor?" Micah asked. Cassandra was dressed in a brightly colored outfit that competed with the generous amount of flaming red hair. Pale eyes beneath ginger-colored brows matched the pale face that was marked by a smattering of freckles across the nose and cheekbones. She knew that Micah's family was from Ireland, but where Micah was dark and brooding, Cassandra carried the high color she always identified with the Irish.

"Of course, how could I have forgotten?" Olivia responded politely, before remembering how distracted she had been when they had left the tattoo studio. She could feel her cheeks burning and was sure she had gone quite red in the face as that memory resurfaced. She hoped they would think it was the wine.

"Micah. Olivia. It's good to see you here tonight." Cassandra offered her hand to Olivia, smiling knowingly at the flustered woman. Olivia murmured an appropriate greeting before hiding her face in her glass, choking on her sip of white wine when Cassandra winked at her in the most conspiratorial way.

"You too, Cass," Micah responded, catching the odd look passing between the two women. She must have missed something, but evidently it wasn't anything Cassandra was willing to share.

Micah and Cassandra continued to chat amicably for a few minutes while Olivia listened to their conversation. They had been friends for quite a while and knew many of the same artists at the show tonight. Her mind drifted off for a moment, caught in the fuzziness of her third glass of wine when something Cassandra said drew her attention back to their conversation.

"What about you, Micah? I saw some of your stuff here tonight. I heard one of the larger pieces already sold."

"Hey, that's great. I wonder who bought it."

"I didn't know you had anything on display tonight," Olivia spoke quietly. It came out as a little accusing.

"She has several. You should see them, they are quite good. As usual," Cassandra babbled on. "I was actually wondering if you would care if I purchased the other one for the shop."

Cassandra peered over her champagne glass at the two women.

"You don't have to buy one, Cass. Tell me what you want and I'll do something for you special," Micah offered.

"Hey, that sounds great, and in return I will finish up your tattoo as payment." Cassandra's smile broadened, pleased at making such a sweet deal.

"Sounds good, I will call tomorrow so you can let me know what you want."

"Actually, I have an opening next Friday if you want to come in and finish your dragon. Plus I need to fix where you had the road rash. We can talk then."

"Awesome, count me in."

Cassandra was drawn aside by another guest with a question. "Excuse me ladies."

Olivia nodded at Cassandra, then leaned closer to Micah. "And when were you going to tell me you put artwork in for the show?"

"It was supposed to be a surprise, Olivia. I've been working on them for the last month."

"Where have you been hiding them?"

"In my gym. I didn't want to say anything, just in case I didn't have time to finish them." Micah leaned down to kiss the slightly peeved woman, conveniently forgetting that they had an audience.

Cassandra fanned herself with her program, then cleared her throat. Olivia blushed. Micah simply grinned and offered no apology. "Well, I guess that's my cue to leave you two alone. I just wanted to say congratulations one more time on a great show," she said, making a show of fanning herself again. "I think I need another drink now. And maybe go find my husband to reaffirm I'm still straight," Cassandra teased, then gracefully made her exit.

"Well, take me to these drawings of yours," Olivia ordered, more than a little out of breath after being thoroughly kissed by her lover in public.

Micah led her through the maze of rooms and people, until they stopped in front of two large drawings, one pen and ink and the other done in black graphite.

"Here you go."

"Micah, these are wonderful. Why have you never done anything for the house?" Olivia found the ink drawing fascinating but not to her taste, the bold lines and stylized work similar to her tattoo art. It was also marked sold. The second drawing, however, was beautifully done. It was dark, brooding, and completely different from anything else she had seen Micah do.

"I really like this one. Were you trying something new?" Olivia asked, the urge to reach out and trace the outline of the lifelike wings made her fingertips tingle.

Micah had drawn what looked like two angels, one dark and one light, in an embrace. It was exquisitely erotic without being vulgar. The dark angel kneeled behind the pale one, holding her in a tight embrace, there was a suggestion of movement in her arms as her fingers travelled across breast and thigh that was echoed in the ecstatic expression of the captured angel. Raven-black wings crossed over and above delicately drawn pale-white feathering. The angelic wings were held down by the weight of the dark angel's wings. Micah's rendering spoke of their true nature—half feathered and half leathery-black like a demon, but Olivia couldn't tell if the feathers were taking over or falling away.

"Thank you, I wasn't sure how it would turn out, that's why I kept it hidden. I am glad I decided to show it, though." Micah stood proudly in front of her work. "I didn't know if you would want something like this in the house."

Micah looked up at her work. It wasn't exactly what Micah would call PG-13, and with Reggie in the house, she was trying to keep her work away from younger eyes.

"Perhaps in our bedroom," Olivia suggested, taking in the half-lidded expression on the figures in Micah's drawing, trying to figure out which angel was most in danger of falling. She leaned up to kiss Micah's neck, feeling her talented lover shiver at her touch.

"You think?" Micah asked.

"I do, it's too bad you put it up for sale." Olivia spoke without thinking, then immediately regretted her words when Micah frowned.

"So, you are getting your tattoo worked on next Friday?" she blurted.

"Looks like it."

"Can I expect a repeat performance of last time?" Olivia asked as innocently as possible. She so loved teasing Micah.

"Are you going with me?"

"Yes," Olivia answered without hesitation, her pulse jumping in response to the anticipation in her lover's voice.

"Then, yes." The low timber of Micah's voice flowed through her, warming her blood more than any wine ever could.

"Let's go home, Sweetheart. I have a need to see you perform in those wonderful leather pants tonight," Olivia whispered close to Micah's ear. The look on Micah's face had ruined all her plans for teasing—now all she wanted was Micah in their bed as soon as possible.

"I am always at your service, Love." Micah bowed to Olivia gallantly, her arm making a large sweeping movement that looked grand in her tight leather pants. "But aren't things all the sweeter for waiting?" Micah teased, earning her a mock slap on the shoulder. "But in all seriousness, I do have to stay a bit longer. Are you okay with that?"

"If you must." Olivia sighed.

"If you're tired, we can always call Robert around to pick you up. I am sure I will be home soon," Micah deadpanned, waggling her eyebrows at her. Olivia laughed at Micah's antics then glared at her.

"Oh, no. There is no way I am leaving you here, in those, with all these women." Olivia ran her fingers along the beltline of Micah's pants, making it perfectly clear to her that she was not going to leave Micah running solo.

"Well, then." Micah coughed, "I suggest we get all of our socializing done as quickly as possible so we can get our evening started."

***

Cassandra watched Micah and Olivia leave the room before returning to the graphite drawing, taking in the dynamic piece with a practiced eye. Micah was a damned good artist and could probably give her a run for her money if she ever wanted to start tattooing. Her pen and inks were bold and daring, and they were what she was used to seeing. This drawing though, with soft lines and shading against the white Bristol paper—this was something unique. Cassandra couldn't stand it. She knew that she had made a deal with Micah over the tattoo, but she couldn't bear the thought of this piece going to a stranger. She made a quick phone call while she stood there, frowning impatiently until an employee of the art gallery scurried up apologetically.

"I'm sorry, ma'am, but the artist pulled this piece from the sale this evening." He placed a small white card at the corner of the display that said "Not for Sale." Cassandra smiled at the nervous man, not upset in the least bit that the piece was going to stay with whom it belonged.

***

Micah led Olivia through the crowded halls, stopping every once in a while to chat to someone and introduce Olivia to her friends. Occasionally they were stopped by other guests who wanted to talk to Micah about her art. She was amicable and witty, and had an unerring knack for extricating Olivia out of conversations she found dull or smacked of data gathering. The few people who recognized her found Micah fascinating, or rather, they found their relationship fascinating. After one such encounter, Micah leaned over and whispered in her ear. "Are you okay with them knowing about us?"

Olivia stopped dead in her tracks, considering for a moment before looking up. "You know, I hadn't even considered it. But now that you ask, I can honestly say I really don't care what they think."

As if on cue, Olivia's father appeared out of the crowds and spotted them. "I didn't know my father was coming to the show."

"I invited him, Love," Micah said a second before the older Holden appeared in front of them. Olivia was caught off guard by her father's enthusiastic hug; he wasn't usually one for public displays of affection.

"Olivia, dear...you look wonderful tonight." He turned and held out his hand. "Micah, I had no idea you were so talented."

Micah murmured something appropriate, giving Olivia time to recover from her shock.

She stood there for a moment, listening to her father and Micah chat. It was wonderful to see them together like this, especially considering Micah's past. A subtle truce had developed between the two of them over the last couple of months; the four of them had even shared dinner a few times, despite Micah's initial reticence.

Micah's phone went off, interrupting the conversation. Pulling it out of her pocket, Micah looked at the message and grimaced. "I know you want to leave soon, Love, but I have one thing I need to do before we go. Are you okay waiting here for a few minutes?"

"Of course, is there something wrong?"

"No, not at all. Just boring details about one of the sales," Micah explained, her fingers moving rapidly over the keyboard as she responded to the message. "But it is something I would rather do now, since we are still here."

"I'll keep my daughter company, Micah. Don't worry; I won't let anyone steal her away while you're gone," the elder Holden quipped.

"Thank you, sir," Micah said, and then turned back to Olivia. "I'll be right back."

Olivia nodded. She had a pretty good idea what was going on, but if Micah wanted to be secretive about it that was fine with her. She wanted that drawing and Micah knew it.

***

As soon as Micah left, an investor their office represented latched onto her father and started talking business. After casting an apologetic eye towards Olivia, he launched into a conversation Olivia felt was better left to the office, during working hours. She was glad her father took over, since she was not really in the mood to talk shop. Tonight was for Micah. It only took one step away to lose the conversation, the din of voices around her subsiding into grey noise with only a smattering of words reaching her ears at odd times.

Left alone with her thoughts in the midst of the crowd, Olivia found herself thinking about the last couple of months. She had found Micah, yes, and won her as well. Like any new relationship, it had been and was still intensely sexual. Olivia had to admit that the "new" Micah was more adventuresome and creative in her sexual outlets than Olivia could have ever imagined. Micah challenged her daily, expanding her concepts of what sex was and how it was expressed.

Olivia had thought she was sexually liberated, especially after she realized and accepted that she was gay. Lesbian sex wasn't exactly "vanilla" by hetero standards, but Micah didn't just step over the boundaries of gender-based sexual expectations, she stomped on them completely, daring anyone to tell her she had to behave a certain way. This in-your-face attitude spilled into her everyday life, where her androgynous looks and choice of dress put it out there for the world to see. Regardless of how she presented herself to the world, Olivia was one of a very few, perhaps the only one she had revealed her hidden self to. This person, this very real and lovable person had convinced herself that she was just the opposite. Micah had once called herself a "broken toy" and Olivia's heart ached just thinking that Micah believed that about herself.

She could only guess at how hard it had been for Micah to take such a risk on her, especially with all of the psychological baggage she had been carrying around. She had worked so hard to convince herself that she was unlovable that she had done everything in her power to make sure she wouldn't be put in a position to test that belief. Opening up to Olivia had dropped Micah in dangerous waters, risking everything while knowing how terrible the consequences of failure could be.

Some people might wonder why Olivia had stuck around, why she didn't wait for Micah to work out her own problems before approaching her. Olivia smiled at this. Micah was such a complex woman—she had enjoyed helping her peel away layer after layer of self-imposed armor to find the exciting, vibrant woman hidden away from the world. Of course, without her armor, Micah had to deal with all the raw openness of her life, much like healing skin after a burn is exquisitely sensitive to even the mildest air currents.

When she looked at her beloved...and she could call her that even after such a short time together, Olivia could see the subtle changes in Micah's demeanor. She seemed more at ease, more comfortable in her own skin than when they had first met. Oh, she would always be and have "cocky" Micah inside of her, but she didn't seem to need her quite as often.

Olivia looked up suddenly, her meditations interrupted by a subtle change in the air around her. The room had become a living being, a living being that had stopped breathing and was holding its collective breath in anticipation of something wonderful happening.

She looked around, searching for the source of such an unusual event. Her eyes landed on Micah immediately. She always seemed to know where Micah was, even in this crowded room, she had no problem finding her. Once she found her, she couldn't look away.

A slow easy smile spread across Micah's face, lighting her eyes with an inner fire as she strode towards Olivia. In a room filled with hundreds of beautiful people, Micah still managed to turn heads as she sauntered past the fashionistas flaunting their jewels and designer dresses. Husbands frowned as their wives openly appraised her lover as she strode confidently across the room. She reminded Olivia of something wild and dangerous, a lioness among a roomful of gazelles. Still, her hazel eyes remained locked on Olivia, never wavering from her goal.

Olivia gasped when she realized that Micah had changed out of her leathers. She was dressed to the nines in a black tuxedo, one obviously cut for her exquisite frame. A woman's suit would not have fit her properly; she was too fit and muscular to pull off wearing the overly slim cuts. The lines of the tuxedo followed Micah's feminine attributes, while the traditionally masculine suit balanced out the androgynous look that she favored. Her dark hair, usually tousled and rakish, was slicked back from her face, bringing the height of her cheekbones out and her expressive eyes into play.

Olivia waited silently, stunned into motionlessness, until Micah reached her. She looked down at her, her eyes dropping down to focus on Olivia's lips.

Olivia felt her lips part in response to that speculative gaze. The promise of a kiss was enough to quicken her pulse. The promise became a reality. She could feel Micah's hands smooth along her waist, her thumbs subtly massaging the sensitive skin just below her breasts.

For one long incredible moment they were alone in the universe, a universe shrunk down to hold just the two of them, to Micah's lips against hers. The silence of this universe shook her, and then she realized that the room had gone silent, a hundred pairs of eyes watching this moment with wonder and joy and yes, even a little jealousy.

"Surprise." Micah's voice caressed her ear, sending a delicate chill down her back.

Micah stepped away and held out her arm. The gallant movement not lost on the crowd or Olivia.

"Shall we dance?" Micah asked, leading Olivia out to the center of the room. The crowd moved aside for the two of them, giving them command of the impromptu dance floor. Somewhere, someone had changed the soundtrack playing in the background to something more appropriate for a traditional waltz. It was a fairytale moment, the cliché not lost on either woman as they turned and faced each other. Micah was a woman of many surprises, and she managed to surprise Olivia yet again when they started moving to the music. Micah was an elegant dancer, taking the lead without hesitation.

The last note of the song ended with a kiss, and they continued dancing to the sound of silence for a few seconds longer before stopping and looking around. Everyone was watching them. It was time to go somewhere a little more private.

"Would you mind if we went outside for a few minutes? I could really use some fresh air."

"Lead the way, Sweetheart," Olivia, said. She was so pleased with how the night was turning out. Micah looked exquisite in her tuxedo...and that dance.

Once out on the balcony, Micah closed the doors, affording them some privacy before joining Olivia at the railing. A pastel moon illuminated the pale stone around them, competing with the soft golden light of the understated lights. The air smelled sweet from the flowering bushes in their decorative pots. It was perfect.

"It's a beautiful night." Olivia gave a contented sigh, leaning into the solid form behind her.

"Yes, it is," Micah agreed.

"Olivia." Micah began fiddling with something in her pocket. "I have something for you." Micah pulled out a long slim box and turned Olivia around so she could place it in her hands.

Opening the dark case to reveal the white satin interior, Olivia found a gorgeous diamond necklace nestled inside.

"Oh, my. This is exquisite."

Olivia turned so that Micah could put the necklace on, her nimble fingers moving softly along the back of her neck to close the clasp on the magnificent piece. A soft kiss along her neckline made her shiver. She could feel the small hairs along her neckline raise, her skin tingling beneath those teasing lips.

"I am so glad you like it." Micah accented her words with a delighted chuckle. "I thought it went really well with this," Micah added as Olivia turned back around. She was holding a small square jewelry box with a diamond ring nestled inside it.

"Olivia, I really don't have the words to express how much I love you. So, all I can say is...Will you marry me? Will you share your life with me? Will you make me the happiest woman in the world?" Micah could feel her heart pounding in her chest as she waited for Olivia to answer her questions.

"Yes. God, yes! Nothing would make me happier," Olivia exclaimed, her eyes shining darkly in the night as joyful tears fell unchecked.

Micah took Olivia's hand in hers and slid the ring onto her finger, lightly placing a kiss on her knuckles. "I love you, Olivia."

"And I love you."

Micah bent down and retrieved a bottle of chilled Champagne from where she had placed it earlier, bringing out two long fluted glasses with a flourish. A pure note rang out when the crystal glasses came together, the only break in the perfect silence while the couple sipped the sweet cool liquid in celebration of their engagement.

"It's beautiful," Olivia murmured, gazing down at the ring on her finger. She could tell it was old, but the setting and design was timeless and gorgeous.

"It was my grandmother's. She gave it to me and told me to save it for the one I would love forever—I guess she always knew I wouldn't be wearing it myself." Micah spoke wistfully. Her grandmother had always been a very intuitive person. There was no doubt in Micah's mind that her grandmother knew she would take a wife rather than a husband long before she did.

"That reminds me, I have something else for you." Micah fumbled in the breast pocket and pulled out an envelope. "I had the paperwork drawn up for the cabin today; as soon as you sign it the cabin will be ours, not just mine."

She clinked her glass against Olivia's. "To us, Love."

"To us. And thank you. I know how much your cabin means to you."

"Dance with me?" Micah set down her glass to take Olivia into her arms.

"Forever and always, Sweetheart," Olivia vowed, knowing this was it for her. Micah was the only one she would ever want. She was everything she would ever need.

***

When they returned home, Micah vaulted up the stairs to the bedroom with an admonition to wait five minutes before coming up. Olivia took advantage of the time by checking in on Regina. Micah had suggested Olivia let Regina go to a slumber party tonight since it was going to be a late night. Evidently, her two girls had been conspiring against her.

Olivia waited the five minutes before heading upstairs. She walked into a bedroom she barely recognized. Micah had turned off all the lights, leaving only the ambient glow of a dozen candles floating around the room. The glow cast a deep bronze and gold hue across the wood surfaces of her furniture while the smell of warm wax and fragrance hung heavy in the air.

"Oh my," Olivia whispered. Anything else she might have said faded away like the small trails of smoke spiraling lazily into the air when Micah came up behind her. Micah's warm breath tickled across her ear, making her shiver even before the younger woman spoke.

"Do you like?" She breathed, taking one velvet soft earlobe into her mouth to suck gently. Olivia relaxed into her lover's arms. Her reward was a slow progression of hot kisses along her neck and shoulder. A sliver of teeth barely grazed her flesh, a tease compared to the sharp nips Micah knew she had developed a taste for. Micah wanted this night to be perfect, wanted Olivia to feel how much she meant to her all the way down to her soul.

Olivia twisted in Micah's arms until they faced each other, their faces mere inches away as she wrapped her arms around Micah's neck. Olivia ran her tongue along parted lips, the invitation too obvious to be ignored.

Smiling gently, Micah tipped her head down to be at a level with Olivia's waiting lips, not kissing her just yet. Instead, she gathered one full lip between hers and used her teeth and tongue gently, teasing Olivia until she felt her fingers wrap tightly in her short hair. The

479

insistent tug of fingers escalated. She shivered against the small points of pain sending slivers of endorphin-laced pleasure crashing through her. She gave up the teasing nibbles to capture Olivia's mouth, finding her tongue with her own. It took a great deal of self-control to not get carried away with that kiss, to not let the kiss take over and rule her passions. She had plans for tonight, and ripping Olivia's clothes off in a frantic rush was not one of them.

"Wait here," Micah commanded; her plans also didn't include silence. She walked over to the stereo and hit the play button.

She had a very specific set programmed just for tonight. The evocative, dark tones of Evanescence filled the room, the haunting rise and fall of the operatic voice a perfect match for the candlelit room. When she turned around, Olivia hadn't moved from the middle of the room. It only took a couple of long strides to return to her side. Micah kissed her gently, making promises with her lips that she meant to fulfill over the next few hours. The house was theirs for the night. Her only time constraint was the burning wicks whose flickering light would eventually fade and send them into darkness, but not until she had bared her lover to the blinding heat of their shared passion.

Micah undressed Olivia slowly, each article of clothing reverently removed from her body only to be tossed aside, discarded and forgotten on the floor. When she stood in front of Micah naked and bathed in candlelight and shadows, Micah paused, staring at the beauty standing before her. Her pale hair fought the shadows, painted with all the colors of smoke and fire in the flickering light.

"So beautiful," Micah murmured, running the back of her fingers down Olivia's smooth cheek. Olivia trembled, not from the cold, but in response to her touch.

Micah felt overdressed. She stepped back a couple of feet and waited until she had Olivia's full attention, then undressed in quick movements, exposing her muscled body to the spellbound woman. Even in the shadows, Micah could see Olivia's appraising look, hear her sudden intake of breath when she removed the last bit of clothing between them.

"Lay down, Love. I have something special in mind," Micah suggested, taking Olivia's hand in hers and leading her to the bed. Her eyes darkened, reduced to black pools that flickered with a dozen gold-red flames.

Olivia laid down on her stomach and listened to the captivating music while she waited. Micah always had music playing, but tonight the haunting lyrics seemed to mean something more. She thought Micah was trying to speak to her through them. The mattress shifted, letting her know that Micah had returned. Soft hands stroked along her back before Micah settled in next to her. The slick, warm sensation of body oil played across her shoulders and down her spine as Micah massaged her with deft movements, working her overly tight muscles. Olivia stretched out on the bed, relaxing under the firm but tender circular movements. A moan escaped her when Micah's hands travelled lower, massaging her back and then her buttocks, finding sore muscles she didn't know she had.

The utter decadence at getting a massage from her naked lover turned into something more when Micah's lips found her skin, starting at her buttocks, she trailed a slow, winding trail of kisses that ended only when her body rested along the entire length of Olivia's body. Olivia could feel the heat from Micah's groin pressing into her backside, the slow grind sending her arousal into overdrive. Micah's lips at her shoulder made her want to squirm, but their position kept her from moving. Olivia started moving against her, but caught as she was between the bed and Micah's hips, all she could do was tease herself.

"Sit up, Love," Micah whispered against her ear. Micah helped Olivia up into a kneeling position, then curled up behind her, balancing both of them as she swayed in time to the slow music.

Olivia had never felt so exposed and yet so completely sheltered at the same time. Micah's strong arms held her close, their bodies' slick and clinging to each other from the thin sheen of body oil. She spread her legs farther apart for balance, then hesitated. Micah somehow read her discomfort and slipped one hand down along her stomach to cup her sex gently, protecting the heat at her core from the cool air circling around them. Micah's other hand caressed her breasts, finding her nipples ready and wanting the attention of Micah's kneading fingertips. She arched farther against her lover, offering her neck to Micah's talented lips in sacrifice to desire.

Micah seemed intent on torturing her. Slim fingers lazily combed through the fine soft hairs at her apex until Olivia moaned in frustration. Micah made an odd noise in her throat in response, her fingernails lightly scratching along Olivia's swollen and open lips before pinching and tugging so that the wet folds slid against her swollen clit. She could hear herself moaning. Olivia bit her own lip to prevent herself from begging for relief.

It was torture, but it was exquisite torture that held the promise of release...if she could only exercise patience.

The music changed as a dark but operatic female voice filled the room, ebbing and flowing through slow hypnotizing sections that would suddenly crash into heavier notes, demanding attention. The rhythm was primal and evocative as it countered the slow, ethereal vocals that nonetheless pierced deeply into her soul. Micah chose that time to slide her fingers into Olivia's waiting wetness, the heat from her arousal flaming higher and hotter as Micah moved against her, the rhythm of her fingers matching the rise and fall of the music surrounding them, adding its ragged beat to the pounding of their hearts.

Olivia was so close, liquid paths of fire and electricity danced through her veins, starting at that point inside her where Micah's fingers moved. She was consumed in wildfire, so bright and hot and pure that she had to close her eyes against the impending implosion she could feel building at the base of her spine. Her body tensed, coiling tightly on itself as if the circling movements of her lover's fingers were winding her up like a toy. Just when she felt like she couldn't hold the tension in her body a moment longer, Micah slowed her movements, backing away just enough to pull her away from the edge of oblivion.

"Open your eyes, Love." Olivia struggled to unclench her eyelids, forcing her eyes to obey her commands and see the outside world instead of the blood red pulse scorching through her brain.

"Look," Micah demanded. Her voice, husky with her own need, caressed Olivia's ear.

So soft, that voice, to be so commanding.

Olivia did as Micah commanded, focusing lust-filled eyes at the mirror image staring back at her. Micah was looking at her from under shadow-darkened brows, her eyes shining black in the darkened room. Micah's tan skin glowed dusky in the low light, her lithely muscled arms wrapping Olivia in an erotic embrace. The visual imagery almost sent Olivia over the edge. She could see Micah's hand between her thighs, feel her there even in her stillness. The smoky image captured their passionate embrace. She gasped, her mind flashing to a similar image—one of a pale-haired angel being ravaged by a fallen angel.

"My angel," Micah murmured, the image in the mirror dipping its head down to taste her skin with its lips. "My saving grace." The image in the mirror shifted. Long fingers slipped between the angel's thighs, taking her with deep thrusts that brought a flush to her breasts and neck. Her lips parted in the beginnings of a deep moan that ended in a series of short gasps and cries that begged for completion. A pale arm snaked up, grasping at midnight-black hair while the dark figure behind her sucked and bit into the pale flesh at her shoulder, drawing her orgasm out with a final thrusting shout until they both tumbled down from their heights, their images sliding away from the mirror.

When Olivia came to her senses, she had two thoughts rolling through her head, one quite simple and the other quite profound.

Wow, and then, *this is how Micah sees us, light and dark together. But who is saving whom?*

Micah curled up next to Olivia, one arm flung around her lover as she worked to recover from the unexpected orgasm. The feeling of her lover clamping down around her fingers, pulling her in deeper as she came undone in her arms had unexpectedly sent her over the edge. Somehow, Olivia's passion had jumped their joined flesh, sending a ripple of Olivia's ecstasy into her and sending her tumbling after her into the abyss.

Despite all that, desire still thrummed through her body. If anything, it fueled her need past anything she had felt before, her body demanding something she refused to ask for. Trying to quell the growl of the huntress inside her, Micah resigned herself to holding the woman she loved in her arms. Tonight wasn't about lust so much as celebration. She had wanted to do this for Olivia and her own need could wait.

Olivia stirred from her semi-comatose state, turning in her arms to face her. Olivia's face held that hazy, heavy-lidded gaze that always made Micah's heart skip a beat. Brilliant blue eyes made that look a lie when they sparked and caught fire as she watched, an evil glint appearing at the same time as the wicked smile that promised delicious punishment for what she had done. Insistent hands pressed Micah's shoulders against the bed, urging her to accept her punishment without argument. She was ready, more than ready, and any potential argument was lost when Olivia's warm mouth descended on her breasts. Her lover ravished her nipples until they were hard pebbles, showing her as much mercy as she had given her...none.

"Ah, Gods, Olivia..." Micah gasped, her hips jerking uncontrollably when Olivia slid quickly and gracefully down her body to find her core with both lips and tongue. She swore the woman somehow wrapped her tongue around the painfully hard bundle of nerves between her thighs, the pressure building as she sucked at her clit with abandon.

Her stomach flexed, neck muscles working, just so she could look down her body. She wanted to watch what Olivia was doing to her. Her face was hidden behind a pale drape of hair that tickled across Micah's stomach but the rest of her? The curve of her back was hard to ignore, but it was her ass that caught Micah's attention. She undulated against the bedsheets, the firm globes flexing in time with every thrust. Micah's hips jerked off the bed, caught up in that same rhythm while Olivia's tongue lashed her on. Fingers curled inside her, finding the sweet spot that made her spasm and fall back onto the sheets.

"There..." Micah gasped. "Right there, don't stop."

"I won't," Olivia promised, lightly nipping along Micah's thigh. "Come for me, Sweetheart."

Goaded on by the subtle pain, Micah didn't so much as fall into her orgasm as it crashed into her, drowning her in its depths as she bucked against the hot mouth lapping at her, drinking from her passion until she had to beg for her to stop.

"Maybe not so much of an angel, after all," Micah whispered, her voice as weak and spent as the rest of her body.

Epilogue

Olivia padded back across the room, her bare feet sinking into the luxurious carpet Micah had put down at her request. The sleek lines of her lover was a visual feast she never tired of partaking in.

Micah was sprawled out on her stomach, one arm dangling idly from the edge of the tousled bed, her head resting on her other arm. Micah's damp skin was still flushed beneath her tan, except where it was hidden by the deep black lines of the tattoo wandering across her back. She was exquisite, the taut muscles and catlike posture better suited to a leopard slung precariously across a tree limb in the Serengeti, lazily observing unsuspecting prey as they grazed beneath her.

In that strange way her fiancé always seemed to know where she was and what she was thinking, the dark mane of hair lifted from the bed. Gold-flecked hazel eyes bore into hers, the hungry look in them revealing her admiration. The intensity of the look gave away something else as well. Without having to say it, Micah's gaze always told Olivia just how much she loved her.

Olivia sat down at the edge of the bed, silently watching as Micah stretched, taking her earlier observation about Micah's catlike posture and giving it movement. A flash of light brought her attention to the white gold band Olivia had placed on Micah's finger earlier this evening. She knew Micah would never wear a traditional engagement ring, so Olivia had found the perfect way to mark Micah as hers, an Irish Claddagh imbedded in a semi-masculine style ring. Micah's eyes had lit up in delight when Olivia brought it out, then explained to her what the Claddagh meant, and how it was meant to be worn. Olivia had been very careful to slide the ring on the right way, the heart turned inward to tell the world that Micah's heart was taken.

Feeling the need to reconnect with her lover, Olivia's hands wandered across Micah's sculpted back, her fingertips tracing the lines of the recently finished tattoo. Cassandra had outdone herself—the dragon danced along Micah's skin like a living, breathing entity. It really was an amazing creature, a mixture of scales and feathers and sleek muscles coupled with intricate loops and Celtic knot work within and alongside the main body. She almost hesitated running her fingers along the sharp claws and curved teeth, fearing their edges would draw blood if they could.

"Cassandra really did an incredible job on this," Olivia said, feeling solid muscles jump beneath her fingertips. "You know, you never really told me. Why a dragon?"

Micah turned over to look up at Olivia. "Why do you want to know now? I don't mind, I am just curious."

"I've just been wondering why you chose a dragon."

"You are in an odd mood tonight." Micah settled on her side, propping herself up on one elbow and pulling the sheets back up around her middle.

Olivia didn't comment. She had noticed a while ago that unless they were making love, Micah still had a habit of keeping her old scars covered. Not that it mattered to Olivia; she loved Micah for who she was. Her scars were a part of her, as much as the tattoo and leathers, and she wouldn't change a thing...except for the reason the scars were there in the first place.

488

A quick surge of anger bordering on pure hatred flashed inside her, twisting sharply in her belly when she thought about Micah's selfish and violent father. She still kept tabs on him, just in case. There was no way he was going to do anything more to Micah than he already had. She didn't like keeping secrets from her fiancé, but she had made a promise to herself that he would never come knocking on Micah's door again.

"Come back to me, Love," Micah said, *caressing* Olivia's cheek softly. "Is there something wrong?"

Olivia shrugged, her face pensive as she pressed her cheek into the caress, taking great pleasure in the loving touch. It was these simple moments that made her heart sing, the quiet times where they lay together and spoke intimately with each other—touching each other for no other reason than to do it. "I don't know," she said, then realized how that sounded. "No. I guess it is just all so wonderful to me. Sometimes I can't believe that we found our way here." She wound her fingers in Micah's free hand, lifting their clasped hands up to her lips.

"Ah, I understand." Micah truly did understand that sentiment. They had come to the cabin for the weekend because she had needed the time away from the city. Micah needed to ride and breathe in the country air before winter set in and her options became limited. She hadn't expected Olivia to present her with an engagement ring, and was touched by how personal she had made it by honoring her Irish heritage. Micah wasn't used to being on the receiving end of romantic gestures, but Olivia's choice of place and timing couldn't have been better. Her cabin had always been a place of refuge, the place where she had reached her lowest depths and hid away from her greatest fears. Now, this place held more joyful memories than sad. It was a fitting way to honor her grandmother's lifelong passion for the land.

"You asked about the dragon?" Olivia had asked her a question and she had been stalling, trying to decide how to explain what had been the driving force behind her transformation. She thought she was ready, now.

"Yes, but you don't have to tell me if you don't want to."

"No, it's okay. I want to tell you." Micah sat up, pushing herself up in bed until her head rested on the headboard. She dragged the covers around her, and then tucked her knees up so she could rest her elbows on them. Olivia scooted up next to her, but didn't insist on joining her beneath the blanket, somehow sensing Micah's disquiet.

"The dragon just came on its own, I guess. I started drawing it here in the cabin, before Jonathan found me. At first, it was angry, violently scribbled across my sketchpad. I guess it represented how I felt...torn, shredded. I felt like the universe was ripping me apart. Over time, it changed. It became something transformative, a symbol of power and change that I was learning to embrace. You know, the Celts believed that the dragon represented all the elements, both feminine and masculine. Water and air, matter and spirit. The dragon offered purification and rebirth. It made sense to me." Micah smiled wistfully.

How could she explain how she felt then? The changes she went through as she discovered the parts of herself that she had been hiding from, the parts that her parents had tried to suppress? Micah leveled a warning glance in Olivia's direction. This wasn't going to be easy.

"You know the rest of the story, how I was when Jonathan found me. There were two things in this cabin that I could have taken back with me to New York, one you know of, and the other...the other was the drawing you saw on my bedroom wall."

Micah stopped then, caught somewhere in the middle of the past and the present. A year ago, she had locked the cabin door and walked away from the cutting. Now here she was in the cabin with the blade safely tucked away, miles away from her in New York. It still called to her on occasion. Micah shook her head to clear it. It didn't do any good to dwell on those dark thoughts; they intruded too much as it was without her going there voluntarily.

"Micah..."

"No, wait. Olivia, I need to finish this," Micah cut in, interrupting whatever Olivia was going to say. Her voice cracked; she felt like she had been talking for a very long time. A Coke appeared in her hand out of nowhere.

"Thank you, Love." Micah soothed her parched throat with almost half the can before starting again. "It was only after I hit rock bottom that I was able to embrace myself, I was free to remake myself into the person I wanted to be...who I really was, not who everyone else thought I was supposed to be. As much as I hate some of the things I've gone through, I wouldn't change a thing. To do so might risk me ending up in a different place than where I am right now." Micah spoke earnestly; she had to make sure Olivia understood how important the past was, no matter how ugly it had been.

Olivia's face stilled. The explanation was both more than she anticipated and nothing she had expected.

Micah laughed then. It was either that, or break down completely. She drew Olivia into a tight embrace, willing her to accept the forced change in mood.

"What? Did you not expect such an answer? I would never place anything on my body that didn't mean something." Brushing away a stray strand of hair from Olivia's face, she smiled at the woman who had captured her heart. "Nor would I draw anything that did not reflect the absolute truth, Love. You will always and forever be my own pale-haired angel."

Micah kissed Olivia then, unfolding her long legs and twisting until she trapped Olivia beneath her. Olivia moaned into the kiss then let out a less-than-sexy squeak when Micah suddenly rolled and Olivia found herself looking down at her errant lover.

"I think, my love, that it is my turn?" Micah grinned wickedly, giving Olivia permission to run with all the possibilities that were included in that grin. Olivia's heart sang with the knowledge of what Micah was offering her. It had taken Micah a long time to open up to her, and even longer before she was able to let Olivia reciprocate. Gazing down into trusting eyes that waited impatiently for her to begin, Olivia laughed in joy. She already knew where she was going to start.

"You are incorrigible," Olivia teased.

"And you are not, Love?"

"No, I am not. But I do think we are well-matched," Olivia acceded, licking her lips in anticipation. She knew full and well what that simple act would do to her. Micah twisted beneath her, broadcasting her impatience with Olivia's teasing ways. "That we are, Love—that we are." The words came out strangled, ending in another moan when Olivia brushed her lips against Micah's neck, then nipped gently. Olivia slid her way down along Micah's body, finding the curving, twisted body of the dragon as it slid across her abdomen and along the sensitive curve inside her hip line. She ignored the rough scars that marked the inkless areas—it wasn't necessary to bring attention to them. Instead, she let her lips and tongue slide across the raised flesh that followed her kisses as the inked skin responded to her touch. She knew how sensitive those areas were, and she delighted in the soft moans and tensed muscles that woke Micah's dragon. When she lay poised above her goal, she looked up at Micah to find fierce eyes watching her.

"This is all mine, no one has ever touched you this way, or seen you the way I get to see you." She spoke just as fiercely, challenging the other woman's gaze. In this moment, this hour, the two women had found their balance. There was no need to claim dominance over the other. This was a meeting of equals who reveled in their love...as well as their lovemaking. It didn't hurt Micah's ego one bit to accede the other woman's right to her claim. Micah knew the same applied to her—Olivia was hers and no others.

"Yes, Love, all yours."

If you enjoyed this novel, please check out more offerings by Rhavensfyre.

Follow on Facebook @ Characters of Rhavensfyre

www.rhavensfyre.com

twitter@rhavensfyre

SWITCHING GEARS

Works by Rhavensfyre

LIFE IS NOT A COUNTRY SONG

This romantic novella is book one of Chase and Rowan's adventures.
Rowan St. John is on her way back home with an empty horse trailer
and down a driver.

Chase Meadows had it all, until she came home one day to find her
lover in bed with another woman. Now she's left with nothing but her
truck, her horse and a definite need to find a new start. California was
about as far away from North Carolina and the past as she could go.
All she had to do was get there with her pregnant mare, Smoothy—
the only thing she had left in her name that she would never give up.

When Rowan St. John responds to her ad for a last minute horse
transport, she thought she had finally gotten a break. A deal is struck
that benefits both women, more than they ever expected.

LOVE IS NOT A ROMANCE NOVEL

This romantic novella is book two of Chase and Rowan's adventures
and the sequel to Life is Not a Country Song.

Chase and Rowan are given some time to learn more about each other
when the last leg of their trip is delayed.

Rowan sees it as a way to show Chase everything the Southwest has
to offer, including her, while Chase is more worried about earning her
keep and making sure one special little colt is strong enough to travel.
Trust and understanding are tested, and some internal demons are laid
to rest against the backdrop of sun-kissed mesas and tall pines.

Both spiritual and sensual, the ladies discover that some journeys
aren't measured by how many miles you travel, but by how far you
are willing to take your heart.

LIFE, LOVE, AND LOYALTY

This lesbian romance is the third in the popular Chase and Rowan Series.

After a few detours along the way, Chase and Rowan have finally made it to California and are settling into their lives at the Flying S ranch.

An urgent call sends them back on the road again when wildfires get close enough to threaten an old college friend's farm. Without a second thought, Rowan agrees to help evacuate her friend's horses, and from there on nothing goes as planned. Rowan and Chase find themselves in a volatile situation that places them both in danger. The destructive force of both man and nature can be terrifying. Will Chase and Rowan find each other and find a way out of a suddenly treacherous landscape?

A CHRISTMAS PROPOSAL: A CHASE AND ROWAN NOVELETTE

Chase and Rowan have been through a lot together but this Christmas will be their first. Plans change and Chase is still learning a lot about family, but when it comes to Rowan, she has a steep learning curve. This romantic novelette is exactly what it says, all you have to do is read till the end to find out if it's a yes or no. Of course, getting there is the best part of the story.

TIE DYE AND FLANNEL

Dr.Stacie Phillips' comfortable, pragmatic life is about to be turned upside down. Dr. Phillips is a young Veterinarian caught up in her carefully constructed life, trying to protect her family, her new career, and most of all-her heart. Her best friend, Josie, only wants what is best for her, and if that means meddling in affairs of the heart she will do it. Josie has her own reasons for wanting Stacie to be happy, and the last thing she wants is Stacie putting off her life to help Josie deal with hers. Stacie meets Maria, a free-spirited herbalist from Arizona, when her goddaughter Rowan literally runs into her at a farmer's market. Unfortunately...or fortunately for her, Rowan's mother, Josie finds out about the chance encounter and things start to spiral out of Stacie's control. If you've ever tried to wear tie-dye and flannel at the same time, or you're a flannel who's ever fallen for a tie dye sort of gal, this is the one for you to read. This stand-alone novella is set in the same world as the popular Chase and Rowan series, only this time we're flashing back to the 1980's.

LADYSMITH

There is a saying among the old ones, "If you dream of a mare, a MacLeod is sure to be near."

Rohanna MacLeod grew up listening to her grandmother's stories of the old world, of Fae and Myth and Magic. Nothing like the mundane world she lives in, or so she thinks. Swirling in the mists beneath her ordinary world lies a prophecy that has shaped her entire life and caused her nothing but loss and pain— until a chance offer and a plain business card sends her to Alexandria Strider, the Ladysmith.

Rohanna is a challenge and a mystery to Alexandria, one she cannot resist. Caught between new bonds and old oaths, Alex must choose her role in a destiny that threatens to change who she is and what they have together. Sometimes stories are more than myth and legend.

What has been forgotten can be found again, and nightmares can come alive in your dreams.

SABRE

During the Civil War, hundreds of women cut their hair and donned the uniform of the common soldier on both sides. History tells us they did it to follow their husbands and brothers to war, rather than stay behind to uncertain destiny. A few, though, found their freedom beneath the heavy wool uniform and shorn hair.

These are the few that are not spoken of, the ones who desired no husband and found liberation behind the blue or the gray. Meet JC. Resigned to a solitary life, an unexpected gift changes everything for this Union soldier.

This short story is a historical lesbian erotic romance.

STEPPING OUT

Enter Micah and Olivia's world from Switching Gears and enjoy a tale of a night out on the town that was so deliciously naughty it was too hot to keep hidden away. Join Micah as she takes a walk through her past, leathers and all, for a night she soon won't forget. What can we say? Some fantasies can't be put to sleep until they are put to bed.

THE POTTER'S WHEEL

Would you dare love a Goddess?
The Potter's Wheel is a lesbian erotic romance. A short tale of epic love, both lost and found, and the undeniable passion between two unique and otherworldly women

THE MISADVENTURES OF TWO RELUCTANT ZOMBIE HUNTERS: ZOMBIES AT THE CON
No one expects the zombie apocalypse…not even those who make a living pretending it exists. When a troupe of Zombie Hunters find themselves in the midst of a real zombie apocalypse they have to find a way to escape. After all, there aren't any real weapons allowed at the Con…and only wits and ingenuity will keep them alive long enough to make it home.

SWITCHING GEARS

SWITCHING GEARS